Praise for *The Reb*

'Another superbly researched and vividly told novel about the gifted and spirited women of Oliver Cromwell's family; full of insight, detail and imaginative richness'
Rowan Williams, former Archbishop of Canterbury

'I cannot imagine a novel that would take me closer to the heart of Cromwell's world . . . utterly convincing'
S.G. Maclean, author of the *Damian Seeker series*

'This affecting, action-packed novel brings a momentous but often overlooked period of history vividly to life'
Carolyn Kirby, author of *The Conviction of Cora Burns*

'It is wonderful to see such familiar historical characters brought so colourfully and convincingly to new life; and the writing itself is of the finest – skilful and vivid – literary standard'
Professor Ronald Hutton, author of *The Making of Oliver Cromwell*

'Miranda Malins has delivered an even more gripping second novel, with each character drawing you in thanks to the depths of their personalities and beautifully articulated views of the world. A joy to read!'
Michael Scott, author of *Ancient Worlds*

'Miranda Malins goes from strength to strength with her second novel *The Rebel Daughter*'
Leonara Nattrass, author of *Black Drop*

'Incredibly rich in historical detail, bringing to life England's most turbulent years through the eyes of a woman at the heart of it.'
Frances Quinn, author of *The Smallest Man*

Praise for *The Puritan Princess*

'A powerful and superbly researched historical novel'
Andrew Taylor, author of *The Last Protector*

'There is much to enjoy in this evocation of a family whose lives are so upended by the convulsions of history'
The Times

'Miranda Malins is a real and fresh new talent. This is beautifully written, exciting fiction from a writer in full command of the history'
Suzannah Lipscomb, author of *A Journey through Tudor England*

'Totally gripping – grab it now. There's a new Cromwell on the shelves!'
Minoo Dinshaw, author of *Outlandish Knight*

'The extraordinary, revealing and moving relationship between Oliver Cromwell and his daughter Frances is brought to vivid life in this masterly historical novel'
Paul Lay, author of *Providence Lost*

'A beautifully written and captivating true story of personal love and loss . . . Malins inhabits her characters and brings them convincingly to life'
James Evans, author of *Emigrants*

'Malins' easy and graceful style makes for a thoroughly enjoyable read'
Linda Porter, author of *Mistresses*

'Dazzling – a brilliant, warts-and-all debut novel'
Lancashire Post

Miranda Malins is a writer and historian specialising in the history of Oliver Cromwell, his family and the politics of the Interregnum period following the Civil Wars. She studied at Cambridge University, leaving with a PhD, and continues to speak at conferences and publish journal articles and book reviews. She is also a Trustee of the Cromwell Association. Alongside this, Miranda works as a commercial solicitor in the City and began writing historical novels on maternity leave. She lives in Hampshire with her husband, young sons and cat Keats. *The Rebel Daughter* is her second novel.

Also by Miranda Malins

The Puritan Princess

MIRANDA MALINS

An Orion paperback

First published in Great Britain in 2022 by Orion Fiction
an imprint of The Orion Publishing Group Ltd
Carmelite House, 50 Victoria Embankment
London EC4Y 0DZ

An Hachette UK Company

1 3 5 7 9 10 8 6 4 2

A CIP catalogue record for this book is
available from the British Library.

ISBN (Mass Market Paperback) 978 1 4091 9486 6
ISBN (eBook) 978 1 4091 9487 3

Typeset at The Spartan Press Ltd,
Lymington, Hants

Printed and bound in Great Britain by Clays Ltd,
Elcograf S.p.A.

www.orionbooks.co.uk

For Mummy

CAST OF CHARACTERS

THE CROMWELL FAMILY

Oliver Cromwell, MP for Cambridge and colonel in the Eastern Association Army
Elizabeth Cromwell (née Bourchier), his wife
Robert Cromwell (Robin), their oldest son
Oliver Cromwell (Olly), the Cromwells' second son
Bridget Cromwell (Biddy), the Cromwells' oldest daughter
Richard Cromwell (Dick), the Cromwells' third son
Henry Cromwell (Harry), the Cromwells' youngest son
Elizabeth Cromwell (Betty), the Cromwells' second daughter
Mary Cromwell (Mall), the Cromwells' third daughter
Frances Cromwell (Fanny), the Cromwells' youngest daughter

THE WIDER CROMWELL FAMILY

Elizabeth Cromwell (née Steward), Oliver's widowed mother, living with the family

Liz Cromwell, Oliver's unmarried sister, also living with the family

Jane Desborough, Oliver's sister

John Desborough, her husband and colonel in the Eastern Association Army

Valentine Walton, Oliver's brother-in-law and colonel in the Eastern Association Army

Valentine Walton (Val), his son

Catherine Whetstone, Oliver's sister, later living with the family

Lavinia Whetstone, her daughter, later living with the family

Edward Whalley, Oliver's cousin and major in the Eastern Association Army

IN CAMBRIDGESHIRE

Reverend Hitch, Vicar Choral and Precentor of Ely cathedral

Sir John Claypole of Northborough

Mary Claypole, his wife

John Claypole, their son

Martha, Cromwell family maid

Matthew, Cromwell family groom

IN THE ARMY

Earl of Essex, Commander-in-Chief of Parliament's forces

Earl of Manchester, Commander of the Eastern Association Army

Henry Ireton, Major in Colonel Thornhaugh's Regiment of Horse

Francis Thornhaugh, Commander of the Nottingham Regiment of Horse

Charles Fleetwood, Captain in the Earl of Essex's life-guard

Frances Fleetwood, his wife

Sir Thomas 'Black Tom' Fairfax, second-in-command of the Northern Association Army, later Commander-in-Chief of the New Model Army

Lady Anne Fairfax, his wife

John Lambert, Colonel in the Northern Association Army

Frances Lambert, his wife

Thomas Harrison, Major in the Eastern Association Army

Catherine Harrison, his wife

Thomas Rainsborough, Colonel in the Eastern Association Army

Edward Sexby, trooper in the Eastern Association Army and agitator

Hugh Peter, minister in the New Model Army

Thomas Pride, Lieutenant-Colonel in the New Model Army

Edmund Ludlow, Lieutenant-General, MP and later Councillor

Earl of Warwick, Lord High Admiral of Parliament's navy

Robert Blake, General-at-Sea in Parliament's navy

George Monck, former Royalist, later Commander-in-Chief of Commonwealth forces in Scotland

Robert Lockyer, trooper in the Eastern Association Army and Leveller

IN PARLIAMENT

John Pym, leading voice against the King in the build-up to war

William Lenthall, Speaker of the House of Commons

Sir Henry Vane, key member of the Independent faction

Denzil Holles, leading member of the Presbyterian faction

Bulstrode Whitelocke, Commissioner of the Great Seal

IN LONDON

John Lilburne, pamphleteer, former officer in Parliament's army and a leading Leveller

Elizabeth Lilburne, his wife and fellow Leveller activist

John Cook, lawyer and later chief prosecutor of the High Court of Justice

John Bradshaw, lawyer and later Lord President of the High Court of Justice

Thomas Simon, chief engraver at the Mint

Margery, wet nurse

Jean, Oliver's valet

ROYALISTS

King Charles I
Charles, Prince of Wales
James, Duke of York
Prince Rupert of the Rhine, the King's nephew and commander of his cavalry
Sir John Ashburnham, courtier
Sir Charles Lucas, Lieutenant-General in the King's army
Sir George Lisle, Colonel in the King's army
Lady Whorwood, owner of Holton Park
Jane Whorwood, her daughter-in-law

THE CROMWELL FAMILY IN 1643

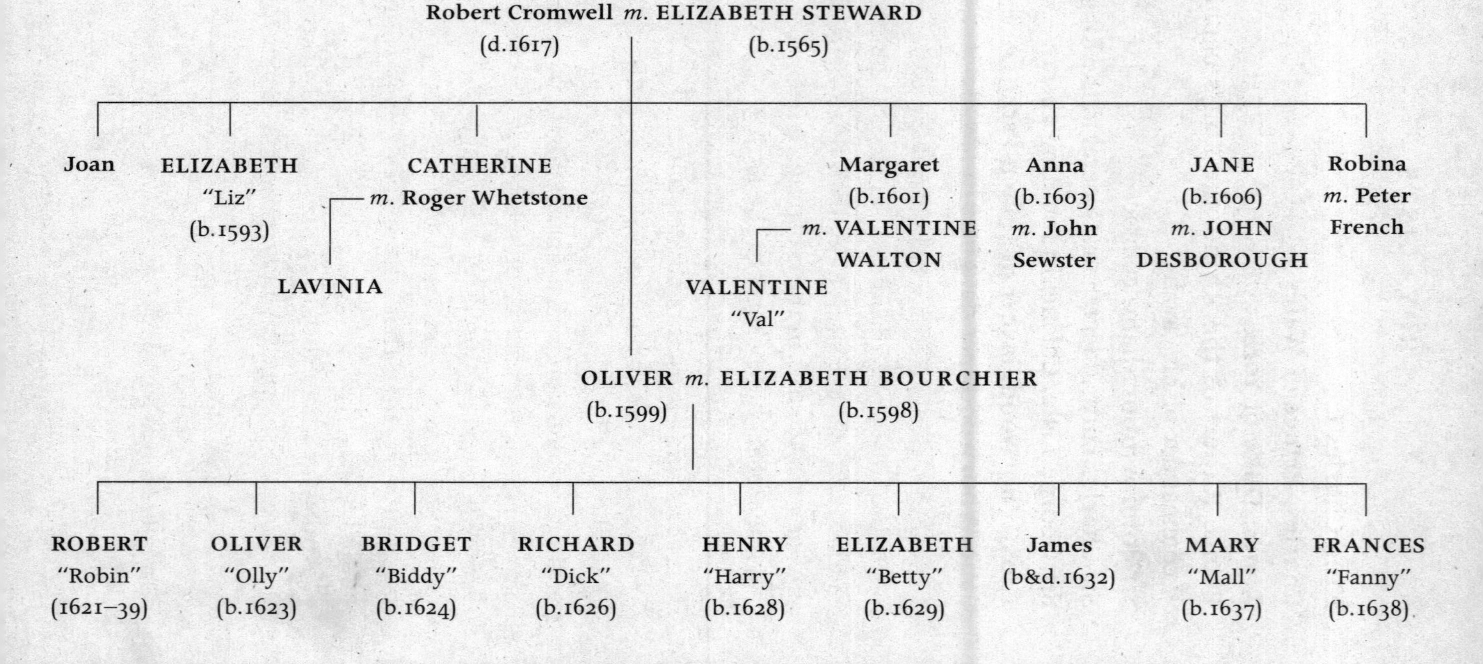

PROLOGUE

JANUARY 1636, THE FENS

I am always the first in my house to wake. Before Mother or Father, before my brothers and sisters. Before Grandmother, who cannot sleep more than three hours together and never after five in the morning.

I even beat the cockerel in the barn.

She rises while it is still night and gives food to her household and portions to her servants.

I like that verse from Proverbs. It is not just the sense of warmth, of bringing light out of the darkness or providing for loved ones that speaks to me. It is the word *She*. She rises. She acts. She meets the day first and on her own terms, restored by a few precious minutes of quiet. She sets the fire and lays the table, yes. But she lays out more than that: she shapes the day for herself and all around her.

And what does she do next? More, even more. *She appraises a field and buys it; from her earnings she plants a vineyard. She girds herself with strength and shows that her arms are strong.* There are a lot of verbs in there. Women do not get many verbs. For once, just for once, the Lord speaks to us not of kings or prophets, of a rich man in a castle or a poor one at his gate. He tells of an ordinary woman. A woman whose *strength and honour are her clothing*. A woman who *opens her mouth with wisdom, and faithful instruction is on her tongue*. A woman whose *price is far above rubies*.

And so each morning I wake first and claim the day for my own.

Yet even so there are some things I cannot do. I cannot find the wages for a servant to help Mother. I cannot conjure bacon when our stock of salted meat runs low nor stop the many-fingered frost crawling through the cracks in the windows. I place dried lavender on the kitchen table and mix the honey and herbs to flavour the porridge now warming in the hearth. But this is all I can do.

It has been a hard winter for us. Though Mother and Father do not like to admit their worries, we children have noticed each little economy as it has crept upon us. When the first beeswax candle stubs were replaced with the pungent tallow kind. When Mother started to take in our neighbours' linen for mending. When Father had to sell his hunter; a horse he loved almost as much as his children. But what use has a farmer for a thoroughbred which cannot work in the fields, even if he is a gentleman?

And the weather has done its worst. The cold has gone to Father's chest, forcing him to wear a red flannel round his throat day and night. And the rain, so much rain. The winter floods have receded for now, but they have left destruction in their wake: mounds of muddy peat banked along the roads that criss-cross the Fens, sodden fields and rotting fence posts. There is no time to lose if we are to nurse the land back to health in time for this year's yield. Tenant farmers in these parts are soon ejected if they don't make their farms pay; whatever their good name, however illustrious their ancestors.

So each day, after taking our porridge in the pink dawn light, we are at our labours, Father anxious not to waste an hour of the short winter days. This morning, as the watery sun climbs above the wide, flat horizon, my hands tingle, frozen inside my gloves. Each fingertip has been unstitched so that I can use my fingers to work alongside my brothers. I sit with my little sister Betty chitting potatoes in the barn at the edge of the field while we watch their brown-coated backs bend over their work. Hours pass as we pick all but the best nobbled eyes off the potato tubers and place them rose-end up in long, narrow crates packed with straw.

I pause for a few moments, chafing my fingertips against each other. They smell sickly sweet with starch and are stained soil-black, the swirling grooves on each so ingrained I could use them to make prints on paper, as I used to when I was a child. I look down at the wheat-coloured curls of my little sister Betty's head as it rests against my arm. At six years old – five years younger than me – she tires quickly. I will send her inside soon, I think. She can have some milk and a biscuit, then help Mother with the mending.

Father is in a good humour today at least, the black mood that claimed him last week has passed for now, though we never know when the storm clouds will gather again. He strikes up a song and I listen as the mixed trebles of my brothers join in, my eldest brother Robert's pitch less steady than the rest as his voice is breaking into a baritone. Betty and I join in and we are quite the choir when a horseman appears on the ridge against the sky. From my vantage point I see him first and fall silent. Betty, then each of my brothers, follows suit when they spot him. Father is the last to cease. The rider stops at the nearest gate, his bay horse snorting frosted breath. Father stands up from the hurdle he is mending and holds a hand to the small of his back.

'You the tenant farmer here? Mister Oliver Cromwell?' the messenger calls to Father, leaning down into his saddlebag. 'I've a letter for you.'

We watch as Father plants his stake in the sodden soil and strides towards the man, his long boots squelching in the mud. He takes the proffered square of paper and thumbs it open, the seal cracking between his gloves. He reads, his face bent low over the page, his brow furrowed like the field he stands in.

It is a long letter.

Idly, Betty juggles two potatoes up in the air and I watch them spin, sprinkling soil on our skirts. But then a great, throated laugh takes our eyes back to Father and the potatoes tumble to the ground as we watch him clasp his arms around himself, his whole body shaking and sagging with a convulsion of laughter and tears.

'Boys!' he shouts when he can speak again. 'Robin, Olly, Dick, Harry!' Father calls them in age order and, like hounds, they bound towards him. 'Biddy, Betty!' He looks for us girls next.

We set off, potatoes spilling from our laps and rolling in every direction across the floor of the barn. I pick up my skirts and hurry into the field, Betty scampering ahead of me leaping the mountainous ridges of mud that are as high as her knees. When we reach Father, our brothers crowding around him, he sweeps Betty up in his arms and she clamps her muddy legs around his waist, nuzzling into the roughness of his thick working coat as I hang back, wishing it was me pressing my flushed cheek against his, before chiding myself for my sinful envy.

'News, my darlings! The best of news!' Father says at last. 'Praise God! My uncle, who you know died last month, has left me an inheritance: leases on a number of properties in Ely, a post as the tithe-collector for the dean and chapter of the cathedral, an income of some three hundred pounds a year. It is not a fortune, but it is enough, more than enough . . .'

His words tail off but I know what he means: enough for Father to climb back to the rank of gentleman, where he belongs. Enough to reclaim his status among the leading property owners of the county. Enough for us to reverse the recent decline in our luck. It was four years ago when Providence began to frown on us and Father was forced to sell up and leave his native Huntingdon. I watched him, exiled from the town and his respectable life there, sink down in the world to the rank of tenant farmer – he, the grandson of the so-called 'golden knight' Sir Henry Cromwell, who had built the magnificent Hinchingbrooke House, favourite stopping place of old King James whenever he took to the Great North Road. Even our current King Charles had visited there as a boy and had played at rough and tumble in the gardens with Father himself. Or so he claims.

But all that will change now. We can rewrite our history.

Robin, my eldest brother, who at fourteen is almost a man himself, beams with joy and relief. As Father's heir, he will have most to gain from this elevation, though I know it will mean a great deal for all of us. For my brothers, university, perhaps a profession – Parliament even, if the King ever lets it convene again. For Betty and me, a better class of husband when the time comes. And for Mother, no more sewing by tallow candlelight.

'Oh my dears . . .' Father's voice returns, heartier than before and I can almost see his body strengthening beneath his working clothes. 'Come, let's go and tell your mother; we'll roast one of the chickens to celebrate! And you, sir,' he calls to the bewildered messenger, 'you'll join us in a drink, I hope? Raise a glass of wine to our future?'

He gathers us to him to walk back across the fields to the farmhouse, the horseman – smiling now – shadowing us along the road. The boys set off at a trot but Father takes only a few strides before pausing. 'This is God's work,' he says so quietly only Betty and I can hear, 'and I will thank Him every day of my life.' Father touches the tip of his nose to Betty's and she smiles. 'God came to me when I was at my weakest, girls, did you know that? When I was at my most broken. And He bid me serve Him through my suffering. And I have – He knows how I have. And I never questioned His plan for me, for all my doubts – but now, ha ha!'

Betty giggles and I find myself laughing too, giddy as Father puts an arm around me and pulls me into his chest. My brothers hear our laughter and spring backwards to cluster around Father's legs once more, the older two, Robin and Olly, grinning and clapping him on the back, the younger, Dick and Harry, skipping and clutching at his coat.

But Father has left us once more as he looks up to heaven, tears welling in his eyes. I tip my face to the sky to look where he does and a watery shaft of sunlight blurs my vision. I hear Father's deep voice once more, feel the words growing in his chest as his heart beats against my ear:

'Now I can serve God by my *doing* and not by my suffering alone. And what things I shall do in the world!'

Father's voice rings out, sending a flock of starlings winging into the air, and the whole field resounds with our rejoicing.

PART ONE

Seven years later, Ely

CHAPTER ONE

SPRING 1643

The dish slips from Betty's fingers and smashes on the flagstones. Somehow I keep hold of mine and we stand frozen in shock staring at the front door. A furious knocking thunders against the oak and the street outside rings with angry shouts and shots. Instinctively, I wait for Father to push past us to the door before I remember that he is away fighting with his regiment, my brother Olly too. My oldest brother Robin lies in the cold ground of course, Dick and Harry are off at school and our groom, old Matthew, will be two jugs down at The Bell now it is gone nine in the evening.

There are eight women in the house, I realise with cold fear, and not a single man.

'Who is it?' I venture forward, the dish of potatoes still in my hands. Mother emerges in the parlour doorway and I glance sideways at her, hoping for reassurance.

'Reverend Hitch,' a familiar voice whispers thickly through the grained panels. 'There has been an uprising in the town, mistress; you must secure the house, put out your lights.'

Mother is beside me now and has opened the door an inch to reveal the clergyman's pinched face. Over her capped head, I can just see townspeople scurrying through the dusk, their heads bowed. The reverend is good to warn us, I think, for we are not always the most obedient of his flock, having a natural independence of religion.

'Royalists?'

'Aye, mistress. About fifty of them have come out for the King. They've seized the gates and are working their way across the town. Six of our Parliament troops have been killed already, another is bleeding out in the cathedral. You must make yourselves safe – they will know this is Captain Cromwell's house and that he is from home. I must press on now.'

'Lord have mercy.' Mother clutches at the single string of pearls at her neck. 'Thank you, reverend, we are grateful. If you come across our groom in the town, please send him back here and ask him to bring any men that can be spared. We will barricade ourselves in and trust to God.'

Reverend Hitch nods and hurries into the gloom, his black cloak flapping around his ankles. Mother closes the door and bolts it firmly. She turns to us, her face resolute, even as her hands fly out in a flurry of instructions. My heart pounds against my bodice.

'Betty, take Grandmother up to her room and see she has bread, small beer and blankets. Then go to the little ones; the knocking will have woken them and they will be frightened. Dress them in case we have to leave suddenly, then sit with them. One candle only, put out the others!'

Betty hesitates, glancing down at the shards of painted earthenware scattered on the floor; mother's best dish.

'Leave that, I'll clear it up when we are safe.'

Without a word my sister disappears into the parlour, the white hem of her petticoat flashing as she takes the step.

'I will go around the back of the house, Mother,' I say, leaving the potatoes on the table by the door.

'Yes, you do the back, Bridget, and I'll do the front. Fasten the windows, close the curtains, lock the doors. Leave one rushlight only alight in each room so that we can see what we're doing.'

'Liz?' Mother calls into the back stairs and my spinster aunt answers from the kitchen. 'Douse the fire. Fill some flasks with beer and make food parcels in case we need to run for it.'

Quickly, I work my way from room to room, ending in the barn attached to the west end of the house, which was Father's tithe office before the war. A mouse scuttles under my feet and I almost trip as I press forward to the large door at the end of the room. I lock and bolt it before dragging some sacks of flour against it. Sweating, I try to lift one to place it on top of the other but it is too heavy and I curse my lack of a man's strength. I can manage Father's chair, so I wedge that against the door instead and pray for the best.

Returning to the hall, I find Martha, our kitchen maid, sweeping up the broken dish and, when she has finished, together we drag the bench from the corner by our boots and coats over to the front door and ram it against the panel. Turning, I am surprised to see Betty coming down the stairs.

'The girls are crying,' she says, her pretty face pained. 'They clung to me but wouldn't believe my promises that we will be safe. They will only listen to you, Biddy.'

The lot of the oldest sister, I think, touched despite myself at their trust. Little Mary and Frances are so much younger than us – only six and nearly five. A second family almost, born to Mother after Father's fortunes turned. I know they worship thirteen-year-old Betty with her fresh beauty and sweetness and find me, now eighteen, a touch severe at times. But we are at war. To be good and beautiful is no longer enough. Without the men here, we must be strong and inventive. Hard work, quick wits and a firm understanding are women's currency now; courage as well as compassion our stock in trade. I used to seek only the comfort of marriage and motherhood in my future, I think, as I take to the stairs, but now I wonder if those will be enough.

We spend the whole night huddled upstairs; a mass of female bodies pressed together in a warm haze of lavender scent and frightened sweat. We are silent, watchful. The girls sleep fitfully, sprawled across Mother's and Betty's laps, while Grandmother lies wakeful in her bed, muttering psalms. Aunt Liz nods in a chair beside her while Martha and I take it in turns to peer through the curtains and, once each hour, steal downstairs to check on the doors and windows.

Outside, the city sleeps as fitfully as a teething baby. Time is tight and tense, with long spells of silence broken by shouts and screams as footsteps thud over cobblestones before vanishing again into the still night air. Alone, the ghostly towers of the cathedral watch over us, their hourly bells heartbeats in the moonlit dark. At around three in the morning, torchlight flames in the street below us and the fiery light filters through the curtains to cast shadows across the fearful faces of my family. In the eerie silence we hear men's voices beneath our window.

'Is this his house?' a man asks roughly.

''Tis,' another answers.

There's a hammering at the door. Not the rhythmic woodpecker knocking of the reverend this time, but a beating of many fists, even a few boots.

Mary wakes and whimpers before Mother clasps her hand over her mouth and whispers in her ear. I listen, the sound of my own breathing the loudest noise I have ever heard. Louder even than the cathedral bells tolling a parish death or a thunderstorm rolling in from the Wash. Closing my eyes, I pray for the bench to hold the door against them.

A minute passes, then the thunder stops and we hear the sounds of the heavy-footed men spreading out around the house as the torchlight moves away. Opening my eyes again, I imagine noses pressed against the glass, men sniffing the night air for the scent of women cowering in their nests. Somewhere there is the sound of tapping and I wonder for a terrifying moment if they are going to break the glass and force their way in, or perhaps light some fuel-soaked rags and throw them through the windows with rocks.

Mother reaches forward for my hand and begins to whisper our Lord's prayer. *Our Father, which art in heaven* . . . I seize her hand in mine and Betty and the girls cling to us both. As silently as mice in church, we all take up the words. *Thy will be done on earth, as it is in heaven* . . . I shut my eyes and lose myself in the prayer. We intone it four, five times before, suddenly, Mother breaks off. The spell broken, we lapse into silence, listening.

The men have gone. Our words, God's words, have seen them off; that and the hall bench. At least for now.

Victorious, I feel my breath return to me as I loose myself from Mother's hand and settle down to wait. Slowly Mall and Fanny slip back into sleep, Betty too, this time. Aunt Liz nods once more, Mother drops her head onto her chest and Martha pulls her ragged shawl about her in the corner of the room.

Alone among us, Grandmother and I do not surrender to sleep. Even in the pitch-blackness we sense our companionship: 'You and I, Bridget,' Grandmother's ancient voice rasps in the darkness, 'we keep the watch now.' Somewhere in the distance I hear a scream.

It is mostly quiet after that, though every so often more shouts and running feet swirl about the house. Mother wakes for a time and we have a whispered conference before she dozes again. After another few hours, the first shy pinks slip around the edge of the curtains, the glass, visible in the gap where they don't quite meet, blurred with mist. I feel a weight in my bladder and tiptoe from the room in search of a chamber pot.

Now I am up and about I decide to check the house and I slip softly down the stairs, pulling a blanket around my shoulders. I am in the hall, almost exactly on the spot where Betty dropped the dish, when I hear a sudden volley of gunshots followed by horses clattering into the street. The horses pull up outside our house and I shrink away from the door. Frantic, I cast about for weapons, alighting on a log from the hall basket and the heaviest candlestick from the nearby chest as the best that are available. I steal myself away under the stairs and hide, my pulse ringing in my ears. I pray to God to spare my sisters and harden my resolve. If He needs help from me I will willingly give it; I will die before I let any man touch them.

Once again the door shudders under fists. There are muffled shouts, as if the men are calling to us inside the house, but I cannot make out their voices from my cave beneath the stairs. It sounds like boots on the door now and as the wood splinters I force myself out of my hideaway. I breathe once, twice, then the door bursts open.

I surge forward with a scream, brandishing my weapons. Flailing, I run straight at two men, now tripping forward over the bench they had forced from the door. I strike each. Then, trapped by their stumbling, heavy shoulders, I fall backwards with them, still clutching the log and candlestick, so unable to cushion the landing with my hands. I lie winded and raging, struggling for breath. But then I look up and see the bulky man standing framed in the doorway.

Father. It is my father.

'Biddy!' He lunges towards me in concern. 'My darling, my brave girl! Are you hurt? Is everyone safe?'

I feast my eyes on him from the floor. 'We are all safe, Father. The others are upstairs.'

'And you the guard dog?' Father asks and I catch the pride that edges his voice and bathe in it.

One of the men who kicked the door in bends over me and I feel his hands hooked under my arms as he lifts me up, catching the rough smell of sweat-soaked cloth and horse hair. He is tall but wiry, quite the opposite of the stocky Cromwell men I am used to. It is only then that I look at him and see that his lip is bleeding.

'Well, Henry, what do you say to my eldest daughter Bridget?' Father addresses the man as he grins and spreads his arms for me to go to him. 'Is she not the bravest, boldest woman you ever met?'

The man he speaks to lets me go and straightens himself tall, bringing a fingertip to his lip. Flustered now, I move from him to Father, whose solid frame and familiar straw-and-leather smell calms me. From the safety of his arms, I look properly at the two other men. They are in their prime – both in their early or mid-thirties, I would guess – and dressed in cavalry clothes; the one with the bleeding lip as dark and stern as the other is fair and smiling.

'She caught me quite a blow sir, I'll give her that,' the dark-haired man replies at length, rubbing his jaw carefully as he eyes me with a shrewd gaze.

'Aye and me too,' the fair one laughs, his fine curls shaking above a lace collar. 'Well done, mistress!'

They speak with a similar accent – Nottinghamshire, perhaps. I am saved the embarrassment of answering them as Mother flies down the stairs, Betty and the little girls hurtling after her. 'Oliver, thank God.'

I stand back, allowing Father to gather his women to him, and smile at the scene as my wits and composure slowly return to me: 'I'll prepare breakfast,' I say, turning for the kitchen.

*

Father has brought his closest officers home with him, our own kin among them, to whom we give the warmest welcome. My two uncles, Colonels Valentine Walton and John Desborough – husbands to Father's sisters Margaret and Jane – loom large in the house. Uncle Walton laughs and chats with Mother and Aunt Liz, shaking off army life like a resting cart horse, his son, my cousin young Val, frisking colt-like beside him, his sword shining at his belt. Uncle Desborough, meanwhile, takes his repose in an altogether different style, his huge form lumbering around the house with the air of a grizzled bear glowering at any of us who approach. Most precious of all to return, though, is my older brother Olly, and I watch him happily as he settles back into the corners of the house, his hands touching every object and surface as if to assure himself he is truly home.

We are a large party at breakfast – too large for the parlour table, so Olly stretches out on the floor with the girls pawing and playing with his sash and sword, while Grandmother keeps to her armchair by the fire. Betty perches prettily on a stool beside her while I am quietly pleased to have been granted a seat at the table. Through the doorway I hear Matthew's hammers and grunts as he fixes the front door.

'Never have I been so glad to come home,' Father says, leaning back in his chair at the head of the table and beaming at us before his brows knit together in sudden anger. 'And to think my little wenches were under attack themselves, in our own house.'

'Do not fret, dearest,' Mother says, directing her level gaze down the table to her husband. 'We were safe enough.'

'And now my son is back we'll be safer still,' Grandmother speaks over her bowl of porridge. 'He left a mere captain and returns a colonel!' She beams at Father with satisfied pride: her only son now proved to the world the golden boy she always knew him to be.

Father blushes under his mother's praise before blustering: ''Tis a welcome promotion, Mother, I don't deny it.'

'Hear, hear.' The other officers bang the table in appreciation.

'The "Lord of the Fens" sweeping all in his wake!' Uncle Walton toasts, grinning, and I sense his pleasure at the levelling of their ranks.

Father raises an eyebrow and then his glass in thanks and drains it, his humour returned.

I slide to my feet and take the beer jug around to refill his glass before scanning the table to see if any of the guests needs more. I am anxious to do what I can to make the two strangers at our table welcome, partly in recompense for the violence I showed them when they first crossed our threshold. So I am pleased that the fair young officer I had struck with the candlestick, whom Father introduced as Captain Charles Fleetwood, smiles a friendly request at me over his empty glass. But the dark-haired officer beside him, who I now know to be called Major Henry Ireton, gives me no such reassurance. Glancing at him, I wonder momentarily if the swollen lip I gave him with my brandished log has inhibited his breakfast, for his plate of bread and bacon and glass of ale are untouched. As I watch him, he fixes his sharp eyes on Father and begins to speak:

'Yet we must not sit idly on our hands, colonel,' he

begins, his voice deep and rounded with a measured authority that belies his junior rank. 'Thanks chiefly to your efforts, we have swept the King's army from the Eastern Counties but Ely will remain a target. The Isle is so naturally defensible the King will have to take it if he wants to regain the region. And now Major-General Grey is bidden west with five thousand of our Eastern Association Army to join the Earl of Essex's forces in the Thames Valley to take the towns defending Oxford, Ely is exposed to the King's northern army.'

Henry Ireton pauses at the natural end of his logical summation. If he is not a university man and graduate of the inns of court, I shall be very surprised, I think, considering him over my cup.

'You speak truly, Henry,' Father nods with seriousness and I note his familiar use of the younger man's first name, 'and the army's high command write to me that they see things as Henry does, my dear,' he continues, addressing Mother now. 'Which is why they have appointed me Governor of Ely to oversee the fortification of the region from a headquarters here. With Grey gone west, I'm left to run things here as I see fit – for now.'

Father stationed at home? I thrill at the news, though Betty is quicker than me to express her delight.

'Then you will remain with us for longer this time, Father?' she asks, her cheeks glowing as she skips over to him and takes his hand.

'Aye, Betty my love,' he replies, kissing her hand. 'I'll likely be based here until after harvest. Though I'll need to lead the men out against any incursions, travel down to Parliament and report to our commander-in-chief the Earl of Essex from time to time.'

'Then, come September, we'll be back in the field again and who knows,' my brother Olly says from the floor and, though I can't see his face and his tone is hearty, I fancy I catch uncertainty in his voice, layered beneath the bravado. He and our cousin Val were so eager to take up arms when the war began last year, like new boys going away to school. But now they each captain a horse troop in Father's regiment, the time for games is over. I wonder if the reality of fighting his countrymen has changed Olly and resolve to press him to tell me what it is really like once we are alone.

'It is a large task they set you,' Henry Ireton addresses Father thoughtfully. 'There will be much to do: liaising with the Cambridge garrison, building fortifications at Wisbech and Earith, raising and training more troops, securing finance, procuring weapons and provisions – with two thousand men that will mean . . .' His coal-bright eyes glaze slightly as his words tail off and I fancy he is calculating in his head.

Father gets to his feet, scraping his chair on the floor-boards, and prowls around the table until he is standing behind Ireton's chair. 'It is a large task indeed, Henry, so large I will be needing a good deputy. Someone far cleverer than I am, with an eye for detail and a head for figures. What do you say?'

For the first time since he burst through our front door, Major Ireton's face softens into a smile. 'I say the Lord has brought me here for a purpose,' he replies and rises to his feet to receive a warm arm clasp from Father, who kisses him on both cheeks.

I watch the display, intrigued at their relationship as I so often am by those my father now forges so easily on the battlefield. What must it be like to ride in a cavalry charge beside another man? To storm into a hail of musket fire and cut men down like reeds and sedge under your blade; a field of harvested flesh. How must it feel for Father, who, until a year ago, had never picked up a weapon but for hunting? Looking around the room, I observe the other men responding to Henry's appointment: Uncle Walton with a joyful banging of the table, Val and Olly swiftly following his lead; Uncle Desborough with a surly nod of approval; and Charles Fleetwood with a shower of soft applause, though I fancy his celebration is a little muted. Perhaps he was hoping for the preferment?

'And you can keep an eye on my family for me when I am from home, Henry,' Father continues, 'if you can keep on the right side of Biddy and her logs and candlesticks! Bidding Biddy, I call her, and you can see why,' Father laughs.

I flinch from my reverie at Father's use of the unflattering nickname and find the eyes of the room turned, momentarily, upon me. Father's levity bruises me but I know he means to show pride in his eldest daughter's capability, not to jest at my expense, and so I sit up straight and set a smile on my face before replying: 'Deputy Ireton will have no trouble from me.'

Henry inclines his head a fraction towards me and I give a small nod in return before rising to clear the table.

CHAPTER TWO

'I don't care much for his looks,' Betty whispers to me later that morning. 'Too severe. Too pointy. What is it he puts me in mind of? I know! A fox. He is too fox-like.'

'What nonsense,' I reply, irritated at her shallowness. 'You can hardly hold that against Major Ireton. It is the content of a man's character that counts, not his features.' He is a little fox-like, I concede inwardly, but I won't demean myself by agreeing with Betty.

We are standing at the kitchen basin soaking our brother Oliver's linen which he has left, as always, in a muddy saddle bag on the kitchen table. It is our task to sponge the most stubborn stains with lye soap before Martha washes the clothes in the outhouse. I scrub at a dark brown stain on his cuff and suddenly wonder if it is blood.

'But he is so serious,' Betty continues, raising the corner of her wrist to smooth a curl back from her face.

I rub the bloodstain between my thumb and forefinger, marvelling at how we can each observe the same characteristic yet judge it in opposite terms. For Betty, Major Ireton's gravity is a failing, whereas I see it as a virtue: *The simple inherit folly, but the prudent are crowned with knowledge*. 'He is a soldier doing God's work, Betty,' I try to explain. 'If that doesn't make a man serious, I don't know what would.'

Betty gives a tiny, tinkling laugh and her elbow finds its way into my side. 'He would be a suitable match for you, Biddy; I could see you being happily serious together, kneeling side by side in prayer before bed.'

I stiffen against her. She could not have said anything better designed to put me off Henry Ireton; her choosing him for me means I could never choose him for myself, even if I do decide to marry. She knows it and I know she is waiting for me to say so. Instead, I hold my tongue in defiance and apply myself with renewed vigour to the bloodstain.

When it is clear that I am not going to oblige her with outrage, Betty trips on with her thoughts. 'Still, at least we have the other young men to cheer us. Captain Fleetwood seems lively and it's clear the war hasn't had the same serious effect on Val.' Betty pauses in her efforts beside me to stare out of the low latticed window through which we can see our cousin Val and brother Oliver in the garden, stretched out on the grass, soaking up the sun, their heads close together. 'I'll go and see if they want to come in for some cake,' she says suddenly. 'My fingers are starting to prune.' Betty dries her hands and removes her apron before swishing through the kitchen door to the garden. I watch her as she glides over to the boys and lowers herself majestically onto the grass beside them, arranging her skirts neatly. Olly doesn't move at her approach but Val sits up smartly.

Watching them chat together, I sink into my own thoughts as my fingers work the delicate lace edging of Oliver's linen collars. They are such small garments, mere slips of fabric in my fingers, and I am taken back a few years to when I used to stand here washing my little sisters' soiled linen squares and lace caps when they were babies. That was a fevered time: at thirteen, and then fourteen, I was old enough to witness Mother's last two childbed pains at first hand and I saw for myself how the burden of yet more children dragged her down once more into the morass of motherhood – the endless feeding, wiping, changing, soothing, her hands never once free for her own pursuits from morning till night. Before then I had had a romantic view of birthing and raising babies, but this was scrubbed and rocked out of me in those servile years. Mother and Father couldn't have been happier, of course, seeing the little ones as a fresh hope and a new start after my great-uncle's legacy had transformed our fortunes and moved us to Ely. They were relieved too, I think, that their last child would not be beautiful baby James who had lived but four days when I was eight, and whose death, coupled with Father's anxieties and plummeting status had laid a cold blanket over my parents' marriage bed for several years.

I wring the water from the last collar and place it in the basket next to me with a small rush of satisfaction at the completed task. My arms, now stilled, begin to ache pleasantly as my eyes drift through the window again to the group on the lawn. As I watch, Betty makes a joke, the boys laugh and Val reaches forward and twists a curl of her hair around his finger, the chestnut lock glinting in the sunshine.

Olly rises at this point and comes loping across the

garden and into the kitchen. He glances at the full basket at my elbow then gives me a kiss.

'You're a good sister, Biddy. I'll be glad of clean clothes free of lice when I am back among the men.'

I smile warmly in return. He is my favourite brother, if God allows such a thing. The closest in age, only a year older than me. The quietest, most sensible among the boys; Mother's good sense coupled with Father's charm. 'You just promise to think of me the next time the man beside you is itching and scratching,' I say.

Olly laughs, then falls silent, his gaze shifting to somewhere in the middle distance. I can almost feel him letting his guard down in my company, almost see the fear as it steals across his boyish face and the relief that follows it like a shadow. I have a sudden urge to wrap him in duck-down and stow him away safely in the chest at the end of Betty's and my bed. But I know he needs strengthening, not coddling.

'You do God's work, you know that, Olly,' I say gently. 'You're playing your part in a just war against a tyrant king. Lord, I wish I could fight – I long to make a contribution besides washing and sewing.' I wring my hands in the towel, grasping at the linen.

'You wouldn't say so if you'd seen what I have seen,' Olly counters quickly, though not unkindly, for he knows my frustrations. 'There isn't much of God's glory on the surgeon's table or in a disease-ridden camp,' he continues, his tone darkening as he summons up chilling memories. 'It's blood and sweat. Shit and mud. It's hard to think of the greater "Cause" when you've woken drenched in rain, your feet are swollen and wet, your belly is empty and there's a twenty-mile ride ahead of you with a musket ball waiting for you at the end of it. I spend each day of my life now either bored or terrified. And always, always hungry.'

His frightening words conjure an alien landscape and I grapple for a way to understand it. The closest scene and sensations I have known are the childbed with its bloody sheets and bowls of mangled, ripe-smelling flesh where one can endure an eternity of moaning boredom punctuated by moments of screaming terror. Olly sinks into a chair and reaches across the table for a piece of currant cake. Slowly, I sit down beside him and watch him eat listlessly, the crumbs tumbling from his chin.

'Oh my dear.' I hardly know what to say in comfort, the war so far beyond my ken. 'I'm sure all the men must feel as you do, sometimes.'

Oliver snorts as he chews. 'Some, yes, those of the ordinary sort. But not our family, oh no. Our uncles are brave as bears; Val thinks the whole thing a glorious game and hurls himself into it with glee; and Father . . .'

'And Father?'

He takes a moment to choose his words. 'Father becomes another person entirely. He comes alive among the men and on the battlefield, as if he was born for this. It is a strange thing to see. Almost unearthly – and yet of the earth too. No, it's just I who am scared and resentful, though I never let them see it. Besides, I have no choice: I'm Father's heir now and if he fights for Parliament, so must I.'

It is the familiar burden we both feel in different ways – the loss of our eldest brother Robert. A memory as sharp as a needle drags me back four years to the middle of a November night when a red-cheeked messenger rode clattering into the street and woke our whole house with his fist at the door. A lantern, a letter, a howl from Father such as I've never heard before or since from man or dog. The headmaster of the boys' school in Essex had written to say that eighteen-year-old Robin, my oldest brother – the heir, the golden boy named for my grandfather – had died suddenly of a fever. Our only crumb of comfort was that our other grandfather, who lived nearby, had made it there just in time to be with him at the end.

There was nothing but pain for weeks, months, as we drew from the deepest well of grief. And then, when we emerged hollowed and squinting into the half-light, we found we had all been transformed. I had been both mother and father in those darkest days when my parents became children in their heartbreak: Father had interrogated God and almost lost his mind, Mother had somehow softened and strengthened. The younger children, Dick, Harry and Betty were made more precious, the baby girls more cheering. And Olly, always so carefree and at home in his comfortable second place among us children, had stepped bitterly into our dead brother's boots, blinking in the limelight.

'What if I die next?' Olly is looking at me now, tears in his eyes and seeming much younger than his nineteen years. 'Robin died the eldest son. Now I am the eldest. What if God cuts me down like the boys in Egypt? Then Dick after me, then Harry . . .'

'Shh.' I hold him tightly, rocking him gently like he was a baby. 'That will not be. It was the first-*born* son the Lord took from each family and only as punishment to the Pharaoh.'

'But the King is our Pharaoh and just as tyrannical.'

'Hush.' I take his hands in mine, mapping the terrain of the war on his fingers: the schoolboy hands smooth but for the bump where his pen had rested replaced now with rough skin and cracked fingers callused from hours gripping reins and muskets. 'We are not in Egypt now but on the road to the Promised Land. We will have our new Jerusalem, you will see. That's what you're fighting for, my dear. Trust in God and he will be kinder to us, I promise.'

'It may be your promises that keep me safe,' Olly pulls back from me, his words spittled and spluttering as he reaches for his bag, still on the table. 'I have a pot of salve here, bought from an apothecary I met outside Peterborough. If I am wounded but can take the weapon that struck me, I'll send it straight to you and you must rub this potion on to the weapon. The veterans in my troop swear treating the weapon can heal the wound.'

I take the pot uncertainly, twisting the lid to examine the dark substance within that gleams like blooded goose fat. I know objects can feel sympathy towards one another but could this grease cure my brother at a distance of hundreds of miles?

'Just promise me!' Olly cries, pushing the pot towards my chest and I nod quickly, covering my scepticism and taking him back into my arms.

'I promise,' I whisper, comforted to have something I could do to help him.

Olly appears quite recovered by the time we gather for supper a few hours later; his careful mask of easy soldier's valour returned as morning dew covers the grass. We are just the family now, with Henry Ireton and

Charles Fleetwood gone off to see about billeting their men, and there's a greater sense of ease among us, as at the end of the day when we take off our stiff clothes to stand breathing freely in our under linens.

We have made a feast to set before the men. Mother has been in command of the kitchen all afternoon, indulging herself making Father's and Olly's favourite dishes: eel pie with nutmeg crust, which Aunt Liz took to the baker's to cook; roast chicken basted in sage butter turned on the jack over the dripping pan; mashed potatoes and boiled carrots; and a milk syllabub flavoured with the first cherries of the season – my proud creation after careful spells with the skillet and birch brush. After we have eaten, we draw our chairs around the fire which is still welcome on a cool spring evening. Mother takes a protesting Mary and Frances up to bed and Aunt Liz sees to Grandmother. The older men lounge and discuss the war – Uncle Walton, I fancy, is a little in his cups – while Olly and Val listen attentively. Betty sits beside Father, her hand in his, while I busy myself mending a pair of his stockings.

'If we can just dig in here in the Eastern counties,' Uncle Walton says as he fills his pipe from Father's pouch on the mantel, 'if we can just hold the territory we have gained, all will be well.'

'No,' Uncle Desborough shakes his head brusquely, pipe smoke curling up his drawn face, 'it won't be enough. We need to hold on to the east *and* help Essex take Oxford and the Thames Valley. Otherwise we'll find ourselves caught between Hopton's forces fighting up from the West Country and Newcastle's army bearing down on us from the north. As long as the King holds

Oxford and the Thames towns, he can strike at London and all will be lost.'

Instinctively, we all look to Father for his view. He takes a deep pull on his pipe and shifts his gaze to the fire.

'Do you know what keeps me from my sleep at night, Betty?' he says at length, turning his face to my sister's and squeezing her soft hand. 'Money. Men. And motives. Parliament must grant us more funds – I'm paying to shoe and stocking most of my men myself. And we need to raise more troops; good, honest men who know what they're fighting for and who love the Lord.'

'And motives?' Olly asks.

Father turns to him and smiles sadly. 'That's the most troublesome problem of all, my boy. Your Uncle Desborough is right. It will not be enough not to lose this war, we must win it – decisively and unequivocally. We shall none of us be safe unless we do. And yet I fear that some of our noble commanders do not see it this way. They want merely to put on a good show in the field and then to use our position to sue for an honourable peace with the King. They shy away from the notion of driving on and on until we win, whatever the cost. It is a great frustration to those of us stuck at the fringes of this war with little influence at its heart.'

I can see his point. From the King's perspective, we who fight for Parliament are the rebels in this war and always will be, however often we may best his troops. But if he beats us fully – even once – our brave men might all be hanged and their estates confiscated, flinging we women onto the streets. It is a chilling thought but one I do not run and cower from but surge towards with greater determination. I glance at Olly, wishing I could transfer some of my strengthening anger to him.

'But surely we want to make peace with the King in time, Father?' Betty asks, leaning into Father and flashing a smile at Val at the same time. 'You did not go to war to remove him from his throne.'

I mean to wait for his reply but feel too strongly to bide my tongue: 'Yes, but if we didn't intend to win the war, Betty,' I say, 'why ever did we take up arms in the first place?'

'You are right, Biddy.' Father rewards me with a grin and I glow under the warmth. 'We must be brave and staunch. We must have the courage of our convictions.'

Betty's forehead pinches in a slight frown but Father banishes it in an instant.

'You too speak truly, my dearest; we want the King to keep his throne, of course. But Parliament must be able to negotiate with him from an unassailable position of strength. We must keep outright victory and the possibility of striking no deal with him on the table. Only then can we ensure we restrain his powers and keep our own heads too.'

'Speaking of heads, I'm for bed,' Uncle Walton says, his words slurring at the edges. 'We'll ride home tomorrow, Val,' he tells his son as Val leaps up to help his father to his feet. He turns to his brother-in-law, my Uncle Desborough. 'John – you'll ride with us? We can see you home and stop in and see Jane and the children before going on to Great Staughton.'

Uncle Desborough nods and strides over to the fire to knock his pipe ashes into the hearth.

'I'll see to the beds,' I say and go in search of Martha

to help me make up the spare truckle beds – Val can go in with Olly and my uncles can sleep in the back room. This takes us some time, what with dusting down the frames, unrolling mattresses and finding clean linen and blankets that aren't being used. So by the time we have finished and Martha has located a spare chamber pot, jug and washing bowl, rushlights and candles, most of my family are in bed and the house has lulled into hushed sleep. Weary now myself, I say goodnight to my uncles – Uncle Walton already snoring and Uncle Desborough giving only the shortest grunt and no thanks in response – and climb the stairs to bed. Opening the door to our room I am surprised not to find Betty already in our bed. Closing the door softly so as not to wake Mary and Frances, I stand still for a few moments, listening.

Outside the wind has picked up and I can hear the loose window on the landing rattle. From my parents' room come the low familiar notes of Father's heavy sleeping and I thank the Lord once more that he is safe under our roof again. And then I catch another sound, this time unfamiliar: a soft murmuring of voices and the rustle of a skirt. Softly, I tiptoe along the narrow landing and peer around the corner towards the boys' bedroom. The sight before me burns my eyes: Betty is leaning against the wall, her chin tipped prettily upwards so her lips meet Val's as he bends over her. I stare at them for a few seconds, mesmerised by the intimate details of their picture. Her hand on his shoulder. His hand cupping her face. The double shadow they make on the wall by the light of their night candles. Suddenly I find my speech returning.

'Betty!' I hiss, not daring to speak any louder for fear of waking Father.

They spring apart and Val drops his candle with a curse, the flame extinguishing in the fall and hissing among the rushes. He drops to his knees to scrabble for it and I seize Betty by the wrist, yanking her away from him.

'Ow! You're hurting me,' she complains, but I pay no heed and whisk her into the safety of our room.

'What are you thinking?' I am about to say more, to let loose my angry thoughts, but Mall sits up in her bed across the room and peers at us, her doll clutched to her chest. I am forced into silence and can only stand in frustration as Betty undresses and flounces into bed, her dignity in some miraculous way preserved.

I motion Mall to lie back down and undress myself slowly, perched stiffly on the bed. Once under the covers, I keep as closely to my edge of the bed as I can and lie rigid like a dead fish, my angry thoughts thundering. Soon I sense that Betty is asleep and I marvel, as always, at the way she can simply banish unpleasantness from her mind in moments. Why can she, who has erred, sleep righteously while I, the innocent observer, am left reeling? I try to calm myself and bring my feelings under control but they are riddled enough to keep me from sleep for many hours. And so I lie in the darkness, listening to my sisters' soft breathing and struggling to understand which it is that upsets me more: that Betty has strayed from the Lord's path or that she has kissed a man before I have.

CHAPTER THREE

SUMMER 1643

Our whole family is on a war footing, our every effort bent to the Cause. So fully does it occupy our days, it is hard to remember what we did before King Charles raised his standard against our Parliament last year. While many Englishmen had struggled when forced to choose between King or Parliament, Father did not pause for a moment. The King was overbearing and autocratic, preferring to rule without Parliament, surround himself with treacherous advisers, levy illegal taxes, censor and punish his critics without fair trial and drag the Church back towards Rome, all in thrall to his French, Catholic Queen and her corrupt court. Only Parliament could stop England sliding into continental tyranny. 'Only Parliament can be the champion of the ordinary people and defender of our ancient freedoms,' Father would say as he pressed the men of the district into his cavalry troop, beer and bible in hand. And it was not only the men who felt the wisdom of Father's words fall upon them like God's truth from the pulpit. I felt it too. It was as if the coming of war unleashed a tidal force in Father and its waves carried the rest of us with him.

And so we work.

Father, home for most of the summer as he promised, organises the defence of the region from his former tax-collecting office in our house or from the back of his horse Blackjack. Every day brings a stream of men stomping in and out of our home – messengers, officers, local officials, Deputy Ireton – their boots muddy and throats thirsty for ale. Our front parlour becomes a sort of waiting room where men pace and plan, meet and rest. And we women do our bit too: waiting on the men, washing, mending, knitting stockings for the soldiers and orange sashes for the officers, shopping for provisions, visiting the bereaved, organising collections, selling clothes, bread and pastries in the market to raise funds for the army.

I am standing with Betty and Mother behind a stall at one such sales when I see Henry Ireton crossing the marketplace towards us. It is a hot, muggy Saturday and the town is full of traders, goodwives, servants and soldiers each pressing about their business, mopping their faces and fluttering fans, eyes shielded against the sun. Henry Ireton alone seems oblivious to the heat as he walks purposefully, his eyes trained ahead while he dictates instructions to a scurrying sergeant taking notes at his elbow.

'Ladies,' he greets us briskly and reaches into his pocket for some coins for our collecting cup. The sergeant melts away behind him.

'Good afternoon, Deputy Ireton.' Mother curtseys. 'How are you today?'

'Well enough, I thank you, ma'am. I have been busy about the town sourcing suppliers this morning. It would astonish you to hear the quantities of provisions troops need when they are quartered: meat, bread, oatmeal, peas, cheese, beer and fodder for the horses – all by the ton or gallon. And that is without even considering soap, candles and firewood, medical supplies . . .' Henry loses himself in his list, his eyes lit by the challenge.

Mother laughs, though not unkindly. 'As a mother of a large household, I can well imagine, sir! The question is simply one of scale. If you would appreciate some local insight into the town's tradespeople, I would be happy to advise you.'

Henry seems surprised by her answer and gives an awkward nod and a half-smile. 'I am grateful, ma'am – I will bring you some names when I next come to the Governor's house and would be glad to take your view.'

'Do, sir.' Mother smiles. 'Bridget here can also advise you – she now manages most of our accounts in the town.'

I am pleased to be given due credit in this and accept Henry's nod politely, though the next moment, a doubt begins to creep into my mind. Is Mother deliberately presenting me as a capable helpmeet?

'And where are you off to now, sir?' I ask, moving the conversation on.

'In half an hour I ride out with your father to drill the latest recruits,' he replies, 'but just now I plan to take a few minutes' reflection in the cathedral. We have some new preachers addressing us; a few of the townspeople and some of my own men are speaking. It does me good to hear them.'

I am astonished by this. It used to be that only Reverend Hitch or visiting clergy could preach in the cathedral and if we wanted to hear another sermon – one more to our independent taste – Father had to take us to a private house or a meeting room. I know Father has been too busy to engage himself in cathedral affairs of late so this change must be of Deputy Ireton's doing.

'Would you like to accompany me, ma'am?' Henry has turned to ask Mother while I am lost in my thoughts.

'I would dearly love to, sir, but I am much occupied as you see.' Mother pauses a moment then turns a bright smile upon him. 'But I do not need *both* my girls here to help me – Bridget, why don't you go and hear the preachers? I know you would enjoy that.'

I set my lips tightly. So Mother has determined Henry would make a good match for me. Have she and Betty been talking of it together? Does Father know? Irritated, I cast about for a polite refusal but can find none that will do. And I would like to hear the preachers . . .

'If you're sure, Mother,' I reply with a deliberate indifference. I turn a level gaze on Henry Ireton who offers a polite nod in return.

'Quite sure. Off you go. Perhaps you could call on widow Thomas on your way home, Biddy; see if there's anything she needs.'

And so that is that. I place a loaf of bread and four currant buns in my basket for widow Thomas, and fall into step beside Henry. He has long legs and a swift soldierly pace so I have to take a little skipping step in every three or four to keep level with him.

'You are fond of preaching, Mistress Cromwell?' he

asks me at length, keeping his eyes ahead. His tone is so flat, even disinterested, I can take nothing from it.

'I am, sir.' I reach for the words through quickening breath due to his pace. 'I like to have something new to think on as I go about my chores.'

'Then you value new teachings? You do not seek the simple comfort of the known and understood?'

I consider his question for a moment, surprised by its direction. 'I seek a blend of both,' I say. 'We need the certainty of the known – the Commandments, Christ's teachings and God's love for us – to order our lives by. But the Word of the Lord is a living thing, is it not? Just as we are? We must always seek to interpret it anew, to learn more from it, I think.'

Henry turns to me then and gives a rare smile; his face is rather vulpine, I think again, though I will never admit so to Betty. I will not give kindling to her furious matchmaking.

'I agree with you,' he says, a little warmth now in his voice, 'and never more so than in the present conflicted times when it is hard always to see our path ahead. We must seek to know God's will more now than ever before and He can reveal Himself to us in the most unlikely places.'

I am interested in his ideas despite myself. 'So opening up the cathedral to ordinary preachers is your doing, Deputy Ireton?'

'It is.' He nods thoughtfully. 'I would have greater freedom for the people of Ely to live as they choose and to speak their thoughts without fear. Why fight at all if we cannot effect such change?'

'You will put a good many noses out of joint by it,' I say, reluctant to encourage him by my agreement.

'I do not doubt it, Mistress Cromwell. But I imagine your family is unafraid of offending such people.'

It is my turn to smile then, though I had not intended to. 'That is true enough. There are those that call my family radical for our reformed views, though we have never courted trouble and always attend church as the law prescribes. Indeed, Father works hard to maintain good relations with all the prominent families of the town, whatever their tastes in religion.'

'Your father is a greater conciliator than I am, mistress,' he replies, 'something I have seen often for myself. I am more inflexible, more impatient than he. Many times I have angered for change and he has placed his hand on my shoulder and urged patience.'

I am intrigued by this insight into their relationship. I have observed how much Father respects his deputy's intelligence and commitment. Perhaps it is the contrast in their characters that makes them work so well together?

I would like to learn more of Father's leadership style but we have reached the cathedral now and fall silent. As Henry leads me up the wide chequered nave, the vast ceiling vaulting over us like a great canopy of stone silver birches, the congregants we pass nod in deference to the deputy and I feel suddenly self-conscious, as if I am his bride. I bury the sensation swiftly as deeply as I can.

A soldier is just finishing his address as we take our seats and he walks back to his place with a salute to Henry. There is a scrape and a shuffle behind us and a figure moves forward to speak next. To my amazement it is a woman and as I peer more closely I realise I know her: she is the daughter of one of our tenants. I have got to know them all better this last year through helping Mother collect the rents while Father has been away. The people around us murmur and take in sharp breaths. Even those of the more reformed Puritan faith like us would for the most part draw the line at a woman preaching. But she is allowed to speak and Henry beside me makes no move to stop her.

The woman speaks for only a few minutes, talking of her own experience of God and praising Him for caring about the little things of our daily lives. I listen, rapt. Merely to hear her voice, to see her standing before us in upright majesty, pouring forth her certainty in her unfolding thoughts, is enough for me. I am lifted high up and into the rafters at the sight and for those few minutes feel all my fears for the future slip from my shoulders. If she can do this, why couldn't I? Might this be how I can make my own way in life, by the Word of God?

'She was extraordinary,' I find myself telling Betty later that evening as we help the little ones with their reading. 'To have the confidence to stand up like that and tell the truth of her faith; explain her own relationship with God.'

Betty raises an eyebrow at me. I do not expect her to share my interest in the woman preacher but I am vainly attempting to draw her away from the subject of Henry Ireton. 'Carry on, Mary, try this next word. G-a-r-d-e-n,' we say together. 'Yes, that's right.'

'But what did you and the deputy speak of?' Betty presses. 'I saw you talking as you crossed the market.'

'Nothing of consequence. Garden o-f . . . now this is a difficult word, G-e-t-h-s-e . . .'

'It's a shame he is not more handsome,' Betty interrupts us, eyeing me as she lowers her chin to rest on the top of Frances's head.

'Fortunately, I do not share your obsession with good looks,' I reply. 'The ability to make intelligent conversation is far more important.'

'Aha! So your conversation was of some consequence.'

I bridle at falling into her trap. 'At least we had some conversation. I do not remember seeing you and Val speaking of much on the landing.'

'Hush!' It is her turn to bridle and she flashes me a warning look.

'Why? What were you doing with Val?' Frances tips her head up to Betty, her picture book forgotten in her curiosity.

'Nothing at all, young missy,' Betty says quickly and squeezes Fanny until she giggles, the book sliding off her lap onto the floor.

'What a charming scene.' Father appears in the doorway and Betty glances at me reproachfully as if to emphasise how nearly I had betrayed her.

'My lovely girls at their studies,' Father observes happily as he sinks into a chair and props his boots up on a stool.

'It is late; have you eaten, Father? Shall I fetch you something?' I make to rise but he waves me to stay seated.

'I ate at The Bell with Henry after we reviewed the

new troops. He told me he took you to hear the preachers, Biddy? If so, you did well to catch him in a moment's leisure; he never stops working. I've insisted he dine with us tomorrow. We'll see if your mother can't fatten him up.'

Betty raises an eyebrow at me.

'He did, Father, and very interesting they were,' I reply, ignoring Betty's arch look.

'Ah, well. Good, good. He's a fine man far from home; it pleases me for you to show him friendship.'

I cannot tell if Father means to reproach me my coldness or to encourage me to accept Henry as a suitor. Or, indeed, if his words mean no more than themselves. But I have no wish to discover which.

'How were the new men, Father?' I move the conversation on. 'Will they do?'

He bends down to help himself to a sugared biscuit from the plate on the floor by Betty. 'They're a mixed bunch. Now the Earl of Manchester is appointed our commander and has brought in conscription, he's opened our ranks to less committed men. I've told him we need men of zeal who love God and believe in our cause; that such men are worth ten of the other on the battlefield. But he is in command. Henry and I will do what we can to mould them and if we promote the best of them, regardless of their social rank, they can set the tone for the rest. Besides, we need the men.'

'Are things so desperate, Father?' Betty asks, reaching behind her to squeeze his knee. I feel Mary tense on my lap as she slips her hand into mine.

'No, my love, not desperate,' Father says, his tone light and reassuring; though I wonder if he would give the same answer to his fellow officers that he gives his worried daughters.

'Not desperate, but delicately balanced perhaps?' I ask, trying by my straight stare to indicate my adult understanding.

Father examines me carefully and I can see him choosing his words. 'Delicate, yes, Bridget. The King is on the front foot; we need all the men we can muster.'

'Bedtime, girls,' Mother's voice summons them from the hall. Mary springs obediently from my lap while Frances crosses her arms in protest.

'I'll take them,' Father calls back and Fanny beams and jumps up eagerly. Betty and I watch as Father herds them from the room, their small hands clutching at his jacket. 'Shall I tell you the story of the big bear again?' I hear him ask as they climb the stairs, his words followed by growls and giggles.

'He is good,' Betty says, taking a biscuit.

'He spoils them,' I reply.

CHAPTER FOUR

We all know that we are living on borrowed time; that very soon Father and Olly will return to the field, leaving us to sink into the tedious, crushing despair of waiting women in wartime. I cannot help resenting them for it, as if it is their fault any more than ours.

I believe Olly senses my growing irritation but is kind enough to see it for the love it masks. On the day before their departure, he asks me to come fishing with him as we used to when we were children. I should be helping Martha in the kitchen and finishing mending Father's shirts but the pull of the wide, waterlogged fields and Olly all to myself is too tempting.

We walk together through the town to the Great Ouse and, crossing it, follow the ridges along the patchworked channels east towards the sun which glints off the still waters. I know the spot he aims for and after twenty minutes or so we come to a stop together and I spread out the blanket as he crouches to bait his hook. We settle down and watch the breeze whisking through the tall bulrushes.

'After the war I'll be happy to do nothing but fish,' he says.

I smile, closing my eyes against the warm sunshine. 'Eventually, you will inherit the house and you can spend every day out here in the Fens if you want to. You'll tire of it soon enough though.'

'I won't,' Oliver replies, almost fiercely. 'I don't long to do great things in the world as Father does, as *you* do.'

'Me?' I look at him and laugh hollowly at the notion though it catches a little in my throat. 'What chance will I have to do anything extraordinary?'

He thinks for a moment. 'I don't know, Biddy. But I do know that you'll seize any chance that does come your way. You must promise me something.'

I raise an eyebrow at him.

'Promise you won't be too proud to take that chance, even if it is dressed up as a husband.'

I stare at him, my thoughts moving quickly from initial indignation at his impudence to settle in reflection on the truth of what he says. How can he know the war that rages within me over my future? My desire to accomplish more than merely a husband's approval at my running of his household and raising of his children in conflict with my innate understanding that marriage is likely to be my only realistic route to independence; the simple pleasure I gain from a chore well done battling my frustration that the properly swept front step of my house may be my only horizon. Have I been born of the wrong generation, or indeed of the right one? What place for me in this new world being forged around me? I turn back to the water, drawing my knees up under my chin as these wild thoughts whirl within me.

'Betty has her eyes open on that score,' Olly continues, more humorously now. 'She won't wait for you to marry, you can be sure of that—' He pauses and rubs the stubble at his chin. 'She's given me a note for Val. You don't suppose she and he . . . ?'

I flinch. I cannot stomach lies but neither do I want to betray my sister's indiscretion, even to Olly. 'She's young and flirtatious,' I say instead. 'She's just begun to feel the power of her beauty and she's training it, flexing it like a muscle. I see it developing every day. I even envy it in my weaker moments, knowing full well how her beauty outstrips my own.' I hold up a hand to thank but stop Olly in his automatic denial of this truth. 'No, no, it's fine. In fact, I see her beauty as a burden too, bringing inflated hopes and expectations, putting pressure on innocent moments.'

'I would never have thought of beauty that way,' Oliver says, shaking his head.

'You're a man,' I reply.

'And Father?'

'Blinder than you. Betty's charm works on him most of all. But Mother can see us clearly. I think she wishes her gifts had been more evenly bestowed in childbed: that Betty had some of my faith and I had a measure of her beauty. That she were a little more serious and I a little less so. Perhaps the future would not seem so uncertain for us both were that the case.'

'Such a bleak assessment,' Olly comments. 'I see we all have our battles to fight.'

His words recall me from my self-pity. 'I'm sorry, dearest. But tell me honestly how the war stands. Father is too careful of our feelings to be open with the full truth, I'm sure of it.'

Olly sighs and takes a few moments to cast his line

back into the water where the bait is caught in a shimmering eddy.

'It's not good, Biddy. The King is winning. It's rumoured he is to form two new armies, one in the west and one in the north, both to advance on London. They'll be reinforced by troops returning from Ireland. And we're in danger here in the east. The Earl of Newcastle's northern army gains ground by the day. They've reached Stamford now – that's only a day or two's march from here. We need help. Our best hope, our only hope, is that John Pym and his faction in Parliament can persuade the Scots to come into the war on our side.'

'And is that likely?'

'It's a long shot. There are plenty in that kingdom loyal to King Charles – he is Scotch himself, after all.'

'But they don't like his religion, his High Church ways?'

'No, they don't. And they showed that just before the war when they wouldn't have his new prayer book. That's our best line of persuasion, though we must hope that any agreement doesn't come at too high a price for the English.'

'Their insistence on establishing their Presbyterian Church in England, you mean?' I bristle at the thought of that foreign Church with its rigid system of governance, its assemblies of elders handing down orders to the ordinary people. Where would the freedom for us religious independents be in that? 'Surely Pym wouldn't agree to that?' I ask.

Olly lays down his rod to fish instead in my basket for a piece of bread.

'Anything is possible now,' he says as he chews. 'We

have come this far, there's no turning back.' He turns his face from me and stares out over the water, his eyes narrowing into the sunlight which caresses the dark curls at his neck.

I should follow his gaze and enjoy the mirrored world which lies before me like an illuminated manuscript of the old Church; its holly-and-ivy greens, bright golds and ink and powder-blues somehow sharper and more real than the world it reflects. And yet I only want to look at my precious brother and drink in his unique landscape of marbled peach and tan skin, the scar on his neck from an old shaving cut white against his conker-brown hair. I wait, knowing there's something else he wants to tell me.

At length he speaks again, his voice as quiet as the still water:

'I saw one of my school friends when we fought in the last hour of Edgehill. He was on the other side, right in front of me. We saw each other in the same instant, through the musket smoke, and I froze in the saddle. I couldn't attack him, could I? But my hand was on my sword, blood roaring in my ears as horses crashed into each other around me. So I swung at the man next to him instead, slicing right through him and he fell from his mount. My friend reined in then stared at me in horror as if I was an animal. And why should he not? His comrade lay sprawled on the grass leaking blood, his body already trampled underfoot. I wanted to tell my friend I didn't mean to do it, that I was protecting him. I wanted him to move, to charge at me, or at anyone, but he just sat there, stunned, his horse pawing the ground beneath him. I moved towards him then, desperate just to take him in my arms and tell him I loved him but the next moment one of the pikemen thrust a pike right up through his chest. He didn't have time to look away from me before the light vanished from his eyes and he fell to the earth. He stares at me still in my dreams. Stares and slips lifeless out of his saddle, over and over again.'

I move across the blanket and take my brother's hand in mine, lacing my fingers tightly through his. There is nothing in the world that I can say in comfort and I curse myself for the limits of my girlish experience. Even more so for the little I can do for our cause. I used to think I could steal away, disguise myself as a boy and join the army as it is rumoured some women have done. Women determined to fight or simply to follow their husbands or sweethearts. But could I stand such sights as Olly speaks of? The mountain of male flesh that we must scale to victory? His words cloud my mind with doubts. How then can I help?

And so we sit, each imprisoned in our own way, so still and silent that a kingfisher flashes past us in a bright blur to take up a sentry post by Olly's fishing line.

The parting is as tearful as ever – despite Father's assurances that he is likely to be home again soon – for no separation in wartime can be counted safe, however short. I kiss Father then leave him to the others who need more of his embraces: to Mother, Grandmother, Betty and the little girls. I move instead to Olly and am the last to touch him before he rides away in Father's shadow to join his men.

'Remember the salve!' he calls over his shoulder and I feel for the pot in my pocket.

It takes fifteen minutes for the eight hundred men to ride out of the town and our arms ache from waving and our cheeks from forced smiling when we can at last retreat inside into our shared gloom. As soon as we women are alone, we sag and droop, our true feelings revealed to one another in one collective exhale of breath. It is always this way when the men leave, I reflect with irritation as I look from face to face. It is as if, without them, we are suddenly shapeless, without purpose, without life itself. We wave them off to the centre of things and relapse ourselves into the quiet trivialities of feminine life, always at the mercy of the next post.

It irks me, this dependence we share, even as I feel it within myself too. I don't think I minded the difference between men's and women's lives, even noticed it much, before the war began, though perhaps the feeling started two years earlier when Father became an MP. Before then, in those happiest years when Father came into his legacy and we first moved to this house in Ely, Father's life – the most central life to us all, even more so than our own – radiated outwards from its four walls. Gradually, he reinserted himself into society, took on more and more local responsibilities. We began to entertain our neighbours, to build a network of influence, and Father was among us each day, running his business from the tithe office.

But then his eyes moved beyond the flat fenland horizon. He became MP for Cambridge – an achievement that startled even Mother, who knew best his talent – sold his tax position and was soon riding to Cambridge and London, away for weeks, even months, at a time. But these were not happy parliaments after so many years of the King's personal rule and Father would return gloomy and brooding, closed up in his study with the important men of the region. I listened as much as I could as I took in their beer and bread – heard them say the King was abusing his power, raising illegal taxes, imprisoning men without trial, taking inspiration from continental despots as his French Catholic wife poisoned his view of the Church. There was rebellion in Scotland, then in Ireland, and the King took soldiers into Parliament to arrest his opponents but they, forewarned, had fled. Thwarted, he left London and lifted his standard at Nottingham, declaring war on his own people. Then, before we knew it, Father was raising troops and seizing Cambridge for Parliament; an act of boldness that made his name.

My life changed too, then, though I did not see it at the time. With Father and Olly fighting and the younger boys at school, I took over some of the work of the men of the house that I would never have done in peacetime. Now I help Mother run Father's business affairs and collect his rents, I arrange payment for the boys' school fees, I deal with suppliers and servants and keep my eyes and ears always open for intelligence to pass to Father. In Father's absence, Mother makes family decisions and she leans on me for advice. Together we often sit late into the evening while my sisters are tucked up in bed, reading letters and paying bills, discussing the latest news of the war and planning our future. I love the challenge even as it has made me long for more from my life.

I know now that I would not be content only with a life centred on hearth and home. I need to live a life out in the world where I can have an impact on more than my children and my neighbours. Perhaps I could find such a life for myself as a preacher or a writer. But I do not want to end up like Aunt Liz, a spare part living in a house that is not my own, deferring to another woman and under the rule of a man who is not my husband. And I can no longer pretend I could run away to war. So it may have to be as Olly said, that I need to hitch myself to a husband in order to travel. But I could never marry a man who would not take me on the journey with him, who did not want me for a full partner. Who did not take my advice above all others. If he will not share his outside life with me, I will provide no inside life for him.

Stirred by these thoughts, I set my lips and take command of the desolate women around me; the man of the house once more.

'Henry! How nice. Do come in.'

It is 'Henry' now that Deputy Ireton is so often in our company. Left behind to govern the town in Father's stead, he sups with us once or twice a week, sits beside us in the cathedral on Sundays and takes Mother's advice and mine in his dealings with the local tradesmen. Apart from our groom, Henry's is sometimes the only male voice we hear for days on end. Mother is very taken with him and is coming to depend on him quite as on an oldest son. The little ones, missing their father, crowd around his ankles for sweets and Betty, through boredom, I suspect, smiles and blushes at him now for all his foxy features. He seems to enjoy all of this female attention, which must be such a contrast to his otherwise martial life, though in his own serious and sometimes brusque way. For myself, I take no special pains to make him welcome, though I do value one aspect of his frequent visits: that he always brings news of the war. This evening he shares the headline in the hall before he has even removed his cloak:

'The Scots have joined with us, God be praised!' He does not grin over the news as other men would but his flashing eyes tell me all I need to know of the importance of this development.

'Thank the Lord,' Mother says, taking Henry by the arm. 'You'll stay to supper and celebrate with us.'

'Martha – another place for supper,' I call down the back passage towards the kitchen before fetching a bottle of wine to replace the small beer we would otherwise have drunk were we alone. In the parlour, I cede my usual place at Mother's right hand to Henry and take the chair opposite him instead.

'The details are still being negotiated,' Henry continues as he carefully draws out his chair. 'But, regardless, this will transform the war. With a Scots army we can win, however many Irish rebels the King allies with.'

'Would it be such a large force, Henry?' Betty asks, her eyes wide.

'Twenty thousand strong, it is rumoured.'

'Praise be,' Mother says, clasping her hands. 'Henry, would you say grace?'

I press my eyes together tightly as Henry intones the grace, praying fervently that this army will indeed take our cause to victory. When I open them again, the table is quiet as everyone helps themselves to food. I seize the moment to learn more.

'And what is the price of these twenty thousand Scots, Deputy Ireton? Will we soon find ourselves bidden to a Presbyterian church?'

Henry examines me before he answers, his knife still untouched beside his plate. 'It is a shrewd question, Miss Bridget. That is the sticking point, I believe, and I know that none of us around this table wish to see our independence of religion constrained any further.'

'Indeed we do not,' I reply. 'Then we must hope that Parliament has found a compromise acceptable to all.'

'Yes,' he agrees, 'some clever wording in the text of the agreement – to promise reform and agree to some demands – for example, following them in abolishing holy days such as Christmas, but without stipulating too closely what the future Church should look like.'

'Nor *when* any changes will be made,' I continue. 'Prevarication and delay – surely our politicians can manage that.'

Henry gives me a respectful look before I catch Mother and Betty sharing a conspiratorial glance and narrow my eyes at them, busying myself with my plate, determined to say no more.

'Your family in Nottinghamshire will be glad at the news?' Mother hurries to cover the silence.

'They're sure to be,' Grandmother interrupts from the other end of the table before Henry can answer. 'It is not easy for the womenfolk left behind.'

'No indeed, ma'am.' Henry inclines his head to her politely. 'And it has been especially hard for my family, as I have been cut off from them by the King's northern army.'

'But then, without that misfortune, you would not be sitting here with us.' Betty smiles at Henry and I grate at her easy charm even as I admire it.

I glance at Henry, expecting the fawning gaze that

Betty's honeyed words provoke in other men, but he seems quite unaffected.

Mother smiles then shakes her head in sympathy. 'Is your father at home?'

'My father died many years ago,' Henry replies quietly. 'When I was thirteen.'

'Oh my dear.' Mother places a maternal hand on Henry's and leads us in collective feminine sympathy. 'And do you have brothers and sisters?'

'I am the eldest of eight; eight that lived beyond babyhood, that is.'

I look up at that, intrigued out of my planned silence. 'And so you became head of the household when your father died?' I ask, thinking of Father, who was put in the same position at eighteen, left to care for a widowed mother and seven sisters. I glance at Grandmother, now leaning towards Henry with more interest, and sense she is thinking the same thing.

Henry pushes at a piece of chicken on his plate before answering: 'Yes and no. Yes, in that I took responsibility for my family and have run the estate alongside my mother these past years while my siblings grew up. But no, in that we have a different system in Nottinghamshire where the youngest brother inherits the estate – not the eldest.'

We are all astonished and can barely conceal the fact. 'I never heard of such a thing,' I manage at last.

'Nor I,' Mother agrees while Grandmother tuts into her glass and Aunt Liz gives a pigeon coo of sympathy.

Henry takes a long drink from his wine glass and it occurs to me that this is an embarrassing conversation he must be well used to. It must be painful for him to admit that though he is the oldest son of a gentry family he has no expectations nor prospects. No wonder he is so ambitious to make a name for himself in the war.

'It is an unusual practice to be sure,' Henry speaks again at length, 'but there is no need to pity me. I have always known this to be the case and have taken pains to make my own way – first at Oxford, then in the army. And now the Lord has seen fit to send me to do his work here. This is a fine time for a man to make his mark, whatever his circumstances – our army is full of spare sons like me.'

For a man, yes, I think, not without some envy. If only I could speak so boldly of my own future, with such certainty that my own abilities will carry me through regardless. I examine Henry carefully, wondering if our sympathy has rattled or comforted him, but he is too hard to read today.

'Well, we will raise a glass to that, Henry,' Mother says, her kindness smoothing any wrinkles in the conversation, and we lift our wine to him. 'I have no doubt you will make your family proud, and I hope that, while you are kept apart from them, you will look upon us as your family.'

'Yes indeed, young man.' Grandmother adds her weight to Mother's words. 'I admire any son who cares for his widowed mother and siblings the way you have – the way my Oliver has. You are welcome at our table.'

'Thank you, ma'am – and you, ma'am, you are most generous,' Henry replies, looking a little flustered as he thanks Mother and Grandmother, though I fancy a degree of pleasure lies beneath his awkwardness. He goes on to confirm my suspicion: 'I must admit to enjoying something of the comforts of family life when under your roof and of being reminded of my own mother and sisters.'

'But I hope we do not remind you *too* closely of your sisters, Henry,' Betty says and the meaningful smile she sweeps over me gives me the mortifying feeling she is flirting on my behalf.

I feel my cheeks redden with embarrassment and glare back at her, but the furtive glance I then give Henry to gauge his reaction reassures me, for his face betrays only polite bemusement; Betty's true meaning appears to have escaped him entirely. Relieved, I reach for my glass, thanking the Lord for Henry's lack of intuition even as I wonder what it says about me.

CHAPTER FIVE

SPRING 1644

'Five pounds a week?'

'Five pounds.' Mother smiles over Father's letter.

'And every week without fail?' I ask, lowering the household ledger to my lap.

'That's what he says. He'll send it to us whether he receives his pay or not. Now he's been promoted again his men are to be properly funded and he hopes things should be a little easier for us.'

'Praise the Lord,' I say, returning to the ledger. I scan the columns and do some quick sums. 'We can pay the term's school fees, Matthew's and Martha's wages and settle our account with the butcher.'

'And Betty can have the ribbons she wants for her birthday,' Mother adds.

I allow an indulgent smile.

'If we let her have them early, she can wear them for John Claypole's visit, which will please her,' Mother continues.

'Then he may pay more attention to her than me,

which will ruin your plans,' I reply, cocking my head at her.

Mother sighs at me. 'You cannot put off marriage forever, Biddy. Your father is anxious you should be settled. And if you will not have Henry . . .'

'I never said I would not have Henry.' It is my turn to sigh as I straighten in my chair. 'Besides, it hardly figures what I think when he has shown no interest in me, for all yours and Betty's manoeuvres. He is only interested in his work.' Though I do not care for him in any romantic way, my feelings need not be the guide of his. It is sinful vanity, I know, but I would enjoy being admired just once.

Mother ignores my reply. 'If you will not have Henry, have John Claypole for a husband. He's younger – about your age – and has better prospects: he'll inherit the house at Northborough one day. And his mother is lovely.'

'What else does Father say?' I ask, refusing to stoop to her merchant talk of marriage.

Mother drops her gaze to the folded page. 'He says Olly has been posted to the garrison at Newport Pagnell, while your father is much in London attending the meetings of this new joint Committee of English and Scots that will now direct the war. It is a great honour that Parliament has appointed him to it, alongside all those great peers and generals; he can barely hide his excitement.'

'Father will be far happier now he has a seat at the top table,' I reply, closing the ledger, intent on bed. 'He'll soon have them eating out of his hands.'

*

Despite my protestations, Mother has her way and her friend Mary Claypole and her eldest son John arrive to stay with us. I know them to be fine Puritan folk – John's father refused to pay the King's illegal ship money tax before the war – but I cannot quieten the voice in my head that cringes at such obvious matchmaking. And so my silent and sullen self is quite unprepared to be charmed.

'Mistress Cromwell, what a pleasure to see you again.' John Claypole sweeps my hand to his lips and lowers his lithe, sporting limbs into the chair beside mine in the garden. He is startlingly handsome, all dark hair and flushed cheeks as he smiles in the spring sunshine. A ginger spaniel lays itself across his boots as I pour him a glass of cordial.

'It is a good few years since we last met,' he continues easily, 'and I hear you are most staunch in your support of the war effort and that you quite manage the house while your good father is away.'

His assessment pleases me and I smile in assent. 'I do my bit, sir, what little I can, that is. And you?'

'I plan to enlist soon,' he replies quickly and I am relieved at this, for his appearing in civilian dress had surprised me in one his age and I had worried for a few moments that he was uncommitted to Parliament's great cause.

A movement by the kitchen door catches my eye and I see Martha show the military figure of Henry Ireton into the garden. I frown momentarily, remembering that Mother had invited him to dine with us – her excuse being that he would help to redress the imbalance of sexes at the table, though I know her true reason is to see if the presence of two potential suitors might not spur one or other of them into making me a proposal.

Henry strides vigorously across the grass and the introductions are made before he takes a seat by Mary Claypole and offers her some conventional pleasantries. I sense that John, much younger than Henry, has already written him off as a dull and shabby soldier and the conspiratorial grin he flashes me as he turns his attention back to me seems to confirm as much. Though I should disapprove, I find myself returning the smile as if we have shared some joke.

We talk lightly of life at his home in Northborough and share news of our mutual friends before, coming to a pause, John stoops to ruffle the long fur of his dog's ears.

'What's his name?' I ask.

'Badger. And you want to ask me why?' He smiles at my quizzical expression, seeing the question already formed on my lips. 'Because he saw off a wounded badger the very first day I had him, as we rode home from a hunt. It was the bravest thing I ever saw. And I resolved on that day that I would call every dog I owned Badger in memory of the gallant deed.'

I laugh, surprising myself. Self-conscious, I stoop to scratch Badger's head, my little finger tingling when it briefly brushes John's in the tangled hair. He glances at me and laughs warmly, something in the sound reminding me of Father. Perhaps we could be a good match after all, I wonder, withdrawing my hand to smooth my hair quickly before John looks up.

'Ah Betty, good girl.'

Mother's voice brings my eyes to Betty now gliding across the grass towards us, the extra jar of honey she had been dispatched to buy borne before her like a queen's golden orb. I feel the change in John before he has even spoken. He drops his hand from Badger and leaps to his feet, leaning away from me as he greets Betty.

There is no hope after that. John is mesmerised by my sister and his infatuation is plain for us all to see. Though I am hardly surprised, his preference pains me and I sink into a sulking acceptance of the all-too-familiar dance where Betty draws a man like a moth to a candle, leaving me to shiver in the darkness. Must it always be this way? I think bitterly as I watch her effect on John. Will beauty, youth and charm always count for more than fortitude and understanding? Even in times of war? Mother, seeing my distress, does her best, seating me next to John at dinner with Betty placed at the far end of the table, but the spark has gone from our conversation and John seems distracted, his attention wandering in Betty's direction. And for her part, Betty seems just as taken with John, smiling at him in much the same way as she does at Val. Henry, sitting opposite me, is also more quiet than usual, though he stirs himself over the raspberry pudding to try his best to enlist John into the army.

I find myself longing to be alone to nurse my hurt feelings. I sense that Henry is restless too, no doubt itching to return to work now that the meal is drawing to a close. He is in the process of making his excuses when there is a knock at the door. Mother makes to rise but Henry puts a hand on her shoulder.

'I'll see to it.' Returning a few moments later, he hands a letter to Mother.

'Is it from Father?' Frances asks, bouncing in her chair with excitement.

'Yes, Fanny, though I would hardly know his hand, the writing is so scrawled.'

Mother begins to read and we wait silently. Seeing Martha hovering in the doorway I rise and begin clearing the plates on my side of the table while she attends to the other. Busy with the task, it is only when I see Betty's face that I know something is wrong. She is staring at Mother, her eyes widening in distress. I follow her gaze to Mother's ashen face, see her hand clutch the pearls at her neck, twin tears carving down the curves of her cheeks.

'Mother?' I find my voice.

But Mother does not speak. Instead she holds the paper shaking in the air and I watch in frozen horror as it wavers there for an agony of long moments before Henry steps forward and gently takes it from her. Mother stares blankly ahead while Henry scans the page. My heart creeps up my neck into my throat and I struggle to swallow. Henry lowers the paper.

'I am so sorry, my dear friends, it is the worst of news.' His voice is soft and reverent as his eyes meet mine and somehow he shares the terrible knowledge with me before speaking it aloud.

Olly.

My dearest brother is dead, I can feel it in the marrow of my bones.

Henry says the words but I don't hear them. I am listening for Olly's spirit, trying to will it back into his earthly body. But there is only silence.

Somehow I find the strength to force my feelings

below the floodwater surging within me and move the members of my family around the house like dolls. I take Mother's arm and urge her to her feet, passing her to Henry with a single word: 'Upstairs.' She sinks onto him and he almost carries her up the stairs. I look to Aunt Liz and motion for her to take the girls. Mary and Frances bury their bawling faces into her skirts as she leads them gently into the back passage towards the kitchen. I look around the table for Grandmother before remembering that, mercifully, she has spent the day upstairs nursing a cold and so I can leave her until later.

Betty next. I find John already on his feet and at her side, clearly at a loss for words as she sobs in Mistress Claypole's arms, her new pink ribbons drooping forlornly.

'You poor, poor girls,' Mary Claypole whispers to me above Betty's hair. 'We will continue our visit another time. Write to me, Bridget, let me know how your Mother does and what I can do.'

I thank her and urge her and John towards a tearful Martha to see to their bags and carriage. At the door John turns back to me. He shakes his head and sets his lips, his expression full of sympathy, though he seems unable to find any words of comfort for me. Just for a moment I long for him to take me in his arms and whisper soothing words into my hair but he steps through the front door in silence.

Alone, my thoughts race hungrily to the next task, not daring to rest for a moment on my deeper feelings, nor leave even a moment's window in which to learn more of how Olly has died. Was he wounded in battle? Had he sent me the weapon as he had said he would do?

Could I have saved him with his salve? I hurry to the kitchen, shaking the questions loose from my head like raindrops from a coat. Aunt Liz is giving the girls warm milk and sugar biscuits as they slump on the bench, rubbing fists into their blotchy eyes. Relieved they are being cared for, I put a pan of brandy-wine to heat on the fire before finding the lavender, honey and camomile and setting about mixing a sleeping draught for Mother. The clip of boots on flagstones brings Henry into the kitchen, a tearful Martha trailing behind him. Swiftly he crosses the room to me and takes the pestle from my hand to lower it into the mortar.

'Martha can do that,' he says quietly, before taking my hand and leading me back to the parlour where he lowers me, numb, into a chair by the hearth and drapes a blanket around my shoulders. I am vaguely conscious of him as he moves softly around the room lighting the fire and then fetching me a glass of the hot brandy. But I can only sit and stare. I feel a thick cloud wrap about me and through it I hear the muffled all-too-familiar sounds of crying from every corner of the house as if the very timbers weep. Olly's face floats before me, his lop-sided smile warming me for the last time.

Someone moves my hand up to my mouth and I feel the glass hot against my lips and a bitter sweetness on my tongue. I swallow once, twice. The person takes the glass from me and tucks my hands together on my lap under a blanket.

'He was a soldier, Bridget, you must hold on to that.' Henry's voice filters through the fog towards me.

'A soldier.' Unthinking, I repeat his words without any meaning.

'A soldier,' he repeats. 'He lived with death every day, he knew the dangers, he was used to them. We all are.'

My thoughts surface for air like frantic frogs. I cannot tell Henry that he is wrong; that Olly was no soldier, that he never accustomed himself to the horror. That he was frightened and unhappy. I cannot show him the pot of salve. He has already given his life, I will not take away his honour too. 'Was he shot? Did he suffer?' I manage instead, my stomach knotting in fear as I imagine him grasping for the weapon that wounded him.

'He died of a fever in the barracks.'

'Fever?' I slump in shock. When I had imagined his death, in my darkest, most fearful moments as I lay awake at night, his pot of potion clutched under my pillow, it was always in violence. And then I would overlay the nightmare with a golden dream that I saved him. But I never saw this. Never thought he could have a slow, bed-ridden death like Robin's at school. I see Olly lying on a mattress, his forehead sweaty and his palms cold, with no one to hold his hand. I never had the chance to help him. I circle my thumb on my skirt, remembering the feeling of his lace-edged linen collars as I washed them for the last time, hoping somehow that something of my love had transferred with them; that he could feel my fingers stroking his neck as he died.

Henry's voice interrupts my thoughts and brings my eyes to focus on his for the first time.

'He was doing God's work, Bridget, and God will gather him to Him.'

I think of Olly, tearful with fear that the Lord would strike him down next, having taken our older brother first. I remember how I promised him God would not be so cruel. I had been wrong. I had let him down in more ways than one.

'God will gather him to Him.' I repeat the mantra, pushing away the devil's thoughts.

Henry takes my hands, then, in both of his. 'That's right. God will gather him to Him.'

I stare down at our bundle of hands and remember the promise I made to Olly as we sat fishing for the last time. I find myself saying words that have not formed first as thoughts but simply spill from me: 'Will you stay, Henry? Will you pray with me?'

'Of course I will.'

Henry kneels before me and bows his head.

CHAPTER SIX

How can Mother bear to lose another son? How can I bear to lose another brother? In recent years, my brothers – so precious to me with their straightforward, masculine ways and whose company I have always found somehow easier than my sisters' – have been cut by half. More than half, if I count baby James, who never had the chance to grow into a boy at all. I had four brothers and now I have two. And so we shrink more and more into a feminine household, which seems even harder in this brutal time of war.

Our pain is raw and bloody. Every conversation, every thought, every room and object in the house has jagged edges we snag ourselves upon time and time again. Here, Olly's fishing tackle; there his old shoes; that, the corner he used to hide in when we played hide and seek; there, his favourite step to sit on when he was bored. He is in my head and my heart, in the voices and expressions of my loved ones, in my dreams and my nightmares. It is as if he lives still, just in people and things and not in his own earthly self.

Our friends keep a respectful distance but family clusters round. Aunt Jane Desborough comes often with her children; she to sit in silent companionship with mother, my younger cousins to cheer and cuddle us girls. Uncle Walton writes often with condolences, himself a veteran of deep grief, having lost both his wife – Father's sister Margaret – and his oldest boy before. Dick and Harry return early from school and I look at them hungrily, the sight of them almost too joyful to bear. They are both quite full grown now: Dick a slight eighteen, Harry a stockier sixteen. Yet they creep around like mice, almost as if they are afraid of their own shadows. Dick seems particularly shrunken and I remember with searing pain how Olly suffered when Robin died and he found himself unexpectedly and unwantedly the oldest son and heir. Could any of us have imagined the dreadful pattern repeated?

Father comes home and our grief expands to include him. He is by turns a drowned man and a raging one. Angry with the King for starting this war, angry with himself for answering the call to arms and taking his son to fight. Angry with God for calling his son to Him, then angry with himself again for doubting the Lord's providence. He weeps for Olly, he weeps for himself and he weeps for England.

We weather the storm as best we can.

Henry Ireton is as strong and quiet as a rock in a tempest and we take our turns dashing ourselves against him. He visits daily, bringing news and provisions, praying with us and taking over what administrative tasks he can from Father. He and I work together to keep the family afloat and find some harmony in this. I do not realise how much I have come to depend on him until he shares the news that he is to leave Ely with Father and return to the battlefield. The Earl of Manchester has promoted him quarter-master general, which will put him in charge of supplies for the whole Eastern Association Army – a monumental task I have no doubt his orderly mind will relish.

'The Eastern Association is to ride north to relieve the troops besieging York,' he explains to me in the garden where I am gathering herbs. 'If we can break the siege and engage the Earl of Newcastle's Royalist army, we may end the deadlock and sweep the King's forces from the north.'

His face shines with animation at the prospect, his voice quickening with eagerness. But I listen with as much pain as pleasure.

'Sir Thomas Fairfax is one of the allied commanders, is he not?' I ask, straightening up from the soil, my limbs heavy and thoughts slow. 'From Yorkshire? Father fought with him in Lincolnshire and says he's a brilliant general. Uncle Walton says it was their cooperation that won that county for Parliament.'

'He is a great fighter, there's no doubt,' Henry replies. '"Black Tom" the men call him on account of his dark, gypsy looks which none expect, given his surname.'

I smile briefly for perhaps the first time in weeks, my skin almost cracking at the forgotten movement. 'And what do they call you?'

Henry shifts his weight awkwardly. 'That is not for me to know – you'll have to ask your father that.'

'Then I will,' I reply, straining to find some lightness between us after all the weeks of sorrow. I take a moment to examine him, the familiar pointed face and bright eyes, the lean frame beneath his ink-stained doublet. He is all angles and trapped energy, like a sparking bundle of kindling. For a moment I think he is about to speak to me of something more. I listen for the words, half hearing them on the wind, but they flit away like ghosts. Instead, Henry bows to me and takes his leave. As I watch him walking away my spirits sink into despair once more, though I cannot pinpoint precisely why. For once, my feelings outstrip my thoughts and I do not have the energy to hunt them down.

I am now the oldest among my siblings. Somehow it is this selfish realisation that stands out for me among the myriad horrible aspects of Olly's death. I am a woman who has older brothers – who loves to have older brothers. The third child of my parents' love, their first daughter. That is who I am. I have always had Robin and Olly above me, to grow and learn ahead of me, to ignore me, to tease and cuddle me, to tell me how things are, to explain my parents' whims and ways. To show me the way. How do I now cease to be that person, forged in that fire? Will I ever forget my brothers and think of myself as the eldest? Without them, I feel exposed, as if I have been pushed forward from the edges of rooms, where I am naturally comfortable, and into the middle. As if I will fall off the page of our family tree.

With this ache heavy within me and Father and Henry gone, I take what burdens I can from Mother. In this I find a welcome helpmeet in Betty, who seems to have grown up overnight. When Robin died three years ago, she was eleven and needed as much caring for as anyone else. But not this time. Her birthday is quite forgotten as she applies herself single-mindedly to caring for

Mall and Fanny, taking them off Mother's hands almost entirely. At night we crawl exhausted into bed and take it in turns to hold each other while we cry, often falling asleep with our arms entwined. Whatever bitterness I felt towards her on the day of John Claypole's visit is swallowed for now by our shared grief.

I cling to my surviving brothers too, even as I curse them for so reminding me of Olly and for being younger than me and needing my care and indulgence. Harry, large and charming like Father, does his best to help around the house and keep our spirits up with tales from school. Dick, meanwhile, spends a great deal of time out: riding, hunting and, I suspect, propping up the bar at The Bell and gambling Father's money at dice in the back parlour. His solitariness irks me – as if I ever have the choice to disappear for whole days – and I snap at him one morning when I see him taking Olly's fishing rods.

I am still fuming come the evening when Dick saunters in just as I am serving supper.

'Had a nice day out?' I do nothing to moderate my fishwife tone.

He does me the courtesy of looking a little sheepish as he holds out his plate for the stew.

'Let him alone, Biddy,' Mother chides me gently. 'We must all bear our loss in our own ways. Besides, it does a man good to be outdoors.'

I grind my teeth and say nothing further.

'Perhaps you will find an occupation in due course, Dick, now that you have left school?' Aunt Liz asks, in a clear attempt to move the conversation along.

It is an innocent question but I know that we are all

thinking the same thing: that Dick is now Father's heir and must rise to the responsibility of his new position of birth, however much he may wish to shrink from it.

'What about the university?' Betty asks.

Dick swallows his mouthful of stew. 'It is Harry's wish to go to Cambridge, not mine.'

I look at Harry enviously. He was always the better scholar of the two younger boys. In the back of my mind I begin a new column in the household ledger for my returned brothers and start totting up the unavoidable expense – a horse each, new clothes, Cambridge fees. And we would have to pay Harry's tuition and lodging expenses up front and in full: Harry couldn't work to pay some of his way as a college servant as he might have done in previous years; General Cromwell cannot have a son enrolled as a sizar.

'Indeed it is – if Father will permit it,' Harry says smiling, 'then I would join the army when I am finished.'

'Of course he will, Harry,' Mother says quickly. 'And you're not even to think of the army for a few years yet.'

I glance at Dick. 'The army for you, Dickie?' I ask, challenging him to refuse what I would not were I given the option.

Dick shifts in his chair. 'Perhaps . . . I will see.'

'No,' Mother cuts in. 'No more talk of the army, I'll send no more of my precious boys to the army, whatever your father says. I did not survive your childbeds to see you into your graves.'

I bite my tongue. Grief has propelled me in the opposite direction and I want to urge Dick to fight and to tell Mother that the Cause is noble and that men are needed. That I would fight myself and avenge Olly's death if only I could. But I see behind her bitter words to the grief that birthed them and say nothing.

It is unbearably hot. Summer has rushed upon us as a roaring fire and the garden wilts in the blaze as flies buzz around the kitchen. We cannot leave food uncovered for an instant and are each constantly on the hunt for muslin squares and string. Frances burns her forearms and cries and moans for two days, skulking in the darkest corners of the house, the iced butter salve Betty applies melting and dripping in a trail on the floor rushes where the cat licks it up.

Despite the glaring sunlight, we remain a household wreathed in shadow, our thoughts alternating from Olly to the new danger facing Father, Henry and my uncles and cousins. News is our only tonic and each letter from Father buys us a few hours, perhaps a day freer from gloom. Betty has a letter from Val which goes some way to reviving her, though she is careful to keep it hidden away from me, in her pocket or under her pillow.

Although it pleases us to receive word of our loved ones, their letters and the newspapers confirm our foreboding that a great battle is coming. The King has dispatched his nephew and commander of his cavalry Prince Rupert north and his army is swelling like a spring fen as it covers the miles towards ours. Helplessly, forlornly, we wait for news. The first snippets of intelligence to reach Ely come in an express message to Reverend Hitch from his brother in York, and the clergyman duly brings the letter around to us. It tells of a battle on the moor at Long Marston just outside the city with many thousand dead, though the writer is unsure of the outcome. Few of us sleep that night. The next day brings the broadsheets which confirm the victory is ours and special mention is given to Lieutenant-General Cromwell's command of his cavalry. We read them in joy until a postscript notes that Father had been wounded by a pistol ball in the neck, which sets Mother and Grandmother fretting about infection and clucking together about how little care he will take over the wound's healing.

Still we have no news of Henry or of our uncles and cousins and no word from Father himself. The letter comes, finally, on the following evening just as I am shutting up the house for the night. The little ones are already in bed, as is Grandmother, but the rest of us are still up and we gather silently in the parlour to read Father's words. I am chosen to read aloud and I crack open Father's wax seal clumsily in my agitation, sending shards of wax onto my skirts, before settling into the comfortable rhythm of his speech. His opening is pure joy: '"Truly England has had a great favour from the Lord in this absolute victory given to us, the like of which has never been seen since this war began."' I can almost feel Father beaming as he writes the words, his happiness and bolstered faith pressed firmly into the page with every stroke of his pen.

'Does he say any more about his part in the battle?' Harry asks, almost breathless with excitement.

I go on reading his account of the fight – how he commanded the left wing and routed the prince's horse. Harry grins and slaps Dick on the back and I can see tears forming in Mother's eyes. He speaks of Henry Ireton and his part; that he too has been commended for his bravery. I continue to read, drunk with pride and relief and lulled into false security, before my tongue begins to trip over sad, hopeless words and I stop, scanning ahead. Truly it is a letter in two halves: a Heaven and a Hell. I glance at Betty then force myself to continue as a lump forms in my throat: '"I am afraid to tell you that God has taken away precious young Val by a cannon shot."'

Betty gasps but I read on quickly, eager to get the worst of it out in one go: how his horse was shot from under him, how they tried to save him by amputating his leg but that he died on the operating table, brave and good-humoured to the last.

'No, no, no!' Betty is wailing now, clutching Mother's arm as Mother shakes her head.

'Poor, poor Val. And his father! He was so kind to me over Olly's death and now his oldest surviving boy is gone too. The pair of them – our beautiful boys gone together just as the older ones did. Perhaps it is a blessing that Margaret is not alive to see this.'

I look down at the floor, remembering the boys lying in front of the hearth playing with the little girls on their last visit. How vivid they both were, how young. I close my eyes against the sight before returning to the letter. 'Father says he has written to Uncle Walton with the news of his son's death and that it was one of the hardest letters he has ever had to write. He speaks of the letter here. That he told him how gallant and brave Val had been, how beloved he was by all who knew him. And he reminded him how God had strengthened him when he lost Robin and Olly. *There is your precious child full of glory*, he wrote, *never to know sin or sorrow anymore*.'

I lower the letter into my lap. 'Father begs that you will go to Uncle Valentine and the children with all haste, Mother.'

'Of course, I will go in the morning.' Mother takes Betty's face between her hands, 'I know how fond you were of Val, my darling, but we must be brave for your uncle's sake.'

Betty bites her lip and I wonder what it is she is longing to say. Did she love him? Were they secretly engaged? I remember how her chin tilted as they kissed in the night light, how he would grin at her across the table. I think of his letter – the paper he would have smoothed out, leaned and written on, folded and sealed, clutched and pocketed – now lying loved and crumpled in our bed; the last object to be touched by them both.

Without a word, Betty leaves the room and pulls herself upstairs. I follow instinctively, like a shadow, anxious as always to go where I am most needed. We sit on the bed together, legs dangling like children floating sticks from a bridge. Betty clutches Val's last letter in a trembling hand.

'Dearest . . .' I begin, but what can I say? She has never explained their feelings for each other to me, never shared her secrets. And why should I be surprised at her reticence? The one time I caught a glimpse of their intimacy for myself I scolded her. Though I know I was right, now I shrink from the memory.

'I loved him.'

'I know. And he loved you, I'm sure.'

'He wanted to marry me. Here . . .' She moves the letter towards me and I take it gently from her fingers.

I skim through it quickly: longing and loathing to

read it in equal measure. It is all I imagine a young man's love-letter to be – loving, vivacious, full of the future. I refold it delicately, closing Val's last words into their paper coffin.

'He was a soldier,' I say, borrowing Henry's words as I can find none of my own. 'He knew the dangers and faced them bravely. None braver, Father wrote.' I place my arm around her narrow waist and she drops her head heavily onto my shoulder.

'He was doing God's work, Betty, and God will gather him to Him.'

I hope that she finds the comfort in this thought that I did. But instead she cries and clings on to me tightly, a small voice emerging from the sobs: 'But I wanted to gather him to me.'

CHAPTER SEVEN

AUTUMN 1644

Mud crumbles and flakes onto the floorboards as Father pulls off his riding boots. His hands shake with the effort, stained and crusted fingernails fumbling with the stiff leather. As he straightens up I see a dirty bandage wrapped around his neck and my fingers twitch to change it. Troopers congregate noisily around the open front door, some leaning against the house chatting together wearily as they shake off the road, others untacking their horses in the street. I shut the door firmly, determined Father shall have just a few minutes of rest.

'Our victory has been squandered,' Father is saying as I turn to him, his voice hoarse and strained while his hollow eyes scan the faces of his women who crowd around him. 'Nothing – nothing – could have made God's support for our cause clearer than such a monumental victory. The Lord is driving us forward now. And what do the Earl of Manchester and the other commanders do? Do they listen to God's instructions? Do they press their advantage, pursue Rupert and capture more towns? No! Instead, we slope home.'

I leave him ranting to hurry to the kitchen for beer and bread. When I bring these to him in the parlour, he draws breath for the first time and seems to gather himself.

'Thank you, Biddy. Any post waiting for me?'

'Yes, Father.' I fetch him the packet of letters from his desk in the tithe office and perch on a chair by the door while he reads them, Mother, Grandmother, myself and Betty settling around him like tired travellers about a fire. After moping and mourning our way through endless wretched weeks of barren life, with only the cycle of household chores to structure our days, Father's return is rejuvenating for us all whatever his temper.

Father thumbs through his letters, shakes his head and sinks his chin into his hand. 'You see' – he waves the papers in Mother's direction – 'news of yet more losses. Sir William Waller's Southern Association defeated near Banbury and most deserted and, in the West Country, six thousand of the Earl of Essex's men surrendered, one thousand dead and my Lord himself escaped in a fishing boat. Ha! A fishing boat! The indignity.'

'You must rest, dearest,' Mother says in her most soothing tone. 'Take a bath. Let us re-dress your neck wound.'

'I will, I will.' Father waves an irritated hand before setting his gaze upon the fire.

Mary and Frances scamper in and, without the adult ability to sense the moods of others, clamber excitedly onto Father's lap. I rise to shoo them away until he is in a better humour but Father lightens at once, wrapping his arms around them and kissing their foreheads. He jostles them one on each knee and they giggle and squeal. Chuckling now, Father takes Mary's doll from her and wiggles it about, pretending it can speak.

'My Lord Manchester,' he addresses the ragged doll.

'Lieutenant-General Cromwell.' The doll bows in response as Father mimics what I take to be Manchester's high-born voice.

'We must put an end to this skulking about and hoping for peace, my Lord. We must get back out there and take our fight to the enemy.'

'Oh no, General,' Father has the doll respond, 'we are quite happy where we are. We must not be too successful. There is no need to go looking for danger. The King is a reasonable man, there will be peace eventually.' He shakes the doll so its head lolls from side to side like a jester.

The girls laugh and urge Father on: 'More, more!'

But Father has fallen silent, staring at the Earl of Manchester in his hand. Suddenly his eyes flash and he smiles. 'Well, little Mall, Fanny. How do we make friends with our dolls if we aren't getting along?'

Mary looks unsure but Frances pipes up straight away. 'We invite them to dinner, Papa.'

Father kisses Fanny's cheek and hands the doll back to Mary. 'Exactly.'

The Earl of Manchester is invited over from Cambridge to dine with us the following day and, once he has sent word of his acceptance, the whole house falls into a frenzy of preparations. He will be the grandest person ever to cross our modest threshold and our neighbours – who have caught wind of the occasion, no doubt, from the servants' talk – pop in throughout the day offering advice and the choicest items from their larders. I am up to my elbows in fish guts and flour, as are Betty, Aunt Liz, Martha and our neighbour's kitchen maid, who has been loaned to us for the day. Mother is quarter-master general, overseeing all of the preparations with the same single-mindedness I imagine Henry has as he goes about his work. Despite the profusion of food, Mother loses her nerve that we will have enough, and orders in extra dishes of game and jugged hare from The Bell.

Henry and Charles Fleetwood are also invited and they arrive at the house early to consult with Father. Afterwards, Henry comes to the kitchen to see if he can help and stands a little awkwardly in the corner of the room, trying not to get in the way. My pleasure at the sight of him runs deep as I remember how much I came to rely on him in the weeks after Olly's death. And to see him here, his body whole and intact, fills me with relief, especially when I hear his harrowing account of the battle.

'It was a brutal affair, Bridget. I can't tell you – wouldn't wish to tell you what it was like.' I remember Olly's horrible story of his friend's death at the battle of Edgehill and recall with a prickle, for the thousandth time, that he too is now dead and gone.

'And we lost Val,' I reply quietly, glancing at Betty who is keeping herself busy with the dough.

'Yes and a great many others. Yet it must all be to a purpose, we must ensure that.'

Henry's voice is fierce and I hear a hard edge to it I have never heard before. It stirs me and I feel a hot flame in my chest.

'I can see that, Henry,' I say, wiping my sticky fingers

now the pastry case is finished. 'The victory must achieve something, else the price paid was too high.'

Henry looks at me thoughtfully and simply nods in reply. The next moment Harry barges through the garden door with a basket of newly chopped logs and kindling. He eyes Henry cautiously before giving him a friendly smile. I remember that they have not met before and make the introduction.

'I hear you've finished school,' Henry says when they have greeted each other. 'Will you join us in the army? We could do with another Cromwell – there's few as can match your father's skill as a tactician, save Black Tom, and John Lambert from his northern forces, who shows a natural aptitude.' He stops abruptly and glances at me as if to check that he hasn't assaulted my memory of Olly's loss.

I give a brisk nod of approval even as tears gather in the corner of my eyes.

'I would dearly like to, sir,' Harry replies, setting the basket down at his feet and running a hand through his hair. 'Though I would, if I could choose it, go to Cambridge first.'

'Oh I see.' Henry folds his hands behind him and leans against the wall. 'Well, I cannot blame you for that; my time at Oxford made me the man I am, though I taught my tutors as much as they taught me. Perhaps you should strengthen the muscles of your mind before you join us in the field. We'll need men of learning in our ranks, especially when the fighting is done and the arguments begin. That's when we'll need the quickest minds.'

This surprises me, for I expect Henry to brook no

opposition to Harry's immediate recruitment. But something in his speech suggests that he is talking more of himself than of Harry; that he considers his talents will play best in the thoughtful formation of a new world rather than in the brutal destruction of the old. I appraise him through the floured air. I am sure he is brave and determined in the field, but perhaps he is no natural soldier as he describes Father, Black Tom Fairfax and this John Lambert to be? This would accord with my impression of him: it is always Henry's mind I notice first – its quickness, lightness, its energy – not his body which is all awkward corners. He certainly does not have Father's physical presence, for all his mental agility.

I bring my focus back to the conversation and notice that Harry seems pleased at the older man's encouragement; he smiles at him admiringly as he makes his thanks and continues into the back passage with the log basket. It would be good if the two of them became friends, I think. Harry is in need of more men to guide him, especially now he has lost another older brother.

Miraculously, everything is ready by the time the Earl of Manchester's carriage draws up outside, save for the layered apple cake which Martha is still decorating with candied apple slices, icing sugar and whipped cream. The food from The Bell arrives in warming dishes just in time, though Betty and I have to rush to dust the flour from our faces and lace each other into our best dresses. We slip downstairs just as Father begins to introduce our family to the earl. I barely have a moment to observe the great man before we make our way to the table, the earl's attendants left to sit on the hall bench with two of his personal bodyguard of scarlet-coated troopers posted at the front door. Once in the parlour, I remain on my feet for some minutes filling the glasses and helping Martha bring in the first dishes.

Eventually, I am free to sit and examine the earl. He is about Father's age with a long nose set in a long face that looks as if it were made for gloom. And yet it is apparent within seconds that our grand visitor is charming and affable, almost gentle in his noble manners; a far cry from the stern warrior I had expected. The earl is all politeness, complimenting Mother on our home and the feast before us, smiling at Betty and me and making efforts to include Dick and Harry in his conversation. Betty is entranced. Fascinated, I can tell, to see such exalted breeding, such refined manners at our country table. For the first time since Val's death, I see her begin to bloom under the earl's munificent gaze and am almost relieved to feel my customary irritation with her return.

Taking in the earl's exquisite green doublet edged with intricate lace, watching him tilt his head left and right in a perfect conversational dance, his ringed fingers nimble on his plate, I can well imagine him the King's boon companion as a young man, when they had travelled to Spain for the then prince to woo the infanta. Father has told me how the prince made him a knight of the Bath at his coronation, in thanks for his friendship. How extraordinary, then, that the Earl of Manchester should become such a committed opponent of the King that he was one of the six members of Parliament the King tried to arrest for treason shortly before the war: five in the Commons and just he in the Lords. There were precious few other peers who stayed with Parliament when the King raised his standard and declared war in

Nottingham – was it any wonder he was given such high command?

I look from the earl to Henry and Charles Fleetwood, who is nodding along to the story enthusiastically, then on to Father, who suddenly seems very rough-hewn and rustic by comparison with his commander. He is quieter than usual, chewing chicken and listening to the earl recount a hunting story to Dick, waiting, I can tell, to bring the conversation around to his own ends. At last he does: 'I have been preparing my family, my Lord, for the news that we shall be on the march again soon. It cannot be your intention for us to tarry here long while the King's way to London lies unguarded. We must go west and support what is left of our armies.'

The earl takes a long sip of wine. 'The men are exhausted, Cromwell, much depleted from Marston Moor, many now diseased. We have hardly any funds remaining. The quarter-master general will tell you.'

He looks to Henry and I can almost see him weighing his words before he responds – caught between two of his superiors.

'That is true, my Lord, though if we wait too long we may lose all advantage.'

He answered well, I think, appeasing both yet tipping the balance slightly towards Father.

'You speak of advantage, Ireton,' the earl replies, 'yet I struggle to see what advantage we can hope to gain by repeating the horrors of Yorkshire and losing yet more men. Looking back, I can see that it was easy to begin the war, yet I now think it harder to know when it will end.'

'We do not know *when* my Lord,' Father steps in, 'but we know *how*: by the sword.'

Charles Fleetwood makes an approving noise before falling silent under the earl's eye. His fair face flushes and he fusses with his napkin to hide his embarrassment.

'I am not so sure, Cromwell.' The earl looks back to Father. 'Perhaps it would be better for the kingdom if it were ended by an accommodation.'

'Accommodation!' Father blurts out the word in blind repetition and the earl stiffens a little in his seat. 'But too much is at stake,' he continues before Mother shoots him a pleading look; I can hear the unspoken conversation between them clearly.

'I know full well what is at stake,' the earl replies, his manner calm but his tone now cooled. 'If we fight the King a hundred times and beat him ninety-nine, he will be King still, but if he beats us but *once*, or for the last time, we shall be hanged, we shall lose our estates, and our posterities shall be undone.'

It is a chilling thought, and in my fear I reach for a proverb: *The wrath of a king is a messenger of death but a wise man will pacify it*. I expect the earl's brutal words to be met with respectful silence, but instead Father bursts out: 'If that is so, then why in God's name did we take up arms in the first place?'

His chair scrapes at the violence of his speech and everyone seems to react at once. Grandmother drops her spoon into her bowl, Charles clears his throat and Betty gasps. My immediate shock gives way to fierce pride as I recognise my own words of a few months ago now on Father's lips. But I am surprised to hear him speak with such fierce argument – while Father is prone to occasional sudden outbursts of feeling, usually it is he who becomes the conciliator in any dispute and Henry has confirmed he takes the same role among the officers. In the silence that follows, my heart hammers in my chest as I feel myself torn in two: the obedient, domestic Biddy, anxious that our conversation has crossed the bounds of politeness even as the angry, committed Bridget thrills at Father's fine words. Of course he is right. Surely to show weakness now is to undercut everything that has been done already? Did Olly and Val die for this? I catch Henry's eye and see my passion mirrored in him, even as he keeps his tongue.

'More wine, my Lord?' It is Mother who steps into the heated pause. 'Bridget, would you refill the earl's glass and Martha, you can bring in the puddings now.'

Silently I rise to my feet and edge around the table, hardly daring to breathe. As I fill the earl's glass, I notice Betty, recovered now, bestow a dazzling smile upon him from across the table and I sense the earl's shoulders relaxing under our combined feminine effort.

'You always were a fierce advocate, Cromwell.' The earl raises his refilled glass to Father and turns his head to me. 'Did you know, my dear, that your father and I first came up against each other in a Commons committee before the war? I was defending my land enclosures in these parts against some troublesome tenants and they chose your father as their champion. He did not give me an easy time then, neither does he now.'

I do my best to smile politely at being so addressed but without Father thinking I side with his ally-opponent.

Father, his temper now under apparent control, nods in acknowledgement. 'Forgive me, my Lord, you know I feel strongly upon the point.'

It is strange to hear Father as supplicant but he himself knows the importance of maintaining discipline and respect within an army's ranks.

The earl inclines his head in response and turns to Dick. 'And what of your sons, Cromwell? Are they made from the same fierce mettle as their father?'

Dick blushes, Harry grins and the earl smiles.

'Have you left school now, my lads?'

'Yes, my Lord,' Dick manages to reply.

'And which school?'

'Felsted, my Lord, in Essex.'

'Ah! I know it well. The school is under the patronage of my in-laws, the Rich family. The Earl of Warwick sends his grandson Robert there. Excellent. And what plans have you now? University?'

'Yes, my Lord,' Harry answers quickly. 'If my father will permit it. Cambridge.'

'Very good,' the earl replies. 'Your father and I were both students there in our time. Same college, were we not, Cromwell? Though I don't believe we overlapped.'

Father smiles, though I sense an unease still about him. 'I believe so, my Lord. You matriculated the year after I left.'

This may be true but it is also a helpful way to save face. I doubt the earl would have mixed much with Father had they been there together: the heirs to earldoms do not tend to befriend the sons of minor country gentlemen.

'Ah. Well, an excellent idea, Cambridge, is it not, Fleetwood, Ireton?' the earl continues, addressing the junior officers now. 'You're Cambridge men, are you not?'

'Emmanuel college, my lord', Charles replies quickly with a relieved smile. 'Happy days indeed.'

'The most godly of colleges, and, thanks to that, grown the largest when I was there.' The earl nods approvingly. 'I believe half the new world is now populated by Emmanuel men. And you, Ireton?'

'Oxford, my lord,' Henry replies minimally.

'Ah, the other place,' he commiserates. 'College?'

'Trinity.'

'Hmm. Most unfortunate now it is so staunch for the King.'

Henry gives a polite smile – like Father's, a soldier's smile for his commander – but offers no further comment of his own.

I sense troubled times ahead. Making my excuses, I go in search of the apple cake.

CHAPTER EIGHT

'Cambridge, Harry? Now?' The earl has barely left, his good humour restored and his wineglass still warm from his fine fingers, when Father turns his frustration on Harry. 'Do you not wish to join up? And you too, Dick?'

We trickle back into the parlour and I gaze forlornly at the mess upon the table before tiredness overwhelms me. I'll sit down with the others, I think, just for a few minutes while Martha and the girl from next door make a start on the dishes.

'He is not to join up, dearest,' Mother replies before either boy can speak. 'Neither of them is. Not yet, I can't bear it.'

'I know your trials, my love,' Father capitulates and coos, 'but did you not hear what we said at dinner? Now is the time to press forward, for Olly's sake, if for no one else.'

'Don't you invoke his name in this cause,' Mother snaps and I exchange an amazed look with Betty to hear her speak so angrily to Father. Betty, the conciliator, hurries over to her and takes her hand before turning her pretty, sad eyes upon Father.

'Please, Father, we could not bear any more loss, not after Olly and Val.'

Father sighs and sinks into a chair. Though still only fifteen, Betty can always silence him with a plea.

'My Lord Manchester thought Cambridge a good idea . . .' Harry ventures bravely before Father cuts him off sharply.

'My Lord Manchester is not committed to winning this war. Surely you could hear that for yourself?'

'I could Father,' I say. 'He has not your fervour, nor Henry's and Charles's, that much is clear.'

Henry clears his throat and, reminded that he and Charles are still in the room, I blush at my warm words and try to counter them with a cool expression.

'Perhaps there may be a compromise?' Henry's calm voice wades into our family battle. 'Harry could complete just a few terms at the university, then join us. He could whet his scholar's appetite and still be with us in time for next summer's campaign season.'

Harry looks at Henry with canine gratitude but Henry keeps his eyes on Father who is patrolling around the room as he does when he is thinking hard. We wait for him to stop and deliver his verdict:

'Very well, Henry. Perhaps that is a way forward. Though I am in a hurry, Harry need not be. We'll be fighting this war for several years yet, I'm sure of it.'

Several years yet. A cold future stretches before me; a repeating pattern of weeks and months of impotence while Father, Henry, even my little brother Harry, have the chance to serve the Cause. My eyes drift to the piles of dishes on the table, the crumbs on the floor, a wine-stained napkin. I used to take joy in my small, everyday tasks; in being useful at home. But that was before the world turned upside down. It is not enough anymore. Now I want to find a way to be useful to my country.

As autumn curls dejectedly into winter, Father's letters to us from the front sink into familiar frustration as he tells of the earl's mismanagement: advantages are squandered, sieges mismanaged and advances half-hearted. Worrying news reaches us that the Earl of Essex, stranded and cut off in Cornwall, has been forced to surrender his troops to the Royalists. When the armies withdraw to their winter quarters, Father returns not to us but to London, convinced that Manchester, Essex and the other noble commanders are now a greater stumbling block to Parliament's victory than the King himself.

With Father and Henry away much of the time and Harry now gone to Cambridge, we welcome the postponed visit of the Claypoles. Mother remains convinced that John could be a match for me, despite his obvious attraction to Betty, and I let her plot and plan as it seems to lift her a little from her mourning. For my part, John lost his initial allure when he had nothing with which to comfort me at Olly's death; and so I hope instead that his visit will cheer Betty and remind her that a future life still awaits her in this world now that Val has gone on to the next.

John arrives on a fine bay mare, Badger trotting at his feet and his mother following in a carriage. Though we wait at the front door with full womanly welcome, we hardly have the opportunity to greet John as Dick instantly whisks him around to the stable to see his own horse, newly bought with Father's hard-earned funds.

Mary Claypole alights and comes inside with us, shrugging at her son's absence. Over the next three days, although Betty enjoys John's smiles and special attentions, she is forced to share him with Dick who, having seemed somewhat adrift of late is clearly relieved to have a fellow sportsman's company and takes John off hunting and to the races for hours at a stretch. On the second night of their stay, the two men disappear to The Bell and do not stagger home until two in the morning, their raucous singing bouncing off the cobbles as they fumble and slur their way into the house. Fortunately, only I am awake to see them and I let Dick have a piece of my mind as I bolt the front door behind them.

I expect John's neglect of Betty to lessen her interest in him but it has the opposite effect. When I complain about the boys' night-time revels as we prepare breakfast early the next morning, she rides to their defence.

'It's good for men to spend time together out of doors,' she says, attempting to sound worldly, and I wonder if her emulation of Mother is intentional.

'Yes, but every day?'

'When they're as fine a sportsman as John Claypole.' Betty smiles over his name and instinctively smooths her hair with a glance in the kitchen window. I know that look.

'And to drink to drunkenness at night and sleep late each morning?' I continue my complaints regardless, soothed by airing my grievances. 'They won't be up for hours, you mark me, and yet Mother will insist we leave the bacon for them. How much is left over from yesterday morning?'

Betty disappears into the larder and returns with the lean remains of the bacon joint.

I sigh. 'Eggs for us, then. I'll make them while you lay the table.'

Betty gathers the plates and cups but pauses as she leaves the kitchen, turning back to me. 'Do not be so hard on Dickie, Biddy. He means well in his way.'

I crack an egg into a bowl, tutting as a chip of shell escapes with the white. Betty still has two older brothers to look up to, I think, as I cast about for a spoon to remove the shell. Dick and Harry will always impress their little sister whatever their flaws, just as Robin and Olly used to inspire me. I crack another egg too fiercely and the slippery gold coats my hands so I cannot wipe away the tear that falls into the bowl instead.

When the Claypoles depart the next day, they leave behind them two entries in our household ledger: a profit for Betty who, for the first time, takes Val's letter from beneath her pillow and presses it instead into the bible that is tucked away in her trunk for want of use; and a loss for Dick, who comes to Mother and me a week later to confess a debt incurred from his losses at the horse-racing with John. It is such a large sum Mother is forced to write to Father for the funds and the money he returns is wrapped in a stern reproof for his new heir.

Father's response also sends news of his fight with the Earl of Manchester, now playing out in Parliament itself as Father gives his account of conditions in the army to the Commons while Manchester responds in the Lords. It is a bitter battle of words, Father says, and powerful factions are coalescing around each side.

This conflict, which, in its own way, seems as far from us as the military battles we have also followed, is brought home to us in a newspaper which carries reports of all the speeches made in Parliament and to the joint English and Scots committee that runs the war. I am pleased to read that Henry has given his own evidence in support of Father; testifying to the earl's stated desire to win the war through accommodation, which he gave around our very own dinner table. But this mild pleasure is dashed when the paper reveals that the earl has accused Father of misappropriating funds by sending us the five pounds each week. Mother is distressed, Betty is mortified and Grandmother clicks her tongue as I fume by the fire. From that day on, each time I spend money in the shops or settle our accounts in the town, I do so with shame burning my frost-bitten cheeks. To be accused of dishonesty, of profiteering from the war, cuts me to the quick and I itch to rescue our family's good and honest name from this indignity. I wish now that I hadn't slaved over the earl's fine meal.

Henry Ireton, returned to Ely to get on with the governor's business, seems to share my irritable mood and when I chance upon him walking past the cathedral one morning, he gives me no more than a raised hat and a stiff nod. I smart at his curt treatment and resolve to treat him coolly the next time we meet. When I answer the door to him early one morning a few days later, I wave him inside briskly and take no pains to ask him how he is. But he doesn't appear to notice my indignation in his eagerness to share news.

'An agreement has been reached,' he says as he removes his gloves.

'With the King?' It is Betty who asks, coming down the stairs carrying a basket of laundry, her eyes still heavy with sleep.

Henry looks momentarily surprised by her question, his foxy face pinching. 'Between your father and the Earl of Manchester,' he corrects her.

'Come in, Henry.' It is Mother speaking now and Henry is whipped away from me before I have spoken two words to him as she and Betty bustle him into the parlour, laundry left forgotten in the hall. Irritated, I linger in the doorway with my arms folded and listen as he explains his news.

'Parliament is to pass a law that no MPs can also be officers in the army.'

'But Father?' My mind whirls. 'He'll have to resign his commission – that can't be what he wants.' At a stroke I feel my sole connection to the war snapping into insignificance. What will our lives be like returned to the fringe of events?

'Yes.' Henry turns to me, raising a thin hand to stroke his narrow beard. 'But at least Manchester and Essex will lose their commands too, as they sit in the Lords. It was the only way to oust them from control and save the war effort. And your father is to take a leading role in remodelling the army along professional lines.'

'So Father will return home,' Betty sighs happily, sinking into a chair with a puff of her skirts.

'Praise the Lord.' Mother clasps her hands together. 'Martha? Some breakfast for Deputy Ireton.'

'Thank you,' Henry interrupts quickly, 'but I can only stay a few minutes. I have much to do today. Oliver and I are to set to work raising and training a new army, with proper funding through taxes and a loan from the City and a clear direction to win this war once and for all. They're to have a real uniform too – the whole army in red coats with only coloured cuffs to mark the different regiments – we'll need your help with that.'

'But wait . . .' It is my turn to interrupt, my thoughts still on the fate of our cause even as I sense Mother's and Betty's fly to the sewing. 'Who will command instead?'

'Black Tom Fairfax,' Henry replies and, though he does not smile, I sense a pleasure behind his response. 'He's a fine choice: determined, brave, a brilliant field strategist. The men love him and he has managed to stay out of this feud so both sides are happy with him.'

'And Father thinks him a good general, I know,' I reply, thinking back over our conversations, uncrossing my arms and folding them behind me as I lean back against the doorframe.

'Yes, your father holds him in high esteem, and he is the finest judge of character I know.' Henry spins his hat in his hand with something approaching excitement. 'For the first time I begin to think we can win this war. And now I really must be going,' he runs on as if embarrassed by his own enthusiasm.

'In that case, why don't you walk with Henry, Bridget?' Mother says quickly. 'We will need to order in as much red cloth as we can – you could call in to the draper's and let them know.'

It is another excuse to push me towards Henry and I bristle with familiar annoyance, though I will not give Mother and Betty the satisfaction of seeing it. 'Very well, I'll just fetch my bag.'

We emerge blinking into a bright morning, the cobbles

sparkling with frost in the cool sunlight. Henry sets off at his usual brisk pace before seeming to check himself and slowing to accommodate me. It is early and the rakers are still sweeping the street, working their way towards the cathedral as wives rush to throw out the night's rubbish before them, pungent smells perfuming the air. Husbands with work to go to tumble from their houses, hats pulled low, bread and cheese thrust into their pockets as shopkeepers open their shutters and roll their tables of wares into the light.

I am about to ask Henry more about the plan to create this new-modelled army before he speaks abruptly.

'I have spoken to your parents about the possibility of our being married when the war has ended.'

My thoughts scramble to catch up and my feet stop working, causing me to trip on the slippery cobbles. His words are so sudden. I take a moment to recover myself before hurrying to keep up with him. Is this truly a proposal? And is this how all proposals are made? As if one is bargaining over a bolt of cloth? *Married*. 'Married?' I echo him unconsciously.

'Yes.'

'To each other.'

'Well, that is the general idea.'

'You are asking me to marry you?' Stunned from my wits, I must make sure of the facts.

Henry keeps his gaze ahead. I cannot believe he can keep walking while discussing something of such magnitude. Surely we should have stopped? He should have taken my hand? I think of Val's hand cupping Betty's chin; of John Claypole smiling sideways at her when he thought no one was looking. Yet here we are almost caught up with the street cleaners, filth trickling between the cobbles like streams towards the Great Ouse.

'Yes,' Henry continues, seemingly oblivious to both my indignation and the unconducive surroundings. 'I wish to marry when the war is done with and that possibility now seems within reach. I believe you and I get along well and your father, whom I respect above all others, approves of the match heartily.' His words are clear, logical, his tone dispassionate.

I expect him to stop but he merely gathers pace as if he can out-run the conversation.

But I stop then, unable to continue this frantic walking while I need to gather my thoughts. Henry continues for a few strides before he notices and pauses, swivelling on his heel to stand and regard me. Am I never to have my own stake, I think desperately as my breath slows, even in my own marriage? Must I always be of use to others rather than an advocate for my own ambition?

'And that, I imagine, is its foremost recommendation for you?' I say at length, feeling a bitterness rising in my throat that his warmest words are of Father and not me. 'I will not marry you simply so that you can ingratiate yourself with my father.'

I see I have shocked him with my out-spokenness, though he ought to know my frankness well enough by now. I know I should draw back, behave more delicately. But I must find a way to shake him into revealing some genuine emotion.

'Is that what you think?' he counters.

'Well, would you wish to marry me if I were not my father's daughter?' I challenge.

He cocks his head to one side to consider my question

before fixing his eyes on me. 'I cannot answer that faithfully and I would never lie to you. If you were not his daughter, I would not know you and you would not be the woman you are. You have all of his best qualities but blended with your own. That is how I see it.'

I am pleased with the substance of what he has said about me yet still confused by its delivery. For the first time in my life I am at a loss as to what to say and at an even greater loss to understand my feelings.

'Well, I have your answer,' Henry says at last, removing his hat to give me a stiff bow.

'I have not given my answer,' I counter, annoyed that he seems poised to leave me.

'You have indicated your feelings on the subject.'

'You have hardly given me a chance to consider my feelings on the subject,' I snap back before lowering my voice as one of the rakers turns towards us, his back hunched over his rake.

'Then, consider them,' Henry says, a touch of irritation now creeping into his voice. 'But right here and now it seems to be a no.'

'I – That is hardly fair. Very well, then, it is a no, if you must have your answer in such a desperate hurry.' My chest burns and I fling the words at him even as he is striding away up the street. Some instinct makes me almost call out to him again to warn him to pick his path around the rubbish, but I set my lips in silence as he ploughs straight through it with total indifference.

'Morning, Bridget.' Our neighbour passes, craning towards me inquisitively, but I just nod in hurried return before disappearing into the draper's.

CHAPTER NINE

SUMMER 1645

'Do you love him?' Betty asks for the hundredth time as we sit in the parlour; she sewing yet another army uniform while I struggle to write a letter of condolence to the latest widow in the town. I sigh and pick up the list of names Father has sent me: only two more bereaved families to write to today.

'No.'

'But you like him?'

'I admire him.'

Betty wrinkles her nose. 'Admire him? That's hardly enough. But, then again' – she pauses mid-stitch, her pretty face posing in thought – 'admiration is akin to liking and liking can lead to loving.'

'Perhaps . . .' My mind slides away from her onto Henry, as it now so often does. It is months now since I have seen him: he kept his distance while he was still in Ely and is now gone off on campaign once more with Father. I have no way of knowing his thoughts. He forced me to answer him in an instant amid the street cleaners on that frosted winter's morning and I said no. But I had asked for time to consider his proposal. Is his offer still on the table?

Father says yes and urges me to accept his favourite's hand while Mother frets and worries at the problem like our cat at the loose threads in the hall rug. Grandmother clicks her tongue and warns me of spinsterhood, driving Aunt Liz from the room in bitter tears. Harry writes from Cambridge to say he thinks Henry a fine fellow and Mall and Fanny complain that he no longer visits and brings them sugared almonds. Everyone has an opinion and I am not allowed a moment of privacy. Even my bed is not mine alone as Betty, fascinated by an imagined romance, asks for my thoughts at night and probes for my dreams in the morning. I feel as if I have unravelled into a confused jumble of parts just as the men of Father's and Henry's 'New Model Army' have been transformed into fierce crusaders.

'We do get along well and I respect his industry and strength of purpose in the service of a cause I love. That could be enough to begin with. And I do not want to end up a spinster like Aunt Liz, living in Dick's or Harry's house and picking up after their children.' Betty has lulled me into a confessional mood as she always does.

'But the way he asked you,' she continues softly, her voice disapproving as I begin to regret telling it all to her. 'So unromantic. It would never do for me – but for you?'

She eyes me knowingly and I have to admit to the truth of her implied point, which does not carry the malice another might read in it. Isn't she right? Though I envy her romances in my girlish moments, have I ever truly longed for my own? Or do I want something greater? A calling? A shared ambition? Honesty and respect. Could that be the foundation of a successful marriage instead?

I take my problem to church each Sunday and listen awe-struck to the rainbow of lay preachers who now speak of their own experiences of God. Sometimes the woman preacher is there and I strain forward to hear her words, thrilling at the female cadences resounding in the lofty cathedral. I long to speak too but each time I resolve to rise to my feet and offer my thoughts up to God and my neighbours, I lose my nerve and then walk home angry and frustrated with my own inadequacies.

When it becomes clear that I am not to find fulfilment in church, or with my needle bent endlessly over the army's new uniforms, I range further afield in search of it. Aunt Liz has begun nursing at the local field hospital and persuades me to join her one morning. Together we walk out of the town and through the water plains to a large barn which has become a makeshift centre for treating the wounded of the Eastern Association, who rumble in from the west by the cartload. I can smell the men when we are still a hundred yards off: the rancid stink of rotten flesh and soiled underclothes. I press a handkerchief to my nose as we thread between the mangled soldiers lying on pallets in canvassed shade. The scene that greets me inside the barn is of so many perpendiculars: male bodies lying prostrate while upright female ones drift between them like swans among the lily pads of the Fens. There is little to suggest a coherent system. Two elderly physicians confer in a corner while a third, a younger man, winds a bandage tightly around what appears to be half a head on a bloody pillow. I recognise a few other women from the town, busying themselves cleaning and dressing wounds and preparing food while a small boy goes from body to body offering water, pausing to signal when he finds that one has gone from man to corpse unnoticed.

Aunt Liz hands me an apron and we set to work taking bowls of porridge among the men. One slight young man is too ill with fever to feed himself, so I sit beside him and ladle tiny spoonfuls into his dry mouth, trying with every breath not to think about Olly. Instead, I listen to the intonations of the older man sitting up on the makeshift bed beside him, reading from a tiny pocket bible clutched in his grimy hands. He turns a page every minute or two and so it doesn't occur to me until I offer him his porridge that he is blind and is reciting the verses from heart.

It is not long before one of the elderly doctors plucks me by the hand and leads me over to the corner of the barn where some dirty sheets have been hung to create a private operating space. 'We need to take his arm off,' he says, thrusting a hot flannel and a plank of wood into my hands as I stare dumbly at the man who lies before us, his eyes lolling with the effect of poppy juice. He is stripped to the waist, sweat glistening on his chest and collected in a pool at his navel, where fine, tawny hairs curl in a line towards the top of his trousers. His body is beautiful, I think, the thought jarring in its incongruity. It is so alive, so vivid, I suddenly long to lay my head on his chest and run my hands over his thick arms. *His arms.* I look with horror as the physicians prepare their butcher's tools.

'Come, Biddy.' It is Aunt Liz's calm voice that brings me back to myself. 'We must help. The orderlies will hold him down, I'll hold the wood between his teeth, you press the flannel to his forehead.'

'Yes, yes, of course,' I say automatically, even as the prospect of maiming this living creature horrifies me. I drift into position and hold the warm, damp cloth in place, stroking the man's dark, matted hair out of the way. Before I know it, the physician is sawing and I bite my lip until I taste blood as I feel each movement of the saw reverberate through the poor man's body and up into my hands. He twists and groans, splutters and bites and I scream inside my head desperately trying to drown out the noise of the relentless cutting. Back and forth, jagged teeth into skin, muscle, then – most hideously of all – into bone. The table judders, the metal scrapes and the air fills with the sickly sweet smell of warm blood as it flows down into the bucket. I fight desperately, trying not be sick and find myself chanting the Lord's prayer as the bile rises in my throat. I will not be sick. I will not let this poor, beautiful half-man down. The arm is off, tossed onto a table with a heavy thud, and the man has fainted. I press the flannel and pray.

After that, I go to the hospital most days. But something inside me that had already begun to change, evolves even further. I had always thought that our war was glorious, had always longed to fight beside Olly and Father, and now Harry, who has left Cambridge and joined the flamboyant, firebrand General Thomas Harrison's regiment. When Harry called home to bid us farewell, I clung to him and pushed him away in equal measure. Proud and pleased he was going to serve even as blind fear and raw jealousy raged within me. I kissed him and punched his arm then wept for Olly the moment Harry turned from us upon his horse and set his eyes upon the horizon. Finding Olly's pot of salve in my trunk that night, I rolled it in my hands, wondering if I should have told Harry to send me any weapon that wounds him. But why should it be always this way around? Why should Olly die and perhaps now Harry too, without me taking my turn to bare my breast before the cannon and cavalry charge? Am I not now the oldest? The next who should risk sacrifice?

But the sight of these maimed bodies in the hospital purges me of my naïvety. And when I learn that the beautiful young man, whose forehead I had stroked as he suffered the agony of losing his arm, had died from the infected wound two days later, I finally accept my limits. We must defeat this wicked king who has inflicted so much pain on his people in lust for his own power. We must ensure more voices are heard by the powerful, bring the lives of ordinary folk like us closer to those who make the decisions that govern our fortunes, stop the injustices that are so casually and uncaringly meted out upon us. And, above all else, we must win our freedom to worship as we like.

So the cause must be served, the men must fight. But there is no place for my weak, woman's body in this theatre of bone and muscle. I can use my hands to help heal, of course, to feed and nurse. But is that not what mothers do each day of their lives? I need to find another way to serve; something more than this. A way to use my mind and my passion. If we do win the war, then words will count for more than swords in the battles that follow. What was it Henry said to Harry? *We'll need men of learning in our ranks, especially when the fighting is done and the arguments begin.* And if Henry survives to set his intricate mind to the task, could I not use my wits and understanding through him?

I think of this, beginning almost to obsess over it, as the very news we receive in each post bag seems to speak to my budding plans. Henry is promoted Commissary-General, making him second in command of the New Model Army cavalry with five regiments under him. At a stroke, he is propelled into the centre of the army leadership with a powerful voice in its affairs – an impressive achievement for a minor gentleman from Nottinghamshire with no fighting experience nor family expectations. And it is my own father, granted a temporary appointment in the army, despite remaining an MP, who champions the man he would have me marry, recommending his promotion to Commander-in-Chief, Sir Thomas Fairfax. Is Providence marking out my path? *O Lord, make Your way straight before me.*

But I know His answer. *Straight is the gate, and narrow is the way, which leadeth unto life, and few there be that find it.* I know it in my heart even before we hear from our neighbours the terrifying news that a fierce battle has been fought at Naseby, some sixty miles west of here. I send Martha to The Bell straight away to see if the morning couriers have brought any letters or papers with news and she returns with the latest broadsheet.

'It was a great victory,' she laughs as she spills panting through the door. But I hardly listen, snatching the paper from her and scanning the pages for Henry's name, despite Mother calling to me from the parlour to bring it to her. Nothing. Nothing. And then – I swallow for breath.

His horse was shot from under him just as Val's was.

He was wounded.

He was taken prisoner.

I press the paper back into Martha's arms and blindly, wordlessly, find my way up the stairs to my room. The excuse of a headache frees me from my chores for the rest of the day and I feign sleep later to avoid sharing my feelings with Betty: I will not open myself up to more teasing, not when I hardly know my own heart. And so I lie cold and silent, Olly's salve clutched in my hand as I worry about Henry and about the fatefulness of my proud rejection of him. If he is dead, will I regret that I had not given him hope? Or am I foolish to imagine he would even give a thought to me on his deathbed when his own attitude to me is so business-like. What will be my fate after the war if there is no Henry Ireton to marry?

The next day brings a letter from Father and I have to dig my fingernails into my palms to stop my hands from tearing the paper from Mother as she reads it, first to herself and then, slowly, aloud to the rest of us. Finally, after what feels an eternity, Henry's name finds its way to her lips and I begin to release my scratched, aching palms.

Henry is grievously wounded, Father's words sound in Mother's voice, and not fit to fight for a good while. My chest tightens as I clutch to separate the good news from the bad.

'But he is no longer a prisoner?'

'No, my love. He fought himself free from the Royalist

army!' Mother lays down the paper and leans towards me, smiling.

'And what praise Oliver heaps upon him for his fierce resistance!' Grandmother takes up the tune, her keen eyes firmly fixed upon mine as all the others follow.

'How brave!' Betty thrills.

'Yes, yes,' I snap, getting to my feet, anxious to avoid any further irrelevant romanticising of his gallantry or interrogation of my confused feelings. Henry is safe, but for how long? And will he ever return to me?

Fortunately, the family is soon distracted from my love affair with preparations for Betty's approaching sixteenth birthday. We are to have a birthday picnic in the Fens and Mother and I have made Betty a new pair of lace-embroidered gloves and a matching shawl, which are hidden in my chest.

My suspicions that Betty and John Claypole have been corresponding seem confirmed when Mother receives a letter from Mary Claypole asking if John can visit in a few weeks. 'Surely it is no coincidence that he is to visit us for your birthday?' I challenge Betty but she merely smiles and winks as she brushes her hair. Dick is as keen for his visit as Betty, though I give him a stern talking to before John comes, insisting that they do not repeat the high jinks of his last stay. He is an easy target, with Harry and almost every other young man of the district away fighting, and I feel more confident now that I can keep my younger brother in check.

Betty's birthday arrives and with it John Claypole, bright and beaming on his bay mare, Badger weaving between the horse's legs. Martha and I have packed the picnic into baskets and we women take one each as we set off for the fields, Fanny and Mall scampering ahead while Mother and Aunt Liz bring up the rear, Grandmother tottering between them, swatting at flies. I watch John and Dick riding ahead and wish, not for the first time, that we had another horse and I could feel the summer breeze in my hair and the speed beneath my legs. I complain to Betty, walking alongside me.

'Yes, me too,' she agrees, before springing ahead towards the men. 'John!'

He looks back over his shoulder, a smile curling up his rosy cheeks as he and Dick draw up their horses.

'We ladies are jealous of your riding.'

'Sorry, Betty,' Dick calls back. 'We can go back and hire some horses in the town.'

'No need for that!' John says and he leans down, offering his arm to Betty.

'But you can't!' I say quickly, hoping my voice is loud enough for her alone to hear. 'Not with him – and it's a man's saddle.'

But Betty ignores me and I watch, horrified, as she hitches up her skirts. Dick dismounts and gives her a leg up. She climbs in front of John Claypole and smiles over her shoulder at him as he tightens his arms around her waist and blows away a wisp of her curling hair which flutters in his face. By any standard, it is an inappropriate intimacy and I turn back to Mother and gesture for her to intervene but she simply shrugs and smiles. I wonder if she still thinks Betty the girl she was; if her maternal view blinds her from seeing how rapidly Betty is growing into her womanly ways.

'You want to come up with me, Biddy?' Dick asks but

I shake my head and trail instead behind John's horse, imagining the contents of the whispered conversation I can see from the small movements of its riders' heads. Something passes between the two of them on the ride, that much is clear from Betty's flushed enjoyment of the picnic and the glances she casts at John under her eyelashes. When they run off with Dick and the little ones for a game of blind man's buff, I turn to the older generation. I have found myself increasingly in their company of late, though whether that is by my own inclination or the lot cast for me by others, I hardly know.

'It's gone far between them,' I begin, brushing crumbs from my skirt.

'Perhaps.' Mother will not commit herself.

'She could do a lot worse,' Aunt Liz observes, biting into an apple. 'He's from a good family, heir to a respectable estate.'

'Yes, but she's only just sixteen.'

'Life can be short, Biddy, especially at the start.' It's Grandmother's turn now and we all turn to her as disciples. 'I waited till I was twenty-two to marry my first husband, poor William, and he was dead and my baby girl too within eighteen months. And now I've been a widow again near thirty years. Life can be cut very short or it can grow very long and we're never to know which.'

'Only God knows,' Mother answers and I wonder if she is thinking of her dead sons.

I lapse into silence, musing over their words, intrigued to hear of the man who shared Grandmother's bed before my grandfather. It was God's Providence that her first husband and baby should die; else we would not have lived. Which woman can know what lies ahead when she enters into marriage? The Lord plainly says as much:

> *For how do you know, wife, whether you will save your husband? Or how do you know, husband, whether you will save your wife? Only let each person lead the life that the Lord has assigned to him, and to which God has called him.*

We are not left to speculate for long. That evening, after supper, John comes to find Mother and me where we sit in the parlour, going over our accounts. 'May I speak to you both?' he begins, running a hand through his hair, and I feel a shiver creep up my spine.

'I will write to the lieutenant-general, of course, but as he is not here . . .'

'Yes, John?' Mother smiles encouragingly while I glare at him.

'I wish to marry Betty. That is, we wish to marry each other. Or—' He seems flustered and I wonder if he has had one too many glasses of wine in preparation for this interview. 'I wish to ask your permission to pay my addresses to your daughter.'

'Goodness.' Mother acts surprise well, I must credit her. 'Well, John, we are all fond of you, I am sure, and I know Betty is. But she is still very young.'

'Sixteen,' I add unnecessarily.

'I know. But what can I say? We love each other.' He grins at Mother and I sense her melt under his smile. She has a soft spot for him already, I can tell.

'Perhaps in a year or two . . .'

'Ordinarily, I would not complain at that, ma'am, but I

am joining up to fight soon and who knows where we'll be in a year or two – I might be dead!'

'Even more reason to wait,' I find myself saying, thinking of Betty a widow before my thoughts slide onto Henry. 'After the war—'

'Ha!' John exclaims in frustration before working to bring himself under control.

'We are only saying what my husband would say, John,' Mother soothes. 'Oliver – well, I cannot see him parting with his Betty one moment before he needs to.'

There is plenty of truth in that, I think, aware even within my own thoughts of how bitter I sound to myself: Father cannot wait to pass me onto Henry but his adored Betty would be another matter entirely.

'Will you at least talk to the lieutenant-general?' John changes tack skilfully. 'Plead my case. I would lavish all the love and respect he could ever wish for on his daughter; I adore her. And she would be mistress of Northborough one day.'

I listen helplessly, trying to imagine Henry's interview with Father about marrying me and pretending that it is he speaking so passionately of his love. But it is a hollow vision. Where this could be a scene of the enchanted lovers of *A Midsummer Night's Dream*, I fancy Father and Henry's discussion would have sounded more like one between the Athenian mechanicals.

'I will write to my husband,' Mother confirms with a smile. 'And he will want to confer with your parents. I hesitate to speak for him in his absence, but I'm sure it will be a matter of time only, John, and not a question of any other objections.'

*

'You cannot bear the thought of my being happy while you are not!'

If John took Mother's answer with sensible calm, Betty has no such reserve. We have the counterpane pulled over our heads and she is hissing at me while Frances and Mary stir in their beds across the room. 'Am I to wait to marry until you do? At this pace I will be an old maid like Aunt Liz before you have deigned to walk up the aisle.'

'Betty, please, listen.' I must say the kind, conciliatory things I wish to before she provokes me into anger. 'I was thinking of you. If he is killed—'

'Don't you think I know that? I have already lost Val. I will not lose another man I love where there is the chance that we could have some time together.'

'But—'

'No, I will not listen, why should I? I might have known you would not stick up for me; that you would take Mother's and Father's part. You always longed to be the eldest, even before the boys died. It is your sole desire in life to please our parents and suffocate the rest of us – better still if you achieve both in the same breath. Look at how hard you are on Dick, how you would not support Harry when he wished to go to Cambridge.'

She goes too far. My breath is sharp as I inhale quickly. 'That is not fair. I am simply looking after your interests. All of your interests. Someone has to take responsibility around here – to help Mother manage things and do as Father would wish while he is away fighting. Life is not the game you make it out to be.'

'And you will not have Henry, so I cannot have John. Or did you want him for yourself?'

'No! And Henry has nothing to do with it!' I snap, before lowering my voice as I hear Mall call out to us. 'I have no wish to stop you marrying before I do. Do you think me so petty? You are only fifteen!'

'Sixteen!'

'By a day!'

'Ha!' She is fuming now; I have never seen her so angry – Betty is always sunshine itself. Even when she is sad, when she was desperate at Val's death, and Olly's and Robin's, she did not rage as I did, but wept. Anger has no currency with her. Or so I had thought.

'Well, you can't stop me,' she continues, regaining her haughtiness even while horizontal. 'None of you can. I have promised John that if he comes back from this next campaign season alive, then he can have me, married or not.'

'Betty!' It is my turn to show anger now. 'You have no right to pledge such a thing! You would commit so grievous a sin?'

She shrugs and I try again. 'You would rebel against Father? You would break his heart?' Now this is the right line to take, I know – Father has always been Betty's weakness whereas God is incidental to her. I watch her wavering even as she quivers with indignation, her slender chest heaving in her nightgown.

'I can persuade him,' she says at last, setting her lips firm. 'I know how to work on Father; I can bring him around.'

This I do not doubt, though I will not encourage her by saying so. Betty turns a cold shoulder to me then, signalling that our argument is ended. And, as always when we quarrel, she is asleep within minutes while I am left to stare at the ceiling and into my soul.

If Betty's birthday is a memorable storm of laughter and tears, mine passes as a desert drought. Where she has turned the 'full age' for women, I, at twenty-one, am already five years past my appointed peak and now advance to what would be the age of majority were I a man and of higher value in the world. Betty, who – never one for grudges – seems to have forgiven my perceived disloyalty for now, fusses over me with a lemon cake, as do the little ones in their own shy way. Father writes hastily from his campaign in the West Country but I have no visitors, no handsome suitors. I hear no word from Henry.

As we pass into harvest time, and the Fens crisp from lush green into burnt gold, I find myself flailing and so retreat into the comfort of chores. I help in the hospital, staunching, mopping, soothing. I keep the accounts, pay the servants, order linen and cloth, meat and wine. I write to grieving families and visit blotchy-eyed widows. I go to church, I pray. I sew, I lay, I clean, I cook, I clear. *She rises while it is still night and gives food to her household and portions to her servants.* Verbs, it is always the verbs that keep me going. But, week by week, I feel somehow as if, with Henry gone, my best chance in life has slipped past me like the streams around the sile of Ely now swelled with autumn rains. With Father and Henry away so long, we women are reduced to observers once more, consuming our news in the unsatisfying morsels of letters and broadsheets, snippets of marketplace chatter and gossip. I hear of Henry's rise as if he is someone quite apart from me: a man of note, a celebrity. He has recovered from his wounds and re-joined the army, helping Fairfax to take Bristol from Prince Rupert who, it is rumoured, is dismissed by a petulant, ungrateful king for his defeat. Henry then becomes an MP, joining that small, elite band of officer MPs like Father, who are somehow allowed to straddle both Army and Parliament, in spite of the agreement forged out of the argument with the Earl of Manchester. Henry is honing his political skills, it seems; increasingly in demand to apply his legal penmanship in drafting terms of surrender and negotiating peace as, one by one, the great towns of England fall to our army.

Then the final blow comes: Father writes with some relief that our friend from Chippenham, Colonel Francis Russell, is taking over the defence of Ely as Father and Henry have become too indispensable at the heart of the war effort. Henry will not be returning any time soon and I am once more beached on the shoreline.

I have missed the tide.

CHAPTER TEN

SPRING 1646

If I have let Providence be my mistress, Betty will have none of her. She makes her own way. Somehow – it is a mystery to me how – Betty gets what she wants, as she has always done. John survives the winter fighting, even distinguishing himself in battle at Newark, and comes home to claim his prize. Mother dithers and tries to delay them. Father writes that it is too soon and I hear the anguish in every line of his letters; his despair that he might lose his most darling girl from his house while his back is turned. Betty woos him with soft words and inked kisses even as she takes to walking about the town hand in hand with John and ordering silks and lace for her trousseau. The engagement is common knowledge now and the union cannot be put off further, even if Father has not yet signed the marriage settlement and cannot return for a wedding.

And so Betty – the sixth of my parents' nine children – is the first of us all to make the earthly journey to the altar, laced and wrapped in ivory satin and fox fur, her hair shining and her eyes moist in the dappled, golden light of the cathedral. I thread her into her gown as the bells ring in our ears and am flattened by her happiness. Even as I love her and long for her pleasure, I loathe that she is leaving me. My wedding day – should it ever come, which I increasingly doubt – will not be the same as this, without her rising from our bed and curling and tucking me into my bridal self, her sing-song voice cheering and teasing me, her beautiful reflection showing up my own plainer version in the glass. No. She will always be the joyful bride and I the mournful handmaid. Those were the roles it seems Providence assigned us.

We toast the couple and I strain my cheeks with smiling; conscious of the pitying looks of our friends and neighbours and determined that no one shall think me anything other than delighted. We eat, I smile some more, and then Betty is gone – rattling off in the carriage to Northborough wrapped in John's arms, Badger nestled between their legs. I watch them until they are gone from sight; Betty's shawl, fluttering in the tailwind of the coach, is the last I see of them as they turn the far corner of the street.

When it is over, I lose myself in clearing up, working until everyone else has gone to bed and the last pewter dish has been polished. My fingers are raw but I hardly notice and I crawl around the kitchen floor prising cake crumbs from the rushes. When I wake from a sleeping stupor in front of the fire, I accept that I can delay it no longer and, with weary tread, drag myself upstairs to my big, empty bed. For all my tiredness, I cannot sleep without Betty's soft warmth beside me and I lie cold and fretful until morning, trying not to think of the heat of her marriage bed.

*

The house shrinks further and further, collapsing in on itself like the withered daffodils that fringe the walls. Without Betty, Father and Harry – always the brightest stars in our firmament – and without Olly, my best friend and ally, I am utterly lost. Mary and Frances, now nine and seven years old, grate without Betty to coddle them. Dick mopes and lazes. Grandmother is confined to bed once more with Aunt Liz to attend her. I am left with Mother, Martha and the chores.

Nothing breaks the months of relentless tedium until Harry barges into the house one afternoon, all smiles and sore feet. 'Home!'

'Harry!' We flock to him like starved animals.

'Just for a night or two of leave.' He thrusts his bag of washing into my hands as he smacks a kiss on my cheek before throwing his arms around Mother. Dick trips into the hall and claps Harry on the back before disappearing to see to his horse – now old Matthew has left us, management of the stable seems the only thing Dick is good for.

'Drink first or bath?' Mother fusses.

'Or news?' I add hopefully.

Harry grins. 'Drink *in* the bath, then supper and news.'

Later, as we gather around the parlour table, a newly fragrant Harry spills over with his updates from the front line. 'The war will be over in weeks. Only Oxford remains in Royalist hands and, after Colonel Thomas Rainsborough's attack, the King has deserted the city, creeping out of it in the night in disguise. He called himself Harry, when questioned – can you believe it!

He's surrendered to the Scots and now General Fairfax and our other commanders surround Oxford, blocking all supplies. The city is under siege – it won't last long. I'm to head there myself tomorrow, or perhaps Friday.'

The war will be over in weeks. I am stunned, my mind empty, my senses reeling. I look around me at the remaining women of my family and wait for their reactions.

'Wonderful!' Aunt Liz says before disappearing to the kitchen for another jug of ale.

'God be praised.' Mother's turn.

'What's for pudding?' Fanny now, tapping her spoon on the table.

'You'll be gone by Monday, then?' Mother is speaking again. 'I only ask because Tuesday is Martha's day off. But Biddy can manage for a day, can't you?' She turns to me expectantly. 'We can have the rest of the chicken for dinner tomorrow and then, if you go to the butcher's in the afternoon . . .'

I stare at my family in disbelief – can this be the extent of their reaction to this momentous news? How can Mother think of catering at a moment like this? *The war will be over in weeks.* 'Take me with you!' I shout suddenly, the words bursting from me in another's voice.

'What?' Harry's knife hovers in mid-air as he gazes at me.

'Take me with you to Oxford. I must leave. I must see the war for myself before it is ended. I must be part of it – please.'

Harry laughs nervously while Mother simply stares. 'Are you mad?' he splutters at last. 'It's a hundred miles to Oxford, half the roads are blocked by the army. You'd need a letter or a pass to get through every staging post.'

I do not care for the practicalities, the obstacles. All I can think is that I cannot bear to be left behind again to lower my thoughts to stretching another day's meals out of a chicken. I see Olly riding off reluctantly with Father, remember the last time Harry trotted away to fight. In my mind's eye, Betty throws me a kiss from her carriage before dissolving into John's arms. They have all gone. And Henry – Henry is at Oxford.

'Not if I'm with you.' I must answer Harry's objections. 'If I am travelling with you, and can prove I am Lieutenant-General Cromwell's daughter.'

'Mother, please?' Harry turns to her now, baffled.

'Biddy, you cannot be in earnest.' Mother bends towards me, ringed hand outstretched, the other running inside her single string of pearls. 'You simply cannot go off across-country, an unmarried woman in the midst of a war. Where would you stay?'

'We could lodge at inns on the way and when we arrive, I will find Father.' I look between them fiercely. I will not be prevented, I will meet Providence in the field. *A man's heart devises his way: but the Lord directs his steps.* Why not a woman's too? 'Harry – either you take me with you when you go or I leave tomorrow morning on Dick's horse with no one to protect me. It is your choice.'

Harry takes me with him. At first Mother said she would come too but I would not let her: the girls need her more than me and with Grandmother sick, Aunt Liz can't be expected to cope alone. And so I strengthen myself to bid her farewell for the first time in my life and leave with my baby brother. We will ride together to Cambridge, where Dick's horse will be sent back and I will take the public coach most of the rest of the way with Harry riding alongside; I can make the final part of the journey on a hired horse.

As I ride out of Ely in the pale morning sunshine, I have never felt more alive or more free. I do not look back once.

It takes us three days to reach the approach to Oxford. Three days in which Harry prattles good-naturedly and I plan what I will say and do when we reach Father and Henry; I had not thought that far ahead when I insisted on coming. But every moment that I waver and worry about what to do is offset by the nourishment I feel at finally seeing the effects of the war laid before me, however painful these are. The desolation is as terrible as the looming victory is thrilling. Each day we skirt around shattered towns with rubble walls and smoke-filled air, pass through villages and past homesteads with crops rotting in the fields with no men to tend to them. Cripples and beggars line the road, refugees argue with grim-faced soldiers at roadblocks, potholes delay us at every turn. At one post, we watch in a queue of travellers as a finely dressed couple are summoned from their coach, searched and arrested. Battalions of weary soldiers march alongside us, singing under their bibled banners, their preachers calling out hallelujahs.

I have never before travelled beyond Cambridge and am amazed at what I see. England, once, I imagine, a patch-worked quilt of fields, streams and hills, with farms, villages and towns nestled in its folds, has become a chain-mail coat; each troop, battalion and regiment, each siege encampment, watchtower and castle, linked by supply chains, the land criss-crossed with roadblocks. Every river is a boundary. Every bridge still standing is a stronghold. Every town is a fortification. Every man, woman and child has been caught up in this war without an enemy. The sights upset and enthral me but, more than anything else, they open my eyes to a life beyond the stuffy confines of our timbered house in Ely. I know now what I had always suspected, that I need an active life that takes me out of my front door and into the world.

At last, with dusk falling on the third day and a sentry's directions in Harry's pocket, we approach Sir Thomas Fairfax's siege headquarters at the fortified manor house of Holton Park, just west of Oxford. I can almost feel the war at close hand, the distant boom of cannon carrying on the wind and the sharp tang of gun smoke in the air. I am stiff and exhausted – the Chiltern Hills a shock for the legs of a woman used to the flat plains of East Anglia – but giddy nonetheless with the exhilaration of what I am about to do. Guards wave us through the gates and we leave our horses with a trooper, making our way past two sentries and through the stone porch into a grand hall. In front of us, a vast oak staircase twists up to a gallery lined with portraits. Fine tapestries cloak the walls and silver candelabra cast a soft glow around the room. It is the grandest house I have ever set foot in, and I might almost imagine it was peacetime were it not for the captain and his clerk sitting at a desk in the middle of the hall, the bundle of muskets and boots propped in the corner and the stale smell of spilt ale, powder and tobacco on the air.

Harry steps forward smartly, salutes the captain and hands over his papers.

'Cromwell, eh?'

'Yes. And this is my sister. She is here to see Lieutenant-General Cromwell and I am to report to General Harrison.'

'You'll find them in there, in council.' The captain waves his pen in the air towards a door on the left before resuming his conversation with the clerk.

Before I know it, Harry has knocked on the door and entered the room. It is a huge drawing room, the biggest room I ever saw in a private house. A throng of lower-ranking officers mill around immediately in front of us; some standing in whispering huddles, others sitting on the edge of chairs and sofas sharing platters of bread and ham and playing quietly at cards. A few of them look up and cast us curious glances but most ignore us entirely. Instead, their gazes flick often to the scene playing out behind them at the far end of the room. Following the direction of their attention, I see Father standing by the fireplace with Uncle Desborough and four younger officers, one of whom I recognise as Charles Fleetwood. The man on their right has exquisitely coiffed curls and is dressed in the finest evergreen brocade cloak.

'That's my commander, General Thomas Harrison,' Harry whispers to me. 'You won't find a godlier man nor a finer suit of clothes in the whole army – "Preacher Peacock" we call him in the regiment.' Harry smiles fondly then gestures to a slim and upright young man with something of the sleek greyhound in his dashing looks: 'Colonel John Lambert, rising star and a favourite of Father's. And the other with the fine moustache is

Colonel Thomas Rainsborough, the hero of Woodstock, the last bout of fighting that prompted the King to flee.'

He glances at me for my reply but I have none. I can only stare at Henry as my heart hammers in my chest. He is sitting with his back to me, his dark head bent over a paper as he writes, a handsome gypsy-skinned, broad-backed and black-bearded man pacing behind him dictating.

'Black Tom,' Harry whispers again. 'The great man himself! We should wait until he has finished.'

But I ignore him and instead barge through the officers, propelled by a sudden urgency to know my future.

'Biddy!' Harry hisses and I hear him scramble behind me as I forge forward.

Sir Thomas Fairfax sees me first and pauses mid-sentence, his bushy eyebrows arching at my approach as he rests his hand on Henry's desk. 'Why, who is this?' he asks good-humouredly. Henry turns and stares at me and I watch, as if in slow motion, a drop of ink falling from his pen onto his lap.

'Bridget!' Father's voice booms across the room. 'Good Lord! Are you here for me?'

Every man waits, paused in a tableau. My mind clears and a single sentence forms on my tongue.

'No, Father. I am here for Henry.'

It feels as if many moments pass before all becomes commotion. 'Henry? Henry Ireton?' Father repeats, bewildered, before he spots his son behind me, then he exclaims, 'Harry, my boy!' and strides forward to greet us both. The others, taking their cue from Father, cluster around us as Black Tom whispers something in Henry's ear and moves away from his desk. I watch

Henry through the swirl of broad backs around me. He puts down his pen and rises slowly from his chair. As he stands, I notice his dishevelled hair, the ink on his fingers and the mud on his trousers. He has been overworking, I think with a lurching concern that surprises me. It is that protective feeling towards him, more than any other, that sets my mind to my course.

Henry moves towards me then, his dark eyes bright as coals. 'Mistress Cromwell' – he bows awkwardly – 'you wish to speak to me?'

I give the merest nod before drifting away from the others into the corner of the room. With a nervous glance at Father and then Fairfax, Henry follows, his steps cautious and confused. When we are out of earshot, I turn back towards him. My face prickles under the gaze of the generals and colonels who watch us with murmuring fascination. I blur the edges of my vision and sink myself instead in the familiar geometry of Henry's face, taking one deep breath.

'Henry. I have come to accept your offer of marriage, if it still stands. I was dissatisfied with how things were left between us and, as you have not returned to Ely and are not likely to do so, I have come to you.'

He gapes at me; the first time ever, I think, that I have him at a loss for words, perhaps even thoughts. His face, usually so shrewd and scripted, is blank. I cannot read him and a cold fear begins to steal through me. Am I too late? I grapple forward frantically into the silence.

'Does your proposal still stand?' I press. 'Do you still wish to marry me? You did say I might consider it.' I know how desperate I sound but I do not care. What have I to lose that I have not lost already? What else waits for me? And so I wait for him, my pulse pounding in my wrists, watching until, finally, Henry's first thoughts begin to show in his face: he is shocked but perhaps impressed; he is unaccustomed to being wrong-footed. He is someone who likes to plot and plan, who likes to walk steps ahead of others, who always looks to the future. I know this of him. He shakes his head a little in bafflement before a wide smile stretches his pointed face into a diamond.

'Bridget, my dear.'

It is all he needs to say. He takes my hands in his and it is done.

I am safe. My future is assured.

Where I feel mostly relief and Henry, I think, satisfaction, it is left to Father to show the deepest joy. 'Oh my dear hearts, my dear hearts,' he says tearfully as he takes our hands and tips his head to hear God's blessing.

The other men crowd around us, shaking Henry's hand and kissing my cheek as Father hastily makes introductions: Thomas Harrison, fierce and flamboyant; John Lambert, lithe and lilting. Eager Charles Fleetwood expresses his pleasure in seeing me again and I him, while Thomas Rainsborough gives me a low bow, removing his hat to send its sea-green and black ribbon trim fluttering. My wits return to me just in time for Father to draw me towards the swarthy figure of the commander-in-chief, Sir Thomas Fairfax.

'My dear Mistress Cromwell,' he sweeps my hand up for a kiss and twinkles at me, 'and soon to be Mistress Ireton. I think the Lord must be smiling on our cause indeed to bring you two souls together just as we near the end of our war.'

'I hope so, sir,' I reply. 'No one prays more fervently for the triumph of our cause than I. It is a great honour to meet you.'

He bows gallantly. 'Then you are a most welcome addition to our party.'

Our party. The words taste delicious on my tongue and I am warmed by an unfamiliar feeling of intense belonging. The kitchen sink in Ely suddenly seems more than a hundred miles away.

'But where are my manners?' Fairfax continues with well-bred courtesy. 'You must be exhausted from your journey. Let us find my wife, who will make you comfortable.'

'Lady Fairfax is here, sir?' I am surprised to feel a wave of relief; though I have long pined for the company of active men like these, in this instant the soothing presence of another woman would calm me after this initial excitement.

'Yes, indeed. My good lady rarely leaves my side. She is as much the commander here as I am! Lambert's charming wife is here too and a few other ladies. Come, let us find them.'

Fairfax offers his arm and I take it happily, throwing a quick glance at Henry before I am swept from the room. The captain and his clerk spring to attention before their chief and Fairfax leads me up the stairs in search of his wife. We find her in an upstairs sitting room where the opened door reveals a strikingly mirrored scene to the one I witnessed downstairs. My gaze is drawn first to a richly dressed woman, dark-curled and handsome, though closer to thirty than twenty, I would guess. The way she paces the room with elegant strides and pointed-slippered toes tells me at once that she is of high birth. The fact that she, too, is dictating a letter, in her case to a younger woman sitting at a bureau, tells me that she is Sir Thomas Fairfax's wife and the slim hand she holds up to him to wait in patience while she finishes her sentence confirms the fact.

'My dearest,' she greets him when she has stopped and, seeing me, sweeps on, 'who have you brought for me?'

'Mistress Bridget Cromwell, my love. Daughter to Oliver and, as of a few minutes ago, the betrothed of our own Commissary-General Henry Ireton!'

'Oh my sweet girl!' Lady Fairfax shimmers towards me, her pink gown rustling slightly as she takes my rough hands in her soft white ones and places a perfumed kiss on each of my cheeks. 'Felicitations. What joyous news.' In an instant she has drawn me away from her husband and into her female realm, presenting me to her companions as the lord general bows reverently and leaves the room. The two other women sitting on the sofa lower their sewing into their laps and smile at me.

'Mistress Frances Lambert, wife of our gallant Colonel John Lambert, who is a countryman of my husband's from Yorkshire.' Lady Anne gestures to a bright-eyed, golden-curled younger woman, only a year or two older than me, I guess, who tilts her head as she eyes me with a shrewd gaze. 'And Mistress Catherine Harrison, herself a recent bride to our glamorous General Thomas Harrison.' The youngest woman nods a shy greeting and I see at once the slightest swell to her stomach which sends an involuntary blush to my cheeks. Besides these two women, the party is completed by a baby sprawling on the carpet at our feet and a nursemaid hovering behind it, but Lady Anne does not introduce them, nor the girl to whom she was dictating. There is a hierarchy in this room as clear as that downstairs, I think, squaring up to the challenge.

It is a familiar female scene, such as those I have spent my life in, and yet shockingly different. These women are of a higher status and political calling than those of my family and I am suddenly very conscious of my dirty riding boots and the musty stable smell clinging to my skirts. Within an instant, the skilful hostess Lady Anne seems to read my thoughts. 'You must be exhausted, my dear,' she says, gliding to a side table and ringing a tinkling hand bell. 'Let us arrange your room this instant and when you have refreshed yourself, we can talk properly. Ah, Mistress Bateson.' A housekeeper enters. 'Could you ask Lady Whorwood to join us for a few moments, if she is not otherwise engaged?' When the housekeeper has withdrawn, Lady Anne leads me to an armchair where I perch carefully, folding my hands in my lap above my travelling bag.

'Lady Whorwood, your Ladyship?' I ask, for I am not familiar with the name.

'This is her house.' Frances Lambert leans forward to speak before Lady Anne can answer. 'The army commandeered it for our headquarters and though she is a Royalist, we like to preserve the common social niceties, don't we, Anne? Simple things like asking her permission when we have a new guest to stay, though she can hardly refuse.'

Anne. I note the familiarity in her address to Lady Fairfax and wonder how long Anne Fairfax and Frances

Lambert have been friends. Does this suggest future preferment for Colonel Lambert?

'We do,' Lady Anne replies. 'We ladies must all get along if we are to have any hope of returning to a civilised society after this war is done with. Far too few of the men appreciate this in their blood lust, though my husband, of course, is a noble exception. Why, only yesterday, hearing of Oxford's dwindling supplies, he sent a present of a brace of bucks, mutton, veal and lamb, capons and butter into the city for the King's son, the Duke of York.'

How strange a thing a civil war is, I think, as I listen to her kind and courtly sentiments. Only a few weeks ago one of our men shot Prince Rupert while he was out on a raiding party, wounding him badly in the arm, and here is our commander sending a hamper of fine food to the prince's cousin sitting out the siege. It is war but often on the most civil terms. Both sides as keen as the other on preserving something precious to them through all the bloodshed. Or at least that is the feeling among the gentry and nobility who will always find a way to meet each other at the top of any divide; I cannot help but wonder if the ordinary rank and file would approve of their commander sending a food parcel to his enemy prince.

I express my understanding with a nod but reach in vain for a courtly reply wishing, with sudden longing, that Betty was here with me to trade in charm. This is the noble society she has always aspired to; a world of such deep-rooted manners that politeness and charm cannot be driven out, even by the most desperate violence. Where civility must outlast a civil war. I will need to think what she would say and do if I am to find a place in this new realm – try to smooth my outward self in her mould even as I guard my inner political convictions.

I watch this courtly dance with fascination a few moments later when Lady Whorwood enters the room, her stout middle-aged frame swathed in violet silk, a tall, red-haired young woman trailing solemnly behind her. Lady Whorwood approaches Lady Fairfax and the two curtsey to one another at a few feet apart while Frances Lambert and Catherine Harrison straighten themselves on the sofa.

'Lady Fairfax.'

'Lady Whorwood.'

It is almost as if they are preparing for a duel.

'Thank you for coming so quickly,' Anne Fairfax begins. 'We must beg your hospitality once more for my young friend here, Lieutenant-General Cromwell's daughter. And, more than a room, I wonder if you would permit her and Commissary-General Ireton to marry here as soon as I can make the arrangements.'

Soon, it will be soon. Merely days? Blood thunders in my ears; there is no turning back now.

'Of course, your Ladyship.' Lady Whorwood keeps her chin high and her tone as smooth as satin and I wonder how much this imposition of her enemy in the sanctity of her home must cost her. 'My daughter-in-law Jane will see the young lady settled and help with the arrangements.' She inclines her head a few degrees to the younger woman standing behind her. 'The green bedroom, Jane, on the second floor. Come, Mistress Cromwell, Jane will take you now.'

'Thank you, your Ladyship,' I say, rising quickly to

my feet and following Jane, who hardly waits before scuttling from the room.

'We will see you at dinner, my dear,' Lady Anne calls after me. 'Eight o'clock. And you can tell us the story of your betrothal!'

The next few days are both the happiest and the strangest I have ever known. I am propelled like a skiff on the tide from my former life into my new one. It takes several days for my fingers to stop twitching for the chores I no longer have to do. Instead there are servants to prepare meals and soldiers to run errands. My time, for the first time ever, is entirely my own. Once I am settled, I spend the mornings in my room reading, sewing and writing home while the married ladies are busy with their husbands. In the afternoons, we women discuss the latest in the Oxford peace negotiations and make arrangements for my wedding. And the evenings – my favourite times of all – see us gathered around the supper table with the gentlemen, where the conversation is as lively and intelligent as ever I could have dreamed.

It is here, in the grand dining room at Holton, that the worlds of the men and women combine in a beautiful swirl of silver satin and iron armour. Here that the army leaders relax and bring their problems before their wives who weigh and measure them with all the skill and application that Mother and Betty would expend in the drapers. Here that every clause of the peace terms Henry and John Lambert are drafting together are pored over as our negotiators go back and forth with the King's while Oxford simmers and waits on the horizon. While the men are hopeful of peace, further violence cannot be ruled out and General Fairfax makes it clear that he is prepared to take the city by storm if needs be. But Henry assures me the commander's bark is worse than his bite:

'He has no desire to damage England's most beautiful city,' he whispers to me at supper one evening. 'And, for me, I am not sure I could do it. Not to my own university town.'

I am pleased by his honesty and sensitivity, though my feelings for him continue to confuse me. It helps to push them to one side and concentrate instead on the truth of our marriage: that it is a transaction, as honest as any other. A suitable wife and helpmeet for him in exchange for a pathway to power and independence for me. Soon, with a husband of my own, I will be able to do as Lady Anne does and visit the generals in their war room to deliver my views on their latest strategy. Before long I will be seen standing in conference with Henry the way I see Frances and John Lambert bring their heads together over a letter or latest dispatch. Then I will have a role. Then I will have a voice.

In the meantime, Lady Anne – or the generaless, as I soon find out she is affectionately called – takes me under her wing like a mother blackbird and protects me from all the changes that would buffet me, assuming complete responsibility for my wedding. I am loath to admit to her how little I care for the trifles of the day and so I nod and smile as she arranges for her chaplain to officiate, plans the menu for our celebratory dinner and fusses over my clothes, obsessing herself with the task of finding me a suitable wedding dress. She, Frances Lambert and Catherine Harrison discuss the topic for hours, running through their own wardrobes and discussing any gowns that might be made up to do. The Royalist Lady Whorwood is even consulted, much to my embarrassment. Eventually, my wedding dress is obtained from a most unlikely source when Jane Whorwood – who is helping with the wedding arrangements as her mother-in-law instructed – offers me her own bridal gown with suitable alterations. I protest that I couldn't be so presumptuous even as I question privately if I could wear the wedding gown of a Royalist bride. But she insists in charming, if cryptic, terms:

'I'll turn it up for you at the hem and take an inch from the bodice and then it will do nicely. Besides, it will please me to gift it to another bride and wish her better fortune in marriage than I have had.'

'Than you have had, Mistress Whorwood?' I repeat, looking up from the luxurious sunset yellow silk to examine her face, noticing for the first time her pock-marked skin and shadowed eyes.

'I'll only say that my husband was not kind to me and, though his leaving brought me hardship and left me here with his mother, it was a blessing too in its way.'

'I am sorry,' I say, lowering myself onto the edge of the bed and thinking with sudden nerves of my own wedding and wondering for the thousandth time what manner of marriage lies ahead for me when Henry and I are finally and irrevocably alone. My parents' marriage is so happy and strong, for all their worldly troubles, I struggle to imagine what a miserable union might be like. Have they ill-prepared me by this? What kind of wife will I be? And what manner of husband will I find Henry be? He cares for little but his work and shows a wanton disregard in looking after himself. And he can be so unpredictable. 'We none of us can know what Providence has in store for us when we take a husband,' I can only conclude.

Jane Whorwood shapes her round face into an unexpected smile, lighting the freckles across her nose, which go some way to masking the pockmarks. 'I'll have none of Providence myself, not after that. I intend to make my own fate.'

'But how?' I ask, shocked at the notion of stepping so far off one's path, though I realise immediately that my coming to Oxford might have represented the same disregard for Providence. 'Surely, with a deserted husband, you will have to stay here with his mother and your children? And now at the mercy of General Fairfax.'

'I'll find a way,' she replies, pressing the dress into my hands before disappearing from the room.

It will be a strange war-time wedding, with only Father and Harry present from my family and none of Henry's. But I make my peace with this and Henry reconciles to it the moment his best friend Colonel Francis Thornhaugh arrives to stand beside him and be our witness. His cheerful presence comforts me too as he grounds my husband in his past, telling me with touching fondness of their escapades as schoolboys in Attenborough and of the day they joined up to Parliament's army together, raising a local troop of horse side by side. I watch their reunion in fascination. Francis calls Henry 'Hal', as Shakespeare does the young King Henry V, and touches him constantly, almost proprietorially: an elbow jabbed in his side at a joke, a fluff of his dark hair at a tease, a squeeze of the arm in affection. And like a bullrush

Henry bends back towards Francis in mirrored intimacy, blushing and almost tongue-tied with pleasure in his presence. Francis is joyful, open-hearted and mocking and I marvel at first at the unlikely friendship between him and my careful, serious fiancé. But I soon realise theirs is a kinship as close as family and that, as with mine and Betty's relationship, it is their very differences that knot them together. Seeing Henry soften in his friend's presence and hearing more of his family and boyhood gives me some last-minute reassurance in my choice as I go to bed for the last time as a maid.

My wedding day dawns in all its bright, summer brilliance, and I am up and out of bed to meet it. Before all else I pray long and deeply, seeking to understand what God intends for me. Am I the one who has driven myself here? Who has rolled the dice as Dick does when he gambles in The Bell? Have I taken my fate in my hands as Jane Whorwood intends to? Or was this the Lord's intention for me all along? I thought it the former but this morning, for the first time, as I hear God's whispers on the early summer breeze, I realise my folly and resign myself once more to his care.

He is with me as Lady Anne and Jane dress and prettify me, ministering to me as I wish, with sudden longing, that Mother and Betty were here to do. He is beside me as Father leads me up the aisle of the tiny chapel on the Holton estate, the sunlight filtering through the stained glass windows to caress the pearl clusters glowing in the sandy folds of my own, so I feel like Miriam passing through the Red sea. And He is watching as Henry Ireton and I exchange our vows in His sight. Olly too, I hope and pray; pleased that I have kept my promise to him. As we emerge into the sunshine, my head full of my husband and my heart full of God, I feel, for the first time in many years, a warmth that must be happiness.

PART TWO

One year later, London

CHAPTER ELEVEN

SPRING 1647

'She is out of danger? The baby too?'

I inhale Lady Fairfax's expensive scent as I kiss her silken cheeks. Orange blossom and vanilla, I think, and a woodier note underneath. Amber? 'Yes, they are both well, thank the Lord.'

'Wonderful. Well done, Bridget. I always like to call on the fifth day after a birth. We usually know where we are by then; if we are heading to font or graveyard.'

I hiss in my breath, though I know the truth in her words, having watched my baby brother James breathe his last shuddered breath on his fourth day in the world. The day when God made the sun, moon and stars. 'Would you like to see the baby?'

'Certainly! I must inspect the heir for myself. See if he is the image of his grandfather.'

Of course Betty has had the first grandchild. Of course it is a boy. And of course she has named him for Father – though I expected her to use Oliver, not the severe Cromwell, which is so hard to associate with the tiny, wrinkled baby clinging frog-like to my little sister's chest. Cromwell Claypole – the name twists around your tongue. As I lead Lady Fairfax upstairs to Betty's room, I feel an answering fluttering in my stomach; I will have a girl, no doubt, when my own confinement comes at harvest time.

'This is a fine house,' Lady Fairfax declares as we reach the landing and pause briefly at the latticed window to take in the gardens where horse chestnuts are just unveiling their spring candles. Turning back to the gallery, she runs her noble eye appraisingly over the dimensions of the space, taking in the ceiling height, the detailing of the moulding and any number of other silent indicators of quality that I would not know to look for. 'Your father's agent did well to find him one of these new houses on Drury Lane,' she continues with approval. 'The air is that bit cleaner and sweeter midway between Westminster and the City, though you have to put up with the constant noise of building works. There is space enough for you all?'

'Plenty, thank you,' I say, thinking back to our home in Ely where all four of us girls shared a bedroom. 'Though the whole family is rarely here at once,' I continue as we reach Betty's door. 'My aunt chose to stay behind with friends in Ely when we moved to London and John and Elizabeth are as often at Northborough as with us. But my sister wished to have the baby here where Mother and I could be on hand and with London's best midwives and physicians close by.'

'I imagine you and Henry will wish for your own establishment in due course.' Anne hides her angling line amid the reeds of a statement, her trick as familiar to me as the truth of my feelings evidently are to her; army wives learn each other's ways in the parlour as quickly as their husbands do in the field. And we have spent much of the last year in each other's company.

'I'm sure we will form our own household in time,' I reply with more certainty than I feel. Though I wished us to take separate lodgings when we came to London, Henry, working daily with Father, argued for practicality and economy. I suspect him also of enjoying living within a large family once more – a taste I had seen for myself last year, when he took me up for a brief visit to his family home at Attenborough to meet his mother and siblings; the new bride for their inspection.

It had surprised me there to find the formal, driven soldier I am used to softened into an indulgent family man almost in Father's mould. An oldest son who thrives on dependencies, the champion of his younger siblings and pride of his formidable widowed mother's heart. Seeing him in his natural habitat explained so much of his character. Even here in London he is constantly acting on behalf of his family: dealing with legal papers and letters his mother sends him and helping his brother John establish himself as a mercer, freeman of the corporation of London and member of the Clothmakers' Company. Just as I wish to break free from the warm but smothering blanket of wider family life, Henry desires nothing more than to belong. And who am I to blame him? If he married me in part to come closer to Father, didn't I marry him in even larger part to come closer to the centre of things? It was a bargain struck as any other and both of us must respect it.

These transactional thoughts of marriage are dispelled on passing into Betty's chamber where we enter a sacred scene. Betty reclines as the Virgin mother, tiny Cromwell swaddled in her arms. Around her, timeless figures pay homage: the wet nurse hovers as Mother mixes Betty a tonic and John watches the scene from the window seat like a latter-day Joseph, though with more of a self-satisfied smile than the adopted father of our Lord must have worn.

'Lady Fairfax,' Mother greets our guest warmly, though with the touch of deference we all show to the generaless.

'Mistress Cromwell, Mistress Claypole. I am glad to see you looking so well, my dear,' Anne Fairfax sinks smiling into an armchair by Betty's bed. 'And gladder still at the rosy complexion of your wet nurse. I always recommend choosing the girl with the pinkest cheeks.'

'Thank you, your Ladyship. My husband procured her for us.'

'I'm sure he did,' Anne replies with the hint of a smile and I wonder if her mind has slipped into the same impure thought as mine: that John will have been quickened in his step by his eagerness to have his wife back in his bed as soon as possible. How will Henry feel about this when my turn comes? My mind drifts back to our wedding night and the awkward meetings of elbows and knees when Henry first brought his body to mine as I lay rigid with nerves. I remember the flickering of Henry's moustache and beard against my skin as his mouth hovered over mine. I see the drops of sweat gathered at the centre of his chest, glistening in the rushlight like those on the body of the poor dead soldier whose arm we had taken off. I feel the imprints of my fingernails in my palms at the wrenching pain. How strange it was at first to share a bedroom with him: to listen to his heavy breathing in the night, watch him spit in the bowl as he cleaned his teeth, to hear the tinkling of his piss in the chamber pot in the morning. It was weeks before I could dress and undress in front of him without raw embarrassment. Agony the first time I explained we should not lie together as my courses had come. Things are better now. More settled. But how well will we face the mortal intimacy of childbed together?

Lady Fairfax settles into the soft talk of women's matters, sliding into the secret, shared language of mothers that I am familiar with but in which I am not yet fluent: feeds, leaks, stitches. Fidgeting, I am relieved when Betty tires and we return downstairs to the parlour where I can have my commanding officer to myself.

'What news from the army?' I ask her as soon as our maid has brought wine and candied cherries and I have shooed Mary and Frances from under our feet. 'You have been at headquarters with the general?'

'Yes, indeed. Though I am glad now of a few days in London; I do declare Saffron Walden a dreary town, even if it is your part of the country.'

It takes no effort to smile gamely at her jest when her slight means little to me. Why is it always so important where someone comes from? For Father, the clay lands to the west of the Great Ouse and marshy fens to its east are Eden. Charles Fleetwood, when he senses he has lost Henry's interest, brings my husband's eyes back up from the page with a single mention of their shared homeland of Nottinghamshire. *What country are you from?*, men ask each other on first meeting, and the answer is never England.

'But are the men so desperate as the papers make out?' I press her. 'Listen to this.' I pick up the *Perfect Diurnal*, delivered only that morning, and read aloud: '"Parliament's rejection of the soldiers' right to petition for indemnity for their actions in the war could lead to thousands suffering imprisonment or worse." And here, on the other side, an account of a soldier convicted of manslaughter for a death on the battlefield and burned on the hand.'

'That's true enough,' the generaless replies, the battle-light returning to her eyes. 'It was a man in Colonel Rossiter's regiment. My lord was incensed at that case but could do nothing to stop it. He tells me his men are owed months of pay and begin to fear Parliament will disband the army before granting them the money and safety from prosecution they sorely need.'

I tut into my glass. 'It's a disgrace that good men who left their families and trades to spend their blood to bring peace and safety to Parliament and the kingdom should be so ungratefully and shamefully treated.'

Anne smiles at me with a touch of indulgence and I colour under her smooth stare. Yet I am not ashamed of the strong feelings I share with my husband. 'You are a fine wordsmith, Bridget.' She purrs the compliment. 'Henry must value your help with his drafting.'

'When he seeks it, which is less often than I would like,' I reply, desire for his trust loosening my wife's tongue even though I know the generaless to be fishing once more.

'No doubt. But you are still freshly espoused. When you have been married as long as we have, he will scarce pen a thought without taking your view first.'

'And until then?' Impatience rubs at the edges of my words, roughening away the fragile London polish to return me to my Huntingdonshire vowels. The child inside me stirs and I know the time I have to devote myself solely to Henry and his work is limited. I must prove my usefulness to him before I am lost in the new mother's muffled, white world of milk and linen.

'Until then,' Lady Fairfax slips into her own maternal mode, 'be sure to always be the one to bring his letters. Busy yourself fussing around his desk while he opens them so he speaks his thoughts aloud to you. And when he is at work drafting his papers, try, if you can, to be at hand – sit quietly with your sewing if needs be. Men often like to practise their words out loud before committing them to ink and if you are there to catch them – oh, and ink – learn how to mix it the way he likes. And how he files his papers too.'

I nod, filing her advice away carefully in turn.

'But now,' she continues after sipping her wine. 'I have told you news of the army, now you must return payment.'

'The news from Parliament, you mean?' I take a moment to order my thoughts before beginning my report. 'Henry tells me it is all faction and division – the spirit of consensus that won us the war quite melted away. Now the governing English and Scots committee is dissolved, the loathsome Denzil Holles leads the Presbyterian majority in Parliament pushing for a spineless peace with the King, paying off the Scots army to return home and shipping half our regiments over to Ireland to put down the rebellion.'

'No doubt he thinks it a way to disband the army

from under our noses, breaking any influence we have and wheedling out of paying the men's wages and granting their indemnities at the same time.'

'Quite.' It is a sore subject for me. As one of the few remaining soldier-MPs, Henry has been trying to put the soldiers' case to Parliament and it is taking a heavy toll as he is increasingly caught in the cross-fire between the MPs and the army. 'Do you know what the other members did not forty-eight hours ago?' I ask Lady Fairfax as I place my empty glass on the tray. 'They issued a declaration that Henry and some of the other officers are 'enemies of the state. Enemies of the state simply for looking after their own men!'

I quiver at the recollection of Henry's face when he told me of this on a late return from Westminster, his very skin seeming aflame above his night candle. Nothing I could say would soothe. Nothing I could offer would tempt him. He would neither eat nor go to bed but buried himself at his desk while I dithered behind him barefoot, unwilling to surrender myself to sleep yet unable to achieve anything material. That Henry should be declared traitor! He who cares so deeply about doing his duty to England and only thinks to protect the interests of his men, his passion for his work blinding him so far that he neglects his own physical needs. He had wept over the words once, finally, he had come to bed, the first tears I had ever seen him shed. They were silent tears and I thanked God I had had the wit to stay awake for him; the minutes I held his dark curled head and soothed him more precious to me than any spent in conjugal embrace.

My words stir the generaless at last and she shakes

her head, placing her wine glass on the table so she does not spill it in her agitation. 'Enemies of the state,' she repeats. 'I can hardly believe it. There must have been some terrible misunderstanding.'

'Perhaps,' I am forced by our ranks to allow her gentler interpretation, though I believe there is more of malice than of misunderstanding in the widening divergence I see between the army and Parliament each day. Henry certainly thinks so, for all Father's attempts to find a less worrying explanation.

I hear the front door bang, the sound echoing off the Delft hall tiles. 'Perhaps that is Father and Henry now returned from the House. They will be able to tell you more.'

But it is neither the bulky form of my father, nor Henry's slim frame that flings open the parlour door. It is my brother Richard who stands, flushed and breathless before us, his bag of legal papers dropped on the floor at his shoes.

'Dick!' I greet him in surprise. 'Why such haste?'

'Terrible news, Biddy,' he says between gasps, sending a hurried nod in Lady Fairfax's direction. 'I have just come from the City where all talk is that your husband and Denzil Holles have gone across the river to fight a duel.'

'What?' I spring from the chair, my thoughts swirling like starlings. 'A duel?'

The next hour creeps by, minute by minute, as uncaring as a woodlouse. Dick knows only as much as the other pupil barristers at Lincoln's Inn and John Claypole, whom we dispatch at once to enquire at Westminster, has not yet returned. Lady Fairfax insists on waiting with us until there is news and Mother joins us from Betty's chamber, her finger sliding round and round inside her pearls – double stranded now Father's pay has increased – as the baby flutters anxiously beneath my stays. Feeling the life within me, my thoughts fly to the worst imaginings: life without Henry, cast into the purgatory of stateless widowhood with a dependant baby. And, more than that, I realise. More than my tumbling status and wide-eyed fatherless child. I would never see Henry again, nor hear his fine words and rich voice – such a surprisingly deep, velvet voice for one so slim and foxy-faced. I would never watch his pen pause on the page as he rehearses a word or phrase in his head, never feel his hand on my cheek in the darkness.

I turn sharply at the noise of the front door, my wild, confused thoughts dropping from my head like hailstones. Men's voices, the door opening.

'Henry!'

He is here, he is alive. I find my feet running to him, my arms around his neck like a blushing girl.

'There, lass,' he says, surprised into soft homely words at my unusual display. 'I am quite safe, we did not fight.'

'What happened?' Lady Fairfax crosses the room to Father, John and Charles Fleetwood, who are removing their hats.

'Holles and Henry had some words outside Parliament, your Ladyship,' Father says, his tone gruffer than usual. 'You can guess what about.'

'The sneering dandy said the soldiers' petition was seditious and accused me of forcing men to sign it,'

Henry spits out the words. 'Said I was a traitor and a coward and he would prove it with pistols.'

'What did you say?' I shake my head in shock. 'Surely you were not going to fight him?'

'He told him to go to the Devil!' Father barks with a hollow laugh, the strain of the day telling. He is still not fully recovered from the illness that laid him low for all of February and he coughs as he blows some hot breath into his hands. 'Holles may be as stubborn as a mule but if there's one who can meet him at the manger, it's Henry.'

'I told him it was against my conscience to fight a duel,' Henry continues, his tone more measured now. 'But that I was no coward and would go with him wherever he chose so he could take a shot at me if he so wished.'

Mother gasps and Lady Fairfax claps her hands. 'Bravo, sir! What bravery.'

'What foolishness,' I counter, provoking a reproving glance from Mother at such unwifely undermining. 'Come, sit.' I try to make amends with a tender gesture and lead Henry to a chair. 'What happened then?'

He lowers his slim limbs into the best cushion-backed chair and, seeing his exhaustion, Charles Fleetwood takes up the account. 'They were on the point of boarding a boat to go across to Southwark fields when the Speaker stopped them with a delegation from the House. They said they would not sanction members of Parliament drawing pistols.' Charles looks to Father, as if for his approval.

'And so you emerge with your honour intact, my son,' Father says, clapping a proud hand on Henry's shoulder.

'It was a fine sight to see Holles so reprimanded and by those he reveres above all others. That man has had no love for me, nor mine, for many years now.'

Martha and the new maid slip in with supper trays during the commotion and I loose myself from Henry to make up a plate for him. Henry is smiling at Father's praise when I return to him, though his eyes glaze as he takes the plate from me. It hovers in the air for a moment before he lowers it to his lap untouched, a cold potato rolling from the edge onto the floor. I retrieve it and blow away a speck of dirt as the men bustle around, falling upon the food while Mother draws Lady Fairfax towards the table.

'No, no thank you, I will not stay,' Anne says hastily. 'Now I have seen the man of the hour safely returned to his wife.' She glides over and gives me a kiss before whisking herself out of the room in one stylish movement, the maid hurrying after her into the hall to find her things.

My eyes return to Henry who is now looking very pale. 'My dear, I really think you should go up to bed, you have had a shock.'

My words shake my husband from his reverie but he bats them away, shifting his full plate onto the side table as he gets to his feet. 'No, I can't. I must work on our vindication paper. Holles has raised the stakes – now our honour is in question and we must answer our accusers swiftly. But my ideas are only half-formed. Where is my bag?' He casts around him.

Normally I would support him in his work-lust; I know he cannot abide going to bed with an unfinished task and the remembrance of a letter unwritten or a paper unstudied will cause him to leap from the bed with a rushlight in search of a candle, pen and paper. But not tonight.

'I must insist, Henry. I'm sure the draft can wait until tomorrow. Or you can dictate your ideas to me from bed? I have your copybook. Come, I will bring your supper plate.'

Henry makes to resist me but then Father's voice commands him from across the room. 'I would take heed of Bidding Biddy, my son, if you know what's good for you. She's right, the draft will keep and Charles and I can take care of anything that needs attending to tonight.'

For once I am grateful for Father's teasing, as his voice has a martial edge to it. Henry seems to hear it too, somewhere deep inside himself, and he turns to the door without another word. Quickly, I seize his plate and follow him, sneaking my arm under his elbow as we climb the wide, shallow stairs. *It is not good that the man should be alone*, the Lord said, *I will make a helper fit for him*. I will be that helper for him tonight: draw his water, fetch his slippers, pour his wine, take his notes. And it will please me to do it.

CHAPTER TWELVE

A baby changes a household. And it seems the first baby of a new generation must change it most of all. Though little Cromwell is but the size of a rabbit, and this a large townhouse, he rules over us all with Betty his pliant Lord Chancellor. The days are punctuated by orders and errands which issue from the Claypoles' room at all hours, drifting along the landing and down the stairs like dandelion seeds to land unbidden on any one of us: Betty must have peppermint oil and has a hankering for sugared plums; baby Cromwell has soiled his cloths again and so Martha must break open the fire for yet another round of laundry; Dick must go to the City for the physician to check a lump in the wet nurse's swollen breast.

Dick, to his credit, is affable enough in his indenture while Mother sinks comfortably into her role as chief lady-in-waiting and Father assumes his halter happily, delighted, it seems, to have a grandfatherly refuge from affairs of state. For my part, I try my best to shield Henry from the mundanity of life lived by the rhythm of an infant while I still can and cower with him in our bedroom whenever I can slip unnoticed from Betty's orbit.

Motherhood suits Betty. She is reborn with a newly bountiful beauty and a soft bedroom voice. She seems elevated. Not smug – she is too generous for that – but enlarged somehow by her achievement. I feel our natural balance of older and younger sister has shifted again, just as it did when I climbed the stairs to find her kissing Val in the witching hour.

I think of that scene as I watch Betty process down our new staircase in great state for her first supper with us since the birth. Father opens a vintage Rhenish wine in her honour and we are a merry party, fingers moist and mouths full, when a knock at the door heralds a visitor. The steward shows in a scowling soldier, fresh from the road. His lobster-tail helmet and buff coat tell me he is a trooper even before I catch the scent of horse sweat and stale hay he brings into the room.

'Trooper,' Father acknowledges him, 'you bring a message from headquarters? If they're expecting a reply by return, leave it with me and I'll have the girl bring you some ale, bread and cheese in the back parlour.'

The trooper takes a moment to reply and I see him shift his weight from one foot to the other. 'It is a letter, General, drafted by myself and other agents elected to represent the men of eight regiments of horse.' He steps forward smartly and proffers the paper.

'Agents?' Father looks to Henry as he takes it.

'Agitators,' Henry answers, his eyes darkening. 'Your name?'

'Sexby, sir, of the Lord General's Regiment of Horse.'

Father hands the unopened letter to Henry, who

cracks the seal and begins to read. 'Well, trooper Sexby,' Father smiles, picking up his knife to set about the ham, 'if you yourself are my correspondent, I should ask you to pull up a chair to my table. You must be tired from the ride.'

Sexby inclines his head but does not move. 'I prefer to stand, sir, if it's all the same to you.'

I admire his restraint, though I wonder if he seeks a greater safety in preserving the semblance of rank as a bulwark against the radical danger in his written words.

'Fair enough. Give me the gist of the letter, then, while Commissary-General Ireton reads the detail of it.'

Trooper Sexby glances at Mother and me before his gaze falls hungrily on Betty. He's about thirty years old, I would guess, with a tradesman's bearing. A capable man, I sense, though with a roving eye and, I'll warrant, a hot tongue.

'Never mind the womenfolk,' Father says brusquely. 'You may speak freely before my family. Besides, I have no mind to be disturbed from my supper.'

'Very well.' Sexby squares his shoulders. 'The letter presents the army's grievances to you and other generals: our arrears in pay and want of indemnity; our objection to being pressed into service in Ireland or disbanded without adequate protection. It seeks your assurance of support in seeing our requests met.'

'Your requests!' Henry looks up from the paper. 'You and the men have my sympathy, Sexby, but you cannot simply break rank like this.'

'That is not how we see it, sir,' Sexby fires back. 'We have earned our say in these matters. Earned it by risking our lives and limbs on the field. Aye, and our necks off the field too, for we are rebels in some men's eyes. We are not a mercenary army who can be paid off but men who chose freely to risk all for a cause they believed in.'

His words speak to me. Does he not ask only for a say in matters which rightly concern him? An impulse I am all too familiar with. I look to Father but he is sitting back in his chair now, watching the scene play out. It is Charles Fleetwood instead who interrupts my thoughts:

'We know your worth, trooper. Your commitment too.'

'Yes, yes,' Henry shakes his head, tossing the letter onto his plate as Charles colours. I snake my fingers across to rescue the paper from the gravy and scan the page as Henry continues to gather his thoughts aloud:

'The more the soldiers speak their minds, the less Parliament listens. With each step you take out on a limb, we lose standing with the House. They see anarchy ahead and they blame us – I almost fought a duel because of your men.' He is on his feet now, prowling around the still figure of Sexby, like a sheepdog around a ewe.

But Sexby shows himself more ram than ewe.

'That may be, sir,' he answers smartly. 'But, if you'll forgive me my plain speaking, the men still feel betrayed. They are nervous that the Presbyterians in Parliament will go over their heads to strike a bad deal with the King. Frightened they will be hung out to dry as the price for peace. You must side with them, if they're not to fall into rebellion.'

The last word brings my eyes up from the page. *Rebellion?* Has it come to it that our own soldiers would rebel against us their commanders as we – the King would say – had rebelled against him? I glance over to Betty whose face, still cushioned with the plumpness of pregnancy, is now pinched in alarm.

'Is that a threat, Sexby?' Charles snarls and I can almost see his taut body prickling. The quiet sympathy of his first words to the trooper has been swiftly replaced by anger as he takes his lead from Henry.

'Peace, peace.' Father holds up his large hands and casts left and right to his two deputies. Both fall silent though Henry continues to pace. 'We must not fight among ourselves,' Father coos. 'We need each other. What undermines the army, weakens its officers.'

'But what undermines the officers also weakens the army,' Henry interrupts, coming to lay a hand on Father's chair. 'Oliver, we must vindicate ourselves from the charge that we are behind these agitators – I held no man's hand over that petition.'

'Your name *must* be cleared, Henry,' I add, no longer able to stay silent. 'Though if it can be done without setting back the trooper's cause, would that not be best of all?' Husband and father break their gaze to look at me and I sense I chose the right moment to add my voice as a bridge between them.

'And so it will be, Biddy,' Father says, his voice soothing as liniment. 'Parliament means to weaken us by driving us apart.'

'*Divide et impera*,' Henry says quietly, crossing his arms.

'They wouldn't be the first.' Father grins at him. 'How's our draft vindication?'

'Coming on,' Henry answers, his tone unusually sullen.

'Well, then, if the lord general agrees, I suggest we present both this letter and our vindication to Parliament together. That way we avoid explicitly endorsing the men, yet the House cannot place a paper between us. Does that satisfy you, trooper Sexby?'

Sexby considers for a moment. 'It does, general,' he says and with his final glance directed at me, he quits the room.

I watch him go, wondering if he thinks he has found an ally in me. As the door swings behind him, there is a palpable relaxation around the table. Mother – who has sat in benign quiet for the whole conversation – leans forward to circulate the wine while Betty shifts in her seat with the tell-tale wince of a recent mother.

Father is watching Henry, waiting for his reproach. It comes a moment later.

'You gave too much ground, Oliver. If we appear to stand with the agitators on this, we weaken our voice.'

'No. I do not see it that way.' Father gets to his feet and sets off to patrol around the table, crumbs tumbling from him onto the carpet as he goes. 'We must offer the men some support, so long as they remain orderly. Lambert thinks as much, Harrison too, and I count their views highly. Besides, if we stand by them now we buy time. Parliament needs us officers to govern the army; without us in the middle, it is powerless. I have something here that proves as much.' Father stuffs his hand into his pocket and pulls out a letter along with a further sprinkling of crumbs that spray onto his leg. 'This is from the Speaker appointing you, Henry, Charles and me as Parliament's commissioners to treat with the army and restore calm.'

I whistle in a breath, imagining the scene. *They went to Joshua to the camp at Gilgal and said to him and to the men of Israel: we have come from a far country; now therefore, make a covenant with us.* Father, Henry and Charles against the men. Could they do it?

'So tomorrow we'll present the army's case to Parliament,' Father goes on, interrupting my thoughts, 'and thereby placate the men. Then we'll ride for Saffron Walden where we'll appease Parliament by putting its case fairly to the soldiers.'

'Excellent.' Charles nods firmly.

'Then I must get to work,' Henry says, springing towards the door, his mind already sunk in his text.

'I'll come and help you,' I say quickly.

'No need, Biddy,' he flings the words back over his shoulder.

'Well done, Father.' Betty smiles at him with admiration as I sink back onto my chair in disappointment. 'You will keep both sides at the table and secure the peace. Then this awful business can be resolved and we can all get back to a normal life.'

'Or, more likely, he'll end up caught in the middle,' I counter, reaching for plates to stack in my fury, her indolence and lack of imagination inflaming me into further hot words. 'There will never be the neat ending you crave, Betty; we cannot go back to how things were, only forward to how things could be. Else why have we suffered so much? The soldiers want their contribution recognised – to have a voice in their own lives. And I know just how they feel.'

If Betty is irritated by our dispute, she does not show it. With Henry gone to Saffron Walden for the next few weeks, she wastes no time in commandeering my room as she flees from her baby's cries and her husband's snores into the cushioning companionship of our childhood. As always, where she leads I unwittingly follow, slipping back into corners of our former life.

'How is it with Henry?' Betty asks, eyes wide and bright as harvest moons as she slips into my bed.

'How is what?' I plead ignorance.

'Married life!' She snuggles closer to me even as I stiffen.

'Oh hush.' I blow out my candle, hoping to extinguish the conversation.

'There's no need to whisper any more – the girls have their own room.'

'As do I,' I say pointedly, nudging her to get out of the bed.

'Well, I shall tell you about John, then,' she says, snaking her hand under the bedclothes to tickle me. 'He talks in his sleep.'

'No!' I cannot help myself. 'What about?'

'Oh nothing of consequence – commands to Badger, mostly. They seem to hunt together most nights. And another thing: his feet are always red and sore. The moment we are alone he kicks off his boots, pulls off his socks and pads around in his bare feet. But does he ever pick them up?' Betty sighs with a mummer's theatricality.

I smile at the image of John shedding clothes around the room and Betty tutting over them just as I used to do with her. 'Henry sleeps like an eel in a basket trap.'

'Really? Worse than me?'

I chuckle at that and the familiarity of the way she has warmed me up into conversation almost pains me.

How I miss these dark confessions. I follow the trail of breadcrumbs with which she leads me out of myself.

'Much worse. He wriggles all night.'

'Does he sleep through or wake for the watch in the middle of the night?'

'He wakes. He likes to work.' This has been one of the biggest adjustments for me; not to have that precious hour in between the first and second sleep to myself for silent reflection and prayer; having to share it with a restless Henry. Betty always slept through, blissful and beautiful beside me.

'Work at that hour?' Betty props herself on her elbow in astonishment. 'John likes to do quite another thing entirely—'

'I'm amazed he can wake you for it.'

'Sometimes. He can be – persuasive.' I feel her smiling in satisfaction. 'And Henry?' I hear her picking words like pebbles from the riverbed. 'Surely he likes to take his pleasure with you? I can see the evidence of it in your growing waistline.'

My mouth dries with embarrassment. How to speak of this most intimate area of life, even to Betty? Especially to Betty, the epitome of men's desires. 'He does, he did. But life often distracts him. As it should,' I qualify quickly, 'as it must.' I run on. 'He has important work to do and he's not John's mindless pleasure in the carnal things of life.'

'You do not surprise me. John lives in his body whereas Henry lives in his mind. But that should suit you, dearest, does it not? For you live in the mind too.'

I fall silent for my thoughts. Two minds together; might they not be as happy in marriage as two bodies?

How well my little sister understands me. And yet . . . If I bring our minds even closer to one another, I think, perhaps a greater intimacy might follow? But what exactly is the intimacy that I crave? I am comfortable to keep matters transactional between us, even in the bedroom. Yet, I would like a greater share of Henry's confidence and trust. I will use this time apart to think, I decide. I must unearth something of value to offer Henry on his return.

Betty reaches across to stroke a wisp of hair from my face. Unbidden, a tear trickles from my eye at her kindness. If I am a mind, Betty is a heart. Perhaps that is why we fight and love together so well.

'You have lost weight. And you were only gone three weeks.'

Henry's pointed face reappears above his jagged collarbone as he pulls off his stained undershirt and hands it to me.

'And I doubt you've changed your linens the whole time you were away.'

He shrugs pleasantly. 'What can I say, Biddy? I do not fare so well without you to tend to me. I forget about the small things.'

'Evidently.' I smile at him, though my good humour masks concern. For all my desire to be an intellectual partner for Henry, he needs my traditional wifely attention to his material comforts more than anything else. Without this he neglects himself.

Ragged with tiredness from the ride, Henry collapses into a chair by the open window, closing his eyes to the breeze. It is so hot he has no need of another shirt, though I find a clean one for him anyway and lay it on the bed, smoothing a crease at the cuff.

'Did you make progress with the army?' I ask, even as my fingers work among his bags, looking for laundry.

'Barely. The agitators have won over some powerful advocates among our fellow officers. Colonel Thomas Rainsborough, the most senior of their supporters, wept and stormed over their plight while Preacher Peacock pranced and prophesised. And John Lambert, though he has no love for Harrison, supports him in this, flinging his best theories at us as your father does ink in one of his play fights. All the while the junior officers and the agitators gaze adoringly at their champions and scowl at us for being narrow-minded middle-men.'

'And the lord general?'

'Fairfax won't dirty his hands with it. He floats above us all like some benign deity. Untouchable.'

'The generaless will like that. So you are at an impasse?'

'It seems so. And now Parliament is proposing to disband the army by force with none of our rights guaranteed. I begin to wonder if Parliament and the army will ever trust each other again. They have stopped fighting the King, and now do battle with one another.'

I stop rifling through his things and turn to face him. This is as good a moment as any to share my idea; my husband is in a pliant, confiding mood, too tired to keep his cards close to his chest or to let work distract him from me. Gently, as if I approach a startled hare, I leave his laundry and come to sit on the stool at his feet.

'Henry, I have been thinking about this conflict between Parliament and the army.'

'Yes?'

'It seems to me that you and Father are caught in the middle like the up-turned egg cup in a pie; if you move it an inch one way or the other, the pastry lid collapses.'

Henry raises a mocking eyebrow. 'A pie.'

'I know, but hear me out. You are there trying to keep the pie intact, holding it up like Atlas did the world.'

'Go on.'

'But what is the most important thing to ensure a pie bakes properly? Not the pastry or the filling, not the egg cup . . .'

Henry spreads his hands in amused ignorance.

'The oven. If it's too hot, the crust burns, if it's not hot enough, the crust disintegrates.'

'And the oven in this baking metaphor is?'

'The King of course!' I laugh despite myself, all too aware of how limited my experience is that I need to reach for kitchen examples to make my political points. 'All he has to do is watch and wait as his enemies tear each other apart and then he can feast on the carcass.'

'On the broken pie surely?'

I cuff him gently. 'Listen. Whoever does a deal with the King first will win.'

'Yes. But we can't get near him. Parliament bought him as prisoner from the Scots.'

'For thirty pieces of silver, no doubt.'

'Quite. And they're keeping us away from him while they peddle their deal. There's talk now that Holles' Presbyterian faction in Parliament may even seize him for themselves. Then they would give him back to the Scots army and together restore him to his throne by force, imposing the Presbyterian Church in England. The army would be crushed and we would lose all hope of religious freedoms then.'

My mind races ahead of his. 'Then the army must stop them. Go to the King and secure him from capture.'

Henry sits forward at this, hands clenched under his chin, elbows on his knees. I wait while he thinks. It is a bold plan, but who is bolder than my husband when the Cause is at stake? If he is the one to take it to Father, it will bind them even closer together. And if I am the one who can facilitate that . . .

Still Henry says nothing, which I know means he treats my idea seriously.

'You could take the plan to my father,' I continue quietly. 'He will be impressed at its simplicity.'

'He will shy at its boldness. He does not like to use force where negotiation will do.'

'I know. But if you present it to him in the right way—'

Henry cocks his head at me, inviting more filial insight.

'I did not spend twenty years under my father's roof without learning something. He responds to two lines of appeal: ideas that ring true to human nature; and those that serve Providence. Link the two together and you'll convince him.'

'This does just that!' Henry says, sudden energy propelling him to his feet to pace about the bed, his bare feet padding on the carpet. 'We know the Parliament-men work against us while the King takes them for fools. But I'll warrant the King will come to the negotiating table if we're on the other side of it; he knows he cannot fool us and he'll want to see what he can get in a deal with the army. And this may be the only way to reach the peace that God has shown he wants for us by leading us to victory in the war.'

He grins at me then with the sudden pleasure of a schoolboy mastering an essay, before stopping still, the smile drooping from his face. 'Fairfax won't countenance it.'

I come towards him quickly and flatten my hands on his bare chest in reassurance. 'Then don't tell him. Arrange it from here. Choose an officer to take on the task discreetly.'

Henry moves his hands over mine while his mind works. 'I'll find an agitator. They hardly need persuading that Parliament is acting against them. They're champing at the bit for us to take matters into our own hands.'

'Then take them.'

Henry looks at me for a long moment before lifting my hands to kiss each palm, his lips like butterflies. I catch my breath. Smiling, he starts to undress me.

It is done. Night after night officers come to the house under cover of darkness, their horses stabled quietly, the front door opened for them before the need of a knock to wake our neighbours. Once again, as in Ely, the house fills with the smell of pipe smoke, sunburnt leather and the sweat of men and horses. Mother and I serve beer and bread while Father broods. Round about him, young men agitate for action – Henry and John Lambert the firmest voices – and soon Father relents. The order goes out, the die is cast.

It is a huge risk. Father knows this and is already packing his bag when a street runner brings the midnight message that the Presbyterians plan to arrest him the next day. He leaves a few hours later, riding away before the first dawn pinks blush the sky. Henry follows the day after with the things that Father could not carry: the travelling desk and papers; his spare boots and medicine chest; and me.

CHAPTER THIRTEEN

SUMMER 1647

I am thrilled to be back with the army. Back in the realm of men. Where the days are measured not in infant sleep cycles and servants' household rhythms but in watches and drill-times. Where the air is heavy with the smell of so many lives: piss and porridge in the morning, gunpowder and sweat-soaked linen during the day and the aromas of a thousand cooking pots and fires in the evening. Where men snatch meals in the saddle and sign papers leaning on their comrades' backs. Where preachers and pedlars wander from tent to campfire and strangers become brothers against the flames. Where men live in the present and long for the future they dream of.

The army is a nation all of itself: with its own language and customs, its jokes and mythologies. Rulers and ruled, buyers and sellers, cooks and carpenters, physicians and priests. And there are other women too in the baggage train: wives and daughters, nurses, laundrywomen and whores. It is even rumoured there are women in the ranks disguised as boys. Girls who have followed their husbands or sweethearts; runaways, paupers and orphans. I think of them often and of the younger Bridget who, in her desperation to count, toyed with doing the same thing. And so I peer closely whenever I pass a fresh-faced cornet or mouse-like messenger, looking for the tell-tale signs of womanhood that only another woman would see.

It is not long before I find my own regiment of women and take myself to the command room to pay court to the generaless. Despite the limitations of our new accommodation at a shabby inn near Cambridge, Lady Fairfax still manages to cultivate the aura of the grand estate and I find myself pleased to rest my now heavy belly in her rooms after the uncomfortable journey north.

'It's a boy,' she says on first seeing me, with barely a preamble.

'A girl, I think,' Frances Lambert counters, cocking her head like a hen, 'the bump hangs low.'

'I thought that meant it was a boy.' Catherine Harrison looks confused.

'Nonsense,' Lady Fairfax pulls rank, 'you can't tell from the bump. Look at the hair and skin. She looks a little sallow but that will be from the journey. The shine on her hair, though, does not lie. Another grandson for the general, Bridget, you mark me.'

I smile awkwardly as I accept a glass of small ale.

'And how it will please him to have his root stock grafted to that of your husband,' she continues grandly. 'All I hear now is Cromwell this, Ireton that. "Cromwell and his son Ireton". "Ireton and his father Cromwell". They grow in stature together daily, like oak and ivy.'

Her words thrill me, though I try not to show it. *He chooses an oak and lets it grow strong among the trees of the forest and the rain nourishes it*. If I can be the rain, I think, how high could the tree not reach?

'How are things here?' I ask to cover my ambitious thoughts.

'Shifting.' It is Frances who answers. 'An army without a war to fight is a restless, ungovernable thing.'

'And a thing never before seen in England,' I add. In the past, armies were raised temporarily by great lords calling in their tenants and serfs, and disbanded just as quickly as soon as a campaign was over. Often the men knew nothing about who they fought or why. But this army – our army – is different. Men joined for their belief in the Cause and, now they have changed the world, they have become more than the sum of their parts: an institution in themselves, a professional army with views and ambitions. And so now they stand strong together and wait.

'My husband Thomas thinks we'll be gone from here before the week is out,' Catherine says, her tone conspiratorial.

'Gone where?'

'London, he says. To bring matters with the Presbyterians in Parliament to a head. To secure their impeachment . . .'

'We must not be hasty.' Anne offers a ringed, restraining hand. 'Reaching accommodation with the King must be the priority.'

'He is nearby now, is he not?' I ask.

'At his palace in Newmarket; not far. Though the manner of his coming was quite disgraceful.'

My pulse quickens and I sip my ale before replying. 'You thought it wrong for the army to seize him?'

'The army didn't seize him,' Lady Fairfax snaps. 'He was removed from Parliament's custody by a rogue cornet with no authority from my husband.'

The other women flinch but I steel myself. 'The lord general did not approve?' I ask though I know the answer.

'Certainly not! Indeed, when he heard what had happened, he rode out to meet His Majesty and offered to escort him back. But the King refused. Said he fancied taking his chance now with the army. My Lord was astonished.'

It is just as Henry had said; Fairfax would never have agreed. I know I should move the conversation on but it is too tempting to defend the plan my commander could never have guessed was mine.

'Surely, however the deed was executed, the result is a good one?' I inch forward. 'We can now treat directly with the King who, it seems, is open to discussion.'

'And a lasting peace is more likely achieved,' Frances Lambert speaks to a ringing silence. I am astonished she has sided with me against the generaless, and Catherine Harrison stares from one of us to the other in wide-eyed amazement.

Lady Fairfax pauses as all eyes turn back to her. After a moment she smiles with all the polished serenity of a great lady. 'Of course your husbands are great friends and rivals now.' She looks at Frances and then at me. 'Lambert and Ireton – I hear they're as clever and wily as each other. And the peppery General Harrison, of course' – she gestures to Frances – 'he grows in popularity with the men. All of this young blood eager for glory.'

'Our husbands all revere the lord general,' Catherine says quickly.

'Indeed, indeed.'

'How is my Lord?' I ask, realising the need to pay homage after my small victory. 'Henry tells me he has been ill.' It is intriguing that Fairfax's retreat with illness followed the challenge to his authority represented by the King's seizure. Was he really as ill as he claimed?

'He is recuperating.' Anne smiles reassuringly. 'He was overly fatigued and laid low by a chest cold. But he will be back in the saddle soon. In fact,' she rises, bringing the rest of us to our feet in response. 'If you ladies will excuse me, I will go to him now.'

Lady Fairfax quits the scene proudly and, as I look at Catherine and Frances, I cannot help feeling that the battleground she has surrendered is now ours. Before, I would have followed the generaless from the room. But now, emboldened, if a little saddened by the distance growing between us, I sink back onto the sofa and assume command: 'Shall we call for another jug of ale and some biscuits?'

When I was last living with the army as a new bride, and under the generaless's care, I felt fleet of foot and light of heart. It is different now. Now I feel the cumbersome weight of the baby in my belly as I walk around the camp and climb the stairs at the inn – a constant reminder of my sex and the encumbrances we must endure. Then, this was a joyful army fresh from a providential victory. Now, the cracks are showing between us: I sense the quivering unease among the officers and men; a nervous tension like the hot, crackling air before a summer storm.

The general and generaless keep their distance, Henry hisses like kindling and Father too is fired by the new energy that always animates him in times of crisis, burning deeply like a well-banked coal fire. He is even, I fancy, a little in love.

'The King was surprisingly gracious,' he says to us as we take a modest supper together in Henry's and my room at the inn. 'Gentle of manner and speech and quick to invite me to speak at close quarters. Not at all how I imagined he would be.'

'He seeks a deal,' Henry says, staring into his glass.

'As do we,' Father reminds him. 'You wait until you meet him tomorrow, Henry; he'll charm you too.'

'I shouldn't think so,' I interject with a laugh, stacking our dirty plates ready for the girl to take back down to the kitchen and wiping my hands. 'Henry cares little for charm, else he would have set his cap at Betty and not at me.'

The smiles I bring to both men's lips please me. Neither insults me by trying to deny the truth in my comparison.

'You're a plain speaker, Biddy, you always were,' Father concedes, with no small hint of pride. 'Henry knew his match when he saw it. And you serve him well with your care and counsel.'

I swell with pride. 'Thank you, Father, I trust so. But I fancy I know what Betty would counsel were she here and not me.'

Father looks at me eagerly, flushing with pleasure

simply at her name, while Henry moves to the window in search of the evening breeze.

'She would urge you to a good shave and a clean collar before you see the King again. Mother too.'

Father laughs fully at that. 'Haha! He expects me to be a provincial "Roundhead", so I should act the part!' Still laughing he bows his head before me like a child before his mother. He loves to playact and reverse our roles; pretend to take instructions from the little girls or call Dick and Harry 'sir' and 'master'. It is one of his techniques for casting off his cares and always signals his desire for a sojourn in our softer world.

I fetch him water and prepare the soap and blade. 'Shall I do it, Father, like I used to? Come here to the sofa, where you can lean your head back.'

He renders himself up to me.

'I saw the King with his children,' he speaks after a time, moving his lips slowly so as not to catch the sharp edge I manoeuvre around the familiar contours of his chin. 'He knelt before them, kissed their cheeks and they clutched at him in turn. It's hard not to like a man who so loves his children.'

It is a strangely human image, which I struggle to match to the cold man on our coins who thinks himself God's representative on earth. He is but a man too, I think, as I skim around the wart on Father's chin. A man with a neck, a heart and a pulse as any other's. 'Then he should want to do right by them,' I reply. 'Find a peace, keep his throne. Secure their future. Appeal to him on that count. Speak to him as one father to another.'

'I will, Biddy. He was grateful to us for allowing him to see them and for granting him his chaplains too.

He's finding us gentler wardens than Parliament's hired guards ever were. And I'll wager the Scots were even fiercer captors. We have laid the foundations for constructive talks. He still rejects Parliament's propositions, thank God. He has no desire for the canting presbytery in England – we're at one on that score, at least. But time is short – the agitators and the radical officers who support them like Harrison and Rainsborough press for us to abandon the King and march on London.'

'I'll start working on our terms as soon as I've finished the document for the new Army Council,' Henry says, coming back towards us and taking a seat by Father's reclining figure. He is so close that I flick droplets of soap-scudded water onto his arm as I continue my work.

'This is a general statement of our position?' I check.

'Yes. We cannot simply continue to list our grievances. We must look beyond them to find positive proposals for how the nation should be governed. This will be a founding text where we set out what we believe should be the basis of a lasting political settlement. It's almost finished – I can read you the draft.'

It is a radical thought: that this army – that any army, raised simply to win a war – should publish a political manifesto. But then this is a new kind of army, as I think so often. One in which the ordinary soldiers have a stake.

I wipe the blade on the napkin, Father's short stubble hairs smoothed in soap onto the linen like ants trapped in butter. 'Then, if the Council approves it, you'll use that as a starting point for drafting the specific terms of agreement we'll put to the King?'

'Exactly.'

'He's a clever man, your husband,' Father's voice floats

up to me from beneath his closed eyes. 'And a good partner for me. He dreams up the ideas and I sell them.'

And I stand between you both, I think, tending to Henry and helping him persuade you of the merit of his ideas. Henry's intellect, my care and insight, and Father's diplomacy: that's how we'll achieve the change we need.

Henry retrieves some crumpled papers from his travelling desk and begins to read his draft. Father and I listen in silence, the gentle, rhythmic swish of the blade on Father's skin layered beneath Henry's sonorous tones. Still, there are some passages of his drafting that are so beautiful I cannot help but interrupt with my praise:

'That's wonderful! Read that bit again.'

'Which?'

'The bit about how much a complete settlement of the liberties and peace of the kingdom means to the army. The quiet vines . . .'

'Oh yes. "*Nothing is more dear to us or more precious in our thoughts, we having hitherto thought all our present enjoyments (whether of life, or livelihood, or nearest relations) a price but sufficient to the purchase of so rich a blessing, that we and all the free-born people of this nation may sit down in quiet under our vines, and under the glorious administration of justice and righteousness, and in full possession of those fundamental rights and liberties without which we can have little hopes, as to human considerations, to enjoy either any comfort of life or so much as life itself, but at the pleasures of some men, ruling merely according to will and power.*"'

'Quite right and well said.'

Flushed a little at my praise, Henry continues to read. Then, a minute later, I cannot help another interruption:

'I like that: "*We were not an army, hired to serve any arbitrary power of a state, but called forth and conjured by the several declarations of Parliament to the defence of our own and the people's just rights . . .*" Very good. But how about "We were not a *mere mercenary* army, hired, etc."?'

'Oh yes!' Henry reaches for his pen and adds the new words in a scrawl above the line.

'Excellent,' Father murmurs, though I can sense Henry's political poetry almost lulling him to sleep.

Quietly, I lay down my tools and move away from Father to settle myself on Henry's other side. 'Go on.'

He turns slightly, angling himself towards me before he continues to read. I try not to interrupt again but listen as he moves on from the preamble to list the army's specific demands: protection for the soldiers once disbanded; Parliament to have prescribed sessions and never to be dissolved by the King without its own consent; electoral reform towards more balanced representation; the people allowed to petition with their problems; prisoners to have swifter trials; a blanket forgiveness for Royalists, with a few notable exceptions; and broad religious toleration. I bathe happily in the vision of a just society Henry paints before my eyes.

When he has finished, Henry lays down the pages and rotates his neck, clicking the joints. 'If the Army Council agrees to this declaration,' he says to me after a few moments, 'we charge the Presbyterian MPs with treason for double-dealing with the Scots and see Parliament purged. Then, once he accepts our terms, we restore the King to his throne.'

Moved, I clasp Henry's hand, smoothing my thumb over the ink stains and writing callouses on his fingers.

'Marvellous, my dear. And I can help you synthesise this into the proposals for the King. If you work from this document, pull out the points you want to include and speak them aloud to me, I can note them down ordered into an outline agreement. We can begin now.'

Henry smiles gratefully, the hollows under his eyes deepening with the creeping evening shadows. 'If we can do a skeleton draft tonight, I can take it to Lambert to work on tomorrow; he'll want his turn with the pen.'

I lean forward and kiss his sallow cheek.

'Truly it is God's work you do here,' I say softly.

'That *we* do.' He kisses me back and my heart soars.

Smiling, I turn around to our companion. 'Do you not think so, Father?'

But he is asleep.

CHAPTER FOURTEEN

I stare at the fire, sealed up now for the night but still glowing through the cracks. 'You will have to break it open again,' I tell the flushed servant girl, with no time to feel sorry for the sleepless night I will cause her. 'We're leaving at first light and will want baked potatoes, bread and meat pies ready for the journey. It will take an hour or two for the ovens to warm but if you start now there's time. You can draw the beer and water first thing, I have brought our flasks, here.'

I hand them to the girl at my elbow who puffs out her cheeks and turns forlornly to the kitchen boy. If this was my house I would help them but we are paying guests at the inn. Besides, I need to write letters, pack and, if I'm lucky, snatch some rest. At least the scramble to move gets easier each time, I think, as I climb the creaking stairs to my room; I could almost do this in my sleep.

The army is not lingering in one place for long. Father and Henry urge patience while they desperately try to strike a deal with the King. But all the while, like a stalking lion, the army prowls from base to base: to St Albans, to Reading, to Uxbridge, to Bedford, its scouts and quartermaster's men ranging ahead to secure provisions and beg accommodation, its tired, sprawling baggage train – we women included – trailing in its wake. And always with one prey in its sights: London. But what will we find when we get there? I wonder as I pack our things for yet another move. Each day, news arrives in the pedlars' backpacks and the messengers' saddlebags of riots in the capital as angry mobs of apprentices and disbanded soldiers rage around Parliament. The Presbyterian MPs whip up this crowd while the Independent members – our allies – look for help from us, now only a day's march away. With Henry paying suit to the King, I lie alone and awake at night thinking of my family sitting in Drury Lane like cowering game birds listening for the beaters and dogs. The city is a powder keg awaiting a lone spark and, once lit, it could consume us all.

I try to press these anxieties from my mind as I stand, bare-souled on a Sunday morning listening to the army's service of worship on an open, windy plain. Here on an expanse of heath, I close my eyes and am back in the plains around Huntingdon, where I was born. Above me, the sky is so much wider than it is in London, arching vast over our heads in every direction so that I feel myself no bigger than an ant. I have always loved that feeling; the nearness to God it brings to be one blade of grass in his Creation.

Over the wind, I can just catch the fiery voice of preacher Hugh Peter delivering his Sunday sermon to the men in volley after volley of Cornish vowels. *'And have we not fought a just war, a righteous war, a war for our liberties and for God himself? Are we not God's people that gather here this day? Who is it who would disband us before our task is accomplished? We will not be cast aside. Christ himself stands beside every man here, speaks to you when you falter, picks you up when you fall . . .'* John Lilburne, the firebrand pamphleteer leader of the new 'Levellers' – a London-based popular movement now angling for political change to secure greater rights for the people – calls Peter the 'journeyman of the army', and I myself have seen his everyman qualities and practical turn of mind. To Father he is a perfect minister. No scholar, preaching the finer points of theology. A man who sees God clearly but lives in the mud among the men.

Soaked in Peter's rich words, I survey the army's gathered church. It is an awesome sight, so many hundreds upon hundreds of broad backs and feathered hats, pikes tall and muskets propped, peacefully parading before Christ. Ordinary men who, before they answered Parliament's call to arms, were labourers, farmers and apprentices, merchants and publicans, butchers, drapers and chandlers. Carpenters, cobblers, coopers and constables. As one, they mumble prayers and raise their voices for the psalms, arms about each other's shoulders. If these are not God's people, I think, I do not know who are. Not the Royalist troops, most of whom would have thought no more than to answer the summons of their lord who himself serves the King. So much service, so much bondage. So little room for the individual man and his beliefs. The men of the New Model Army serve a lord but it is *the* Lord and they do so freely out of love.

It is then that I see them coming over the horizon: small black and brown shapes like beetles crawling along the skyline. Carriages. Many carriages. I nudge Catherine

Harrison, standing between me and her husband, and she lifts her eyes from her prayer book. On my other side, Frances Lambert stares too and, beyond her, the general and generaless whisper to each other behind their hands.

'Who do you think it is?' I ask the Harrisons. Preacher Peacock squints then shrugs, the elaborate feathers of his hat quivering in the breeze, before slyly adjusting his cloak and brushing a speck of mud from his sleeve in anticipation of the new arrivals. Hugh Peter continues to preach but as the coaches draw near us, his voice fades away and, row by row, the soldiers turn their heads to see what is happening. Fairfax sends some men to push back the crowds and allow the carriages a clear passage to where the senior officers and we ladies await them. Another minute and the first panting horses draw level with the general. Instantly, the door is flung open and the figures inside spill out, like distressed damsels almost falling into Fairfax's arms.

'My Lord Speaker,' the general says in astonishment, greeting a flustered, black-coated middle-aged man who must be William Lenthall, the Speaker of the House of Commons. The man who famously defied the King's attempt to arrest his most prominent opponents in Parliament in the spiralling months before the war. Behind him I see another more familiar figure, the graceful Earl of Manchester, Father's erstwhile sparring partner whom we had feasted once in Ely. Looking past them, I see scores of other men alighting in agitation from the other carriages: fifty, perhaps sixty in number, well-dressed though rumpled from the road and clutching armfuls of papers and travelling bags.

'We seek sanctuary, general.' Speaker Lenthall bows, launching without preamble into an explanation of their arrival. 'My fellow members of Parliament and myself. Matters in Westminster have become intolerable. The mob held me down in my chair and forced me to do their bidding. I could no longer perform my office and so Parliament can no longer be held to exist. I will not return until the House is freed from this Presbyterian tyranny and it may be the army that needs to do it.'

'God's teeth!' General Thomas Harrison explodes beside me before Fairfax can answer. He turns urgently to his commander. 'Surely now, sir, we must march on London. We tarry here too long awaiting the King's pleasure when the man cannot be trusted.'

'He dealt with us rudely when I attended on him yesterday and I left in protest,' the rising star, radical Colonel Rainsborough adds, having pushed through the crowd to stand shoulder to shoulder with Harrison. 'We'll have no settlement with him, mark my words.'

I feel immediate concern: I had no idea he had returned early, nor that the meeting had gone so badly. Father and Henry were full of confidence in the King when we last spoke. Everyone reacts to this intervention: Fairfax drops his chin to his chest and Speaker Lenthall and Manchester take a hasty step back at the sheer force of these two young officers who, together, seem to represent the whole power of the army. While I watch them with anxious admiration, the generaless sweeps upon them in fury.

'Of course we must treat with the King,' she says sharply, drawing herself up in all her own majesty. 'He is our sovereign, for all he has been led astray. Is that not right, my Lord?' Having cleared the way for her husband, Fairfax steps smartly into it.

'It is, my dear. His Majesty must be part of any settlement for the sake of all of our security.'

Manchester nods vigorously while Lenthall strokes his pointed beard, his thin fingers anxious. Behind them, the other MPs mutter to each other, some nodding in agreement, others shaking their heads.

Inspired by Lady Fairfax's boldness, I find myself speaking next: 'My husband and father say we can trust the King, my lords; that they are making progress – they are with him now and have every hope he will accept their terms which are agreeable to the Army Council.' I pray God I am right even as I speak. Father and Henry are staking everything on reaching a deal with the King and while they are gone I must be their mouthpiece.

'*The Army Council*,' the commander-in-chief repeats my words, and then lunges forward suddenly, as if they have stirred him into action, like a wakening wolf. 'Quite, Mistress Ireton,' he says with purpose. 'And it is as the Council that we must discuss this further. Come, my Lords' – he gestures to the MPs – 'you must be tired from the journey. We will set about finding you some accommodation – my dear, perhaps you and the other ladies could see to this?'

He delivers this last over his shoulder to his wife as the men make to move off together. So we wives must turn ourselves to billeting and wait to hear what happens, I think, turning to Catherine in disappointment. But then a shout goes up and everyone stops at the sight of Father, Henry and their negotiating party riding into our midst.

'My Lord Speaker!' Father calls to William Lenthall warmly, still in the saddle. 'What brings you to us?' He draws alongside the knot of grandees, his boots almost in their faces, and swings himself heavily off Blackjack, Henry dismounting from his horse more carefully behind him with an anxious glance at me. His brow is heavily knit and his fists clenched within his riding gloves; I know he carries bad news.

'We had no choice but to leave the capital, general,' the Speaker replies. 'The mob forced our hand and we seek the army's protection.'

'Good Lord!'

'How went it with the King?' Fairfax addresses Father before he can voice any further opinions on the astonishing arrival of half of Parliament in our midst. Out of the corner of my eye I see Manchester squirm slightly and I wonder if he still smarts at Father's rise.

Father squares his shoulders and considers a moment before he speaks. 'Our meeting today was a grave disappointment and it pains me to tell you. The King – I do not think he trusts us, not yet – he seems disbelieving that we ask no personal honours for ourselves in our bargain. I tried to explain that we simply want to live quietly as his free subjects but he just shook his head in bafflement and turned to his advisers as if to say: "You see, how can I deal with these men?"'

'You are too charitable, General,' Henry interrupts, glaring darkly. '"You cannot do this without me!" he said to us. "You will fall to ruin if I do not sustain you."'

There are a few whistles and sharp intakes of breath.

'What did I say?' Rainsborough barks in triumph, the

sea-green and black ribbons of his hat flung from side to side.

Henry offers him a half-smile of apology before continuing his angry account. 'The King baulked at our proposal for a stronger Council of State to check his power. He smiled when we spoke of free elections, laughed when we demanded freedom for MPs to disagree with the Lords and the King should they feel the need. He sneered at our desires for toleration in religion and shouted when we said he would not be allowed to control the army for another ten years.'

I watch my husband in horror; all those careful proposals that we had laboured over, agonising at each provision, amending every other word from draft to draft. I look past Henry to the sleek figure of John Lambert, who looks almost as pained as he does. It is a bitter rejection for all of us who at one time or another held the pen.

'True, true.' Father is extending a calming hand in Henry's direction and I look from one to the other frantically.

'Surely this is merely his opening position?' Fairfax, visibly shaken at the news, casts about him for agreement, his voice booming in his agitation. I am fond of the general and take no pleasure in seeing him at a loss.

'It must be,' the Earl of Manchester weighs in, swinging his gold-tipped cane in emphasis.

All look to Father. 'I do not know,' he confesses at last. 'I want to believe we can win him around. We must try. But for now—'

'Now we must ride to London, surely?' Preacher Peacock surges forward towards Fairfax, Rainsborough at his heels. Black Tom, boxed in, almost disappears from view. 'Surely, my Lord, now?' They address themselves to the commander-in-chief, but they glance sideways at Father.

With Harrison and Rainsborough's thick, jostling backs blocking my view, I cannot see the lord general's face, but the seconds that stretch away tell me he is thinking hard. I look instead to the generaless, who gives the merest shake of her head, her eyes fixed on her husband. But she is separated from him by Father, by Henry, Harrison and Rainsborough, with Lenthall and Manchester looking on. The knot about the commander-in-chief tightens, imperceptible perhaps to all but me.

One. Two moments more. Then the only command he can really give:

'We march for London.'

It begins as a regular march but ends a Triumph worthy of Caesar. In conscious echo of him, some of the men pick laurel sprigs for their hats as they make their way through the last miles of open country before the city. We have no slaves, nor conquered treasure, as the Romans had, but different spoils of our war which are their equal: the Speaker himself with sixty waving MPs calling from their carriage windows for a 'free Parliament', our preachers and their Bible banners swaying atop God's soldiers, and the New Model Army itself – eighteen thousand of them – a new and wondrous machine the like of which has never been seen in England, nor anywhere else in Christendom.

The Lord is our Emperor. His Providence our gods. And the Thames is our Rubicon.

Father knows our victorious army's entry into London will be a glorious sight and sends to Mother to travel out ahead to join us. It matters to him, I know without him having to speak it aloud, to have her ensconced in the fine velvet upholstered carriage alongside Lady Fairfax; to have his wife welcomed into the generaless's coach with all that it represents. Black Tom is still our Commander-in-Chief and respected by all, but Father is now the heart of the army. And the younger generation comes up fast in his wake, with the presence of Frances Lambert, Catherine Harrison and myself in the coach following that of Lady Fairfax testament to that.

We cover the miles slowly, like a long river meandering along its set course. Swaying and rattling in the August heat, I am soon stiff and my heavy belly presses on my bladder. We are hungry too and buy bread, cheese and strawberries from the hawkers who sell to us through the window as they walk alongside the carriage. It is a long, hot journey, but I do not complain.

The city lies down before us like the lamb with the wolf. Southwark opens its gates; the mayor and aldermen welcome us at Hyde Park; the Common Council of the City at Charing Cross; and cheering crowds line the route. When our carriage stops in the outskirts of Westminster, a trooper rides back down the line and tells us through the window that up ahead the Speaker has been set back in his chair and Parliament reopened. There will be a public holiday of thanksgiving and the army will be paid. I hear men cheering.

Relieved and exhausted, Mother and I eventually find our way back to Drury Lane. As I step down from the coach into the dry, dusty road and look up at the latticed windows, I replay my conversation with Henry when we had parted that morning.

'We must find our own house now, Henry,' I had said – telling him this time, not asking. 'I cannot return to my parents' home again. It may suit Betty, but it doesn't do for me. I must be mistress of my own four walls before the baby comes. Promise me.'

And he had.

CHAPTER FIFTEEN

AUTUMN 1647

We are trying again; round two of the peace negotiations. It has begun well. In an expansive gesture of renewed goodwill the King has invited the army leaders to bring their wives into his presence at Hampton Court where he is now permanently lodged; notionally under the guard of Father's cousin Colonel Edward Whalley and his men, but really in a return to full regal splendour. He may not be free to leave but he is at last back in one of his own palaces and in all other ways living in grandeur: his youngest children, closest advisers and personal chaplains with him, Presbyterian emissaries awaiting an audience, and scores of liveried servants to attend to his every whim, the court's bills sent to Parliament.

Though I had prepared myself to be unimpressed by my first encounter with the monarchy in all its mystery, I am overwhelmed at the scale and magnificence of the palace. We approach by river, the vast brick walls the colour of dried blood rising above us, topped with a forest of chimneys, like the massed pikes of one of our infantry regiments. We alight at a canopied jetty, then a gravel path leading to a wide drive takes us through a great castle gate into the first of many courtyards. At this point Mother has to pause to remove a stone from her shoe but, luckily, there is a shadowed doorway for her to do this unobserved, leaning on my arm for support. I, in turn, am grateful for a few moments to rest my heavy stomach.

Father and Henry are clearly well known here as – stone removed, breath caught and hair swiftly tidied after the Thames wind – we sweep unchecked past the guards and up the marble staircase to follow a maze of tapestry-lined corridors. Everywhere I look there is a new marvel: statues and china figurines, intricate clocks and ornate mirrors, silver and glassware atop gold-painted tables, all gleaming in the candlelight from huge gold scones.

'What need has one man of such riches?' I ask Henry who merely shrugs in response.

Each room boasts brightly coloured walls lined with gilt-framed paintings – monarchs hang next to hunting scenes, Christ twisted on the cross beside nude nymphs and goddesses, their rosy faces and pink, swollen bodies leering out at me. In one gallery, we pass a sequence of huge painted canvasses depicting the Triumph of Caesar and I am cast back a few weeks to the long hot day when our army processed into London. Will someone paint us one day?

Father lingers before these for a few minutes, pacing back and forth and shaking his head in wonder and admiration. 'Are they not marvellous?' he asks, his back still to us.

But I cannot reply. The rich colours blind me and strip me of speech. The Word of God leaks from my mind as the graven images take its place.

We move on. Stunned, I pass through gilded chamber upon chamber until we emerge, like water gushing from a fountain, into the magnificence of a room Henry whispers is the Presence Chamber. Looking around me at the colourful, swirling figures, it is clear that courtiers have begun to orbit the King once more, as planets around the sun. How can any man who lives like this believe himself normal or look at others with a level gaze? I squeeze Henry's arm, marvelling anew at his and Father's boldness for putting themselves forward to negotiate with him man to man. What was it Henry had told me he said to the King when he had first refused to negotiate? 'Sir, you have an intention to be an arbitrator between the Parliament and us and we mean it to be between your Majesty and the Parliament.' Henry had not been cowed that first time, and neither must I be.

He stands before me. He himself. Father to his people, a god made flesh. This man over whom the war was fought. The man who caused Olly to die.

Short in stature but resplendent nonetheless, the King carries his head as carefully as if it always wears a crown. Indeed, I can almost see it, glimmering there atop his coiffed curls as he sweeps his gaze over me. I burn in his heat, and, searching for some fixed point to guide my faltering steps, train my eyes on the space where the crown should be as I move, trembling, towards him.

Brightly coloured courtiers hover about the King like butterflies about a lavender bush, then one pink-painted figure flutters into my view. It takes me a few moments to place her face before it comes to me in a flash: Jane Whorwood. Can this bright creature be the sad, mistreated daughter-in-law of Lady Whorwood who had lent me her wedding dress at Holton Park? What is she doing here at this pretend court? She sees me in turn and dips a little acknowledgement. I long to hear her news and am about to move towards her when the King's closest adviser, Sir John Ashburnham, approaches us. Taking Mother and me on each arm he leads us forward to meet our sovereign and I put Jane from my mind. As Father and Henry watch from a pace behind, we draw near to the King, who bends gracefully towards us like one of the classical statues we passed in the grounds.

'Mistresses. What a pleasure to meet the wives of gallant General Cromwell and Commissary-General Ireton,' he purrs, his soft faintly Scotch voice lilting. I think for a moment that he speaks in irony but he is perfectly sincere – as if he is speaking of his own generals and not those raised to fight against him.

'Your Majesty,' Mother curtseys and I follow suit, dipping my eyes to his buckled shoes, 'it is a great honour to attend upon you, Sire,' Mother continues so smoothly Father must have coached her.

King Charles inclines his head in acceptance of the essential truth of this. 'I must apologise for keeping your husbands so often away from you while we discuss this tangled business,' the King continues smoothly, circling his ringed hand in the air as if to distance himself from the late troubles and giving a little laugh. Thus signalled, a polite chuckle ripples around the room in answer. Somewhere close by a harpsichord tinkles.

I have to bite my lip to prevent a hysterical laugh escaping my mouth along with the response: *You do owe us an apology but it is not for that*. I just manage but the effort leaves a bizarre grin on my face.

The King seems pleased with it and continues his munificent musings with a broad smile of his own. 'But I will reassure you, mistresses, that I shall not be keeping your husbands with me too much longer, for I am almost resolved to move forwards with their proposals and not those of Parliament.'

A murmuring immediately washes around the room. Behind me Father and Henry fidget with relief, while Colonel Whalley murmurs a 'bravo'. Across the room the knot of Parliamentary commissioners shake their heads and whisper.

I am so relieved I find my voice: 'That is welcome news indeed, your Majesty,' I say, and without thinking, touch my swollen stomach as if to pass his assurance to the baby. My gesture alerts the King to my condition and, before I know it, he steps forward and places his own hand firmly on my bump. It is such an extraordinary liberty I flinch, but his continued smile tells me he thinks my movement a gasp at the honour he does me. For a moment, I stare into his hazel eyes and breathe in the same warm air he has just exhaled. His beard smells of perfume and I feel dizzy at the scent.

'You will be pleased, no doubt, General Ireton, to have the business settled before you become a father,' King Charles says, giving my stomach a proprietorial pat before withdrawing his hand and briefly inspecting the lace at his cuff.

Henry mumbles an awkward reply but I am too distracted to catch his words.

It hardly matters as the King's attention begins to wander from us. 'Do enjoy your day, ladies,' he says in dismissal. 'Mingle, look around. Cromwell, you must take them on a tour after we have dined.'

The King we defeated is once again the gracious host and commander-in-chief and I retreat from him, confused. Has nothing changed? Did Olly and Val die for this? Now I have seen him for myself, I cannot escape the feeling that the King has somehow floated above the recent horror. I imagine him only ever pushing pieces of an army about a board, where my beloveds are on the board themselves, fighting and dying in the dirt.

I do not speak to the King again, but watch him from a distance, fascinated despite myself. First at the lavish feast, where I am invited to sit only five places along from him and am served from the same dishes. And later in the gardens into which everyone spills to follow the King who, having just received the new tennis suit he had ordered, declares he must try it out on the court at once. I look, too, for Jane Whorwood, but she seems to have disappeared.

It is while we are standing at the back of the viewing gallery beside the tennis court that Sir John Ashburnham finds us once more. I know him to be one of the chief go-betweens with Father and Henry over their negotiations, so I draw closer to hear what he says. It is an opportune moment for a quiet conclave while the King is occupied and everyone else is watching as he scurries around the court.

'Is he in earnest?' Henry wastes no time.

'I believe so,' Sir John replies quietly, his eye on the King as he takes a serve. 'This latest version seems to have persuaded him.'

'Thanks to you,' Father says and I know from seeing

each draft of the proposals myself that Sir John had a private hand in this last iteration – tweaking a word here, a clause there to ensure it better appealed to his difficult master.

'As long as he is not leading us in a merry dance,' Henry says as the King shouts in triumph at a winning volley. 'You know what opprobrium we face from all sides for continuing to deal with him. Our own soldiers call us traitors while the London presses claim we have sold out our men for our own ennoblement.'

I tut, thinking of the scurrilous broadsheets I have seen: 'They write that the King will make Father Earl of Essex,' I add. 'Reclaiming the title King Henry gave to our forebear Thomas Cromwell just before his fall. It is such an insult.'

'I know, I know,' the courtier says soothingly. 'The newspapers seem as baffled as my master that you do not ask for titles for yourselves as part of the bargain. But believe me, your efforts in the face of such hostility from your own side do not go unnoticed. The King read your recent speech in Parliament defending the monarchy, Cromwell. He heard that you were instrumental in the Army Council deciding to expel Major White for claiming the only power in the kingdom is now the sword. He knows you go out on a limb for him.'

'As long as he does,' Henry says before Father can reply, his narrow face pinched with anxiety.

Father grips his arm with a reassuring hand. 'All will be well, my son, I'm sure of it.'

A flurry of clapping and riotous cheers interrupts us and we turn back to the game. The King, of course, has won.

*

It is dusk by the time we leave, the air still so warm after such a hot day that the breeze on the river is welcome. As it is too late to travel back to London, Mother and Father come to stay with us at our new home; a little rented house in Kingston, just around a bend in the river from Hampton Court. I am thrilled to host them under my own roof, to hear Mother's little comments of approval for my domestic arrangements and to see Father kick off his boots in my parlour while Henry pours him a drink.

The town of Kingston was a good choice: close to the King for the renewed negotiations but only a few miles up-river from the army's new headquarters at Putney. And, crucially for me, not so close to my family in London that my home would become a mere satellite to theirs. Henry's army pay just covers the rent and I am able to use some of my dowry to hire a local groom and girl to help us. Fortunately, the landlord let the house to us furnished, which was a relief as neither Henry nor I own many things. And even now Henry is reluctant to acquire too much furniture before the peace settlement is finally struck; as long as he remains on active service in the army he must be ready to be dispatched elsewhere at a moment's notice. But I, at least, take pleasure in the small acquisitions of a newly married woman establishing her first household: my own account book, ledgers and pen; my own sets of best and everyday linens; my own household purse and set of keys.

We move in just in time for we have been but a fortnight under our own roof when a dull, swelling pain wakes me in the night and sends me for peppermint oil and hot brandy. I know, with dread, what it is; I have not helped at the birth of five babies without learning how the dreaded process begins. It could take days and so I try to sleep while I still can, reciting the psalms when my eyes refuse to close. Deep down, as I listen to Henry's peaceful, unknowing breaths beside me, I hope the daylight will not come. That I will not have to enter the terrifying battlefield of the birthing chamber, climbing for perhaps the last time into a bed from which I may never rise.

As soon as Henry wakes at dawn, he is all action, as I knew he would be. He sends the maid for a midwife and the groom to the city to fetch Mother and Betty and sets about the hot water and towels himself. Meanwhile, the contractions grow more quickly than I expect, punching the air from my chest and pinching my back until they are so painful it is as if a rapier pierces my spine each time. Fear washes over me.

'What if Mother and Betty do not arrive in time?' I pant the words at Henry. Though relief floods me in the next moment when the midwife arrives.

She is brisk and efficient. I am taken upstairs, stripped to my shift and examined, her large, cold hands massaging my belly to find the baby's position, summoning it to her like a soothsayer. 'It is breached,' she says with no preamble and a cold weight drops into my stomach. 'A physician—'

She looks at Henry who flails. 'We are new to the town and have not yet found a doctor. Do you know of one nearby?'

'Only one and he is across river attending another birth – twins.'

I look wildly at Henry, willing him to return to his normal commanding capability. He does not disappoint.

'I'll go to army headquarters at Putney – find a physician there. I'll ride, it will be quicker than going by boat. I won't be long, my darling, I promise.' Snatching his bag, he plants a heavy kiss on my forehead before disappearing around the door.

He is gone an eternity, though I think I pass out for the last stretch of time as his face, when it eventually returns, is blurred with others – a white-bearded man's, which looms over me before I feel new hands on my stomach; the maid's, as she comes and goes with hot water. Next, the tinkling sound of medicine bottles rattles in my head.

But then a familiar voice cuts through the fog: 'He's my personal physician, my dear, the best. Do not fear, all will be well.'

I smell orange blossom, vanilla and amber. The generaless. I reach for her hand in despairing gratitude and she squeezes it fiercely. Relieved, I sink back into the pillows. By the time I hear Betty's voice and feel my mother's cool, familiar hands on my cheeks, I no longer know who or where I am.

She comes in a rush of blood, her first wail piercing my soul. And I feel myself reborn alongside her.

We live, both of us. The pain bewilders and unmans me and I leak and ooze from every crevice, my skin sweaty and sticky, the air thick with such sickly sweet smells my stomach heaves. But we live.

CHAPTER SIXTEEN

My world shrinks so baby Elizabeth and I float in my bed like the survivors in the Ark riding on the floodwater. I gaze at Liza for hours on end, tracing the half-forgotten faces of my dead brothers in her tiny features. Perhaps it is fancy: I had not known Robin and Olly as babies, of course, and only held baby James twice before he died. But still, I am sure she has Olly's high forehead and the set of Robin's mouth. With her wide-spaced eyes and plump cheeks, she is certainly more Cromwell than Ireton.

Nothing around us reaches me and I exist only from feed to feed, each time passing Liza with some reluctance to the wet nurse. I had mentioned my desire to feed her myself but Mother and Betty over-rode me in my weakened state, and before I knew it our maid had found a willing girl from the town.

'It is a fad among the godly to nurse one's own children,' Betty chides me. 'Much better to have a girl do it while you focus on recovering your strength.'

My breasts swell with pain, harden and leak for the first few days, but then they slacken again and I stop longing to press my baby into them.

Henry is delighted and something else – humbled, I think – a rare emotion to see from him when he is always so sure of himself and his intellect. He seems to look at our baby with awe and at me, now, with reverence. I find his hand taking mine more often, his lips grazing my forehead. And for me, the fact that Liza is a soul made up of one part me and one part him endears him further to me, even while I know that our baby really belongs to God and is only on loan to us for as long as He can spare her. I hope, I pray that this is for the rest of my life on earth, though it is not for me to ask this of Him, nor to question His providence.

Those first painful but peaceful days do not last. As soon as I am lucid, I am confronted with a stream of well-meaning but tiring visitors. Mother, of course, who has been staying in our guest room to help; Harry, when he gets leave from the army; Dick, when the law bores him; and Father, who drops in for a drink and gossip as he travels back and forth to the King. Henry's younger brother John visits from the City to bring Liza some fine white linen baby clothes from his cloth-making company.

The visitor who most pleases my husband is his childhood friend Francis Thornhaugh, who arrives in the rain one evening, bearing a beautiful carved wooden horse for Liza, painted piebald to look like Henry's favourite mount – the one who carried him all through the war until she was killed beneath him at Naseby.

'Magnificent!' Henry says, examining the toy so lovingly I think he will hardly let it out of his hands.

'It's for the babe, not for you, Hal!' Francis laughs.

'Such a likeness of Juno,' Henry continues to marvel. 'You should have another made of Trent.'

Francis laughs again – it seems to be his default reaction. 'No, she's an ugly old mare. Juno always showed her up when we rode together.'

'But she has a stout heart and never flinches at gunfire,' Henry counters indignantly. 'I'd take bravery over beauty any day. She was the best horse in the troop.'

My mind fills with the image of the two of them, riding boot to boot as they criss-crossed Nottinghamshire, going from village to village to raise their troop for the war. I lean forward as Francis crosses our room to the cradle and picks Liza up lightly in his arms. I half expect her to cry at the feel of this large, loud stranger but instead she lies soft and contented in his arms. Francis grins at Henry, motioning his success, and Henry raises a dark eyebrow.

'Beginner's luck,' he says.

'A natural gift,' Francis counters. 'And remember, I did not have the multitude of younger brothers and sisters to practice on that you had.'

'Hardly!' Henry interjects. 'You spent as much time with them as I did. You were so often at our table, Mother would plate up for you even when you weren't there!'

They hark back to their boyhoods again and I lie back happily, grateful for the company so long as I'm not required to say much. In my mother's time, it was the custom for new mothers to be 'churched' – forced to stay isolated in bed for weeks after birth and only allowed to re-join their communities after a cleansing ritual in church. Thankfully, brave Puritan women like Henry's mother objected so strongly that the custom is dying out and I can choose for myself who to see and when I feel ready to move around. But still I feel a lingering aftertaste of the sacred in my room: that it has become a confessional, as if something in the sight and feel of the new baby lulls pilgrim visitors into sharing past remembrances and future concerns.

A few days after Francis's visit, Dick speaks to me of Father's early negotiations for his marriage to a godly girl from Hampshire called Dorothy. Not, perhaps, the grandest heiress Father's climbing status could have secured, but a pleasant girl from a Puritan family he likes. Dick has met her twice, the second time taking her riding. Finding her a natural horsewoman with witty conversation and offering him the prospect of a sporting, country life, Dick throws down his law textbooks, declares himself in love and asks me to push Father not to swerve from the deal, whatever the niggles.

'They're haggling over money, of course,' he tells me as he perches on my bed swigging Henry's best madeira. 'Father says he can't pay too much else he'll have nothing left for the girls' dowries. But there's some other sticking point, I wager.'

'What other point?' I am only half listening but touched that he wishes to confide in me.

'Doll's father confessed to our go-between that he's nervous of Father's equivocal position – the way his reputation tosses back and forth on the tide. Do many see Father that way, do you think? Will Father win him around?'

I look at him with a tenderness that surprises me. For all his unreliability and fondness for easy living, my little brother is clearly set on this girl. 'Perhaps,' I say, shifting Liza in my arms. 'In continuing to treat with the

King, Father is trying to hold the middle ground but the longer it goes on, the more he merely angers both sides. It will come to a head one way or another and then we'll all know where we stand.'

While Dick comes to me to confess his love, Betty comes to satisfy her curiosity. Returning, this time with John and little Cromwell. Once she has cooed over the cousins' first meeting, she swiftly opens the conversation she has really come for. 'What was he like? I've been longing to ask.' She flicks her wrist to shoo John from the room and he leaves, rolling his eyes, chubby Cromwell dangling awkwardly in his arms like a puppy as he goes in search of a drink.

'Who?'

'Who!' She tuts and slaps my wrist in mock rebuke. 'The King, of course. Was he extraordinarily glamorous?'

It is my turn to tut, though I cannot help a sneaking pleasure that I have visited the court when she – to whom it would mean so much more – has not. 'He was well dressed,' I concede.

'What colour was his doublet? How was his lace?'

I shake my head before indulging her. 'Pale blue, I think. And French lace perhaps? The trailing kind, closely stitched.'

She sighs with pleasure at the second-hand description.

'You ought not to be so impressed by worldly things, Betty.'

'You sound like Father,' she says, pouting.

'He's right. A man's graceful manners and expensive dress count for little against the content of his character. If the King betrays our trust, I'll have none of him, whatever his lace.'

'You can't mean it?' She stares at me, her cornflower-blue eyes wide with horror. 'And besides,' she regains herself a little, 'it is not for us to have or not have him – he will always be our king.'

'Perhaps not,' I say, the first time I have even thought this treason, let alone said it aloud. 'Not if he does not deserve to be.' Is it having the baby that has opened my eyes to this, I wonder? Shown me how possible it is to create something new and perfect?

Betty shakes her curls at me, for once lost for words, if only for a few seconds. 'Without the King, we will continue in chaos. You have been too long with the army, Biddy, the radical rank and file have polluted you. You're spouting treason!'

'I'd rather take my chances with a raw recruit who stands by his word than a king who does not,' I say, a touch haughtily, beginning to anger now. Can she not see I am tired and just want to hold Liza and lay my head back on the pillow? Why must she always goad me?

'That talk can only lead to further bloodshed and I'll not have my John pulled back into the field to satisfy the army's swollen vanity. I hope you do not say such things to Father or Henry.'

'I'll say what I like to them when they seek my opinion.'

She flounces to her feet to pace grandly before the bay window. Watching her makes me dizzy and I notice for the first time a throbbing in my deadened arms. 'Hold the baby, would you? She's asleep now.'

I watch Betty try and maintain her offence but one glance at her pink and swaddled namesake and she softens, taking the bundle from my arms which ache with relief and bereavement all at once. 'Go on, then. Get some sleep. Maybe you'll be clearer-headed when you wake,' she says. I know she is raising a fine eyebrow at me and hoping for a last retort, but my eyes have already closed.

Sleep has become a slippery thing. A flashing fish to be snatched and gripped tightly before it slithers away yet again. A fenland eel thrashing in a moonlit basket. Being already accustomed to dividing my night into two sleeps is helpful and, selfishly, I try and stir Liza for a feed in between, taking her into Margery, the wet nurse, even when she is sleeping deeply. Yet still there is no rhyme or reason to her waking, nor the length she suckles for, so each morning sees me hollow-eyed with an aching head. Margery tells me to leave Liza in with her and to sleep through but, though I am not feeding her myself, I want her close by me.

I worry for Henry – never one to sleep enough anyway – who must spend his days battling tiredness along with the agitators in the army and the King. Even in my nursery cocoon, I sense how matters are spiralling away from him, spinning in all directions like a St Catherine wheel on Gunpowder Treason night, now just a fortnight away. The consensus we worked so hard to secure within the army in the spring has vanished, thanks to the King's prevarication, Parliament's continuing failure to address the soldiers' grievances and the growing influence of the radical London Levellers whose ideas spread daily through the ranks. Their impact is clear when the agitators in the army draw up a radical manifesto of their own which Henry reads to me in bed, shaking his head angrily.

'It proposes an entirely new system of government to reflect their opinion that sovereign power should reside in the people of England rather than with the discredited King or Parliament. *An Agreement of the People*, where every citizen has the right to give his own agreement to the government. But who will this new electorate be? Not servants, women or children certainly, just vast numbers of militant soldiers with no permanent stake in the country but the ability to vote their Parliaments in and out on a whim. Without property there can be no independence of action, nor consequences from it either. I know how it will be: rule by the sword the only possible power. That's what Harrison, Rainsborough and their rabble want.'

'I sympathise, dearest,' I say, laying a half-sleeping Liza in her basket so I can brush my hair before bed. 'Yet these divisions within the army serve the King above all. And you must keep some sympathy for the men who have been so ill-served by their political masters. They're still awaiting the pay owed to them and guarantees of their indemnity for the things they had to do in the war. You must give the soldiers a fair hearing for all their Leveller leanings; try to find some common ground.'

'We have, we are. There's to be a series of debates among the General Council of Officers at Putney where representatives of all the regiments can have their say. Your father is to preside.'

'Not Fairfax?'

'He is still ill, apparently. Though I suspect he just wants to stay out of all this.'

'I wonder what the generaless thinks of that?' I reply. Anne had been so kind to come to me at the birth and bring her own physician; I'm sure she saved my life. However much I think her too forgiving of the King, I would not wish her disrespected or ignored. I determine to write and send her a box of the sugared plums she loves. 'Invite them here for dinner,' I say, suddenly struck by the idea.

'The Fairfaxes?'

'No, the Leveller leaders in the army. Rainsborough. And – who's the other agitator you often speak of? Sexby. And you can ask Thomas Harrison too, as you all get along with him.' I know Henry often shares a room with Harrison when they are billeted with the army – perhaps he could be a mediating presence. And I could invite Catherine too, as a further buffer.

'But to have them here?' Henry remains unconvinced.

'You remember when Father was trying to reconcile with the Earl of Manchester before the army was reorganised? He had him join us for dinner, just to see if a friendly, familial setting might not warm relations between them. Do the same with the Leveller leaders. You could sound them out, test the water, probe the gulf between you before the debates begin. It would be a gesture of goodwill to show that you will deal with them in honest faith.'

Henry looks at me thoughtfully, twisting the fine hairs at the end of his beard. 'It's not a bad idea. Just to show there's no ill will. We must reunify the army, whatever happens, else we will all be lost.'

'We'll need Father here.'

'He'll never agree. He and Rainsborough are at

loggerheads now. They can barely stand to be in the same room.'

Colonel Rainsborough must be a forceful man, I think. It's rare for Father to fall out so violently with anyone. He is usually the conciliator at any table; the man who fetches the ale.

'Leave Father to me,' I say and, replacing the hairbrush on the chest, I sink to my knees beside the bed for my nightly prayers. *Dear Lord, let not your true servants fall out among themselves. Reveal yourself and your wishes to us and we will do your bidding.* I open my eyes, distracted by sudden practicalities. 'I wonder if the butcher has any of that venison loin left?'

They come. Awkward, glowering. Watching their words and weighing every one of ours. But they come: Preacher Peacock Harrison with his wife Catherine; the fiery Thomas Rainsborough, triumphant at his new appointment as vice-admiral of the navy which he mentions every few minutes; and Edward Sexby, who I remember, when I see him, was the stern trooper who brought the army's letter to Father to us at Drury Lane that first time Betty came downstairs after her lying-in.

This is my first proper society since my own lying-in and I find myself nervous and oddly tongue-tied, the rapid flow of conversation whirling past me like a fast-flowing stream flooding the winter fens. I forget about Liza for a time and am then shocked by the sudden remembrance of her, summoned by the feeling of warm blood trickling between my legs. I am forced to withdraw and search for clean pads, wondering, as I hastily change my linens, how much longer I will suffer these intermittent bleeds; how long it will be before I feel my body return to its familiar self once more.

I serve the venison but it is not a success. Everyone is too tense to show any real enjoyment of the meat. Still, it matters to appear generous hosts. The currant pudding and brandy butter prompt at least a glimmer of pleasure around the table as Rainsborough follows Catherine's compliment to me on the pudding by revealing a little of his own past. 'I used to trade in currants, before the war,' he explains with admirable frankness, flushed with a proud pleasure at the remembrance of the honest trade he was born into. 'These are excellent, Mistress Ireton,' he continues, 'but you must let me know if you have a fancy to try any of the more exotic fruits. I still have my contacts at Wapping docks – they can get you dates and mangoes, even a banana, should you wish to see one for yourself.'

'How wonderful!' Catherine Harrison claps her hands in pleasure.

I smile, pleased to have discovered one doorway into Rainsborough's good humour. For all his opposition to my kin, I find it hard to dislike him. He is so open and unafraid. 'I will, sir,' I say. 'I should like to taste a banana. Raised in Huntingdonshire, I am still amazed at the sheer variety of food to be found in this city. We had a vibrant trade with the Dutch, of course, and plenty of produce from the North, even Scotland. But here in London there are spices and sweetmeats from all corners of the world. As a Londoner yourself, I'll warrant you'll be pleased to return to the high seas once you take up your appointment with the navy.'

Rainsborough smiles at me before shifting his smile

onto Father, a hint of triumph creeping into it as he does. Henry has told me how Father had blocked his appointment at first, but changed his mind when he realised it would at least take Rainsborough far away from army politics. Father inclines his head and tips his glass in stiff politeness. He is being unusually quiet this evening. To me, who knows him as my own flesh, I sense an embarrassment in him. As if he hates to be thought by his godly colleagues to be on the wrong side of history in his willingness to settle with the King. Henry, however, perhaps emboldened by being the master of the house, is feeling no such reserve and misses no moment to plunge into choppy waters.

'Whatever the merits of some of your individual proposals – and I admire their spirit – I will support no plan that destroys either King or Parliament,' he says a few minutes later, when we have exhausted our small talk of fruit.

'But if that is what it takes to secure our freedoms?' Rainsborough counters, his gaze trained on Henry clear and direct. 'Do not the poorest in our land have a life to live as much as any of us and deserve a say in how that life is governed?'

Although Henry scowls and Father remains silent, I cannot find a fault in this and determine to say so. 'It is a brave sentiment, sir, to insist all men's lives are invested with importance. I would add, though, that all women's lives be credited just as dear.'

Rainsborough turns back to me, his eyes shining. 'It's a fine notion, Mistress Ireton, and there are many wives among the Levellers who would agree with you.'

I long to learn more but I am denied by Father

choosing this moment of all others to lay down his thoughts, as if my intervention has driven the debate to its very limits:

'But all this is so very far from why we took up arms in the first place,' he says, rising to his feet to walk about the room as he likes to do when thinking aloud. 'Which was to show where the true supreme authority lies. We have proved that on the battlefield and now must establish it constitutionally. What you propose tears up the whole social contract under which we've been living these thousand years. It pits faction against faction with any group entitled to press for the form of government they fancy. A settlement with King, Lords and Commons must be best.'

'Men who have the vote should have a propertied interest – some stake in the kingdom.' Henry picks up Father's tune. 'What you propose is to replace civil rights with natural rights and anarchy can be the only outcome.'

'Anarchy!' Rainsborough loses his veneer of civility with one outraged word.

'Not anarchy but justice.' Sexby sits forward in his seat. 'The men who risked their lives in this war should not now be told that they have no rights in the kingdom. I'll warrant the outcome more beneficial to the common men than any backstairs agreement you make with this false king.'

It always comes back to the King and to Father's and Henry's trust in him. Father, I think, is shocked by this realisation as he drops his gaze to his boot where, supposing to see a stain, he scuffs a toe on the hearth rug.

Henry pushes his chair back in a scrape of frustration

though he stays seated. 'How many times must we tell you that we have done no secret deal with the King?'

Sexby tilts his head in half-acknowledgement but will not admit the truth of this in so many words. He turns instead to address Father again: 'I am of your own regiment, general – you must know the men feel strongly upon the point. Charles Stuart will never be satisfied until we have cut our own throats.'

Blood runs before my eyes.

'The soldiers see him as a man of blood who has rained horrors upon them and must be tried for his crimes. And can you blame them?' Harrison blusters, red wine spilling from his glass as if in echo of his words.

I watch the ruby drops fall. *A man of blood*. The phrase chills my own veins. Tried for his crimes – the King? I think back to the proud little king and his waving wrist flicking away his responsibility for the war.

Henry goes very still, his features narrowing. 'I will not have that talk in my house, Thomas, for all our friendship.'

Catherine and I exchange nervous glances as Harrison's face puckers with anger. This is not going at all how I had planned.

'Then I will bid you good evening,' Preacher Peacock says grandly and sweeps to his feet, holding out his arm for his wife.

'And we will follow suit,' Rainsborough adds quickly, rising to his feet and making a small bow in my direction. 'Thank you both for an – enlightening evening.'

'Until Putney,' Sexby adds, laying down his napkin. And this is all the sign-off he gives.

CHAPTER SEVENTEEN

WINTER 1647–1648

Henry is ladling a boiling egg into my bowl, the toast crisping in the fire behind him, when the messenger comes. Supper had fallen to him, with Margery and the maid both out and Liza taking an age to go down, so he had cooked the only thing he knows how; the meal that saw him through his student days. As I open the door to the breathless rider, cold air, still smoky with bonfire ash from the Gunpowder Treason revels, rushes into the house, sending the candles guttering. Hot wax blows onto my hand and I brush it off quickly as I nod the army messenger into the house, the groom leading his horse clattering round to our stable in the twilit gloom.

'The King has escaped Hampton Court?' Henry stares at the trooper open-mouthed while the man warms his back at the parlour fire, the egg pan bubbling behind him.

The story comes out in bursts: the King took fright at reports of the army's anger in their debates – one of which came in a letter from Father himself; he feared an attack, being only a few miles downriver from Putney;

breaking parole, he fled into the night in disguise with Sir John Ashburnham and another courtier, making, it's thought, for the south coast.

I cough from the smoke and shock, shaking my head, still rubbing at the candle burn on my hand. It is a disaster and a betrayal of gigantic proportions. Once we are alone, Henry storms and rages, his cool head blazing in a way I have never seen before.

'It is the end,' he keeps saying, hurling the words into the fire as he paces before it. 'The end of everything I have worked myself to the bone for. I cannot deal with this king ever again. No reasonable man could. I placed myself in peril among the army time and time again for that man. Risked every ounce of my reputation. Reassured the men endlessly that of course he was to be trusted. I will be a laughing stock.' His hurt pride leaks from his voice and I feel a hot rage of my own rise to meet his.

Betty visits the next day, her unfailing nose for drama bringing her to my door at the worst possible time. And so she is there when Father calls, pouring into the house like a cooling flood come to douse Henry's unextinguished anger.

'All may yet be well,' he says to Henry's snorts of derision. 'This forces our issue with the Levellers just as it removes the King from any danger they might pose to him. We cannot be expected to continue with these debates amongst ourselves now. And if the King is secured on the Isle of Wight under the eye of the governor, my cousin Robert Hammond, as the latest intelligence suggests, he'll be kept secure and a long way from Parliament and the Scots.'

I examine Father closely. He sounds as if this plan suits

him almost too well and my mind clouds with suspicion. 'You had no hand in this, Father?' I ask him, my heart thumping as I step into a chasm opening between us. 'We know you wrote to the King two nights ago to warn him of the Levellers' growing ire. Did you provoke his flight?'

I hear Betty gasp at my irreverence. Though we are a plain-speaking family, I know I am taking this privilege further than ever. Where we may have disagreed before, none of us has ever questioned Father's integrity. I glance quickly at Henry and see an answering suspicion flickering in his coal-black eyes which strengthens my spirit. I must put him and our cause before my fondness for my father.

'Children, children,' Father holds up his hands good-humouredly, 'you credit me with both too much guile and too much influence. Of course I had no hand in the King's flight, I merely seek any advantages in it for us.'

'So all is not lost between you and the King?' Betty sips her sweetened cider neatly though I sense the panic underneath the polish. 'You may still reconcile and avert our sliding even further into unrest and misrule?'

'Surely not!' Henry turns a flashing face to his father-in-law, who seems to shrink a little under it. I have never before seen Henry lose his temper with Father and it frightens as much as thrills me.

'We gave him every reasonable chance of peace,' my husband rages on, 'and he has thrown it back in our faces. We have lain ourselves in the dirt for him and this is how he repays us?'

I must lend my voice to support his and think quickly of my previous advice to Henry on how best to appeal to Father: human nature and Providence. 'It is in the

King's nature to play this as the bookmaker at a horse race,' I say, trying to speak to him in a language he understands. Father has always loved the turf and I have picked up enough from him and my brothers to know something of the sport, though the gambling side of it was always more in Dick's line than Father's. 'He places bets each way,' I go on, 'by turns raising and shortening the odds, praising and then casting doubt on each horse and rider so that, in the end, the book makes the profit. He can never be truly sincere in his dealings with you, or indeed with Parliament or the Scots, so long as he is looking over his shoulder for a better deal, sure in himself that – as he said – none of you can do without him. Perhaps this escape – just his latest throw of the dice – is the moment God has marked out to reveal him in his true colours. Perhaps this is Providence at work strengthening us at last to move against the King?'

Father looks at me thoughtfully and I glow to find myself his intellectual equal. But then Betty leads him away from me into false sunshine.

'If the King was afraid of a Leveller assassin, then surely we can understand his fear and his flight,' Betty pleads her sovereign's case prettily, turning her big eyes on Father; always her truly intended audience. 'And why shouldn't he be afraid when faced with such militant radicals?'

I glare at her while Henry merely scoffs. 'How convenient for the King that the best answer to such a fear should be his own covert escape rather than conveying his fears to Colonel Whalley and asking for extra protection from the army.' His tone is bitter and I long to take his hand.

'Father?' Betty ignores Henry.

We all three turn to him, two glowering faces and one pleading one.

Father sighs and threads his thick fingers through his hair, dislodging tiny particles of dirt from the road to sprinkle his shoulder. 'We simply must reach a settlement that incorporates the throne,' he says at last, touching a fond finger to Betty's cheek. 'All else leads to anarchy. I will give this King one more chance to prove he deals fairly, my dears, as I still believe – I still hope – he does.'

Anger and jealousy duel within me as I glare at the sister I love almost above all others. What right has Betty to opine on the army's affairs when she has never deigned to live and work among the men as I have? What is her husband's contribution to the peace effort in comparison with Henry's? She married for a hot passion where I wed for a cool conscience and to please my father. Am I not to feel some benefit of this from the exchange? Should Father not listen to me more than her?

As I look at Father and Betty I feel the gulf growing between we three who used to be Cromwells cut from the same country cloth. But Betty is now a Claypole longing for a return to the comfortable, civilized life Lady Fairfax once spoke of, while I am an Ireton striving to carve a better future for all.

And who is Father now?

Mutiny stirs in the army and anger settles on our house like evening mist. Henry snaps at me and tiredness poisons my tongue in return. Liza senses our simmering and mewls for me at all hours but then refuses to settle in my tense arms. When news reaches us that Father and Commander Fairfax have confronted the violent troops and shot one of the ringleaders, drawn by lot, as an example, Henry's mood blackens further. By day he rages at this chaos, by turns blaming the King and the Levellers, while the nights see him morbid and morose at the thought of the dead man. 'He was one of us,' he says over and over again, shaking his head as if he still cannot fathom how it came to pass. The year darkens as the winter nights curl towards Advent and England gropes in the black.

And then, at last, Providence takes a lantern to the thorny path ahead. I am not expecting Henry, due to stay with the army at its new headquarters in Windsor, for at least a week more. So I am in one of my workaday gowns, hair thrust in a bun, apron about my waist and the baby lolling in my arms when he and Father clatter into the yard one afternoon. I mistake them at first for common troopers as they are not wearing their own officers' dress but the shabbier clothes of the rank-and-file soldiers. I move quickly to the door to answer the riddle, my questions loud on my lips before a raised arm from Father bids my silence. I retreat into the hall and say nothing until they are safe inside and the heavy door swung shut.

I look to Henry for explanation but it is Father who rushes in first with a schoolboy's excitement.

'We are in disguise.' He grins, thrilled at the escapade.

'Why?' I turn to Henry for sense.

'We have received intelligence from one of our spies among the King's laundry maids that he has been smuggling out secret correspondence to the Queen,' he says as he removes his cloak and takes Father's from him.

'Correspondence that reveals his true intentions regarding the peace settlement.'

My mind floods with questions. 'How has he managed it? What are his intentions?'

'His intentions will be revealed in the latest letters,' Father answers, 'but the how will amaze you. It transpires his courier, his secret agent, is none other than Jane Whorwood, whom you met at Holton.'

'No!' I gasp at this. Sad, abandoned Jane Whorwood a spy for the King? I remember her swirling among the courtiers at Hampton Court in a pink dress and what she had said to me when she gave me her wedding dress: *I intend to make my own fate.* 'I was married in her gown!' I blurt out in shock, before sinking into the nearest chair.

Father laughs at this though Henry's face remains dark.

'And your disguise?' I ask, my mind still racing.

'We plan to intercept the bearer of the message at an inn in the City.' Father's words spill out in excited agitation as he takes my arm conspiratorially. 'Our agent tells us he will enter the Blue Boar in Holborn at ten o'clock tonight carrying a saddle on his shoulder and that the letter is sewn into the saddle. We mean to be there ourselves to seize it.'

'You?' I must inject some sense into this plan. 'But the City is crawling with soldiers. You will be recognised. The two of you together especially.'

'No!' Father is boyishly confidant. 'We'll order some jugs and swagger it off.'

'But what if Mistress Whorwood comes herself? She knows you.'

'She won't risk coming herself. She'll have sent the

letter on with a courier, possibly an innocent traveller who knows nothing about it.'

Henry looks slightly less sure but determined nonetheless. I guess he hopes the letter will be the final proof he needs to convince Father of the King's duplicity and he wants to ensure nothing goes wrong.

'We'll lay low here for a few hours,' Father continues, dropping into a chair in the front parlour, 'then ride up to the City. Can we take your groom with us to keep watch? Is he to be trusted?'

'Certainly – he seems an honest man,' I answer for Henry who is far too distracted by work to have noticed the capabilities or otherwise of our new staff.

Margery pops a head around the door and I beckon her to take Elizabeth. 'Could you ask the maid if she could manage some supper for the master and my father too? I can come and help.' My arms now free, I drop my hands to remove my apron before I am struck by a sudden thought.

'I could come with you.'

'You?' Henry turns back from the corner where he is already rifling through the desk looking for his post.

'It would aid your disguise,' I say, warming to my idea. 'I am dressed plainly today anyway – look. And if I take off my necklace and rings and borrow the girl's cloak, I could easily pass for a servant or shop assistant. Then if anyone looks twice at you, my dear, they'll see a trooper taking his sweetheart and friend out for a drink.'

It takes a good deal to persuade them. Father worries for my safety, Henry for my health. But I am not called Bidding Biddy for nothing and within half an hour they have given way. We determine to hire a hackney carriage so that we will have somewhere private and concealed to wait and to read the letter should we secure it (though my foremost reason is to avoid several hours in the saddle so soon after labour). A few hours later, fed and even more drably dressed, we set off.

It is a long journey, made longer by Father's complaints about the poor condition of the coach – a common problem among the hackneys, he says, which would be solved if they were properly licensed and regulated. I am relieved when, at around half past eight, the carriage trundles into Holborn. After a rant to the driver about the loose wheel-arches, Father presses some coins into his hand and instructs him to wait in an alley a few corners from the Blue Boar so we are not observed travelling in a luxury far beyond a common trooper's reach. Pulling our hats low over our eyes, we scuttle through the blustery evening wind to the welcoming warmth of the inn, whose windows glow in the dark street below the creaking sign.

Our groom stations himself outside with a pipe while we go in and find the quietest corner. Henry orders small beer and we drink deeply, keeping our voices low but not so conspiratorial as to attract suspicion. When we have relaxed a little, our play-acting improves. Father lounges against the wall while, conscious of the part to play, I shift closer to Henry on our bench and loop his arm about my shoulders. Yet my heart continues to hammer as I wonder if the King's agents weave among us or if anyone here has recognised the famous men sitting alongside me. Once or twice curious heads turn towards us but each time I plant a kiss on Henry's cheek or Father laughs, clinking his tankard with Henry's, the faces turn back.

Though for the most part I try to keep my gaze lowered to avoid the eyes of others, I cannot help sneaking glances around the bustling room as it is such a novelty to sit so freely in the front room of an inn. When I have visited a tavern before – purchasing food from The Bell, travelling to Oxford or when billeted with the army – I have usually waited outside, kept to my room, or at least to the private back parlours requisitioned by visiting gentlemen. Sitting here, among the ordinary customers for an hour, is a riotous assault on my senses and I struggle to keep conversation with Henry and Father as I soak up all the life around me. Soldiers, apprentices and merchants drink and jostle while their women thread among them waiting at tables or sitting on laps. Drinks are spilled, laughter ripples around tables and curses are thrown across the room. Someone falls over in the corridor outside and a gentleman complains to the landlord that his horse has been fed rotten oats.

Observing it all, I almost forget my nerves but then the sight of our groom at the door, his eyes raking the room for us, sends my heart down into my stomach.

'He's here,' Father whispers. 'Quickly now.'

In a few moments we are in the yard of the inn, damp, pungent straw underfoot and horses' white breath snorting in the cold air. A young man is crossing the yard with a saddle on his shoulder and nearly jumps out of his skin when Father and Henry draw their swords upon him. He drops the saddle and raises his hands.

'What's this? Who?'

I scan his bewildered face and wonder for a moment if he is the right man. But the church bell close by chimes the hour of ten o'clock and there is no one else here who fits the description.

'Is he alone?' Henry speaks sharply to our groom who is lurking in the shadow of the archway entrance, blocking the man's escape.

He nods.

'Do as we say, my man, and you'll have no trouble from us,' Father commands the frightened youth. Who are you?'

'Just a trader from the Solent, sir. I deal in wines and spirits from the continent.'

'What brings you here?' Henry takes up the questioning.

'I travel up to London every month to take orders from the City. Nothing more than that. Is there something wrong?'

'Let's see that saddle,' Father says and the man shrugs in confusion.

'The saddle? If you like. I mean no trouble, sirs.'

Henry beckons to me and I cross the yard to where he stands over the saddle. He motions me to feel the seams of one side of the saddle while he examines the other. Father watches us from over his drawn sword. I inch along the stitching, my fingertips well versed in the feel of old and new stitches, those that have been lately unpicked and re-stitched, those that are of practical use and those merely ornamental. Those where the thread differs for just fractions of an inch. It only takes a minute for me to locate the traitor needlework and I wonder, for a moment, if it is Jane Whorwood's own stitching beneath my thumb; the same stitching as along the hem she took up for me on our wedding dress.

'Here.'

Henry turns the saddle around and quickly slits the seam with his sword. He reaches inside and pulls out a small, slim paper with an expression of triumph. 'Ha!'

Father's flushed face crumbles in shock as if he never really thought this would happen. As if he is in awe of the magnitude of the moment, now it has finally come.

The vintner whimpers, frightened now. 'I had no idea. I do not know what the bit of paper may be!'

Henry moves towards him and the man shrinks back, his eyes wide and wild. Henry scans his face for a few moments before giving the merest nod of his head towards the archway. Father drops his sword and the man scampers away, half tripping in the straw at his desperation to get out of the yard.

'He was no agent,' Henry says, more to himself than to us. 'Just a hapless courier. The real recipient is like to be here somewhere, though, so we must leave.'

Almost on cue, I hear the bubbling sound of voices approaching from within the inn and see a face pressed at the window.

'Quickly!' Father grabs for my hand as Henry picks up the saddle and we hurry out into the night. I half expect to hear the sound of footsteps pursuing us but none come and we are safely inside the carriage a few moments later. Our groom climbs up beside the driver and in an instant we are off.

'The letter.' Father crooks his fingers to Henry, who relinquishes it to him. He examines it closely, peering at it in the yellow light of the carriage lantern. From where I sit I can see that it has been folded in an intricate locking pattern, designed, no doubt, to prevent it being opened, read and easily reconstructed by prying eyes. Father slides his thumbs into the seams and breaks it open, his brow furrowing as he reads.

Henry and I jolt along in heavy silence, waiting. Eventually, Father speaks, though the words that come don't sound like his voice. I have to strain forward to hear him he is so quiet, all his former excitement at this heroic escapade flown.

'The King writes to the Queen,' he says, simple and sparse, with no single word wasted. 'He tells her that we in the army and the Scots Presbyterians each vie for his attention.' Father pauses and again we wait. Up ahead one of the horses whinnies. 'He says he thinks he'll close a deal with the Scots.'

It is a clap of thunder in our midst. Even though I had lost most of my faith in the King already, to hear his false dealing in his own hand, to see the looping writing with my own eyes, shakes me to my bones. I reach for Henry's hand and squeeze it. He says nothing but I know his thoughts match my own: this means he will ride to a second war.

Glumly, we watch Father.

The general's face is blank and unusually pale, the voice dead in his throat with a whisper. He does not move for a long time until, slowly, I notice his large hand begin to close, white-knuckled, over the paper. Quickly, I pluck the page from between his fingers, anxious lest our proof be damaged. My hand shakes to hold it as if it burns my skin while Father's hand closes, empty, into a throbbing fist.

'This man is no longer my king,' he says and I feel the earth move.

CHAPTER EIGHTEEN

SUMMER 1648

The boy is so young. Seventeen? I stare into his blue eyes, glazed with a deathly film, as I make my decision; I have reached the last woman of the day and she has space for only one soldier, yet there are six wounded men left festering on the cart.

'Take the lad,' one of them says: a middle-aged man with bullet wounds in his shoulder and waist, blood seeping into the ragged bandages. 'The rest of us are fine.' He has to breathe between each word, such is his pain.

I look among them, rapidly assessing their chances of survival. Three of them have mere flesh wounds that we can attend to here. One has died already, flopped over the side of the cart. That leaves the older man who spoke and the boy. I long to send the boy, to give him a comfortable bed and a warm woman to nurse him and send him home to his mother. But it cannot be. He has only a few hours to live, if that. The man with the bullet wounds, on the other hand, might live if his wounds are cleaned and treated daily, with fresh linen and herbs. He may have a wife and children who need him to survive.

'Take him.' I point to the older man who begins to shake his head violently.

'Please!' He is almost sobbing. 'Tom's just a boy. He's our cornet – carries our standard into battle.'

Tom. Not Olly or Val. 'I'm sorry,' I say, spreading my hands as my heart aches. 'He will not survive, but you might. You must go. I'll have him brought up to my room here, I promise; I'll make him comfortable for his last few hours. I'll look after him myself.'

The other injured men urge their friend to go and the local woman beckons to him kindly. But still he will not move, one hand gripping the side of the cart, the other cradling the boy's face. The love between soldiers is like no other, I know that now. I summon two orderlies and instruct them to carry the boy to my room and it is only once they have lifted him gently from the cart that the older man climbs painfully down after him, wiping his streaming eyes as he shuffles towards his new nurse.

We are at war again: this time a grinding, brutal conflict with fighting stretching from the Solent to Scotland, from Wales to Newcastle. Father and John Lambert have gone north to fight the treacherous Scots, now turned from our ally to our enemy as they invade England at the King's invitation. Meanwhile, Henry and I have found ourselves fighting the Royalists in the south, first in Kent and then driving them up into Essex, now finally to Colchester, where they are making a last stand inside the desperate town. For all the horror, I am glad to be here. I could not stay in Kingston; we were forced to give up the lease when Henry was recalled to the field

– which turned out to be a lucky escape as there was fighting around Kingston in July in which the Duke of Buckingham's younger brother was killed. I could have returned to the soft safety of my family at Drury Lane – a course pressed upon me from all sides, not least as I am pregnant again – but I would not wait out another war living from letter to letter. That was not why I married Henry. Besides, there is work here for me too.

Finding myself billeted near Colchester for a lengthier stay, I have created some proper employment at last, conceiving a new scheme to help both our wounded men and the local people. The essence of my idea is to match injured soldiers in need of nursing with local women who are happy to take them in for fair pay. The generaless secured me a budget from her husband and I use the first portion to have an advertisement printed which is distributed around the locality. The natural Parliamentarianism of the region – and the promise of two shillings a week plus expenses – helps bring scores of women forward and my days find a new, professional rhythm.

Each morning, once I have found Henry some breakfast and sent out our laundry to the army washerwomen, I assess the latest cartloads of wounded who are brought into the stable yard of the coaching inn which Fairfax is using as his headquarters and where we are staying. There they receive initial treatment from a troop of camp followers I have assembled: the publican providing bread and ale and the women bathing and dressing wounds. Then, in the afternoon, I take the day's casualty list into the back parlour and allocate the wounded among the queue of local women waiting in answer to my advert, paying their first week's salary up front. It is a delicate job: listening yet deflecting the women's constant pleas for their friends and family in Colchester; matching their discernible skills and available house room to the variety of the injured; choosing who is best equipped to take the dying and waving the men off to a kinder death. By evening, most of the injured have trundled away with their foster carers and I retire to my room too weary to do anything but cuddle Liza and sing us both to sleep – the days of my waiting up for Henry gone for now.

The dramatic events at Colchester are making the national press with partisan pamphlets recounting the horrors and bravery of either side flooding the public imagination. These broadsheets filter to us who are there on the ground, reflecting our own madness back to us as through a shattered mirror. It is clear to us all that the people of Colchester are starving. A few weeks ago they ate their cats and dogs. Now, we hear, they are reduced to eating soap and candles. The Royalist army squatting within the town's walls has stripped it of everything, even taking the thatch from roofs to feed their horses, and children are dying in the streets. I imagine it is my family and our neighbours trapped in Ely and weep. I think back to Oxford and General Fairfax sending a hamper of delicacies into the city for the Duke of York. How very long ago that seems. This second civil war is a new horror beyond anything I ever dreamed. There is no civility left.

All supply lines into the town from the surrounding countryside are cut. Parliament's ships blockade the harbour and mouth of the River Colne. The town council petitions our besieging General Fairfax for relief but he refuses. The knowledge that the town and people of Colchester supported Parliament in the first war renders these decisions even more painful both for him and for those of us close by who witness them. But he has no choice, I see that. The town has become the last stronghold of the southern Royalist army and, in spite of every opportunity offered to them, the Royalist commanders refuse to surrender. When Fairfax clears the suburbs of the town and sends a trumpeter to announce terms of surrender to the Royalist leaders, they say they'll hang the man if Fairfax sends him again.

After ten grinding weeks in damp summer heat, it seems that both the besiegers and those under siege are losing their minds: in desperation, the Royalists send five hundred starving townswomen to our lines to beg for relief and former Vice-Admiral Rainsborough – newly returned, having been ignominiously expelled from his own flagship by Royalist mutineers, his command now restored to the Earl of Warwick – has some of them stripped naked before his laughing troops. I cannot look at him after that, whatever his honest charm and talk of poor men's rights. Women should have rights too: the right not to have their clothes ripped from their bony breasts; the right not to starve alongside their children.

I look at the cornet boy Tom, pale and almost lifeless on the stretcher as the orderlies carry him away to my room then turn at the sound of a rider clattering under the archway into the stable yard. A messenger. He leaps from his horse onto the stable straw and I know it is vital news he carries. Could this be the end finally? I watch the effect of the news he bears ripple through the inn: the shouts from Fairfax's command room in the front parlour once he reaches them; the troopers bursting out of the side door to go and tell their friends. I run in search of Henry and find him at Black Tom's right hand. It is the general who tells me:

'Your father has won a remarkable victory,' he says, smiling broadly, his dark eyes shining like wet peat as he strides forward to take my hand. 'He has routed the Scots at Preston – once and for all, it seems.'

'His first battle in sole command,' Henry adds, with a note of pride in his voice at his adopted father's achievements. I have often wondered if his love for my father springs in part from the loss of his own when he was young. That perhaps Father fills a void in Henry's life: the older mentor, model and confidant he lacked as a boy.

'Indeed,' the general agrees. 'Lambert too has proved his worth in the field. Between them, they have the Scots on the run.'

'And my brother Harry is safe?' I ask, barely able to form the words. 'He is with my father.'

'I believe so,' Fairfax pats my hand, 'I have news of the battle from your father himself and he would hardly omit to tell me if anything had happened to his own boy.'

I swell with relief, gripping the back of a tall chair for support, suddenly aware of the heavy child growing in my belly. Perhaps God has finished taking my brothers back to his glory. 'Colchester must surrender now, surely?' I ask once speech has returned to me.

'Yes, thank God. Now we can lift this damned siege.' The general sweeps around to Henry. 'Come, Ireton, there's not a moment to lose. We must send the news into the town at once, speed their submission. But I dare not send a messenger, not after they threatened to hang my last one.'

'We can use kites,' Henry says, his face lighting at the idea. 'Print the news on large pamphlets, attach them to string and float them over the town walls. That way the commanders cannot keep the news from the people who will pressure them even harder to surrender.'

'Brilliant! And we'll fire salutes from our surrounding forts.' Fairfax beckons to two junior aides and motions them to set to the plan while I go to my room. Perhaps now the war will finally end and we can begin, once more, to build a peace.

But first I must help a boy to die comfortably. The peace will come too late for him.

Beaten and broken, Colchester surrenders within hours of our kites floating overhead. The commanders seek to negotiate terms, but Fairfax is resolute: they had their chances, this would be surrender on his terms alone. An example must be made to show that this second bloody and needless war is over once and for all. The next few days are frantic and messy. The town pays us a fine – bartered down from £14,000 to £12,000 – to avoid further pillage and I help Henry to organise emergency relief for the town's poor and the demobilisation of the common Royalist soldiers. With nearly three thousand men to process, this takes some overseeing and queues of rake thin and tired men snake through the city waiting their turn with the New Model officials who, with brisk efficiency, take their weapons, record their names, witness their oath not to fight against Parliament again, then issue their passes home. Henry buzzes about behind the tables for hours answering queries and issuing orders.

I go into the town with some of the other wives, camp followers and medical orderlies as soon as the general gives us leave and I weep and rage at the sights that burn before my eyes. Colchester is no longer the prosperous wool town famed for its Bays and Says cloth and bountiful oyster catch but a vision of Hell. The town's walls gape and crumble like rotten teeth, the priory just outside them smashed and smoking. And from inside I can hear a deathly chorus of wails, moans and shouts, the occasional clash of steel or scream tearing the air. Within the town, every corner turn brings a new vista of desolation: houses torn in two, churches with crumbled towers, their ancient masonry filling the streets where skeletal children clamber on the rubble like rats, choking on the plaster dust. I pass through narrow, smoke-filled streets where starved and charred human corpses huddle on steps and in doorways, their rotting flesh swarming with flies. Royalist soldiers cower from our sight awaiting their fate while wide-eyed, ragged townspeople claw at us, knuckled hands outstretched for aid. An old man pushes a blanket of bones into my arms and I realise it is a baby, only recently died.

My mind is in freefall and I grope around in the darkness for God. How could He let us do this to one another? A year or two ago I would have thought of the Cause; the great purpose that lies behind our conflict. But now instead I wonder who is to blame? Who must pay? And how we can prevent this ever happening again.

While God must answer these questions in Heaven, and Henry and I pray daily for him to reveal his wishes, it is General Fairfax who must answer them on earth. The fate of the defeated Royalist commanders hangs in the balance. Where his terms for surrender granted parole to the ordinary soldiers, Black Tom demanded the officers surrender themselves to his mercy. Convention dictates that Parliament decides the punishment for the nobles among them, but the four common commanders will face Fairfax's military court. One manages to escape and another is reprieved on the grounds that he is an Italian, leaving two to face Fairfax's judgement: Sir Charles Lucas and Sir George Lisle.

'It is a nasty affair,' Henry explains to me as we climb into bed after another exhausting day. 'Under the code of war officers like them who continued to hold an untenable position and so cause unnecessary bloodshed, forfeit their claim to quarter. And they are doubly guilty for breaking their parole given at the end of the last war that they would not take up arms against Parliament again. Sir Charles Lucas also executed prisoners of war, which is a capital offence on its own.'

'Death, then?' I whisper the grim words as Henry snuffs out his candle.

I watch the wisp of white smoke curl up to the bed's canopy and wait for Henry's answer. Even without the light, I know he is setting his mouth. 'It has so rarely come to this before, it is hard to fathom,' he speaks eventually. 'It is one thing to know what is just, what is legal, another actually to carry it out. To shoot a man in the heat of battle is far easier than to give the order for the firing squad in the harsh sunlight.'

'But it is the lord general's decision?' I check.

'Ultimately. But he will seek advice from me,

Rainsborough and the rest of the General Council of officers. The hearing is tomorrow.'

'Sleep on it,' I urge. 'See what you think in the morning.'

Morning comes and with it a letter for me by overnight post. It is in Father's script so I tear into it eagerly, brandishing it to Henry as I swallow the last of my breakfast roll. As I open the paper, another smaller square tumbles out and I look at it in confusion.

'Perhaps it's for me,' Henry says and plucks it from where it has landed on my bulging belly before I have had a chance to scan Father's letter. Knowing no better, I begin to read and, within seconds, my stomach churns and I raise unwilling eyes to Henry, seeing the very moment he learns the terrible news written across his face in lines of pain.

Francis Thornhaugh is dead. Killed in a mopping-up operation after Preston.

Father had written the news to me and asked me to break it gently to Henry before giving him the separate letter in which he pens his condolences.

'My darling,' I say uselessly, rising numbly, reaching for Henry as if, by my touch, I can drain some of his pain.

He does not answer in words but with a howl. I shrink with bitter memory as the animal noise transports me back to Father when he learned that my oldest brother Robin had died at school. I look at Henry, tears blurring my eyes. My husband does not need to tell me what is in his heart. How Francis was his boyhood friend, the brother-in-arms with whom he rode to this war six years ago. How they had raised their local troop of horse together, pamphlets in their hands, prayers in their mouths, riding abreast on Juno and Trent. I think of Francis holding Liza lightly in his arms as he teased Henry over the toy horse. He was the only person I have ever seen with whom Henry completely and utterly relaxed; the one who first saw through Henry's coolness and stern swagger to the raging heart and brilliant brain beneath, just as I do now.

Henry cries, hunched in a chair, fists rubbing at his face like a child. 'This war,' he sobs, 'this King.'

I hurry over to Liza's cot and pick up the toy model of Juno. Retuning to kneel before Henry, I push the carved horse into his hands and press my own on his knees, trying to offer the comfort he once gave to me. 'God will gather him to Him,' I say, closing my eyes in my own prayer for the lovely Francis Thornhaugh. Henry stills a little. 'God will gather him to Him,' I say again. And then again and again I intone the words while Henry begins to rock backwards and forwards to the rhythm of my voice, the little horse clutched in his white hands.

When I attend the court martial in Colchester Castle a few hours later, I keep my eyes on Henry, who sits bleak and blank-faced as if all life and hope has drained from him. There is no flicker of emotion when he votes for the officers' deaths, no sadness or compassion when they plead gallantly for their lives.

Sir George Lisle and Sir Charles Lucas go to their fates bravely, facing a firing squad in the courtyard of the town's castle, their friends and enemies gathered solemnly about them. I decide to watch, determined to see all the brutality of this war for myself, and find a place out of Henry's eye-line with some of the townspeople. A hush falls over us all like mist as the death moment arrives. Lucas faces the muskets balls first and dies fiercely, baring his chest and calling us rebels. Lisle springs forward to catch his friend's body as it falls and kisses him tenderly. I watch the two men – one dead, one alive – wrapped in each other's arms and think back a few days to the wounded solider holding the dying cornet boy in the cart. I had thought the desperate love of soldiers for their brothers in arms a feature only of our army, united in its brave rebellion; had assumed our enemies were not made of such tenderness. But I was wrong. A painting of Mary, mother of Jesus, holding her dead son brought down from the cross, which I had seen at Hampton Court, comes unbidden into my mind as I gaze on the fallen men, lying either side of death. I know in that moment that this will become a modern martyrdom. That I watch the death of two new saints who will be added to the heretical Royalist canon.

Lisle lays the body of his friend down gently and rises, taking a step towards his executioners, crooking his finger at them to come closer.

'We'll certainly hit you, sir, have no fear of that,' the commanding officer says to stop him, his words half threat, half joke.

Sir George Lisle curls his lips into a smile almost from beyond the grave. 'I have been nearer to you, friend, when you missed me,' he says with a swagger that must cost him every last inch of courage, before he too bares his chest and calls for death. It comes for him in answer. In the next instant he is extinguished like a candle in a sudden puff of smoke.

CHAPTER NINETEEN

We have won the second war, just as firmly we did the first and with more ferocity. But, like a hammer blow on a horseshoe, the impact sends us flying in all directions, hot as sparks of fire. Our capitulating Parliament changes its mind again and reopens negotiations with the twice-defeated King, sending commissioners down to him on the Isle of Wight. The army – bloody and victorious – returns from Hell to react with uproar and the Levellers in London take to the streets. All across the country, county committees issue petitions demanding negotiations be abandoned until the King's conduct has been investigated. In the midst of it all, at the eye of the storm, sits General Fairfax, emboldened by victory but nervous as before to march onto the political battlefield. Naturally, he looks to his Council of Officers for advice.

'With Father still stuck in the north, you must take control of this,' I urge Henry. 'We cannot make the same mistakes we did after the last war.'

'We will not. Not this time.' Henry looks at me and I see a new determination scored into his face, a clarity and purpose shining almost from his skin itself. It has taken him a month to recover from Francis's death and the trauma of Colchester and I have had to nurse him mind, body and soul: bringing him soup when I knew he was hungry; mixing the ink and putting the pen in his hand when his fingers twitched; giving my body to him at night when he needed comfort, for all my swollen stomach. But now he has risen phoenix-like from the ashes with God's Providence clear in his mind: Parliament must be dissolved and re-elected and the King held to account before we make a new future for England.

We draft some template ideas together and Henry uses these to write letters at all hours of the day and night, constantly sending our new manservant out for more paper and fresh candles. He writes to Fairfax, to Colonel Hammond, the King's gaoler on the Isle of Wight, to each regiment and to every county committee. At his instigation, his own regiment refuses to comply with an order that would disperse them throughout Surrey, Sussex and Hampshire and petitions Fairfax instead for the King to be brought to justice. This will be the most important campaign of our lives and I sense, as I order in provisions to our new rented house in the precincts of Windsor Castle and block the stairs from crawling baby Elizabeth, that we are digging in for another kind of siege.

When the lord general writes rejecting Henry's advice, Henry paces about our tiny house, his boots loud on the floorboards. 'I must look elsewhere for allies,' he says and we both know who he means. I bring him pen and paper but he puffs and sighs, sitting down at his writing desk, then standing up again the next moment. He dances like this all day until some tragic news in the evening post makes up his mind.

Once again, Father's swirling hand brings death to the house.

'Rainsborough has been murdered!'

'What?' I drop a pile of newly dried linen and rush to Henry's chair.

'At Doncaster. He was slain in the street. Your father says it was a Royalist kidnap attempt that went awry.'

I reel in shock, thinking of the fierce young colonel, lying on blood-soaked cobbles. He was so vivid, for good or ill, his face turned always upon the future – a future that could be remade. And now he would not see it.

'But why would the Royalists target him above others?'

'Revenge for his part in Colchester, your father guesses.'

I stare at him in horror. 'Then you too could be in danger? You agreed to Lucas's and Lisle's executions just as Rainsborough did. And Fairfax gave the command!' We need protection – can you arrange some guards from the garrison?'

Henry gives a gesture of impatient dismissal: a half-shrug, half-shake of the head. 'No need when we are here within the castle walls.'

I move to object but see there is no point; Henry's mind is already moving on to more important matters.

'The Levellers will be devastated,' he says, sitting back in his chair despondently. 'He was their most powerful supporter within the army, their champion.'

'Their hero.' I sink onto a stool by the window and turn away to look out into the courtyard. Listless, I watch a constable as he moves from torch to torch lighting the flames against the gathering gloom, the vast walls of the castle looming above us. As he lights the lamp opposite, two beggar veterans cluster beneath it, inspecting the day's takings in their grimy palms. I draw the curtain with a shiver, half expecting to hear the clatter of assassins' hooves on the cobbles outside.

When I turn back to the room, Henry is writing furiously and I know without looking at the letter to whom he writes.

It is an invitation and we only have to wait four days for the visitor to come.

John Lilburne, the Leveller leader, firebrand pamphleteer and former New Model Army officer and friend of Father's, arrives too late in the afternoon for dinner and too early for supper. So I serve him small beer, bread and apple cakes.

Henry – who never thinks to eat at all unless I place a plate in his hand – is glad to be able to talk without the distraction of a formal meal. He has gathered all his wits for this meeting. 'You know what they say of him?' he had asked while we awaited Lilburne's arrival, Liza on my hip. 'That if the world was emptied of all but John Lilburne, Lilburne would quarrel with John, and John with Lilburne.'

'I might say the same of you,' I had said, smiling in reassurance and passing him Liza. 'You took on Denzil Holles, then poor Thomas Rainsborough. You even parleyed with the King himself. You can manage "Honest" John Lilburne.'

'Rainsborough's funeral held me up,' Lilburne says irritably without preamble or apology as he removes his hat and cloak in the hall. 'You should have seen it, Ireton.'

The absence of the word 'sir' takes me by surprise,

but then I remember Lilburne was a lieutenant-colonel himself before he resigned his commission in protest at our alliance with the Scots in 1645. For all his commanding confidence, he is a small, spare man, the thin arm that hands me his hat evidence of the months he has spent recently in prison.

'Three thousand mourners processing through the London streets,' our guest continues, the pride almost edging out the sadness in his London voice trimmed with northern vowels. 'And all with sea-green ribbons for him – his personal colours. I think we'll adopt it as our sign in his memory.'

I have a sudden recollection of Rainsborough's hat edged with sea-green and black ribbons which he swept off his head when we first met at Holton Park, the day I came to claim Henry. 'Where was he buried?' I ask, thinking next of our conversation about his London trading heritage.

'At Wapping, beside his father.'

The thought moves me: that the political adventurer and lover of the high seas returned home at the end, to lie among the traders and world travellers he so admired under the spiced air of the docks. I hope Heaven has mangoes, dates and bananas ready for him.

I break my reverie to offer Lilburne an armchair by the parlour fire. Henry pulls up the other and I flit between them with the food and drink before perching on a chair in the middle.

Lilburne eyes Henry shrewdly over his beer glass, Rainsborough's name hanging awkwardly in the air over us all. I will Henry to tackle it straight on and he does not let me down.

'Rainsborough was right,' he says quietly but with resolve. 'It brings me no pleasure to say it for we quarrelled most bitterly at Putney. But he saw some truths about the King and about the radical change we need that only became clear to me afterwards.'

After Colchester, he means. After Francis died.

'So you claim Rainsborough for your own now that he is dead,' Lilburne replies quickly. 'Would you be so quick to support him were he still alive, I wonder?'

'You are unjust, sir,' I cannot help leaping to Henry's defence. 'My husband was not to know the King sought another war; since this became clear, he has been coming around to some of your Leveller way of thinking.'

'But has your *father*, Mistress Ireton?' Lilburne swivels his gaze onto me, changing tack as adroitly as a skiff. 'Is it not rather convenient for General Cromwell that Rainsborough – our most powerful supporter in the army and the first man to call for the King's trial – was killed so unexpectedly? The assassins came from Pontefract, I believe, where your Father is stationed . . .'

I leap to my feet in outrage while Henry barks a curse. How could Lilburne think that Father was involved in something so despicable? I may have doubted him of late – over his role in the King's escape from Hampton Court, for example – but Father is no murderer.

Lilburne spreads his hands in an emollient gesture. 'I merely speak what I see, I mean no offence by it. Can you blame me if I am slow to trust you all? Your father had one of our leaders shot last year – or had you forgotten? The army you revere is after its own power.'

I expect Henry to leap after this shocking accusation like a hound after a hare but instead he puts a restraining hand out towards me and I sink back onto my seat. I turn to him and read his face as the swift anger drains from it to be replaced by determination. *Lilburne is testing us*, Henry's expression tells me. *He has landed the first blow, as he meant to. He had to pitch his stall at the outset. But now he will listen.* As if in silent answer, Lilburne replaces his glass on the table at his arm and links his fingers together. It is Henry's turn to pitch.

'The King must be put on trial,' he begins, 'and I am persuaded by your argument for a new written constitution.'

'First the new constitution, then the trial,' Lilburne interrupts. 'I will not countenance a purge of Parliament or the King's head on the block before the people's rights are guaranteed. Else what is there to stop the army stepping into the void to seize power for itself?'

Henry tilts his head but neither agrees nor comments. He continues: 'The new government will be based on the understanding that true sovereignty lies with the people.'

I listen to the heartbeat as this statement lands. It is a huge concession – just a few words showing how far Henry's thoughts have travelled this last year. I thrill at the revolution promised in this one simple idea: that sovereignty comes not downwards through the heavenly clouds from God to the King but upwards through the honest earth from the people to their representative Parliament. I expect Lilburne to leap for joy but he betrays no emotion, listening to every word Henry says, his eyes narrowing in the firelight.

'We must have a new Parliament,' Henry goes on, 'frequently elected and answerable to the people.'

'All of the people,' Lilburne interrupts again. 'All men to have a vote.'

'All *men*,' I echo without thinking.

Lilburne turns to look at me with new interest. 'You should hear my wife Elizabeth on that subject,' he says with a fleeting fond smile. 'The fiercest advocate for your sex you'll ever meet.'

I grin at him, momentarily forgetting our delicate task in my enthusiasm. 'I should like to meet her, in that case.'

Lilburne smiles fully at that and inclines his head to me politely. I glance quickly at Henry and am rewarded with the slightest nod in recognition of my diplomacy before he presses on, the rights of women shunted to one side of course.

'The King is to be elected.'

'No king,' Lilburne interjects with a pointed finger, his attention snapping back to Henry. 'No monarch or House of Lords.'

Henry holds his hand up this time. 'Wait to hear my proposal. We have an elected king – either this one, depending on the outcome of the trial, or another one of our choosing in his stead – and he has no veto nor power over the Parliament.'

'So he is a figurehead only?'

'If you like.'

'Then why bother with a king at all?'

Henry gives a small sigh, his patience starting to fray. 'If we cut too far and too fast, we will lose the people as we go. They understand kings; they are what we have always had.'

He is right of course.

Lilburne shrugs as if at the stupidity of the people for whom he advocates and reaches for an apple cake. He takes a bite before speaking again, still chewing as he begins. 'You intend to commit this to writing?'

'I am working on a manifesto now.'

'If you want our support, you must let us work on it with you; bring it around a little closer to our own *Agreement of the People*.'

I look at Henry, half expecting him to refuse; he guards his pen jealously. Only Father, John Lambert and I are ever allowed near his drafts. He let the King's man, the treacherous Sir John Ashburnham, play with his words once and that hardly turned out well.

'A committee,' Henry says after a moment's thought. 'Comprising Levellers, army officers, London Independents and MPs.'

'Sixteen men,' Lilburne specifies.

'As you wish.'

'If we send summons to them tonight, we can meet tomorrow at the Nag's Head in the City.'

'Very well.'

Sensing a fragile agreement approaching, I fetch the jug of beer and refill both men's glasses. They drink deeply, regarding one another carefully as they do, as if each measuring the other's commitment in the depth of his draught. As I watch them, I feel something inside me lightening; a delicate hope beating its wings like a fledgling. Could we yet pull this off? If the army leaders and the Levellers worked together, then perhaps we could build something lasting from the rubble.

Lilburne sets down his glass and rises to leave. I offer him some supper before he rides but he waves me away, so I fetch his hat and coat while Henry calls from the back door to the groom to fetch Honest John's horse. We gather in the narrow hall and Lilburne bows to me in gruff thanks for the hospitality.

'I'll send my wife to you when you're next in London,' he says suddenly. 'If you were in earnest?'

'Indeed I was,' I reply with genuine feeling. 'I would be delighted to meet her.'

Lilburne looks to Henry. After a moment, Henry puts out his hand and the Leveller takes it firmly. John Lilburne steps though the door but pauses on the threshold, his face lantern-lit under his hat in the growing gloom.

'You will have to persuade Fairfax and the Council of Officers. Can you do it?'

'I can and I must,' Henry answers, gripping my hand so tightly that my knuckles crack.

This becomes Henry's God-given mission and all else falls before it. By day, he works on his *Remonstrance* and hammers out each draft with the Leveller committee; by night, he writes to Father and Fairfax and prays to God for guidance. When, at last, the *Remonstrance* is ready, he rides to army headquarters at St Albans and presents it to the Council of Officers. They reject it swiftly but Henry does not back down and for day upon day he argues on his feet, sending me updates by the evening post if he is not too tired to lift his pen.

I do what I can to help: I write to Father to enlist his support but he replies from Pontefract, where he is still bogged down in the interminable siege of the last Royalist stronghold, to inform me he has pressed Fairfax to wait for one last appeal to the King to accept

Parliament's latest proposals. He pins his hopes on his old friend and ally Sir Henry Vane and the Independent MPs among Parliament's negotiators who are committed to securing the rights won in the war. But this is naïve. I agree with Henry that his old nemesis the MP Denzil Holles and his Presbyterian commissioners will win out over Vane in their eagerness for a deal with the King. It is clear that Father's thinking has not advanced as far as mine and Henry's and I crumple the letter in frustration at his irresolution. Surely he must see the way God has laid ahead now?

I apply to Lady Fairfax too, though I have less hope of agreement from her, for all our friendship. She has ever been a private admirer of the King and keen for his restoration on Parliament's terms and a return to proper and civilised society. She and Betty have that overwhelming desire in common. Anne responds with brief platitudes and I determine to do better when I next see her in person. There is nothing else I can do. Beyond these meagre efforts, I must watch from afar and wait, Liza crawling around my legs and the baby kicking furiously within me.

As the days pass, I feel the baby dropping into position and I know that the birth is near. Determined not to be caught short this time, I secure a local midwife and identify a doctor. When the first pains start I send a messenger for them and dispatch our groom to Drury Lane for Mother. Margery is on hand to help too, though the tottering Elizabeth must be her first concern. I feel the familiar creeping fear but resolve not to send for Henry.

Mother, when she arrives, is aghast.

'You must send for him! Why haven't you already?'

She twists the pearls around her neck in frantic agitation. 'You'll be having the baby tonight and if you had sent for him already he could have ridden here by the morning. What if something goes wrong? And we don't even have Betty here – she's at Northborough. Let me send a messenger to Henry.'

'No, Mother, absolutely not.' I pause to breathe deeply, bent over the back of a chair in writhing pain. 'The timing could not be worse. He is in the midst of persuading the army Council to accept his *Remonstrance* – every day matters. I won't be responsible for forcing him to choose.' I do not add that part of me doubts he would come, even if I did give him the choice, and that I would rather not put him to the test.

Mother is right as always and the baby bursts bloody from me in the deep black of the November night while I scream and howl at the moon. Minutes earlier, I kiss Liza and hug her to me in the last moments I can, frightened as before that I will not live through the birth; terrified in a different way this time at the prospect of abandoning my little girl. But I survive and the baby is born living. My own Betty has a sister and I am grateful for it, not just for her sake but for Henry's, for he would otherwise have missed the birth of his first son.

As before, I pass the first few days in a haze. Margery, still nursing Elizabeth once or twice a day, has milk for the baby and, once it is clear that her supply will increase sufficiently she takes the babe, and I sleep, seemingly for days on end, with little Liza curled up against me, too frightened by the screams she heard from my room to leave my side. This is how Henry finds us when he returns and I wake the instant I hear his low voice.

'Henry!'

'Dearest.' He bounds over to the bed. 'Why didn't you send for me?'

'But why are you home?' I look at him in confusion. He is haggard beyond description.

He grins then, his foxy features softening. 'The Council has agreed to the *Remonstrance* and the army is coming to Windsor. I did it, darling, I did it!'

I sink further into the pillow in relief and satisfaction at the correct decision I made to leave him be. 'You convinced them?'

'Most of the way,' he takes my hand as sleepy Liza snuggles towards him, 'but the news that the House of Commons was to bow to the King's request to come to London "in honour, freedom and safety" pushed them over the line. Holles and his faction were about to out-manoeuvre us again. Now we have seized control of events. My *Remonstrance* was put to Parliament two days ago and they have deferred considering it until they know the outcome of the negotiations with the King. They played right into my hands – even Fairfax concedes the need to force Parliament to dissolve now. It has sat uninterrupted and unaltered for eight years and believes itself immortal. But we must have fresh elections. We'll be marching on London within days, I guarantee it. It's a nuisance your father isn't here but Fairfax has summoned him to return south.'

I sigh happily, too tired to do more than smile at Henry with pride.

'But enough of all that,' he laughs, flopping down on the bed beside me and kissing my forehead as Liza clambers on top of him. 'Where's my new daughter?'

*

Henry is right. The troops come to Windsor but within days Parliament rejects the *Remonstrance* and the General Council of Officers orders the army to march into London. We go with our brothers: even though I should be lying in to recover from the birth, I sense the climax that is coming and refuse to be left behind. And so, wedged with cushions, sitting on a pillow and swaddled in blankets against the December cold, I jig and jolt the sixty miles to my parents' house in Drury Lane with Liza cuddled to me and Margery opposite holding baby Jane as Henry rides alongside us. I smile as I look upon my two girls, one named for my mother, one for Henry's, and close my eyes against the pain of the journey.

Within minutes of our arrival, while our trunks are still being unloaded, Henry disappears for Parliament without even a meal or a change of clothes. We hardly see him again for several days as the House sits all day and night furiously debating until – to our amazed horror – it finally votes to carry on dealing with the King. In despair, the MPs who lost the vote meet with the army officers to demand they take armed action against Parliament. Henry and Preacher Peacock suggest they force Parliament to dissolve itself and hold fresh elections. But the MPs – wary of their own seats – insist on a targeted purge of their opponents instead. Henry is not easy with the plan but sees no alternative.

Neither of us sleep much that night and before the Advent dawn has even broken, I watch by the low stubs of the candlelight as Henry dresses. He leaves solemn and silent and I kiss him farewell as if he goes to war. We both know before it happens that this is the day that everything will change. Father is still away from London but events cannot be delayed any longer. On instructions from Henry – though with the broad approval of Fairfax and the Council – Colonel Thomas Pride stations his men outside Parliament and bars scores of MPs from entering at the point of a musket. Those who object are arrested. London falls eerily silent as the city and the country teeters on a knife edge. In the space of hours, Parliament is reduced to a rump of members who support our revolution and the constitutional balance of the kingdoms shifts like thin plates of ice on a frozen fen. We are a ship forging into dangerous, unchartered waters and Henry is at the helm.

When, eventually, Henry returns to Drury Lane, he can barely speak, though his eyes are lit with fire. It is past midnight but still he goes straight to his desk in the corner of our dressing room to continue working. When I bring up a supper tray a little later I find him asleep in his desk chair, his body still rigid and alert for all his slumber, a paper clutched in one hand and his pen in the other. I lower myself quietly into a chair close by and guard him, though my watch is in vain when, minutes later, a loud banging and heavy tread up the stairs precede the flinging wide of the door. Henry wakes with a startled jolt and we turn together to the large figure, candlelit in the doorway, a weary smile on his lips.

Father strides into the room and looks from one of us to the other.

'What have I missed?'

CHAPTER TWENTY

WINTER 1648–1649

Preacher Hugh Peter is asleep in the pulpit. He is standing high above us, in the stone box that soars like a ship's prow over the congregation, his resting face peaceful among the carved angels. There are soldiers stationed up the winding stairs to the pulpit, two even wedged in beside him, their closely shaved faces staring fiercely out at us. And yet Peter stands still, silent and seemingly asleep.

I am sharing a confused look with Henry when a sudden shout rings out from the pulpit.

'I have been woken by a voice from Heaven!' Preacher Peter booms, his thin moustache quivering as gasps bounce around the church. 'The voice – an angel's voice – sang a song of music so sweet to my ears. This army, she said, this glorious army will dash the King and his kind to pieces, like rocks hewn from a mountain. If we do not act now, this King, this Barabbas, will go free while you, my brethren, the soldiers of Christ, will be crucified in his place.'

Noise ripples through the pews – sounds half cheering, half wailing – as Peter's flock sways to his voice in the bitter cold of the frosted church. I look around me, mesmerised at the effect and feel something swell within myself at the power of his prophesies. On my left, Henry stays quiet but the set of his face tells me he shares Peter's fears and urges, for all the violence of his language unsettles him. But Father, on my right, shifts crossly, shaking his head at his friend's fervour. Still, even after the King's betrayal we discovered in the saddle-bag letter, even after the savagery of the second war, he clings to the hope of saving his sovereign. It is as if he has advanced so far with us only to turn back from the precipice in fear at the last moment. While Henry has admitted he was wrong and embraced the Levellers' calls for change, Father cannot quite bring himself to do the same, even now. I turn away from him and inch closer to my husband, pulling my gloved hand from its muff to find his.

All London is gripped with wild fervour. Like Rome approaching the Ides of March, a madness of fear and anger builds. Prophesies are printed daily – those warning of coming Armageddon mingle with those promising a new Heaven on the booksellers' tables in St Paul's churchyard. Rumours of the army leaders' corruption and debauchery swirl from the presses onto the frozen streets: my father aims at the crown himself they write; Preacher Peacock has a new suit of red velvet paid for from the King's plundered coffers.

We women are also caught up in this cruel censure. My mother and the generaless are targeted in the press with the Royalist newspaper *Mercurius Melancholicus* accusing them of cuckolding their husbands, misappropriating money and competing to become Queen. They both feel the attacks keenly. Mother, frightened more than she will let on, keeps to the house while Anne writes to me that she has had a dream of her husband's head on a plate. Angered at this hounding, I show myself around the city running errands and paying calls until a wild pack of rabid apprentices spits at me in a narrow passageway behind St Paul's and I run from them onto Cheapside, fleeing home in a hackney. A prophetess, Elizabeth Poole, has dire visions of the King's death and warns the men now in power at Whitehall. Her vivid words and spectral scenes keep Henry from sleep while I am wrenched from our bed night after night by repeated bleeding as my body recovers from the birth. Pausing to look out of the window while I search for clean rags in the moonlight, it seems to me as if the whole white snow-laced city cries out to be spattered in blood.

Father and Henry splinter in different directions under the pressure. Henry spends his days speaking in the vast assembly of soldiers and Leveller civilians now convened at Whitehall with General Fairfax presiding to hammer out a final agreed text of *An Agreement of the People*. His focus is on John Lilburne and their conflating visions of the future. It is clear to him that the King must be tried, and a new government erected in his place. 'We have conquered the kingdom twice.' He spits the words out at supper. 'Enough is enough.' But he has not quite convinced Father of this necessity for he, meanwhile, seeks yet more compromise: securing the release of most of the arrested MPs and restoring many of them to Parliament and working quietly with the House of Lords to put a final offer to the King, now at Windsor: would the King accept a figurehead role? If not, would he abdicate in favour of one of his sons?

'It will fail,' Henry chides as Father fills their pipes in the witching hour before bed. 'The King will not have it, or have you learned nothing of him these last years?' Then in the privacy of our bedchamber, Henry reveals deeper complaints about Father to me: 'I have done his dirty work for him, conjured the arguments, attacked Parliament itself, pushed us forward, and now he can sweep in and act the conciliator.'

'But that is the secret of your partnership, the reason you can achieve so much together,' I cajole, seeking to smooth the wrinkles between them and hoping it continues to be true.

Once again, our house at Drury Lane becomes a hive of activity and barter, even drawing the dark-eyed courtier-lawyer Bulstrode Whitelocke, the Commissioner of the Great Seal, to our dinner table to gossip and charm before speaking soft words of a mediation to cool the temper of the army. Betty too comes with John from Northborough in a spirit of peace. She claims they have come to see in Christmas with us even though the feast day has now been abolished altogether by the Presbyterians in Parliament as a sop to the Scots. The ban on Christmas is no great loss to me or my parents who, like other Puritan families, never celebrated it much, believing it an empty holiday invented by Rome. But Betty, Dick and Harry still harbour a fondness for the old trimmings of the season – the mincemeat pies and plum pudding, the holly and ivy garlands and folksongs – while Mall and Fanny complain they never got to enjoy them.

Betty's yuletide explanation for her arrival at Drury Lane is thus a plausible one, though I suspect her true motive is to pressure Father on the King's behalf. I know she clings as fiercely to the idea of saving the comforting charms of the old world as I do to finding the clean equities of the new. We recognise this inverted mirror in each other instinctively, and a new coolness creeps into our relationship. We no longer flatten a lace edge, pluck a stray hair or brush a crumb from each other's clothes as we pass. Neither do we seek each other at the end of each evening, weighing the day in whispered words in a shared pool of candlelight as the servants close up the house around us. Betty consents to coo over baby Jane in her holy innocence but otherwise she spends her charm on Father, whom she asks daily for updates on the latest negotiations with the King.

She is in this posture on Christmas Day, which has been a working day as any other, and so it is not until close to ten in the evening that we are all together and she can drape herself on the chair closest to Father for a late supper. Despite myself, I cannot helping drawing her out; motivated as much by missing her companionship as by my irritation with her blind-sided views and obsequious attentions to Father.

'I hope the King has enjoyed keeping Christmas today in contravention of the law,' I say. 'I hear he ordered a new suit of clothes for it.'

'How lovely,' Betty says smiling, 'I wonder what cloth and colour it was. Do you know, Father?'

Father chuckles at Betty's customary interest in worldly vanities. 'I will make sure to tell you, my dear, if the Earl of Denbigh has seen him today and sees fit to include a description in his letter. I expect it will arrive any minute.'

Henry shakes his head with a tut. 'The King won't

receive him or, if he does, he'll dismiss the offer out of hand, mark my words.'

'He may not,' Father says placidly. 'I will retain this hope to the last – that we can salvage something of monarchy from this king.'

Betty places a soft hand on Father's arm. 'It is admirable of you to continue to try for a deal, Father. A traditional settlement must be best to heal the country.'

Dick smiles in agreement across the table, thinking, no doubt, of the simple country life with Dorothy he longs for. Harry, by contrast, frowns a little and glances at Henry who is staring down at his plate.

'Nonsense,' I counter Betty, braving the clouds I see darken Father's face at my outburst. 'We have all been through enough to dance this dance to the King's tune again.'

'You would have our world torn down around our ears.' Betty turns to me, her tone surprising me in its fierceness. 'You would have us ruled by soldiers in the streets and the pulpits.'

'I would have us governed fairly under a new constitution,' I fire back, 'with the men who fought and died for our liberties given some share in a new age. You were not at Colchester, you do not understand. Did Olly die for nothing to change?'

'It is you who do not understand!' Betty cries, tears springing suddenly into her eyes. 'How can you claim Olly so? What do you know of Val? I can tell you neither he nor Olly went to war to upend our lives. You invoke their names simply to stir Father to your own ends.'

John shifts uncomfortably in his seat and I wonder if

it is the argument that unsettles him or his wife's emotional mention of the boy she loved before him.

'Enough.' Mother speaks firmly, her own voice choking at the mention of Olly. 'Your father has had a tiring enough day without you haggling over him like wives in the market. And think of the girls,' she gestures at Mary and Frances watching wide eyed at the far end of the table.

I glance at Father and see he has left us, his eyes vacant while his mind and heart fill with memories of his dead sons. I think for a moment of going to him and taking his hand, but my loyalty lies with Henry now.

The sudden entry of a messenger shakes us out of our argument and I watch with my heart in my mouth as Father, roused from his reverie, unfolds the letter and sinks his eyes into the page.

'You were right,' he says at length, each word growing in volume. He keeps his eyes down and for a few moments none of us knows to whom he speaks. Am I right? Is Betty? Is Henry?

Henry.

Father raises his gaze to his son-in-law, his broad face twisted into something halfway between a smile and a snarl. 'The King will have none of us. He sent Denbigh away.'

Henry sets his face in a wordless expression: *I told you so.*

Father looks up and down the table, his eyes searching each of ours in turn before they rest on Betty. I think he will turn to her, but his gaze lasts only a few moments before it sweeps on to me, where it stays. It is an invitation and I seize it.

'Press on, Father,' I urge. 'Leave the King to the fate he has chosen and listen to Providence. Enter the Promised Land, do not turn back to Egypt.'

He stays silent and I search my soul for Scripture to lay at his feet. 'Think on Gideon, vanquishing the Midianites, killing their king then refusing the crown to return to his farm. He was ever your hero, think on him.'

Henry rises to his feet and walks around the table to Father. Placing a hand on his shoulder he takes up my tune: 'We did not know last year that he was not negotiating in good faith. But now we know he was playing us off against each other so as to divide us, drive down our terms and play for time until he could prosecute another war to reverse the outcome of the first. That war was his undoing. "*You shall not defile the land wherein you are: for blood it defiles the land; and the land cannot be cleansed of the blood that is shed therein, but by the blood of him that shed it*",' he quotes from the Book of Numbers.

Henry's words hang low and bloody over us all. Awed, we await Father's judgement as if he were Solomon himself. Seconds stretch like pulled dough. Thinner, thinner. Then a snap.

Father speaks.

'The King told us last year we could not do without him,' he says, his words low and painful but sharp as knives. 'Then, perhaps we could not. But now, by God, we can.'

'No, Father, no!' Betty clutches at his arm, frantic tears coursing down her cheeks.

But he does not turn his eyes from me. Once again I feel the earth move, although this time I think and pray it is for good.

CHAPTER TWENTY-ONE

Jane wriggles howling in my arms, her face wet with tears, wrinkled and flushed red as her little fingers claw the air. Helpless, I bounce and hush her, one hand plunging into pockets and down the side of the sofa in search of a linen square to wipe her streaming nose. Lost in the immediacy of calming my baby's raging despair, I do not notice the strange woman at the parlour door until she speaks.

'She has gripe. Give her sugar water with chamomile. My youngest, Tower, suffers from it greatly.'

'Tower?' I am too stunned by the name not to ask.

The woman smiles, stretching her thin face under a pretty but tattered mob cap. 'Named to honour my husband's being wrongly imprisoned there when the babe was born.' Her plain speaking matches her plain dress and finally the pieces fall into place.

'Mistress Lilburne.' I offer a small curtsey and gesture to her to sit while I ring the bell for Margery to take Jane. Freed from my squirming armful, I relax gratefully on the sofa beside my guest, worried the next instant that she will judge me a poor mother. Something about her unnerves me and I find my social advantage a sudden embarrassment, pained at how rich and gaudy my red silk dress appears draped besides her sturdy brown cloth skirt. I offer her small beer and biscuits but she refuses.

'I would not hold you up long on this of all days, but I promised John I'd come,' Mistress Lilburne begins firmly, and I glance at the clock, seeing only ten minutes remaining before I must leave. 'John speaks of you as being a friend to our cause so I thought I would see if you can intervene with your husband.'

'I know Master Lilburne has given up on the debates at Whitehall,' I say, joining her in coming to the point swiftly.

She sighs, though whether this betokens weariness with her husband or with the situation it's hard to tell. 'He is a stubborn fool. But an honest one. And he sees what will happen here. He maintains that Parliament must be dissolved and a fresh House elected before anything more is done, else it will conspire to guard its own power.'

'My husband agrees with him,' I say quickly.

'Aye, him, but none else. And he alone cannot carry it. This Rump Parliament will perpetuate itself and if this court they have convened to try him executes the King in the coming weeks, who's to stop its members ruling hand in iron fist with the army in perpetuity. Why else would your General Fairfax and so many other high and mighty men called upon to judge the King hasten out of London? They see what's coming and want no part of it.'

I smart, knowing the seam of truth that runs through her words. But those men are cowards in my eyes: unwilling to gamble their earthly futures and risk their immortal souls to do what must be done. 'But I understood your husband was presenting the new *Agreement of the People* to Parliament today,' I press on, unwilling to accept her bleak view of these events. 'If they accept it—'

'They won't. They will set it aside for "future discussion".' She twitches her fingers around the phrase to indicate irony. 'And why would they not? This is the Parliament that prosecuted and won the war. The remaining MPs don't want to subject themselves to biennial elections by an expanded electorate and then half of them lose their seats. They have power now and the army wishes them to be seen to keep it, to mask their own tyranny in a respectable cloak.'

I am shocked both by her lucid forcefulness and by the subject of her words. 'My husband, my father and the General Council would not abandon the Levellers now,' I urge. 'Not when they have achieved so much together. They do not aim at tyranny of any kind.'

She looks at me with an almost kindly indulgence and shakes her head. 'The officers will side with the MPs – the men of their own class who share their bone-deep conservatism, not my John and his London apprentices. You mean well, no doubt, mistress but you are misguided.'

Normally, I would bridle at such a criticism, yet somehow I do not mind it from Elizabeth Lilburne. I recognise I am in the presence of a higher political being – a woman who has spent her life petitioning, protesting and pamphleteering, regardless of her sex – and I have too much admiration for her to care how she addresses me.

'You are truly your husband's confidant and helpmeet,' I observe.

'As are you, I am led to believe.'

We smile at each other as if some deep understanding and sympathy has passed between us.

'I will do what I can,' I assure her with a rush of confidence.

'And I will ask no more,' she replies, rising to her feet. 'You should join us women next time we demonstrate – you'd find it interesting. Let me know how the chamomile water takes.'

We are approaching the door when it opens before us to reveal the elegant figures of my friends Catherine Harrison and Frances Lambert with another lady I do not recognise following behind. They curtsey automatically before examining my guest closely. I prepare to introduce them but Elizabeth Lilburne merely nods before slipping from the room.

'Who was that?' Frances Lambert asks as soon as the door closes.

'Elizabeth Lilburne.'

'Goodness! "Queen Besse", they call her in the press, just as they call my Lady Fairfax "Queen Anne". Which one of them is more after a crown, do you think? Or is it in your mother's sights?'

'Nonsense,' I snap. 'She's a fine woman and a selfless one at that.' I brush her silliness away and Frances draws herself up proudly in response. She has a new confidence to her, I have noticed, since John Lambert swept the Scots before him in the last campaign. He has just bought a mansion in Wimbledon and I've heard it's a palace to rival the King's; Lambert – and his wife – no doubt expect great rewards in the new government.

'Bridget,' Catherine Harrison interjects sweetly, coming forward to kiss me. She draws her companion forward as Frances sweeps past us to take the best spot on the sofa, where she sets about preening herself like a cat. 'This is Mistress Fleetwood.'

'Charles Fleetwood's wife? I am glad to meet you,' I say, hurrying to recover my civility, 'I know your husband well; a brave man and staunch to the cause.'

'Mistress Ireton,' the young woman curtseys with a shy smile, her wide face framed with blond curls not unlike Charles's own, 'my husband tells me the first time he met you, you took him for an intruder and struck him with a log. Or was it a candlestick?' She gives a little tinkling giggle and I cannot help joining her, my bad temper gone.

'Indeed I did and he was most good humoured about it.'

She beams with a new wife's pride. 'Charles worships your father and admires your husband greatly, I am so pleased to make your acquaintance.'

'I thought I heard voices.' Father's shaggy head appears around the door as if his ears had been burning. 'And what do I find but all my best young ladies in one place!' He swings into the room. 'Mistress Fleetwood, Mistress Harrison,' he bows in turn but his eyes light up when he sees Frances Lambert. 'Frances! My dear,' he strides across the room and takes her proffered hand, 'how is my favourite friend from the Scots campaign?'

'Very well, general, thank you kindly.' Frances produces a dazzling smile and Father pats her hand.

'Do you know, Biddy, your friend Frances gave us excellent company on our last campaign, really lightened our evenings and kept us from brooding. I was immensely grateful to young Lambert for bringing her.' He turns back to Frances. 'I am only sorry he does without your company now, my dear, as he finishes up in Pontefract.'

Frances smiles. 'It became such a drawn-out business, general, that he suggested I return to London and oversee the move into our new house with the children.'

'Ah the Wimbledon mansion! I hear it has a great garden which Lambert will love. I look forward to seeing it,' he replies, laughing. 'In truth, I could do with John here to join us at the trial but someone has to mop up the last resistance in the north and I can think of none better.'

I watch them closely, alive to the particular jovial closeness that Father loves to strike up with pretty and witty young women; a reflection, I have always thought, of the uniquely female household he grew up in and perhaps, I hope, a slight compliment to his fondness for Betty and me. Looking from Father's smiles to Frances, Catherine and Mistress Fleetwood, I realise that these are the women who matter to him now; the wives of his closest army colleagues, the bedfellows of the new rising stars of the army. The general and generaless's time is over.

Father takes his leave of Frances. 'We must have a hand of piquet and a catching up, my dear, when this grave business is done with. But for now I must hurry back to Westminster; I only popped home for these papers. Jean!' He calls for his valet and the Frenchman hurries into the room and helps Father into his hat, gloves and cloak, pausing to brush a hair off his master's shoulder.

'We are coming too, Father,' I say quickly. 'I've ordered a hackney carriage; ride with us and save time.'

He pauses, taken aback. 'You mean to attend the King's trial, Biddy? I cannot believe your mother would wish you to go: it will be a grim business.'

'We are resolved, general.' Frances comes towards me and takes my arm in sudden friendliness, our spat seemingly forgotten. 'This has been our war too and we mean to see this end for ourselves.'

Father spreads his large hands in acceptance and gives a little bow to us. 'Very well, my dears. I will come with you. Though let me check the carriage over first – you never know if these hackneys are roadworthy and I won't have any harm come to my ladies.'

The King looks so small. Plucked from the whirlpool in which he usually lives with courtiers and servants circling him, dogs at his feet, glass of wine in his hand – stripped of every aspect that renders him a monarch – alone he sits. A man only. One figure so easily lost in the huge expanse of Westminster Hall. Yet he cannot be lost. For all that the worldly signs of his kingship have gone, the King retains an aura about him; a dignity and importance. Perhaps it is the way he draws all eyes from the room and holds them, stunned in his spell. Maybe it is the black velvet suit and cloak he wears; solemn in aspect but the most expensive colour of dye and cloth that any of the hundreds of souls in the great Hall has ever seen, set off magnificently by the shimmering star, badge and shiny blue ribbon of the Order of the Garter.

How Betty would feast her eyes upon him, I think, for all that he is the prisoner at the bar.

He sits at one end of the vast Norman hall, facing his judges arranged in rows along benches – Henry and Father frowning among them. All about, great stands of seats have been erected on scaffolding to contain the swelling, noisy public who murmur and point, some clasping their hands in happy expectation, other shaking their fists. From where we are sitting, in the top row of one of the public galleries, I tip my head to the huge banners that stream from the hundred-foot-high hammer-beamed roof: the King's colours captured by our army at Marston Moor, Naseby and Preston – great pictures hanging in the heavens with all the symbolic power of stained-glass windows in a cathedral, the story they tell every bit as potent. The Hall drips with history, the stones remembering earlier trials: the rebel William Wallace, the traitor Guy Fawkes, the King's friend the Earl of Strafford in the prelude to the war. Each ended in death. Yet none of their ghosts can rival God's anointed come to be called to account as any common criminal. Could any future scene ever match it?

The names of the judges are called first – the whole list, even those who are absent – and I am settling on the hard bench, wishing I had thought to bring a cushion, when General Fairfax's name is given. Suddenly a woman's voice cries out from the stand, a few rows below us and at the other end: 'He has more wit than to be here!' The whole Hall erupts in commotion and I strain forward, catching a glimpse of a masked woman at the centre of the swell. The mask does not fool me, I would know the shape of her shoulders and the set of her head anywhere: the generaless.

'She said she wouldn't come,' I whisper to Catherine. 'What is she thinking of?'

After the initial flurry of excitement the court settles down and the rest of the judges' names are read before the prosecutor, an obscure lawyer called John Cook, reads out the charge; a document of such legal complication Henry and the other judges have been poring and sweating over it for days, vainly seeking for some mechanism within the Common Law with which to try the King who is its fount.

'Tyrant, traitor, murderer, the author of the second war . . .' Cook pronounces to stunned silence until the King, roused from inaction by his words, reaches forward to tap him on the shoulder with his cane. Instantly, the silver top knocks off, falling to the stone floor with a heavy clanging thud. Hundreds hold their breath while the knob swivels and circles on the flagstones, rolling and rolling as time swells around us, until eventually it comes to a stop. The King looks about him as if in full confident expectation that one of the assembly will spring forward to pick it up for him, as someone has done in every moment of his life before this one. But no one stirs. I watch in amazement as the King sits there, the seconds stretching silently around him. Eventually, when none of us can hold our breath a moment longer, he rises and slowly steps to retrieve the top from the floor, retreating to his chair and fixing it to his cane with short, deliberate twists of his fingers, his eyes lowered to the task.

Cook, recovered from the shock, reads on. When he

has finished, John Bradshaw, the president of the court, leans forward to demand of the King how he answers the charge put to him on behalf of all the good people of England.

'No!' Lady Fairfax bursts out again from our gallery. 'Not the hundredth part of them! Oliver Cromwell is a traitor.'

I gasp in horror and glance at Father, who sets his face like stone. How could she? Frances and Catherine rustle awkwardly on either side of me as I gape at my first friend and mentor; my second mother. The court officials, their patience gone, hurry to where Anne sits and attempt to prise her from her seat. She struggles at first then relents, climbing down the stands with her head held high, shrugging off her guards as she continues to shout outrage at the trial. And so our generaless is ejected from the scene. I watch her go with equal parts horror and sadness, for I do not see how we could ever meet as friends again after what she has just said about my father. Despairing, I turn fresh hate upon the King for sowing such discord among the friends who first united to face him in the field. Will there be no end to the casualties of his stubborn pride?

But the King maintains his pride in the face of all. Undeterred, he asserts and reasserts his position. What lawful authority is this ranged against him? How can he enter a plea when he does not recognise the legitimacy of this court? Again and again President Bradshaw urges him to answer the charge, else they cannot proceed. But he will not. Eventually, Bradshaw has no choice but to press on nonetheless, calling for Cook's arguments and evidence. The King sits back in his chair and watches, silently, as his emboldened subjects unpick the stitches of his life.

Though I now loathe him with every inch of my being, I must admit some admiration for the King's calm persistence. And as we reconvene day after day with the drama of the trial playing out before us, he remains staunch and stubborn in his position. Meanwhile, behind the scenes, his accusers think and plan, argue, fast and pray. They gather in Whitehall, cloaked and hatted against the cold draughts of the old palace state rooms, to peer over candlelit paper and into each other's souls as they nudge one another onwards. It is a campaign as any other with powerful enemies and former friends on all sides pleading for the King's life. Anxious men visit our house at all hours and letters pour in with each post; even one from the French King Louis, which I see for myself on Father's desk – deeply inked and grandly embossed on rich satin-smooth perfumed paper. Even the sanctuary of Father's bedchamber is breached: evident in the bags under Mother's eyes and Betty's tiptoeing tread up the stairs each night with warmed wine, a filled pipe and private pleas.

But now that Henry and Father are once again of one mind and united in their cause, they carry all before them. Henry sober and stern, Father driven by an almost giddy mania. Together they defy their opponents and strengthen their allies.

Nothing can save the King now.

We all march, as if in dreaming sleep, towards the execution of our sovereign. Sentence is passed upon him, the death warrant signed with trembling hands: Henry ninth on the vellum, Father third. The King bids farewell to his children but this time Father remains unmoved, convinced of what God intends be done. We slip deeper from reality into unimagined dreams. And it is when dreaming, indeed, that Henry wakes with a start in the dawn light of the King's appointed day of death shouting for pen and paper.

'The King is dead, long live the King!' he babbles as I stir beside him, fumbling for the rushlight.

'What?'

'If we kill him before we have abolished the monarchy itself, nothing will stop the world proclaiming the Prince of Wales King in the very moment his father is extinguished.'

And so in the last hours of the King's life, he waits with a communion of red wine and bread while the Commons passes an Act to blot out his line. All that is left, then, is to take his body.

I go. Alone. None will come with me but I do not care. I have to see for myself the axe fall upon his neck. I dress warmly, a baked potato in my muff that scents the frosted air around me, and wait among the crowd in the street of Whitehall beneath the Banqueting House, wriggling my toes in the cold. The King, dignified in the fading light of his looming death, steps through the window of his father's mansion and onto the scaffold, mouths words that I cannot hear, prays and, Christ-like, blesses his killers. Frozen, in deathly silence and groaning dread, we watch the sky fall in on all we have ever known.

I pray with my eyes open. As the axe, high in the air, flashes cool in the thin January sun, I speak to God, asking him not to look on Charles Stuart in this instant of his death but to think of other sacred souls instead. I tell Him of the starved of Colchester and Tom the cornet boy, remind Him of Francis Thornhaugh and Val, dead in violent blood and anguish. I raise Olly to His sights, not fevered now but smiling in the fenland sunshine.

I pray for a new world as the blood runs.

CHAPTER TWENTY-TWO

SPRING 1649

'Lord, what do I know?' Father stares at the template coin shining fresh as a baby's skin in his palm. 'Henry, you deal with this, you have a view on everything. The Council wants a recommendation.'

Only I notice Henry bristle slightly at the mention of our new executive body. In a grievous oversight Parliament has not nominated him to the powerful Council largely, Henry suspects, in punishment for his urging its dissolution alongside the Levellers. It is a hard medicine to take for the man who, more than any other, brought us to this place. Harder still for the ablest administrator in all the new Commonwealth. But Henry does not take it personally. Putting his disappointment aside, he plunges into the ocean of work that accompanies the founding of a new government with undisguised relish.

Each day he buzzes between the new committees that spring up like saplings to manage the administration of the state, agendas and minutes stuffed in his bag. He sits on the committees for answering the Scots

Commissioners; for preparing a Declaration explaining and justifying the King's trial; for tackling public criticism of the new Commonwealth and the High Court of Justice; for surveying the crown lands and considering what is best done with them; for the courts and assizes; for abolishing the Deans and Chapters; for appointing commissioners for the Admiralty, amending the impressing of seamen and mariners for the fleet and settling martial law at sea.

The more Henry takes on, the more he finds time to do, as if the Lord has given him more hours in the day than anyone else. And to my joy, he apportions some of those hours to me to help him. With Jane – now recovered from her gripe, thanks to Elizabeth Lilburne's remedy – sleeping most of the day, I leave her every instant I can to lose myself in Henry's world. He brings me problems, shares his questions, his doubts. He runs things by me, checks my views. I read, I listen, I draft, I think, I advise. And each day I feel closer to my husband; fond, trusting bonds growing and knotting between us like woven willow branches. At last, at long last, I sense I have proved myself to him. As if the King's death has freed us from the old world to emerge into the new one together.

Henry takes the coin, examining it closely before setting about a detailed discussion with the engraver Master Simon, now hovering at his elbow. I watch him fondly; he is as skilled at taking tasks onto himself as Father is at delegating them.

I shake my head in wonder. 'New coins, new Seals, new liveries for the bargemen, new names for our ships. A new Council of State and committees for foreign affairs, the army, the navy and Ireland. So much created in so little time.'

'And so much destroyed,' Betty mutters, cuddling little Cromwell on her knee as he turns the page of Mother's conduct book looking for pictures. 'Monarchy, House of Lords, Privy Council, Star Chamber, Court of Wards . . .'

'I fought for the Lords; you know that, my love.' Father leaps to his own defence. 'It was not my desire they be abolished.' He looks reprovingly at Betty and their eyes meet for a moment of rediscovered sympathy.

'Yes, but what have we left?' She is undeterred in her complaints. 'A rump of the Commons with no fresh elections in sight, nor written constitution to constrain them. A Council and sub-committees managing day-to-day government with the army behind their shoulders.'

I look at Betty with surprise; her political understanding and interest sharpens by the day. Her words recall to me those of another Elizabeth – Mistress Lilburne – warning me in this very room that these events might happen. Linking them both, I marvel at this topsy-turvy time when the views formerly widest apart as theirs had been can now meet around the back. Though it is always easier for those in opposition to government to unite this way than for those who govern. We were a broader coalition when we fought the King than we are now we rule in his place.

'There is some truth in what Betty says,' I speak, warmed briefly by the slightest hint of a surprised smile I receive from her in reward; a faint echo of our former closeness when life was simpler and so were we. 'It would be better, surely, to have secured a new constitution first – put Lilburne's *Agreement of the People* to the people to give this new government the broadest possible base of support.'

'It wouldn't have washed, Biddy,' Father says swiftly, rising from his chair and walking over to Betty to tickle little Cromwell under his chin. 'Whatever is given the Levellers, they would demand more. And who knows what would have happened with new elections at such a volatile moment.'

Henry looks up from the coin and catches my eye. 'I feel uneasy about it, Oliver,' he says carefully. 'They were our allies when we needed them. And now they're saying we have betrayed them and we are worse tyrants than the King. I don't like it. "England's New Chains", Lilburne is calling this government.'

'He stirs up mutiny,' Father's tone is short. 'It's a plain fact that we cannot please all. For every concession we made to them, we'd face criticism from many other quarters. We must strap down the hayricks and strengthen the Commonwealth as best we can until all the storms of opposition and rebellion are defeated. Then we can experiment at our leisure. You know I am not wedded or glued to *forms* of government; all that matters is that they are fair and just and do the Lord's work. Here' – he springs towards Henry with a sudden thought and plucks the coin from his hand, returning to his grandson with it hidden in his fist – 'which one?'

My little nephew laughs and looks from left to right and back again before patting Father's right hand.

'Ahh!' He opens the palm to reveal the coin. 'Clever lad. You ask your mother to keep this safe for you. An heirloom, if you like. A reminder of the day when we saw the King's piece gave way to the Commonwealth coin. I'll give it to you and you can give it to your grandchildren. You can tell them you were there at the beginning of the new age.'

Cromwell snatches up the treasure and puts it straight in his mouth.

I lunge forward with a mother's instinct but Betty has whisked it out before any damage is done. 'Not in your mouth! What have I said? Only food and drink go in your mouth.'

Cromwell grins and looks up at his grandfather who chuckles back at him in answer.

Everything and nothing has changed. I stare into the future with equal hope and anxiety and entirely bewildered. I know, I feel that we must drive forward and forward. But to what? Restless and unnerved, I re-examine the landscape of my life, its contours at once familiar and unknown. For the first time in many, many months, perhaps years, my whole family is under one roof save for Aunt Liz. With Father and Henry working every day in Whitehall, Grandmother, Mother, Betty and I are reunited in domesticity – Mary and Frances skipping about us and the grandchildren on the floor. It is hard not to think back constantly to our lives in Ely before and during the first war, back to when we all shared the same small rooms, back when my days were structured by chores, back before I had been beyond the fenland horizon or had seen into the depths of men's souls. Back before Oxford, before Colchester, before I had watched the King's blood drip from an axe.

Mall is happiest of all to have the entire family together and she wanders in and out of rooms checking us off on her fingers, always wanting to know where each of us is. Fanny, meanwhile, is even more precocious. Now ten years old she has become a student of politics, always carrying a book and declaiming her latest muddled understanding to anyone who will listen. She is a firm favourite with the men, often to be found on Harry's or John Claypole's lap or hovering at Father's elbow while Mall cleaves to Mother and Betty. Betty looks set to stay at Drury Lane for at least a few more months before she and John return to Northborough. Harry is on leave from his regiment, while Dick is serving time in Lincoln's Inn eagerly anticipating his wedding to Dorothy and his new life of country squiredom.

Old patterns emerge and new ones too. John, at a loose end after having resigned his commission in the army, goes out drinking and gambling in the City with Dick; one day picking up a vast debt from a bookmaker, the next coming home with a new hunter to stable. They drag Harry with them when he has nothing better to do but, if Henry is at home, Harry stays in, hanging on his every word. Henry is fond of him in turn – tutoring him in the finer points of administration and governance when he has a few spare minutes. But Henry has little to do with Dick or John; their light and easy lives a world away from his own so heavy with responsibility.

We women, meanwhile, slip into our familiar positions. Mother discusses the household management with me; Mary and Frances watch Betty as she dresses each morning, learning the secrets to her easy beauty; and I take Grandmother her supper trays once again, relishing the quiet of her company in the candlelight while we pray together for the day to come. But though our roles are in these ancient ways familiar, living in London, and now in the public eye, has changed the very fabric of our lives and pulled Betty and I further apart from each other. Where Betty once spent her meagre allowance on ribbons in Ely market, now she whisks Mary and Frances off to the Royal Exchange for a cup of sweet chocolate and to watch her spend money that John does not have on Venetian glasses and French perfume. Talk now is of new fashions and romances and what pattern of wall-paper Frances Lambert has chosen for the garden room at her Wimbledon mansion, and while Mother indulges this, I scowl at it, retreating to my papers and prayers. Occasionally, we snap at each other: I tell Betty she is spoilt and naïve and she blames me for pressing Father towards the King's death. 'The midwife', she has taken to calling me, since our last argument when she accused me of helping the birth of this 'new and terrifying future'.

It is as if our living among the fighting all these years has taken its toll on us. That somehow we have emerged having learned different lessons and found conflicting places in a new world. Our rancour wounds so deeply because of the love and understanding that will always live between us. I still look at her and know her as my second self, reading her every mood and thought, her feelings reflected in every choice of outfit and how she has arranged her hair. But we do not chat over our chores as we used to. We have servants now to attend to the jobs we used to share and we look to our husbands for the late-night conversations we used to have in bed. Although we are under one roof and sharing the same table, we belong to separate households and families now; we are mothers and wives before we are daughters and sisters – the same flesh pushed into a new mould.

I am confronted with another female mould one morning when I receive a scribbled note from Elizabeth Lilburne. Restless at home, I check on the girls with Margery, snatch up my cloak and set off on foot for the rendezvous she suggests. Betty would never step into the London streets without a servant, I think as I hurry along the Strand, but nothing can frighten me after the hellish streets of Colchester. Mistress Lilburne bade me meet her at a tavern near the Charing Cross and I push open the door expecting to search among a sea of men's faces for hers. But an amazing sight meets my eyes. The front room of the inn is full of women, many dressed in Rainsborough's sea-green colours or with sea-green ribbons in their hair, some clutching glasses of small beer, others holding children, some with their heads bent together over tables strewn with paper. The wall of sound that greets me is at a higher female pitch and I stop at the thrilling sight and sound of the largest number of women I have ever seen in one place.

'Mistress Ireton,' Elizabeth pushes through the crowd towards me. 'I hoped you'd join us. Come, have a drink.'

'Mistress Lilburne! I cannot believe my eyes.'

'Ha! So many women, you mean? A good sight indeed, a sight to please God.'

I smile and nod, hoping the Lord is indeed pleased and not affronted by so many of Eve's daughters striding into the world of men. 'What is the occasion?'

'My John has been arrested again, and some of the other Leveller leaders too.'

'No!' My shock is genuine and I believe she sees it.

'I knew he was unhappy with the new government and becoming a thorn in its side, but I never thought—'

'Well, luckily I did,' she cuts me off, impatient not with me but with the task in hand. 'I saw it coming and the girls and I have been preparing our petition to Parliament for their release. We march with it any moment now. Will you come with us?'

I pause, torn between the thrill of joining them and the fear of what Father or Henry would say if they saw me. To show some sympathy with the Leveller interest in private is one thing, to march with their women openly in the street quite another. And what of the terrible things the Levellers are saying about our army leaders in the press?

She is watching me, testing my position. 'Here,' she reaches to a table and hands me a copy of the petition. 'Read it for yourself and if it doesn't stir you to action, go home to your children with no hard feeling from me.'

I take it from her, dropping my eyes to the page. A child barges past me, a woman carrying a placard comes the other way, knocking my shoulder as she goes, and I thread my way to a space by the wall so I can read in peace. The words leap from the page and into my soul. The general content I sympathise with – demands for the release of Lilburne and the others, calls for lower taxes, more work and fair treatment by the Government – though I baulk at the criticism of the Army Council. But it is the preamble claiming the women's right to speak that blazes through me like fire: *Since we are assured of our creation in the image of God, and of an interest in Christ equal unto men, as also of a proportionate share in the freedom of this Commonwealth . . .*

I am jostled again and look up to find the room emptying as the sea-green maidens slip into the street like mermaids into the sea. I find Elizabeth's face in the crowd. 'I will come!' I shout towards her, 'I will come.'

We march down Whitehall to the palace of Westminster in the spring sunshine with arms linked and songs of praise on our lips. Children scamper beside us and women wave from windows as their husbands scowl from doorways. My heart hammers in my chest as we swell onwards and onwards, crowds parting before us like the Red Sea; and I Miriam leading the women of Israel in our song of deliverance. As a spring tide we crash into the doors of Parliament, waves breaking on rock as the Sergeant at Arms bars our way.

'Go home to your husbands!' he shouts, batting at us as if we were a swarm of flies. A knot of MPs gathers about him, attempting a show of solidarity. 'Go wash your dishes!' one of them heckles, to which a woman in front of me replies, 'We have no dishes left to wash' to much nodding and agreement from the rest. 'We are handing out free corn and coal to the poor,' a more sympathetic MP says before he is shouted down by a colleague: 'It is strange for women to petition.'

'It is strange that you cut off the King's head!' Elizabeth Lilburne calls back instantly, 'Yet I suppose you'll justify it.' There is much laughter at that and I chuckle along with a light-headed giddiness, even though I will maintain my support for the King's death to my dying breath. 'Let us through!' Elizabeth shouts and we push and heave until the sergeant bends before us and we burst through the door, through the passage and into the lobby of the Commons itself.

Immediately I see Father's familiar broad back and curling hair as he stands in earnest conversation with a group of men. I duck from view, hiding my face with my hand, but the crowd behind me surges forward, pressing me closer and closer to him. The women a little ahead of me reach him a moment later and pull at his cloak, bringing him whirling around to face them. Angrily they shout and brandish copies of the petition in his face, chanting the names of Lilburne and the other prisoners. Father throws up his hands half in peace, half in exasperation and I see his hat knocked to the floor.

'What will you have?' he cries, scanning the sea of faces anxiously until, through the chinks in my fingers, I see his gaze stop on mine. He stares at me, his words dying on his lips, then he frowns and shakes his head.

'Those rights and freedoms of the nation you promised us!' a woman shouts in reply to him while around me chants of '*Agreement, Agreement*!' rise into the air. The girl beside me pulls a copy of *An Agreement of the People* that my husband and John Lilburne worked so hard on, and brandishes it over her head as a preacher does a bible, sea-green ribbons fluttering in her hair. My mind empty and my heart full, I tear my eyes from my scowling father and gaze up at the pages, clutched creased with love in her hand. Watching the paper soar in the air I wonder, for the first time, if those words, each weighed and measured so carefully and now stamped in determined ink, are what we fought for all along.

CHAPTER TWENTY-THREE

'Do you know where I have been this night?' Father asks me back at Drury Lane. He stands there in the hall, his face set in hard sadness, the eyes when he can bring them to look on me lit by anger.

I had been waiting for him, determined to face his wrath squarely, and step forward to take his hat and cloak as I have done so many hundreds of times before. I hear Henry's familiar steps on the stairs behind me but I do not turn, neither does he speak. He knows this is between Father and me.

'Where?' I ask despite my fear at the answer.

'Quelling a mutiny,' he states plainly, dropping onto the hall bench to remove his riding boots and search for his house shoes – something he only does when his feet ache with weariness. 'Your friends the Levellers took up arms against their officers in Bishopsgate. They're owed pay and are reluctant to be sent to serve in Ireland, I know that, but there are plans to sell what we can of the King's luxuries to raise funds and we cannot ignore the Royalist threat gathering across the Irish Sea. Besides, the men must learn they cannot draw weapons on their commanders in any circumstance or else we are all lost.'

He thumps a gloved fist on the bench with each word as if to stamp it in stone.

I must speak my mind, I owe him that much. 'But if their leaders had not been arrested for sedition, they would not be so angry,' I say, biting my lip.

'If they did not call us tyrants in print, they would not be arrested!'

'If Parliament had considered the *Agreement* and submitted itself to the people in fresh elections, they would not think you tyrannical. You spoke warmly of them once.'

'They must trust in Parliament.'

'But a Parliament it is now treason for them to criticise, just as it was once treason to speak ill of the King!'

Henry steps between us, trying on Father's usual habit as conciliator for size. 'What will happen to the mutineers?' he asks calmly, a hand on my arm as he brings us back from the spiral we have tumbled into with practical concerns.

Mother emerges from the dining room, drawn out by the sound of Father's voice.

Father sighs when he sees her, exhaling some of his former anger like an ancient dragon of his family's native Wales expelling a puff of fire. 'Fifteen arrested. Fairfax wants the leader shot. I've pleaded for clemency but he is adamant.'

'The poor man!' Mother exclaims though her thoughts turn at once to rest on Father as they always do and she kneels beside him and strokes his hand.

I watch their tenderness gaping in horror. John Lilburne returns to me – his voice angry as he reminded me at Windsor of Father's shooting one of the Leveller leaders the year before: *The army you revere is after its own power.*

'Surely you can prevail over him?' I ask, marvelling that the lord general still has such standing after his avoidance of the King's trial and the generaless's shocking outburst.

'Believe me, I've tried,' Father says. 'Not least because the man will become a martyr to his people. To your people.' He shoots me a dark look and Mother turns to me confused.

'Like Rainsborough,' Henry mutters, shaking his dark head, and I shiver at the thought.

Two days later the soldier Robert Lockyer is shot against the wall of St Paul's cathedral and his iconic martyred status is sealed like the strongboxes built by the locksmith who bequeathed him his name. Thousands take to the streets for his funeral, though I do not join the Leveller women on their march this time. Shockwaves pulse through the army and regiments rise in mutinous answer in Salisbury, then Burford. Father and Fairfax ride west to quash them – without Henry, to the relief of us both. There is fighting in the cobbled streets of middle England and, once again, ringleaders are shot. But this time the Leveller presses go silent and no sea-green flood washes through London. The Levellers are cowed, Father is angry and I no longer see Providence's lamp lighting the way ahead.

Burned and bruised I slip back into the safety of my family, clinging to little Liza and baby Jane and avoiding Father as, over the coming weeks, all about us enemies rise to challenge our fledgling Commonwealth. Our ambassador Isaac Dorislaus is murdered in cold blood by Royalists at the Hague; an act that shocks all of Europe. The Scots, who have proclaimed the dead king's son King Charles II, threaten our northern border, while Prince Rupert's fleet clashes with that commanded by our General-at-Sea Robert Blake off the coast of Ireland – a vengeful Royalist invasion from Ireland or Scotland is only a matter of time. Meanwhile, Father's name is dragged through bloody ink in the press, attacks coming from all sides: he aims to become King, according to a scurrilous broadsheet called *A Coffin for King Charles; a Crown for Cromwell; a Pit for the People*; he is having an affair with Frances Lambert, another rag claims, and, morbidly fascinated, I read the dirty paper in secret and spirit it out of the house before Mother sees it. For all I have disagreed with him of late, Father does not deserve such vile hatred and, softened and saddened, I begin to fill his glass and take him his pipe once more – whenever I can reach him before Betty or Fanny, that is.

I know we do not have long left together. With the growing threat from Ireland, Father is appointed to lead an expedition to cross the sea and prevent the Royalist forces invading our shores. I know too that wherever Father is sent, Henry will follow close behind. And so I prepare to lose both my father and my husband to a third civil war.

'Let me come with you,' I plead to Henry as he bustles about his preparations, stuffing his trunks so full of books and papers he leaves no room for his linens or wash bag. 'You won't look after yourself properly,' I scold, starting to repack his things, 'not without me to make sure you eat, wash and sleep.'

He pauses to smile at the truth of what I say. 'And yet I am unmoved,' he says, planting a kiss on my cheek. 'Jane is far too young to be left by her mother, Elizabeth too young to travel. And it wouldn't be safe for you to be on campaign in a foreign country.'

'I could manage,' I urge, 'I'm used to the privation of army life. And if you set your face against the girls coming, I could leave them here with Mother and Grandmother.' In truth I know I am pregnant again, but I do not tell him in case it makes a difference.

It doesn't. Henry will not be moved.

Henry is not to depart for a few weeks yet but Father leaves sooner. The boys are solemn at the parting, the girls cry, Mother draws deeply from her wife's well and Betty prepares to return to Northborough with John, as if there is nothing left for her at Drury Lane when Father is gone. I shed no tears, but beneath my armour I convulse with feelings. Frustration at Father's inability to see things as I do blends with fear for his safety. Anger that, once more, he steps onto the world stage while I must melt back into the shadows mixes with pain at our parting with less than the full friendship I had begun to enjoy with him. But I say none of this, of course. Together, for the last time, we give Father a private farewell feast before Parliament dispatches him publicly with prayers and pomp in a carriage drawn by six grey Flemish mares. As we watch him transition from our family realm to the public, we abandoned Cromwells draw closer together, as pearls threaded tight on a string. We do not know when, or if, we will see him again and the heavy knowledge binds us as nothing else could.

*

'Lilburne is to be freed on bail,' Henry tells me when he returns from Parliament late one night not long before he is due to leave.

'Really? I am pleased to hear it.'

'I thought you might be. For myself I do not know what to think. He is no enemy of mine and yet I seem to have become an enemy of his.'

'And yet, for a short time, you were so near to one another,' I say, wishing that the pragmatic pressures of politics had not interrupted their collaboration. 'Why has he been released now?'

I am crossing the room to pick up Jane from her crib when Henry's answer stops me in my tracks.

'His wife and children are dying.'

'What?' I wheel around, the room spinning.

'They all have the pox and there's little hope, I believe. We in Parliament felt that he should be allowed to be with them.'

I think of Elizabeth and her blazing hope, of baby Tower and his gripey tummy.

Henry reads my face. 'You're not to go near there,' he says, his tone dropped into severity. 'I'll not have you place yourself and my children in danger for them.'

I do not reply but busy myself with the baby instead; I will not lie to my husband.

The next day, of course, I go. I enlist Dick to my service, sworn to secrecy, and he manages to discover the Lilburnes' address from one of his drinking pals and insists on taking me himself. We take a hired hackney carriage across London to a squalid area east of the Tower and leave it a street away, so we can approach the house on foot. It is a small, timbered building, wedged between a printers and a pawn shop, buffeted by clouds of dust from clattering carts passing on their way to the docks. We pick our way across a stream of filth and hover at the door. Steeling myself, I knock.

After a long wait, the door opens a foot and I recognise the haggard face of John Lilburne peering out at us. 'You can't come in,' he says shortly before he seems to recognise me and opens the door a little wider with a wild, malevolent look, 'though, on second thoughts, do come in, then you can carry the pox back to your husband and father – it's they who should be lying here, not my Liz.'

It is a vile thing to say but I sense he is not in his right mind, so I merely press the basket of food, medicine and clean clothes I have brought with me into his surprised arms while Dick shifts from one foot the other behind me. 'Can I see her at least?'

He shrugs and pushes the door open to its full extent. Peering over his shoulder, I can just make out Elizabeth's blond head in a bed across the room, in the far corner. Beside her is baby Tower's cradle and two small pallet beds with a prostrate child on each, an old woman leaning over them with flannels. One of them is sobbing but Elizabeth does not move.

'Does she live?' I ask, my voice choking on the pitiful sight. 'Do the children?'

'For now. But for how long? At times I can hardly tell if they are still living.'

'Have they seen a physician? Is there anything I can do?' I press.

But Lilburne is already closing the door upon us. 'God bless you,' I call through the vanishing crack – loudly enough, I pray, for her to hear me.

I hear nothing further until some days later when Henry, incensed, thrusts a thick pamphlet into my hands on the very steps of the house as I open the door to him. I stare at it, taking in the title with mounting horror: *An impeachment of high treason against Oliver Cromwell and his son-in-law Henry Ireton*. I stare into Henry's scowling face, my own an open question.

'Lilburne. Denouncing us for tyrannical traitors. The Government will take no notice, but still . . .'

'Still,' I repeat, staring once more at the vile bundle of pages in my hands. 'But what—'

'Look at the preamble,' he interrupts.

I drop my eyes once more to the horrible thing and turn it over with disgust to the reverse of the title page. There, in tiny scrawling print, is a letter from Lilburne to the reader and I only have to read a few lines to understand what has happened:

> *God's wise hand having thought it fit to exercise my faith and patience by taking away both my sons from me, who were the greatest part of my earthly delight in this world, and brought my wife and daughter even to death's door . . .*

My heart lurches to think of little Tower dead in his cradle. I think of my own dear girls and Henry's love for them. As I read on, the print beginning to swim before me:

... I am resolved to be as prodigal of my pen and life for the future as my bloody and tyrannical adversaries are of their oppression, cruelty, tyranny and blood-thirstiness ...

With a yell I fling the pages from me, watching as they whisk away from each other and spin into a dirty drain further along the road.

Henry steps forward to take my arm and I cling to him fiercely, crying for us all.

The next day, I beg Henry not to go to Ireland. 'To leave London now, after that!'

But he merely pats my hand and calls for his horse. 'I have no choice,' he sighs, swinging into the saddle. 'I go where I am sent. And there may be some good work I can do after the fighting is done.'

He is about to click his heels when I lunge forward to tell him about the baby – if something happened to him, I would never forgive myself if he hadn't known. Gripping the top of his boot in both hands I force a smile, though it is like pulling teeth.

His smile, though, is one of genuine joy. 'I hope it's another girl!' he says, leaning down to kiss my cheek tenderly. 'My brave, brave Biddy,' he whispers. '"*A house and wealth are inherited from fathers, but a sensible wife is from the Lord.*" I didn't inherit anything from my father, but you came to me from God.'

And then he is gone.

I watch him ride away along the street with a foreboding that grows even as he fades from view. How many months or years will it be until I see him again? What if he falls in battle? For all his bravery and strength, he is not a natural soldier. I had thought myself happy with Henry rather than deeply in love. But as my heart squeezes from my chest and rides away with him, I know the truth at last.

PART THREE

Eighteen months later, Ireland

CHAPTER TWENTY-FOUR

WINTER 1650–1651

The sea surrounds us, swelling grey and mysterious, filling my vision and assaulting all senses. The fathomless depths below call to me as one water-born in the Fens, though countless trips across the gentle streams of East Anglia in wide-bottomed barges and shallow punts hardly prepared me for this: to cross the Irish sea in a warship. Having only ever seen the sea in the distance, as a haze on the horizon, I had no idea how vast, how vital it would be up close, nor how it would feel to place myself at its mercy.

Liza is sick constantly and so I spend most of the journey above deck, holding her hair back from the biting wind as she stands on a barrel retching over the high side of the massive hull. I clutch her fiercely and stare out over the waves. As we surge forward towards a new land, I think of all the riches of God's creation: *so is this great and wide sea, where innumerable small and great beasts creep. There go the ships: there is that leviathan, whom Thou hast made to play therein. These wait all upon thee; that thou may give them their meat in due season*. And I wait upon the husband whom I have not seen for almost a year and a half. Not much further now; I can see the cliffs through the salted clouds of sea spray, white with snow like icing atop a cake.

I land an adventuress, though the party of officials and soldiers who salute our arrival upon the jetty with bows, fanfare and cannon treat me as a visiting dignitary. In part this welcome is for me, as wife to the new Lord Deputy of Ireland – the civil and military ruler of the country. In other parts, though, it is in tribute to my escort: Lieutenant-General Edmund Ludlow, one of the king's judges, now a councillor of state and sent to be Henry's new second in command; the hundreds of reinforcements he has brought with him under his command; and the three commissioners who travelled with us, come to investigate and report back to Parliament on the condition of Ireland. I had met Ludlow before and am pleased with his competent escort. Yet he is brusque and I find him hard to like, for all I admire him and all the others who stood their ground, took their own immortal souls in their hands, and signed the King's death warrant.

Tired, hungry and with dusk approaching, I am relieved that the formalities pass quickly. In only a couple of minutes Liza, our maid and I are helped into a carriage that takes us the few miles to the inn where we will pass the night before travelling onto Henry in Dublin – a three-day journey, perhaps four. It is a restless night. Liza sleeps in my bed and drapes herself across me in utter exhaustion while I lie wakeful and strangely nervous about my coming reunion with Henry. Though I have written to him every week for all these months – and he replied whenever he had time or a ship was sailing – still the time and distance between us has loomed large, especially after the birth of baby Bridget ten months ago. Since then I have struggled to hold onto my old self as, once again, I emerged from the birthing chamber a new physical being with another baby grown and squeezed from me. Would Henry find me much changed? Would he notice the lines, sags and marks etched on my embattled body which has made three babies in less than four years?

These thoughts worry away at me as we set off for Dublin after an early breakfast of small beer and hot rolls. Yet this self-absorption is soon driven from me by the sights through the carriage window. Working our way up the east coast of the island, we encounter habitations no more than burnt-out shells, beggars crouching under rubble walls and ragged families straggling along the roads, their worldly possessions strapped to their thin backs.

'Where are they all going?' I ask Ludlow when his horse draws close to my window.

'They are being moved on. We are forcing the Catholic Irish from any land deemed strategic. Your father battled hard to conquer this eastern part of the island, we'll not risk losing it now he's gone to Scotland.'

'But surely?' I struggle for the words as a man pulls a skinny little girl, not much older than Liza, from the path of our coach. She rights herself and watches me pass, her father's tool bag clutched in her hands as if it were a precious doll. I know that as Royalists these people are our enemies, and as Catholics they are beyond the salvation of the Lord. But still the little girl's thin face lingers in my mind after it has gone from my sight. 'To turn families like this off their land' – I ask – 'is it really necessary?'

Ludlow gives me a hard stare and I resent the assumptions about my weak and feeble womanhood which I watch pass across his face. 'Your husband must do what is necessary to secure this country and bring it safely within the Commonwealth,' he says brusquely. 'You may feel sorry for these people but it was they who massacred our Protestant brothers in 1641 and dragged us into these endless wars in the first place.'

Of course he thinks that; he has always been on the hardest fringe of the army. I consider challenging him: some say the stories of those massacres were grossly exaggerated by John Pym and his party as they marshalled the country to arms against the tyrant king; but I cannot believe our glorious cause was erected like the house the foolish man built on shifting sand. Whatever the truth is, can this really be the destination we aimed for? To burn villages and turn little girls out onto the road? I sit back against the shabby leather seat and take Liza's hand.

Worse is to come: it is hardly nine in the morning when our procession turns sharply west and we travel some miles inland before regaining our northerly course.

'Why the diversion?' I call once more to Ludlow when he is within earshot.

'The Lord Deputy instructed us to skirt around Wexford,' he answers, steering his grey horse's neck closer towards my door. 'It is still in a ruinous state and we cannot be sure you would not see unburied bodies by the side of the road even now.'

Wexford. I shiver. I know the name, of course, all England does. It was one of the only towns that refused to surrender to Father's army, with dire consequences. Some two thousand died, it is rumoured, though we in the Cromwell household far away in London could never bring ourselves to ask Father or Henry how this had happened in our letters. I shift across the bench seat to look out of the other window. Across the furthest treetops, on the pink horizon, I can just make out the jagged lines of the tallest buildings of the cursed town. In between lies a blackened patchwork of scorched fields, still scored by the deep trenches of siege warfare I remember from Colchester. Against the skyline, I make out the unmistakable swinging forms of corpses hanging from a gibbet and I close my eyes against the sight. Liza presses her doll against me and begs a story and so I lose myself gladly in a fabled fairy-tale world.

I am relieved beyond measure when another two nights' broken sleep and days' rumbling journey bring us clattering into the cobbled streets of Dublin. Within minutes we pull up outside a smart townhouse with a blue-painted door at the top of a wide flight of steps. I lean out of the window, blinking in the sunlight. There, framed in the doorway, is Henry.

It takes me a moment to recognise him. He is even thinner than before, his vulpine features pulled tighter across his cheekbones, his high white collar looser around his neck. And the linen no longer a sharp white but a dirtier cream shadowed beneath a straggly beard flecked now with grey. The effect of the wispy peppery hair set against sallow skin gives an altogether marbled look to his face, in contrast to the strong black hair and bright, pale cheeks I remember. Henry's grey suit is fine – new, I assume, as I do not recognise it – while a chain of civilian office hangs gleaming against the fabric. The initial effect is impressive but I know to look at his fingernails (dirty), his cuffs (frayed) and his old boots (scuffed). My gaze returns finally to his eyes: these at least are bright and smiling but ringed with fine lines, pools of dove-grey skin sunk beneath them.

I have left him too long, I think, pasting a smile onto my face.

'Is that Father?' Liza whispers, though it is not the change in him that confuses her but a three-year-old's lack of memory.

'Yes, darling,' I whisper back and I hand her out of the coach first so that she can climb the steps and clamber into his arms, fearless for all she does not remember him.

'My dear Bridget,' Henry addresses me over Liza's head, the formal note in his voice occasioned, I hope, more by the ranks of servants and officials ranged around him to welcome me than any cooling in his affection.

'Husband.' I drop a curtsey as custom dictates and draw up my skirts to tackle the steps.

'Welcome home,' he says and, taking my hand in his, draws me up and into the house.

I feel myself at sea once more. This is not my house and yet I am mistress. I did not engage the servants, arrange the furnishings, nor choose our suppliers. I struggle to understand the accent of the housekeeper and hardly know how to address her. As soon as I have refreshed myself and sent Liza with the maid to the kitchen for milk and biscuits, Henry takes me on a tour of the house. It is large and grand – palatial even, as befitting the formal residence of a nation's governor. And yet the rooms are cold, the air scented with lemon water and the surfaces gleaming: evidence that an army of servants has spent days cleaning and dusting rooms that had lain unused. Dust motes fill the air, glimpsed like showers of rain wherever the crisp January light falls through the windows, telling me that carpets and sheets have been shaken out hastily before my arrival.

I am touched at the efforts, touched too at Henry's eagerness to show me my new home as he flings doors open and talks a little too quickly. But more than that I feel an unease that he has clearly been living here as if in a glorified office. Only his private study, the front reception room and one of the bedrooms show any sign of previous habitation. I know he has spent most of the last year traversing the country on campaign, living in tents and alehouses and that this grand house is only the Lord Deputy's official residence when the army is in winter quarters. But other men would have relished the luxury after the hardships of campaign life, would have ordered in the best food and wine, filled the rooms with fine society and settled into a few months of comfort. Not Henry: the tour around the house tells me all I need to know of his long working days and Spartan living and the strong smell of tobacco that lingers about him suggests he is smoking too much.

He leaves me to wash, rest and dress for supper while he returns eagerly to matters of business. 'You don't mind, do you?' he says, already leaving our bedroom. 'I have a delegation from the town's metalworkers' guild coming to see me about new regulations; then a meeting with a committee of justices of the peace to discuss the administration of local courts; and then I must debrief Ludlow and introduce him to the other staff. Oh and some letters to write. You have everything you need? We will catch up at supper.' And he is gone.

It is nine o'clock before Henry has finished work and we manage to sit down. I had seen Liza to bed already and had a joyful reunion with my brother Harry who has been over in Ireland for the last year deputising first to Father and now to his brother-in-law Henry. It is clear the two have become close and the sight of them with their heads bowed close together over the evening's dispatches, sentences begun by one finished by the other, gladdens my heart. There could be no stouter companion for Henry than Harry, who was always a bright and eager soul even as a boy, with none of Dick's lethargy nor Olly's shyness. He's the most like Robin, I think, looking across the dinner table at his confident, shining face which grows more like Father's by the day. Where Robin was Father's golden boy before the Lord took him, I suspect Harry is now his nearest replacement. I am struck silent and winded by a sudden longing for my older brothers who, even in memory, feel so very far away from me in both time and space. What would they think if they could see us here at this grand table governing a foreign land?

Talk turns naturally to the condition of Ireland as Henry and Harry seek to bring Lieutenant-General Ludlow up to speed.

'Only three towns remain to be taken,' Henry says, 'Limerick, Athlone and Galway: all to the west and south-west of here. We had to abandon them when winter set in, but we'll be able to take them on in the spring.'

'So few?' I am quite amazed.

'Father's campaign was astonishing,' Harry says, waving a bread roll for emphasis. 'When he arrived with the main force, the vast majority of Ireland was held by the Royalists under the Marquis of Ormonde, in bed with the Catholic Confederate groups. Prince Rupert's piratical ships blockaded Kinsale in the south waiting for their so-called "king" in exile, the dead king's son, Prince Charles, to sail from the Continent and lead an invasion force against England. Only this area around Dublin was controlled by an army loyal to our Parliament. Our new Commonwealth was in grave danger. Then, in a matter of months, Father captured twenty-eight towns, all but two of them with little loss of life and generous quarter always granted to the defeated when it was accepted.'

'Thanks to him,' Henry takes up the story, 'Charles Stuart turned his hopes from Ireland to Scotland. He abandoned his deal with Ormonde and the other Irish leaders and struck a dirty deal with the Scots, renouncing his own religion and – as his father had before him – promising to establish Presbyterianism in England if they would invade on his behalf.'

I know the rest: the Council of State summoned Father back to England last summer and we saw him briefly in London before he rode for Scotland with the newly promoted Major-General Lambert and Lieutenant-General Fleetwood at his side. He is there still and, when I left for Ireland, Mother and Grandmother were once more nervously awaiting every post for news of his safety. Only when Parliament sent Father on his latest campaign to Scotland was he himself promoted Commander-in-Chief of the army after Lord General Fairfax refused to fight his Scottish brethren. The general and generaless had finally quit the scene and Father – risen all the way up from his humble start as a local cavalry captain – was in charge. And, with him gone, Henry is left to complete the conquest of a hostile country and set about its rebuilding and return to prosperity and good governance.

I go back to Harry's words, determined to understand the horrors of this third civil war completely for myself. 'All but two towns?'

There is a momentary hush and Harry flicks a glance at Henry for guidance.

'Drogheda and Wexford,' my husband speaks at last, the names heavy on his tongue. 'They refused to surrender, despite Oliver's warning that they would receive no quarter, and when we sacked the towns, there was a great loss of life.'

'Thousands, we heard in London,' I press. 'Civilians too.'

He nods slowly, his eyes refusing to meet mine. 'The troops were ordered to spare none in combat, nor priests. And in the confusion, it was hard to tell the ordinary folk from the combatants.' His words come uncomfortably and I can tell that he is uneasy with his own account.

I feel a sickness creeping up into my throat: Not my father, not our army.

'Perfectly reasonable,' Edmund Ludlow interjects, his tone bullish. 'Entirely in accordance with the rules of war, and nothing to what the armies on the Continent have been doing to each other for decades. All the veterans from those wars, whom I met as mercenaries in the ranks of our New Model Army, were amazed that we always granted quarter in the civil wars in England. And, furthermore, I understand that the tradition here in Ireland has been not to grant quarter even when it has been promised.' He takes a long drink of wine and sets his glass down with a thud, certain in the rightness of what he has said.

'But so many lives taken,' I say quietly, 'and civilians too.'

'Though more lives were saved in the long run,' Harry replies softly, as if he can spare my feelings. As if I deserve to have my feelings spared when women and children have died. 'After Drogheda and Wexford, the other towns surrendered quickly and accepted peace terms. Else this would have been a longer, bloodier war of attrition.'

It is all very rational, these words, these explanations and justifications of men sitting in safety around a table, wine in their hands. I know there to be an intellectual truth in much of what they say. But I cannot help the questions in my heart: what of the women, what of the children? What of the lives destroyed in blood and fire?

Later, when Henry and I are at last alone, I sense his wanting to return to the subject in the privacy of our confessional chamber. I decide to help him towards it, once the lamps are low.

'Can you tell me about the sackings?' I keep my voice soft.

'I can barely speak of it to you, Biddy,' he answers in the gloom.

'Was it worse even than Colchester?'

'Much worse.'

I am shocked, scarcely able to believe that any scene of war could have been more hellish than that I saw at Colchester. But I want to help my husband come to terms with it. 'I heard what Ludlow and Harry said: there were rational reasons for it.'

Henry clicks his tongue. 'Maybe. Certainly. Perhaps reason was there beforehand in the decisions taken and afterwards in the justifications drafted. But in the moments of bloodshed themselves – I can only tell you that some spirit of vengeance entered into your father.'

I shiver, despite the fire being banked up high against the winter cold. Vengeance. It is a notion I cannot reconcile with the father I know. Something I had thought not in his vocabulary.

'He felt as I did after Colchester and after Francis's death, I think.' Harry hears my bafflement and etches his words carefully, as if writing them on a page in pencil and not in ink. 'Only more, even more. Mad things happened.'

'We heard a rumour in London that at Drogheda Sir Arthur Aston was bludgeoned to death with his own wooden leg.'

Henry sighs then blows out his night candle and climbs into bed beside me, his cold hands feeling for mine.

'You have to understand, Biddy. This new war – this third war – is even worse than the last, as that was than the first. The canvass of fighting has broadened again, the violence has deepened, the stakes are raised. This is no longer a war between a king and his Parliament in

England seeking to bring each other to better terms: a war between gentlemen with the lord general sending hampers to the Duke of York. This is a war to defend an infant state against enemies who now have spilled out beyond our borders into Ireland and Scotland, across Europe and into the new world itself. Gradually, the great powers of Europe are recognising our Commonwealth – Spain is the latest. But still our ambassadors abroad risk their lives to represent us. We face a pirate fleet at sea and a new Royalist invasion from Scotland. You won't have heard while you were travelling, but only two days ago, Charles Stuart was crowned King in Scotland on the ancient Stone of Scone. He will invade England when the campaigning season begins again and only your father will stand between him and our utter ruin.'

Henry sighs, long and deeply, his whole body moving with the exhalation.

This is truly a confessional, I think. He has been carrying these weights on his chest and has been waiting to unload them to me. I squeeze his cold hands with my own and decide to offer comfort in the ways that only I can.

'I understand,' I say simply. 'I see your heart, I see your burdens. I am here now and I will take care of you. Shall we pray together?'

Silently he climbs from the bed and comes around to my side to help me down. We kneel beside the bed, the carpet unfamiliar under my knees, and bring our foreheads together until they rest against each other, our hands clasped, separately, beneath. Neither of us speaks – this is a moment for silent, personal prayer – but I catch the merest whisper of words on his lips: 'The bodies, the bodies—' I place a hand on his fingers and wait until, gradually, our breathing falls into rhythm, my own heart calling to God to stop the bloodshed and to save my husband.

Eventually, when I am sure he is at peace once more, I take his bony face in my hands and kiss it tenderly. Relief and warmth flood through me as when a hot compress is set upon grazed skin. I am with my love, where I belong. We have found each other once more: now he has unburdened his conscience, now we are alone with God. I think of the words of marriage advice Father wrote to me a few months after our wedding: 'That which is best worthy of love in thy husband is that of the image of Christ he bears. Look on that, and love it best, and all the rest for that.'

When Henry's hands, which come first to my face and into my hair, range down over my chest and waist, I remember with a start my changed body and the baby left behind in the rocking crib at Mother's feet. I realise that Henry hasn't even thought to ask about her or about how I am after bringing forth a third babe from my womb. But as he lays me down on the floor of our room, our desperate kisses finding tears on each other's cheeks, I do not mind.

CHAPTER TWENTY-FIVE

The months I spend in Dublin are an unsettling time for us all. Reunited with my husband after so long, I feel the kind of bridal love for Henry that I did not feel when we were first married. Then, our marriage bed felt like a marketplace: our coupling a transaction accepted rather than relished. But now I flush under his gaze and cherish his embraces; the sight of him playing on the floor with little Liza stirring my heart. My one sadness is that such moments are all too rare as both she and I must compete for Henry's attention hour by hour, day by day. In the battle between us and the concerns of the army, the local government of Ireland, the people of Dublin and of Munster in the south, the Council of State and Parliament, we will never win.

Henry is working more furiously than ever before: up all hours; receiving ten, sometimes twenty, delegations and petitioners a day; riding out to any summons; inspecting broken walls and rotting farmland; poring over maps and builders' plans; hardly changing his clothes and smoking furiously – not as Father does, occasionally taking a pipe for sociable relaxation, but quickly and without seeming pleasure, as if he needs the tobacco to get through each day. As always, Henry's powers as an administrator overwhelm me: he can turn his hand to anything, moving seamlessly from discussing the drains of Dublin to farming regulations, from provisions for prisoners to knotty legal disputes; he always knows exactly the amount of money in the coffers, the weight of grain in the town's store; and can lay his hand on any paper, letter or book within moments.

As before, the New Model Army's old quartermaster lacks only one talent in his political arsenal: the ability to delegate. Though Harry and Ludlow plead to take on more of his work, Henry bats them away with a litany of excuses: *I have already read the paperwork on this; I know the Master of Works, he'll want to deal with me personally; I'm riding out that way anyway . . .*

'He will never command anyone to do a thing that he will not do himself,' Harry complains to me, 'and so, too often, he takes the short-cut to perform the task before even asking it of another.'

There is nothing he nor I can do to change Henry. And so, for my part, I content myself in becoming familiar with the household and in assuming the supervision of Henry's care: taking him supper trays; prising the pen from his fingers at night; sending his clothes and under linen to the laundry every week and his boots to the cobblers; and hiding his tobacco. Slowly, the circles under his eyes recede, he regains some colour in his cheeks and puts on a little weight.

Beyond my domestic duties, Henry bids me travel out and explore Dublin. And I do – calling on the wives of all the town's most important citizens and accompanying Henry to dinners, church services and civil ceremonies, as my newly elevated position here dictates – but I find myself strangely trepidatious and, for the first time in my life, feel homesick for the England I know and the family I take for granted. I am not used to such attention nor do I feel sufficiently versed in the nightmarishly complicated politics and conflicts of this foreign land. All the confidence I felt in the months leading up to the King's trial and execution, and in my dealings with Elizabeth Lilburne and the Leveller cause, seems to have evaporated in the face of this new, confusing theatre of war so far from the cause I know. Though Dublin is sympathetic to our Commonwealth, I cannot help my nerves at the prospect of encountering hostility or at seeing again sights such as those I saw on my journey across Ireland. Henry is doing his best to perform a monumental job against huge odds but his powers are limited and the land itself so deeply unhappy I can feel it almost in the air itself. And he himself is frustrated constantly at the limits of what he can achieve.

'In agreement with the Parliamentary commissioners, I wrote to the Council of State proposing a permanent settlement to assure the Irish people of their lives, liberties and estates and they have ignored me,' he says to me one evening as he takes a bath – at my insistence – before the fire in our bedroom. I pass him the soap stick and he rubs it absently across his body, the white suds gleaming in the dark curled hair of his chest.

'I told them in no uncertain terms that, after all the bloodshed, without such an assurance the soil would continue to be untilled, the flocks untended, the war lengthened indefinitely, and the financial burden on England incalculable. And yet they will give me no leave to make these assurances, without which Ireland can have no hope of prosperity. It seems no one besides me gives any proper thought to the future,' he finishes, dropping the soap stick into the bath water and throwing his head back, spraying droplets of water from his shaking hair to fall, glowing like fireflies against the backlit hearth, onto the carpet below.

'Write to Father,' I urge, 'though he's been ill,' I add, remembering, remembering Mother's latest letter and saying a quick prayer for his recovery. 'He's not a young man anymore; these campaigns take their toll on his health.'

'It's lucky he has Lambert and Fleetwood with him to help,' Henry says, distracted momentarily from his own problems by thoughts of the challenges in Scotland. 'Lambert is very able, both as a military man and as a political thinker—'

A genius by all accounts, I think but do not say, knowing the friendly rivalry between Henry and the only other man in the army who can match him for brain-power.

'—And Charles Fleetwood is loyal and earnest, if rather suggestible.'

I remember Charles's pretty wife and her pride in him before turning my attention back to Henry's problem. 'Speak to Ludlow' – the idea occurs to me – 'he's on the Council of State, surely he can have some influence.'

'He's written too, it's no use,' Henry growls and I know the words he has bitten back: *If only Parliament had appointed me to the Council. I know how to get things done, how to use pen and paper, men and tools to build new structures from rubble and ash. I know how to look into the future and see better worlds waiting to be created, not an empty void to fall into.*

I take a towel and, kneeling at the head of the bath, start to rub his hair dry.

As each day passes, and the potted snowdrops on our front steps give way to crocuses and then daffodils, I know our time is running out: that we must part when the fighting season begins again in the spring. But I am determined to stay in Dublin for at least the length of the next campaign, to see Henry safely out of the saddle. It is a hard decision, torn as I am between my desire to look after him and cleave to his side and my longing to return to Jane and baby Bridget, but at least I have Liza with me. I find, to my pleasure and amazement, that Henry himself is not entirely against the idea of my staying for the rest of the year, though he mutters about my safety. But then, with a horror that grows unnatural and unwomanly inside me, my courses stop and I feel my waist thicken.

Another child? I greet the notion with the weariness of the innkeeper finding a familiar and troublesome traveller at his door after closing time. Just as the last time, I keep the news from Henry, half wishing the baby will disappear before scolding myself for such unchristian and unmotherly thoughts. Henry calls a Council of War at Clonmel to discuss the new campaign and it is decided that he will lead a force south-west to take the Royalist stronghold of Limerick. Over the coming days, I help him prepare for war: getting in supplies, summoning and refitting the regiments, sending out dispatches. I will him not to notice my growing belly and busy myself around him like a bee, never settling long enough for him to look at me properly. But it is only a matter of time.

The prospect of imminent departure momentarily brings my husband's attention back to me and, a few nights before he leaves, he draws me to him and runs his hand up inside my shift. I hold my breath for an instant and he stops.

'Biddy.'

'Mmmm?' I close my eyes.

'Are you pregnant?'

I sigh.

'Darling!' Henry is jubilant, kissing me while hastily pulling his weight off my stomach. 'How splendid. How hopeful. A gift for the future coming out of all this—' He shakes his head in wonder before his eyes cloud. 'You know this means you will have to return to England.'

'No! Henry, no—'

'Yes, Biddy, yes. It was one thing for you and Liza to stay here while I go on campaign, though you know my reservations on that. But I won't have you have a baby here, with all the danger that brings. Here, among strangers, with only servants to help you? And what happens if the Royalists regroup and Dublin itself is taken? Do you not think the pregnant wife of the Lord Deputy will be a fine prize for them?'

'But—' I try, but I know it is of no use. When Henry has made up his mind to do something, even Samson could not have shifted him.

'I'll make the arrangements in the morning,' he says, kissing the end of my nose.

*

Henry organises my departure with all the precision of his own: an escort is found, a ship is readied, Liza and me are packed. With the forces all over Ireland now mustering for action, Henry does not want me to travel across the island and so he arranges for me to sail from Dublin itself, though this will mean a longer journey across Wales and England at the other end of the crossing. At least Harry and Henry himself will be able to see us off together.

I barely let my love out of my sight for the last day and night before I leave and, though he has even more work to do than usual, I prevail on him to spend a few hours of our last afternoon with Liza and me in the garden. I fetch a blanket and summon some glasses of beer and honey cakes and we laze on the grass together, soaking up the late May sunshine and listening to the blue tit fledglings nesting in the hedge.

'I will come back over as soon as the baby is old enough,' I say, though the prospect of so many months apart again fills me with dread. 'And you must promise me that you will look after yourself properly while we are apart. You must eat well, sleep both halves of each night, bathe as often as you can, change your clothes every week, send out your linen, share your work with your deputies – you hear me? I won't be pleased if when I next see you, you've lapsed into the parlous state in which I found you this time.'

Henry nods at me with a smile. 'Yes, Bidding Biddy.'

'I mean it.'

'I know you do.' He looks at me fondly but with a gaze that tells me he will forget all I have said the moment I step from the quay onto the deck. I do not trust him to look after himself and so I must find a way to bring him within my care. 'Perhaps you could come to London before then?' I say. 'You must want to report to the Council in person at some point? Press your case for the proper settlement of Ireland?'

'Yes—' Henry acknowledges the truth of what I say with a smile, his eyes now closed against the warm sun. 'It would be good to present to them in person, and to sit in Parliament again and take the temperature there. I could see the children and visit Mother in Attenborough too.'

'And you can leave Ludlow here to deputise, Harry too.'

'I could, I could. And it may be that if we're lucky in our siege of Limerick and the other towns, all of Ireland might be at peace by next year. Then I may feel it safe to leave for a few months, to come home. Home,' he repeats with a sigh and I wonder, suddenly, where he thinks of as home. His childhood house at Attenborough? The Cromwell house in London? Though we have moved now from Drury Lane into lodgings in the Cockpit within the precincts of Whitehall Palace, so our rooms would be new to him. Our little house in Windsor Castle, perhaps? Or the rented one in Kingston? We have never been allowed to settle truly, to have time to build our own home and household, to nurture our children as a true family. The wars have always got in our way. Living among my family in London, exhausted by donning the habits of mother, daughter, sister and granddaughter every day, I have longed for the time when I could run my own house again with only Henry and my girls to please: to be wife and mother from sun up to sun down, leaving room even for something more – to be a woman of my own.

'Home is where you are,' Henry answers my unspoken thoughts, his eyes still closed. How well he understands me now, I marvel.

'I'll be forty in November,' he says, turning on his side and opening his eyes to gaze at me fondly and tickle Liza's chin which is covered in cake crumbs. 'Can you believe that, Liza? I'll be forty and it's your birthday in October – how old will you be then?'

'Four!' she says happily.

'So we'll both have the number four in our age!' He lifts her up and lies on his back holding her high over him while she kicks her legs and squeals. 'I tell you what. As soon as I come home to England, we'll have a birthday party for us both and we'll put the number four on everything: on the cake, on the buns. Your mummy can cut it out in icing and in pastry.'

I laugh, full and deeply, the fresh spring air filling my lungs until I think they will burst. 'And it's Jane's birthday too,' I remind them, 'midway between you.'

'Oh yes.' Henry flashes a sheepish smile at having forgotten. 'Well, we can have some number threes for Jane too, then. Threes and fours everywhere!' With outstretched hand, he pulls me down on top of him and Liza. We cling to each other giggling, Liza's face pressed between us, her sticky hands in my hair. Time stands still. After a few moments, our laughter subsides and we lie there tangled and breathing against one another.

'Do you remember when you came for me at Oxford?' Henry asks suddenly, his voice soft and low through Liza's hair. 'Your father asked if you were there for him.'

I think back to another girl and another life. 'And I said *no. I am here for Henry,*' I say, smiling at the memory of my own bravado.

He grins at me boyishly, once again in that moment the young, quiet major I first met, and my heart swells.

I journey home half in agony, half in hope. Every mile that takes me further from Henry brings me closer to the girls and I swap the Ireland I do not understand for the England I know. But if I have left one set of dangers across the Irish Sea, I have only exchanged them for another. For news reaches me when we change coaches at Birmingham that Charles Stuart's Scots army is mustering north of the border and likely to invade England within weeks. I send my prayers and thoughts north to Father, John Lambert, Charles Fleetwood and the army and we cover the remaining miles to London as quickly as the horses can travel and we passengers can bear, desperate to out-run the invaders.

Mother and Grandmother welcome us home with tears, cuddles and kisses, little Jane clambering into my arms as baby Bridget stares at me, her fingers in her mouth. Betty – newly arrived from Northborough with John and little Cromwell – welcomes me with cool smiles. And I find the women of the family have grown by two more with Father's widowed sister, my Aunt Catherine, and her daughter Lavinia at the Cockpit too. We huddle together over the hot weeks of July and August watching my growing bump and praying for Father, Henry and Harry, always listening for the knock at the door that brings the post. Beyond the door, London simmers in intense heat and summer storms flash in an ink-dark sky. We eat, we sleep, we wash, we talk, we wait – then, at last, our prayers are answered. A messenger arrives in early September with the news we longed for: Father had won an extraordinary and providential victory in battle at Worcester on 3 September; the so-called 'King' has fled, his Scots army destroyed; the Royalist cause is dead. Letters and tributes pour in through our front door: old friends resurface, new ones call. Bells peal, thanks is given and Parliament votes Father £4,000 a year in gratitude. When the great man himself rides at last into the city, the streets are thronged, crowds mass along Whitehall and even gather outside our own house where we arrange ourselves with banners to welcome the lord general home. Here is our Alexander, our Caesar, the papers roar, our Moses, our Gideon.

We women flock to Father as we have always done, like doves to their cote. He cries, clutches us, kisses cheeks and dangles babies and I shake my head in ceaseless wonder that this public hero and private father are one and the same person. That the man who stormed Wexford and Drogheda in furious blood is the same gentle soul who cherishes his grandchildren and remembers everyone in the house down to the lowliest servant, seeking out each within hours of his return to ask how they do. His fondest embrace is reserved not for me, nor even for Mother, but for the widow and children of his faithful valet Jean who nursed him through his sickness in Scotland and then died himself in his master's arms. Father being Father had written to Mother immediately to send for Jean's family and to take them in and care for them. And Mother being Mother did just that.

If I am confused as to who exactly my father is now,

I am not alone. His public position on this triumphant return is unclear as muddied water. The conqueror commanded the army to its greatest – and hopefully final – victories with absolute and unshared power, God shining on him and his actions lauded in prose and poetry. He left Henry behind to rule Ireland and General George Monck to rule Scotland and they both answer to him. Yet back in the shadows and spider webs of Whitehall, he is simply one of the elected Council of State (who also direct Henry and Monck themselves and are ultimately answerable to Parliament) and so unable to guarantee success for any of his favoured policies: the Rump drags its feet on legislating for its own dissolution and new elections, much-needed law reform, establishing a new, broad and religious church and showing the forgiveness for Royalists that Father and his allies would like to see. Under Father's brilliant command the army settled the military argument but a lasting political settlement seems as frustratingly out of reach as ever.

Even our domestic arrangements are muddled. We live in a warren of grand lodgings in the renovated buildings surrounding the old Tudor Cockpit within the grounds of Whitehall Palace – half in public, half in private. Some of our servants and income is our own, some of it provided by the state. Crowds of visitors and petitioners throng at our door at all hours and all the foremost purveyors of London clamour to supply us with fine food and wine, lavish furnishings and clothes on credit. Yet we are objects of derision as often as desire and have been heckled and spat at walking in the park so often the Government has closed the Spring Gardens. Mother, uncharacteristically upset by these attacks, whispers to us of her secret longing to quit this public life and return to the quiet backwater of Ely.

Father, meanwhile, remains entirely unshaken by all these changes. Though he accepts some inflation of our fortunes and added comfort in our lifestyle with pride and pleasure as his just desserts, he is not swept away with his own grandeur the way I hear the Lamberts are in their palatial home in Wimbledon. He lives among us, in just the same manner as he has always done: his muddy boots in the hall, his pipe on the mantel, eel pie for supper. This simple way of living seems to baffle our foreign visitors who arrive at our door bearing the papers of the kings and dukes who dispatched them assuming Father must be the great power in the land. After he has received them and offered them nothing finer than small beer and bread – or perhaps wine and biscuits, if they visit in the evening – I watch them leave shaking their heads in astonishment and bending their steps to the nearest alehouse to meet their friends and gossip about this Puritan prince. And every action Father takes, every attitude, every detail of his dress and habits, friendships and foibles, is observed and recounted, enlarged and embellished in a press that cannot get enough of him.

With such swelled status comes new opportunities for Father to enrich himself but he retains his sense of moderation, surrendering his income as Lord Lieutenant of Ireland, for instance, now he no longer needs it. He insists some of the pay go to Henry and I am secretly pleased as Henry has no inherited wealth or estates of his own out of which to provide for the girls and nothing beyond his pay of £3 a day and the income from some land he has bought for himself in Ireland. But, if my father is modest in his tastes, my husband is saintly and Henry writes to tell me he has refused the £2,000 from Parliament, asking that it be given instead to his soldiers, who are owed pay. Mother and Betty are horrified when I tell them but I bury my selfish disappointment in a genuine pride and admiration at Henry's contrasting selflessness. The other accompanying emotion that I choose to hide from them is concern. This latest action is symptomatic of Henry's unfailing elevation of the needs of those who depend on him above his own. He will stop at nothing to see that right is done by the army and by the common people it represents and I pray, now that the fighting season is upon us once more, that he does not endanger himself in this quest.

Constantly nervous for news from Ireland, I distract myself over the coming weeks with preparations for all the approaching family birthdays. As autumn creeps on, I enlist my sister Mary's help to knit sets of clothes to dress the wooden dolls I have bought for Liza and Jane. Then, for Henry, I bustle around town ordering presents, thinking back to Colchester for what provisions he might welcome best in a siege. All goes well: Liza and Jane love their dolls and the wooden animals and hobby horse my family give them; and I send off Henry's trunks of presents, delighted at the treasures I have sourced for him: new boots, thick socks and fresh linens, a lice comb, books, paper, ink, copies of the London newspapers, candle holders, biscuits, letters, drawings from the children, birthday cake decorated with threes and fours as we had promised and – best and most useful of all – a new travelling medicine chest. Our celebrations swell when a letter arrives from Henry to tell us Limerick has surrendered after a long and disease-ridden siege. That was the great stumbling block, my love writes on a dirty, crumpled sheet of paper. With Athlone already fallen, only Galway now remains and Henry can see a delicate peace on the horizon at last and the prospect of keeping his promise to come home next year.

I rest a little more easily then, allowing myself to think, for the first time in a long while, of the future. Even Father takes some time from work to reacquaint himself with his grandchildren, bursting into the parlour like a bear and crawling around on the floor with them. I am watching him do this one Sunday afternoon at the end of the month, with little Bridget in my arms and Jane and Liza at my feet playing with their dolls when the steward approaches me with a letter in his gloved hands. My heart leaps at the prospect that it is Henry writing with pleasure at his presents which he should now have received, telling me how they showed him how much he is loved and missed. But it is another hand, though as familiar as his, inked on the outside.

'It's from Harry!' I say, recognising my brother's rounded writing in an instant.

'Oh good,' Mother says, coming into the room with a tray of lemon cakes and I recognise the relief in her voice whenever she receives written word from one of her beloveds who is in harm's way. 'What does he say? Is he taking care of himself?'

I pass baby Bridget to Mary as Liza props her elbows on my knees to see her uncle's words, her new doll dangling by my leg. The room waits while I slice open the folds and unpeel the page.

I read the first line, then the second. A greeting, a

prayer and then words that wrench my heart. Henry's name. I go back a few lines, confused.

And then the world collapses into darkness.

'What is it?' Mother is by my side in an instant, cakes forgotten.

'The children,' I say, clawing the two words past the daggers in my throat while I concentrate every fibre of my being on keeping my expression still.

The women understand immediately. 'Come along, darlings.' Grandmother staggers forward for Liza's hand and, at a glance from Mother, Frances swoops for Jane and Mary takes baby Bridget away in one collective act. They bustle from the room, leaving Mother and Betty with me. Father has shrugged off his imaginary bear and kneels stiffly at my feet, his whole body drooping and head bowed as if already in prayer.

'Henry!' I cry his name, the moment the door has closed. 'He is dead. He is gone. He has left me behind.'

I hear a groan and don't know whether it came from Father or from within myself. Darkness overwhelms me, my love's face swimming before my eyes in clouds of smoke, and I reach blindly for my mother. I slide, screaming, into nothingness and do not know if she catches me.

CHAPTER TWENTY-SIX

WINTER 1651–1652

'God will gather me to Him,' Henry's voice pierces my dreams, his arms reaching out to comfort me and I wake screaming, scrabbling for him in the darkness. But he is not there. He is lying instead in my mind, a corpse laid out on a bier beside Robin, Olly and Val, beside his great love Francis Thornhaugh, beside Tom the bugler boy from Colchester, Sir Charles Lucas and Sir George Lisle and the handsome young man whose arm we cut off near Ely. All those lovely men and thousands like them, all those bright, bold, bursting bodies running, riding and striding through the world talking, laughing, doing, doing, doing until a breath comes that God decides is their last and they are cut down to nothingness like threshed wheat still gleaming in the sun.

Henry had comforted me through the loss of them all and now he is not here to help me cope with the greatest grief of any. I scratch at my eyes, at my cheeks, trying to claw my way to the wounding thoughts so I can rip them out. But it is no use. I exist in a hated half-light where days and nights blend and I see Henry beside me in bed, feel the warmth of his side of the bedsheet under my hand, hear his low voice in my head. I warm and swell at his imagined touch, writhing towards him and pricking myself hollow on the emptiness.

The candles cast blackened shadows on the walls, creating shapes which move and lunge around me and as I watch them, my whole body pulsates with questions which will never be answered: How did he die? How was I not there? How did he slip out of the world without my realising? What was he thinking in his last moments? What might he have wished to say to me? The questions press inside my head as if they would force the skull itself to explode; they wait for me behind my eyes like needles to prick me the moment I wake or try to turn my tumbled thoughts from one direction to another. I feel as if my body is fighting its own civil war within itself: my head – angry, disbelieving, searching for answers – warring with my heart – broken, fragile, full of love – within a body that cannot function – a tongue, tripping and throbbing, that cannot form words; a mind that cannot hold onto thoughts; hands that drop things the moment others place objects in them. I am a corpse wishing for nothing more than to lie down and die.

I long for my girls but I cannot bear to be with them; their every glance and action something more that Henry will not see; he, who having lost his own father young, would have walked across hot coals to stop his own children suffering the same heartache. How unfair it is on Henry, I keep thinking, that he should be the unwitting cause of his children's misery. I think of him fussing about our house in Windsor making the stairs and furniture corners safe for tottering Liza, loathing the idea of the merest scratch on her smooth skin even though her tumbles caused no more sorrow than swift seconds of tears instantly forgotten with a biscuit. Yet now he and he alone has placed a canker in the children's hearts that will last until their own deathbeds. And he can never undo it, can never take it back. His death is the first thing that any of us will think of when he comes into our minds; his memory is tainted forever.

How cruel of God, too, to take the one from among us who set his face most to the future. Who rode to war and took on a king and then a Parliament to make a better world. How could the Lord bring him safely through all these years of war to kill him at the very end, just as he was coming into his own? Unlike Father, unlike Betty, unlike Fanny, even, who always has her head in a book, Henry never cast back, never looked into history for answers, never accepted the argument that something should stay how it is because that is how it has always been. The past did not comfort his soul or move him to tears. He respected it, learned from it, of course. But it held no special magic for him. It was what men before him had done and nothing more. The present and the future before it that Providence marks out in flashes of divine intervention: that is what mattered, that is what captivated him. That was his realm. While others apportioned blame, he made plans. When others turned west to the setting sun, he turned east to the rising orb. As others lay abed he rose early to greet the new day and shape it for himself: we were like each other in this and this is what I loved most about him.

Am I only realising this now, I think frantically, seeing

for the first time the similarities that bound our souls? But how much of myself had existed before Henry? We have grown so entangled I can no longer separate his branches from mine, his roots from my own. I had longed for the future these last years and had found new ways to claim a share in it, learning from the other women I looked to for lessons – Anne Fairfax, Elizabeth Lilburne, Betty and her own particular skills in effecting action and coaxing confidences from others. Even Jane Whorwood, who took her life in her own hands to spy for the King. But had I always looked forward and not back, even as a child, or did that come from Henry? Was it Henry who gave me the strength and the confidence to march for my beliefs with the army and the Levellers or did I fall in love with him because he called to that spirit already within me?

'Would you wish to marry me if I were not my father's daughter?' I had asked him when he first proposed marriage. I swim back in my memory, battling against the current, to retrieve his reply and preserve it in stone: 'If you were not his daughter, you would not be the woman you are. You have all of his best qualities but blended with your own. That is how I see it.' I watch the scene replayed as at a mummers' fair, the players' lips sealed from telling each other what fates lie ahead for them. I watch young Biddy proud and uncertain on the Ely street, skipping to catch up with Henry's long stride and I want to shout to her down through the years: he will die! He will leave you behind! This is what I cannot comprehend, above all, and what frightens me the most. The next day and the one after that. Henry was always my future, rising ahead of me like the sun lighting my way. But what future do I have to look forward to now? Our shining new Commonwealth had seemed a beginning, but Henry's death feels like the end.

I turn in, I turn west, I stay abed. The past – my past with Henry – is where I will stay, curled up safely like a kitchen cat. Unsleeping, unwashed, round and round I go each day and night, losing Henry, losing myself, losing all sense of time and place, tossed on the ocean like Noah's wife. For all my confused torment, somewhere deep, deep within me I know my cherished withdrawal from the world cannot last. As a woman – as a mother – my grief is an indulgence. My little girls need me, and Henry's baby now nearly fully grown inside me kicks and writhes in protest at another bowl of soup turned away cold and untouched. At least Jane and Bridget are too young to know what has happened, I think, clutching for straws of comfort. It is only Liza, who had just fallen back in love with the father she had forgotten, who cries with confusion, though she cannot understand fully what death means.

I long for my born and unborn children and resent them in equal measure, scared at the new cracked fault-lines that have appeared in my fragile maternal instinct. But somehow the women of my family seem to understand the frightening feelings swirling dark and light within me like blackberry jam mixed with cream. Grandmother sits by my bed and reads from my favourite psalms. Mary, seeming older than her fourteen years, gladly takes charge of Liza, Jane and Bridget, bringing them to me for swift cuddling visits before whisking them off for a game with their dolls or a story – Fanny trailing behind, uncertain of how to help.

Meanwhile, Mother and Betty feel their way forward as they nurse me, slowly inching, part comforting, part chiding in their care, towards the day when they rip the covers from me, carry me to the bath and sponge me like an infant. I rail against this injustice, crying to them that I wish to be left in peace, as I know Father is, closeted up in his study praying and crying for the son-in-law he loved like his dead firstborn son. But they merely smile, kiss me and place baby Bridget in my warm, dry lap where she nestles against my huge stomach with her thumb in her mouth. Something about the feel of her skin on mine, of her heavy warmth against my legs, calls to me and I wrap myself around her, shouting to Betty for some clothes. She powders and perfumes me and I get dressed, my limbs unfamiliar and heavy, and sit for the first time in the chair by the window, turning my face to the dull, unpolished pewter sky.

Only now I am up and lucid, my mind functioning, albeit in a limited way, do I turn, terrified, to learn how my love was taken from me. I have Harry's letter, then Father has one from him too. Colonel Ludlow writes to us both. I tear at all of them, plucking at the pages for information, piecing together Henry's last days like shards of glass, cutting myself on the edges as I assemble them into a nightmare scene. At the beginning of November, the weather had worsened and he succumbed to a bad cold. Ludlow and Harry urged him to relax his work and recover but he ignored them, of course, refusing to rest and riding through a storm to the garrisons besieging Galway when he could just as easily have sent another in his stead. His body exhausted and driven into the ground by overwork and lack of care, he was unable to fight the plague that came for him when he returned to Limerick. Fever stole through his body but still he worked on from his tent within the siege encampment in the boggy fields before the town, his final act to oversee the court martial of one of his favourite officers whom he had dismissed for violence to the Irish.

I read the accounts in raging sadness. Angry with Henry, for taking too little care of himself. Bitter at the selfishness of his selfless devotion to work which has come at such a terrible price for those who love him. Devastated to think that I could perhaps have saved him had I been there. No one could persuade him to go to bed until he had finished his work, Harry writes. He bled and sweated but would not cease applying himself to public business – receiving delegations and dictating letters and instructions from his damp, festering sickbed. Ludlow sings the same tune: '*The Lord Deputy neglected himself,*' he writes, '*not changing his clothes for the whole siege, except his linen, so the malignant humours that clung to his body could not escape.*' He had lived – just – to see his fortieth birthday, though by this time he was too ill to know it. None of the letters mention anything of his receiving my birthday presents and I weep bitterly to think that they arrived too late for him to see; that he did not have that last contact and comfort from my own hands. Henry died happily and without pain, Harry tries to assure me, '*his hand in mine and his thoughts on God*'; though I read the hollowness within the lines of his letter and can never know how truthful his beatific version of the story is.

The scene he paints swims before me. Canvas flapping

in winter wind, candles guttering and the lantern strung above the camp bed swinging with a creak. Ludlow hovering in the shadows, whispering instructions to orderlies and consulting with the army physicians carrying bowls of Henry's dark blood. Harry crouched at Henry's side, his long legs bent around a stool, his head bowed low over the dying friend and brother whom he had loved so dearly, ever since the day he persuaded Father to let Harry go to Cambridge. And Henry – my Henry – thin and sheened with sweat, lying in dirty linen, bloody bandages about his arms, slipping in and out of consciousness, staring at the light hovering above his head, talking to God and thinking – perhaps – of me. I bury myself in dark depths once more and refuse to eat.

But this time I am forbidden. Mother sits before me, her knees wedged between mine, spooning broth into my mouth while Betty and Mary block my escape. They feed me together for two days, in between which, exhausted and wrung out like a dishcloth, I have almost a normal night's sleep.

In so doing they save me just in time. For the next night, the baby comes.

He is early. But Henry's son clamours to come into the world to fill the void left by his father, to bring another Henry Ireton into my bed and my heart. Clever like his father, he knew to seize the brief window in which the body that housed him was nourished and rested to push his way out. Afterwards, my world shrinks back once more to the four posts of my bed – the year turns but I do not notice. I hold the baby each day bewildered. I hate him for causing me to leave his father to his death. I love him for summoning his father back to life in his narrow face and dark, wise eyes. I cannot bear to hold the son that Henry will never see. I cannot bear another to take him from my sight in case he is lost – not even Margery – and so I feed him at my own breast, losing myself in the painful pleasure of his latch. Betty tries to dissuade me from nursing him but I do not care. I want my baby all to myself.

I worship him as a miracle. And I sleep.

CHAPTER TWENTY-SEVEN

The first time that baby Henry Ireton leaves the house, the first time he feels the sunlight on his face and hears the chatter of other voices besides his family's, is to see his father's coffin.

Henry's body has been brought back from Ireland with great care and ceremony. It is said four thousand people greeted him when he arrived at Bristol and half the army turned out to march as his deathly escort across England and into the streets of London. And now he lies in state at Somerset House as princes used to do, the box draped in black fabric and guarded by a wooden effigy of my dead love, its marble eyes watching the hundreds of people who pay six pence to traipse past his coffin each day for six weeks.

'It is idolatry,' I rage at Father, 'Henry would have hated such empty pomp. He would have wanted his earthly remains to be buried in the ground where he fell, not to be exhibited and worshipped.' Nevertheless, as the weeks pass, and I think constantly of Henry's body, lying alone but half a mile from me, I will myself up and out of my childbed for my own private vigil before I lose him again to his public funeral.

At a note from Father, the authorities close the macabre exhibit early one afternoon and we Cromwells arrive as evening falls, choosing the river entrance and not the main one on the Strand to avoid attention. I agree with Mother to leave Liza and Jane behind with her and my sisters but I insist on taking Bridget and baby Henry: 'It will be the only time in their lives that they and their father will be in the same room,' I say, wrapping another blanket around the baby, 'and I will not deny any of them that.' Arrived, I carry Henry with me up the wide staircase and through a sequence of ever-grander rooms, my way lit by silent, candle-bearing servants, until I enter the guards to enter. Father follows me in with Bridget on his hip but Dick and John Claypole wait behind in the anteroom to give us space for our goodbyes.

My arms full of our warm son, I cross the marble floor to the giant bed. A bridal bed for death. I start in shock when I see Henry's shape lying high upon the bed in the gloom, before I remember that it is his graven image and not himself. That he lies instead in the coffin beneath the effigy, hidden from my sight. I glance upwards, seeing the diamond shape of a funerary hatchment hanging above the bed and read the words aloud: '*Dulce et decorum est pro patria mori*. It is . . . sweet and fitting for his country that he should die?' I struggle with the Latin, blinking in horror.

'No, no my love.' Father is beside me in an instant. 'It is sweet and fitting to die for one's country.'

I shift baby Henry across into one arm and grasp sideways for Father's hand with my other. He takes it firmly and we stand together, joined as one, little Bridget's hand in my hair.

'Will you pray with me, Father?' I ask him, as I had once asked Henry, my voice now small as a child's.

Father kisses the top of my head then raises his booming voice to God and tells him of the great man we both loved above all others. He remembers the battles they fought, the arguments they had and the work they did in the Lord's service. He speaks of Henry's hardness – of his dedication and determination, of his stubbornness once he had found the right path. And of his softness – his love for his family, for his soldiers, for the poor and their needs. He speaks of his own love for Henry and the void in his soul he has left behind. He commends him to God and he says goodbye.

I listen through all this private eulogy with love, willing the words somehow to pass as balm to soothe Henry's broken body and hoping that his soul hears us from Heaven. When Father has finished, I tell Henry how I love him, thinking I do not speak aloud until I hear the echo of my voice ring from the marble and realise my thoughts have formed into words. It is time now to say goodbye. I hold up baby Henry and reach for Bridget's tiny hand. 'These are your children, my darling,' I cry, 'the ones you never saw. But they are here to see you, to honour you and to bid you farewell. They live. They love and are loved and they will thrive and remember you all their days. You are home with God now, He has gathered you to Him. Be at peace, my love, and do not worry about us.'

I fold myself into my father and close my drowning eyes.

*

After that parting, the funeral itself feels as if it is of someone else. In its extraordinary extravagance it could be that of a king, perhaps, or a prince, but not of plain-speaking Henry Ireton from Attenborough. Not the man who lived in the saddle and slept with his pocket bible under his pillow. Weeks of government work have gone into planning a mournful pageant the likes of which have scarcely been seen on the streets of London since the funeral of the dead king's father King James: a spectacle I cannot reconcile with the modest man I loved.

And so on a crisp and clear winter afternoon, I play my part in the performance, waiting on the steps of Westminster Abbey for the muffled sound of drums to signal my husband's final approach. Harry, returned from Ireland for the funeral, stands beside me and I hold his hand, as I have done every waking moment since our reunion. As if, in holding the hand of the one who held Henry's hand as he died, I can transfer myself somehow into his shoes – can reach out and touch Henry one last time. Henry's mother is on my other side, pulled tall by Puritan pride even as her lined face is smashed by grief for her eldest boy, as much husband to her as son since her young widowhood; she has spent as much of these few days in London with Henry's lawyers, executors and bankers disentangling all the family's affairs that Henry managed for her, as she has with her grandchildren. Now, still and silent, she grips the arm of her second son, John Ireton, now a prosperous alderman of the City, who mutters prayers for his brother as he rubs the fine cloth of his cloak between his fingers for reassurance.

We hear the army approach long before the first

regiments of horse and foot emerge from the crowds, their reversed arms marching above the heads of the spectators like the teeth of a comb. The mood is solemn, denoting the death of a hero but also disquiet with the Rump Parliament, and darkened still further by the growing fear of the impending eclipse of the sun due to occur on Monday next – 'Black Monday', they're calling it on the streets – which people worry could portend unimaginable events. The end of the world? The coming of the fifth monarchy of Christ? Such is the panic, the Government has had to issue a pamphlet explaining that eclipses are natural phenomena. But there is no parting the ignorant from their superstitions.

It is the army that appears first, though we hear them long before the first regiments of horse and foot emerge from the crowds, their reversed arms marching above the heads of the spectators like the teeth of a comb. I glimpse Father and the other senior officers leading the official mourners, black mourning bands around their hats, their clothes dark and sombre: among them John Lambert, stately and grand, Charles Fleetwood, solemn and sad, Uncle Desborough, frowning and awkward, and 'Preacher Peacock' Harrison in full, sorrowful plumage for his former bed fellow. Many of the Rump MPs file alongside, men carrying the mace, sword and other symbols of Henry's office in Ireland aloft, his favourite horses following behind, though Juno of course is reunited with him in heaven. And then, only then, does my love come himself on a carriage drawn by six horses, his coffin draped in black velvet and footmen carrying a funeral pall above to shade him. I think of my own humble procession up the aisle to meet him on our wedding day, my fingers pressed tightly into Father's sleeve, and of how I had loosened my grip when I saw Henry's smile.

As I watch the people gape at the sight, mouths open and pastry flakes falling onto their clothes, I understand why the Council of State and Parliament have organised this public display: they have chosen this unwanted occasion to tell a grand story about our new Commonwealth. An origin myth of sorts. Here, arrayed before us are the leading men of the nation, the men who cut their way through the forest of our past to clear the path to the future. The soldiers, the politicians, the preachers, administrators, artists and philosophers. And, among them, Henry is forced to play the part of the fallen hero, the slain Achilles, the talisman of a nation. The best example of a Commonwealth man.

Watching the spectacle, I hardly know how to order my feelings. Imagining a royal procession were parading before me instead – a blood-born prince, a throng of fat and foolish nobles swarming around him, powerful only because of their fathers' names or their mothers' pretty faces. I feel pride at this new elect, chosen for their skills, bravery and vision, with no thought for their name or inheritance; so many spare sons, as Henry had called them. The state, not a puffed-up king, their love and master. The common wealth of the people of England their purpose. But, with Henry gone and the Levellers cast out of the tent, I also sense the inadequacy and fragility of this new state and cannot help resenting how this extravagant, expensive display somehow cheapens Henry's memory.

Harry interrupts my thoughts to pass me a pamphlet.

'It's the text of the funeral sermon Dr Owen is about to preach, printed so the people can read along outside while he delivers it inside.'

I take it in numb fingers and lower my eyes, snorting in bitterness at the appropriate title: *The labouring saint's dismission to rest*. 'He dedicates it to you,' I say, surprised, though caring little beyond this.

'I know, he told me. He didn't want to upset you further by dedicating it to you.' Harry gives me an apologetic smile but he should know me well enough to know I would not be bothered by such a worldly trifle.

I press the pages back into his hands. 'Keep it for me, for the children. I will not look at it now, I want Dr Owen's words to come to me unfiltered just as they will to Henry.'

I am pleased not to have read ahead as the sermon is startling and vivid – the one and only aspect of the whole funeral which brings me any comfort and which I believe Henry would have wanted, though he would have baulked, perhaps, at the preacher's lionising of his memory. As I stand in the cold majesty of the marble palace of Henry VII's Chapel of Kings, I need feel none of Henry's modesty but pure and simple pride and love in him instead. Dr Owen takes Daniel: chapter 12, verse 13 as his text and I summon the words to me like old friends: *But go thou thy way till the end be, for thou shalt rest, and stand in the lot at the end of the days.* Henry was like Daniel, Owen tells us: wise both in civil and spiritual matters and I nod, thinking of our days of political discussion and nights of prayer. But above all, the preacher says, Henry could see God's dispensations in earthly events – he understood Providence. He differed from most men who '*like swine following acorns under the tree, do not look up to the tree from whence they fall*'.

He always looked up, I think, feeling tears of sadness pricking my eyes at the thought of Henry's gaze on the horizon and tears of joy at his being reunited now with the God whom he always sought. God will gather him to Him, I think as I watch my husband disappear below the Chapel floor. God *has* gathered him to Him.

That night I seek out my father's company, drawn to him to share our love and our grief. We are home very late from the abbey and after checking on the children and changing out of my stiff mourning dress and into a looser house gown, I pad down the stairs and along the corridor towards the strip of light under Father's study door. I knock gently and enter.

He is sitting in a pool of firelight, hunched in his tall-backed armchair, a glass of wine angled precariously in his hand. The light is dim and the air perfumed with tobacco but in that moment this space of manly contemplation seems a haven. On seeing me, he holds out a hand and I cross the hearth rug to him. He gestures to me to take the other chair near the fire and I kiss him on the forehead before curling into its corners, drawing my slippered feet up underneath my gown. He points to his glass but I shake my head – I could not stomach wine tonight. With that, we return our gazes to the fire and sit in companionable silence.

'I am struggling to see the Lord's work in this, I must confess it,' Father interrupts my thoughts some minutes later. 'To take Henry from us and now, in this way.' He shakes his head, mystified, and runs a thumb under his eye. 'What does it mean?'

I reach for an answer to soothe us both. 'All I can learn from it is: what is of this world is only ever transitory.'

'Yes, that's true enough.' He nods heavily. 'You're a wise girl. You saw in him what I saw, and loved him as I did. You made him a fine wife, I'm proud of that.'

I blink back my own tears at his words; to sit on Henry's right hand and Father's left was all I ever wanted. To live between them. What do I want now? Will I ever want anything ever again? Can I even want any more? I sink my face in my hands and smooth my cheeks, the firelight winking through my fingers.

'It's all gone wrong,' Father speaks into the flames. 'And I cannot see the way forward anymore.'

'With Parliament?'

'And without Henry.' He nods and I feel a sudden and overwhelming double loss: for my love and our cause, which I feel withering on the vine. 'We must put the country on a solid, lasting footing,' Father goes on. 'The wars are won; now we need a permanent settlement. What we did in the months after the King's execution, we did in a hurry, looking over our shoulders at our gathering enemies. But it was mere expediency, not deeply thought planning. We tore down and set up. But we merely bandaged the wounds of the wars, we did not find the medicine to heal the body for good.'

'Henry thought so too,' I say quietly, whispering his name as if in prayer.

'I know, we wrote of it often. I need him here, now, to advise me, to advise all of us.'

I have a sudden vivid image of Henry, sitting at the

desk in our room in Drury Lane, a pen in his hand, ink on his knuckles, his other hand snaked in his hair as he scratched and scribbled out draft after draft of his latest treatise.

'He would read men and God, then write and write until he knew the answer,' I say. 'And then he would urge action, boldness.'

'I know. But to what end? We must have a new representative to replace this hated Rump of a Parliament if we're to have any legitimacy and lasting peace. And yet this limp, indolent Parliament refuses still to dissolve itself and call fresh elections.'

'But are new elections what you want?' I ask, feeling the familiar interest in politics stir within me like a sleeping tiger woken from a dream. 'At least the Rump as it is preserves a link to the Long Parliament for whom we won the war. And think of the army! If there are new elections, what would stop the landowning voters returning a House of Presbyterians and Royalists? We would never see a tolerant Church then, nor reform of the law and franchise. What hope for the ordinary people would remain?'

Father tuts. 'It is a choice between the devil and the deep sea, as men say now. And my friends are not what I thought they were. Sir Henry Vane thinks me too powerful now, thinks the army not submissive enough to Parliament, and has begun to court the Presbyterians once more. He, who was always on our side against Holles and his faction!'

'So return to those friends who are true,' I urge him, casting about for a glass and helping myself to some wine. 'The army. Surely they represent the people of

England more closely than these selfish, corrupt politicians?'

Father shifts in his chair. 'I do believe that,' he says after a few moments, 'and even more so after the miracle of the battle at Worcester. What if the victories we need now must also be achieved by the sword? It is we who triumphed and so is it not our responsibility to shoulder the settlement?' He throws himself out of his chair suddenly and begins pacing about the room, his chin low in his hand.

'Go with God and the army,' I say, the warm wine clearing my head.

'Well, I would expect you to say that,' he replies. 'For all your flirtation with the Levellers, it's the army and its cause that worked its way into your heart.'

I bristle a little at his casual dismissal of the Levellers, thinking of Elizabeth Lilburne's women's petition and of little Tower dead in his cradle. 'I believe that the good of the people as a whole should be the supreme concern,' I clarify carefully. 'And right now I see little concern for the people in the selfishness of the lazy and greedy MPs.'

'Ha! You shouldn't have Betty hear you say that. She's always for Parliament, said so to me again only yesterday.'

Of course she did, I think, picturing her swishing into this room with a supper tray and placing her ringed hand on Father's as she whispers her misunderstandings in his ear. He always has Betty and me arguing on each of his shoulders, the good and bad angel. But which is which? I sigh but say nothing, watching as Father sinks back into his quandary as abruptly as he surfaced and waiting for the next stage in his thoughts.

'But then would that make me no better than the dead

king?' he asks the room, at last. 'To move against the Parliament-men with soldiers at my back? And if I did so, what government should we erect in their place?'

I spread my hands, shaking my head at the tangled web we have woven. He does not see, does not even look to me for an answer as he is lost in the fog of his own argument. I take another sip of wine and turn my face to the fire, searching the flames for the outlines of Henry's foxy face. It is only after a few minutes of quiet that I realise Father has stopped pacing and is standing before me like a schoolboy.

'What if a man took it upon himself to be king?' he asks, his voice no more than a whisper. 'The people want a king back on the throne and to know where they stand. They want a new government but along old and understood lines. A government that won the war and learned its lessons but promises healing and settling. We cannot have the young Charles Stuart now we've defeated him in battle. And his younger brother, the Duke of Gloucester, whom we have in custody, refuses to take his place . . .'

I see with a sudden, terrifying clarity where he is tending. 'Father, no.'

'I don't want it, Biddy! Not for myself. I'd be happy for it to be another – Fairfax, perhaps? But if there is no other alternative?'

'No!' I repeat, sterner this time. 'All those men did not die, Olly did not die, Henry did not die, so that we could pull down the House of Stuart and replace it with the House of Cromwell.' I splutter over the final words, my disbelief turning into frantic laughter. 'King Oliver! And what – all of us living in the royal palaces?

Of course Betty would love to be a princess, so would Fanny. How could you contemplate it? And the army! What would they say?' I think back to the dead baby I held in Colchester, to the swinging bodies on the gibbet at Wexford.

'John Lambert has started working on a constitution now that could—'

Lambert! Of course. Who else but Lambert would fill Henry's shoes as the Government's chief theoretician. 'No, no, no.' I shake my head and a few drops of dark wine spill onto my white linen.

'He could use some of Henry's ideas from the *Remonstrance*—'

'Henry would not want this.' The past tense chokes in my throat.

'We do not know what Henry would have wanted! He understood how the ground beneath our feet constantly shifts, how we must bend ourselves to the wind.' Father comes towards me and seizes my hands, kneeling at my feet, his knees creaking as he does so. 'He worked as hard as anyone to keep the King on his throne. He had nothing against monarchy itself.'

'But then he saw there was a better way,' I say, my voice softened now by tears. 'He saw the truth in *An Agreement of the People*: that men, more men – perhaps someday women too – need to consent to their own government.'

'He purged Parliament.'

'With your blessing! We both know that. And because he thought that, with the King out of the way, we could find a better way. He did not do it to betray the Levellers. He was with them in wanting to dissolve

Parliament and re-elect fresh MPs, not to purge it into the self-serving husk it is now.'

Father drops his head and pats my hand to put an end to our debate, all the wind gone once more from his sails. 'It is just a thought, just a thought,' he says softly. 'We must consider all options. Bidding Biddy, I've always called you and so you are. You'll keep me to the straight and narrow if no one else will.' With a sigh at his sore knees, he levers himself up and hobbles across to his own chair, sinking into it with an exhalation.

I watch him through narrowed tear-rimmed eyes, loving him as I always have but now fearing him too. Which way will he turn at all the vital junctions that he'll face over the coming months and years? Who will he listen to? And can I spend the rest of my life a powerless, dependant widow lost in his huge household, watching him take the wrong turns?

CHAPTER TWENTY-EIGHT

SPRING 1652

The daffodils bend cheerfully towards me, their brash yellow trumpets surging from the carpet of spring greens in a mocking cacophony of new life. I shrink back, shielding my eyes from the bright colours too harsh for the liminal landscape of my grief.

'I would be much happier in my room,' I moan to Betty, thinking of my snug seat in the bay window of my chamber where I nurse baby Henry, turning my face from the sunlight if it burns me.

'Nonsense.' Betty tightens her grip on my arm. 'We must get you out into the fresh air. Your colour is better already.'

Too tired to argue, I let her steer me through the private palace gardens at the back of our Cockpit lodgings and out into the swell of St James's Park. The park bursts with people: footmen walking their masters' dogs, nursemaids running after scampering children to keep them away from the gardeners felling two more trees for firewood for the poor. Nearby soldiers, lounging together in the sun after a shift on palace guard duty, whistle at the flower girls who patrol the paths with baskets of fresh blooms on their heads, trying to catch the eye of fashionable promenading couples.

I look at the strolling lovers with loathing. This is a silly, courting season, even in our own home where romance has gone to my sister Mary's head as she tried her hand at matchmaking Harry to her friend Lord Wharton's daughter. It ended, inevitably, in a muddle and tears when the couple did not take to one another and Mother and Father were forced to step in and rescue the situation from Mall's meddling. As for the couple, it would have been a good match but Father will never contemplate a marriage where there is not love, whatever its advantages, and so he urges no more spoken about it. And, as ever, his patience with his 'little wenches' Mary and Frances is endless: 'Spare little Mall's feelings,' he bids me when I complain of the mess she has made, 'and save her losing a good friend.' For all her fourteen years, Father still treats her like a child.

I am hard on her, perhaps, on Fanny too. But they irritate me in my tender grief with their new airs and graces, their fine clothes and whispering behind their fans about the latest objects of their affections. I cannot help but hark back to when Betty and I were nearer their ages and the simple lives we lived in Ely before the war, before Father was a great man on the edge of the throne itself, before all the luxury. We thought nothing of doing chores all day and climbing into our shared bed at night. Marriage to a good, Puritan neighbour was all the elevation we could hope for. And now Mall and Fanny skip about Whitehall, ordering new silks and satins and dreaming of noble matches, our beautiful cousin Lavinia, who now lives with us, urging them on. Can I really live the rest of my life as the widowed older sister like Aunt Catherine, I think for the thousandth time, never truly free to run my own household and my own family as I would wish – and dependent on a father or brother's generosity for the roof over my head and the food in my children's mouths? Am I to dance at my sisters' weddings and sit beneath them and their husbands at table?

I try and shake these thoughts from my head, bringing my attention back to Betty, who is prattling on about the children's new nursemaid as we skirt some trees to emerge onto a wide gravel path. I struggle to hold onto the sense of what she is saying but the simple sensation of her voice and presence comforts me deep down to my core. It reminds me that, for all her faults and misguided views, she is the only true companion of my old life; the only one who watched my love for Henry grow, even saw it before I did myself. We have found an uneasy truce in this hour of my need with no talk of politics or the future, staying safe in the shallows of each day's domesticity.

'Goodness, it is Frances Lambert!' Betty's sudden words yank me back into the moment and I look up at the vision before us on the path. Caught in the middle of a laughing anecdote, Frances has paused, an entourage of friends and admirers gathering about her like courtiers around a queen. She looks radiant, dressed in a wide deep-blue gown and lace-trimmed shawl and I feel Betty beside me feast her eyes on her.

'Mistress Lambert.' I curtsey to my old friend with a weak smile, clumsy with the lack of practice at any social interactions for months and conscious of my drab mourning dress.

'Mistress Ireton,' she replies without warmth. I clutch for the pleasantries that would once have come easily to me but find my mouth empty. Where then I would have engaged in confident chatter, now I stand raw and nervous as a country girl, wishing Betty would step in and cover my lapse. Cloaked in the dreadful silence, I stand quietly waiting for Frances and her friends to move aside and let us pass. But she does not.

'Oh no, Bridget,' she says, standing her ground and drawing herself up a little straighter. 'I am afraid you must make way for me now.'

I stare at her in confusion, my mind blank, aware that passers-by have stopped to watch us. At the edge of my sight, a smartly dressed couple whisper to each other behind their hands and a wolf-hound barks at the steward who has paused him in his walk.

'You will have heard,' Frances breezes on, 'that my husband is to be made the new Lord Lieutenant of Ireland, and is to rule in your departed husband's stead, Lord rest his soul,' she adds as a casual afterthought. 'We have already made a great many preparations for our life there as the Lord and Lady of the country. There has been so much to order! A new carriage and six, tapestries and plate, a full household of servants and the whole house in Dublin to be decorated, of course; I heard your husband had neglected it most shamefully. And you, my dear, are returned to being plain *Mistress Ireton* and so must stand aside to let me pass.' She finishes her speech with a flutter of her fan and a pitying smile that pierces me like an arrow.

I am struck dumb at the cruelty of the slight, my mind reeling and my heart pounding. I feel naked, as if Henry's death has stripped me of all my clothes, my purse empty as all my worldly currency has drained away. Is this my future now? To be without household or status, to be invisible and overlooked? I shiver, despite the warm spring sunshine, and feel a sickness overwhelm me as pink and white blossom petals swirl about us, blurring my sight. Beside me, I feel Betty wind herself up like a clock on a spring.

'Really,' she begins, the words puffing from her in indignation as she grips my arm protectively. 'Forgive me, Mistress Lambert, but I think, in your excitement at your new position, you have forgotten my sister is in mourning.'

Frances arches an eyebrow at Betty. 'Mistress Claypole, isn't it?' she asks, emphasising John's relative insignificance.

I press my hand on Betty's arm to steady myself before stumbling as a stream of tears comes sudden and unbidden to my eyes. I am angry with myself that they come at such a vain and superficial incident. The next moment, I feel a firm hand on my arm and a man's support on my other side.

'Mistress Ireton,' a familiar voice speaks smartly beside me. 'Would you do me the signal honour of walking with me the rest of the way to your father's? I could do with your wisdom and counsel – yours and none other's.'

I turn towards the voice and make out through my blurred vision the fair curls of Charles Fleetwood dancing in the blossom breeze.

'Lieutenant-General Fleetwood,' Frances Lambert

purrs in his direction but Charles merely gives her a stiff nod before turning a dazzling and admiring smile upon me.

'Shall we?'

I take his arm gratefully and, with Betty flouncing on my other side, we walk calmly and confidently away back down the gravel path towards the Cockpit gardens.

'I am so sorry you suffered such a cruel insult,' Charles says softly once we are well beyond Frances' earshot, bending his tall head down towards me, his russet army coat stiff and familiar under my hand.

'I do not know what to make of it,' I say, bewildered. 'We used to be friends, at least I thought we were. And she's a great favourite of Father's,' I say, before remembering too late the ridiculous, scurrilous rumours that they had had an affair.

Betty tuts loudly on my other side, anger, pride and jealousy audible to me in a single click of her tongue.

'She has grown grand beyond her station,' Charles says, his Nottinghamshire accent warming me in its familiarity: such a similar voice to Henry's, just a little higher in pitch. 'All London knows that she and Major-General Lambert tilt at ever higher offices. Much as I respect him – we fought side by side against the Scots and I would have had no other beside me in the field – I fear he is susceptible to worldly vanities. Not like your good husband,' he adds, slowing his pace a fraction, and I draw a little closer to him at the warmth of his kind words that bring Henry fleetingly back to life.

'Nor like you, General Fleetwood,' I return the compliment, remembering the good words Henry always had for his comrade. 'Henry spoke often of your godly ways and devotion to the cause.'

Charles smiles with genuine pleasure at that, his fair face flushing with colour. I find myself matching his smile and then unsettled at the unfamiliar sensation in my cheeks.

'Well, we are most grateful to you, general,' Betty inserts herself into our conversation with the coquettish tilt of her head so familiar to me. 'You will come home and dine with us?'

I look up at Charles and with a silent encouragement from me he nods in thanks.

Betty glances between us and then loosens herself suddenly from my arm. 'I will go ahead and tell Father to expect you,' she says quickly, 'do please keep my sister in the fresh air for a few minutes longer, general – she could do with regaining the colour in her cheeks before returning to the house. If you're all right, that is?' She looks at me and I nod, feeling stronger and more recovered with every passing moment.

It is only once we are left alone and Charles steers me through some budding shrubs to a bank of buttery daffodils and primroses that I notice he is dressed in mourning himself; a black bombazine band about his hat, matching gloves clasped in his hand and a mourning ring on his finger. 'But you yourself are in mourning?' I say, confused as his dress cannot still be for Henry, not now we are in the final formal stage of public mourning.

Charles stiffens a little beside me before he answers. 'I lost my own wife a few weeks before your husband's death,' he says, the words slow and painful. 'It is because I share the peculiar grief of the newly bereaved spouse that I felt your slight by Mistress Lambert so keenly and had to intervene. I know what it is to lose one's second self and to flounder.'

I stop walking and he halts in response. 'I am so sorry, Charles, I did not know,' I say, thinking painfully of the pretty woman who sat with me at the King's trial. 'I met her once, she was lovely. And so very proud of you.'

He bites his lip at that and drops his gaze to his boot, scuffing a piece of gravel. 'We were happy,' he says at length, without looking up. 'I have children to raise on my own now, and they look so like her.' His voice drifts away and I think of baby Henry and his pointed face waiting for me to reclaim him into my arms when we return from the walk.

'I have four of my own,' I say, my thoughts on them. 'Three little girls and a new baby boy born—' I struggle to complete the sentence.

'After Henry's death, I know.'

We lock eyes with the unspoken sympathy of two lost souls recognising each other bobbing in a flood.

'Are you recovered enough to return?' Charles pulls himself back from wherever he had gone and offers his arm once more.

'Yes,' I reply, bending down to pluck three daffodils to take back for the girls. 'Yes, I am.'

Charles Fleetwood stays for dinner, then calls again a few days later and again two days after that. Both times he comes to see Father and Father snakes an arm around his shoulders and pulls him into his study for a smoke and a talk. But each time he finds his way to the parlour afterwards and sits to share a glass of wine with me. On his third visit, I take him to the nursery and he declares the girls enchanting and little Henry the spit of his father.

'Will you come for a walk with me in the park?' he asks, as I close the nursery door behind us. 'The daffodils have given way to tulips now.'

My feet feel heavy but he is kind. 'If I can brave the park again without fear of further slight,' I say, attempting a joke to cover the pain still held in that memory.

'You can brave it, you've faced far worse,' Charles says, smiling and leading me down the stairs to the hall. 'You came at me with a candlestick once, if you remember.'

I am thrown back through the years in an instant. Back to the frightened girl crouching under the stairs, to the shouts of soldiers echoing in the streets, to the door bursting open and two men surging into the hall to collide at her either side: Henry, dark and scowling. Charles, fair and smiling.

Charles opens the garden door for us and I half expect to find Henry on the other side of it, nursing his bleeding lip. I step through into the silent sunshine, still watching Henry in my mind. But it is Charles's voice beside me which returns me to the present.

'Will you marry me, Bridget?'

My heart stops beating. I turn to him in astonishment, dropping the shawl I was still wrapping about my shoulders.

'I'm sorry, that was sudden.' He shakes his head as if at his own foolishness, his blond curls catching on his white collar before dipping to retrieve my shawl. 'I had thought to ask you in the park – or to wait a few weeks' more. It's just that I suddenly remembered you charging at us all those years ago, how brave you were defending your family, and it rushed out. Here.' He takes my elbow and steers me around the side of the house to a bench against the wall, framed by an espaliered cherry tree, blushing pink with blossom.

I sink onto it, still staring at him in blank bewilderment while he paces before me, gathering his thoughts. At length he begins again, his hat now in his hands.

'This is no romantic whim but a practical proposition,' he says quietly. 'I have a broken family and I need someone to help me put it back together and protect it. Someone with children of her own whom I can love in turn. Someone who understands loss. Someone who loves the cause I love and will serve it beside me. We have always been friends, have we not, and been comfortable in each other's company?'

I struggle to move my lips in answer, stunned. Raw and numb, like a fish iced and waiting for a buyer on the fishmonger's trestle table in Ely market, I fancy that if another man touched me, I wouldn't even feel his fingers on my scaly skin. And yet, and yet . . .

'Can I take some time? Will you leave me to think?' I put a hand to my head as if to show him the need and he bows and retreats along the path, his last words, 'Of course, of course, take your time' trailing behind him like gun-smoke after an infantryman.

I drop my eyes to my lap where some feather-light pearl-pink blossom petals have gathered in the stiff black folds. Where is Henry, I wonder, picking a petal and turning it over in my black-satin gloved palm. Where is God? What would they have me do? Once more I am on the flagstone floor of our house in Ely, Henry helping me to my feet while Charles chuckles beside him. There they will stand forever in that instant rubbing their wounds and talking in their Nottinghamshire accents, Father laughing behind them. Is this what Providence means for me? What if Providence has led me back to that first meeting as if to show me another road I could have taken then but which I can return to now? As if to show me I can have a second chance at life. Perhaps not at love, but at life? I cannot imagine it now, wreathed in sorrow and pain, but perhaps I don't have to. Perhaps I merely need to take a leap of faith and let the future be what it will.

'He has asked you, hasn't he?' Betty appears beside me on the bench, her rosewater perfume drifting about me as a spring mist.

I turn to her uncomprehending and she tilts her head as she always does when I have caught up with her at last.

'I knew he would from that moment he saved your dignity in the park.' She sighs, happy at her vindication. 'I used to think him sweet on you years ago,' she goes on, 'but which of us would ever have looked at him beside Henry? Henry had such power, such force of will. Even I could see that for all his foxy features.'

'He is not Henry,' I answer numbly, voicing my thoughts aloud before they even form. 'He is not my love but a pale copy.'

Betty purses her lips in thought and we sit together in silence, a shared sadness lying between us. I remember how we held each other in our chilled bed through all the griefs of our youth and my fingers twitch for hers. I long suddenly for her to fling her arms around me as she would once have done but she keeps still and contained beside me: my companion still but now too often my opponent.

'It gives me little pleasure to say it,' Betty begins her reply at last, 'for you know I do not share your blind devotion to the army and its acolytes. I'd love you to marry a friend of John's, a Parliament-man who would work to settle the country in its old ways—'

I stiffen bedside her and she edges her gloved hand onto my skirt: 'But your path was always going to bend away from mine. Charles would suit you well. For all I dislike his politics, he is an army man through and through, a colleague and admirer of Henry's, trusted and loved by Father.'

Her gentle words settle into my own thoughts. How had Henry described Charles? I conjure him back from the dead to re-pronounce judgement: *loyal and earnest, if rather suggestible*. Suggestibility might be a welcome change in a husband after Henry's stubborn, unchanging ways. I would need any second husband to be flexible and to accept me for who I am and how I have loved. And Charles knows my deep feeling for Henry – had a strong love himself for his wife – he would not expect the same from me any more than I would from him. Henry would look to the future as he always did and he would bid me do the same.

Squeals and cries tug me out of my reverie and Betty laughs as the children spill around the corner into view, the older ones running and shouting as the nursemaid trails behind them, baby Henry asleep in a shawl in her arms. Betty leaps up and skips after her boy across the lawn, catching Cromwell about the waist and swinging him into the air, Liza and Jane clutching at her skirts as Bridget totters to catch up. The maid nears me and I signal for her to give Henry to me. I ease him into my arms, settling his body in the folds of mine, my movements tiny and precise to keep him in precious sleep.

I lean my head back against the warm bricks and watch the children. Do they not need a home of their own, a mother who runs her own household and shapes her own life, a father to provide for them in my stead? And what of me? Do I want to live as a girl again, my fate tied to my father's? Will I withdraw from the world, wedged into the corner of his house – or when he is gone, Dick or Harry's – like Aunt Liz or Aunt Catherine, slighted in public by the married women who have taken my place? Jane Whorwood's voice flutters into my head: *I intend to make my own fate.* I wonder, in a frantic moment, if I could set up on my own. I could become an agent like Jane or take a leaf from Elizabeth Lilburne's book and use the widow's pension granted to me by Parliament to become a preacher or pamphleteer, as I had once dreamed. With my wartime experience I could do as some of the widows of Colchester did and open lodgings offering nursing, childbed and deathbed care. Or perhaps I should leave England entirely and find a new life in the New World.

But my children could not live like that and, besides, I think with a sudden stirring, the old world has given way to the new here in England and I must stay and see if for myself, shape it, even, if I can. With Charles, I could do that: could form my own household, rebuild my family and claim my place again in the world. If I have learned anything in these last years, it is that it is women's work to carry on, whether to keep the flame of civilised society alight in times of war, as the generaless told me when I first met her, or to fight themselves for greater freedoms like the Leveller women. Or – I smile at Betty when she looks back at me – even simply to help a lost sister to a new husband and a safe shore. We can preserve things or we can change them, but we must act. A woman must get up in the morning even after she has buried her husband or her child.

My thoughts pull back to Henry as they always do and I remember his sudden, abrupt proposal – as unromantic in its way as Charles's was – and how I squandered it in my pride and confusion and would have lost him forever had I not seized him for myself. Then Olly breezes into my mind, his face sparkling, under-lit by the sun-soaked water of the fen. *Promise you won't be too proud to take that chance, even if it is dressed up as a husband,* he had said, and his advice had pointed me in the right direction once before. Baby Henry stirs awake in my arms, his coal-bright eyes calling me back from the past.

'I promise,' I whisper to Olly in farewell and he smiles.

EPILOGUE

DUBLIN, DECEMBER 1653

I am always the first in my house to wake. Before my husband and my children. Before the household servants and office staff. Before the kitchen boy who breaks open the fire and fetches the kindling.

I am even up before the baby.

She rises while it is still night and gives food to her household and portions to her servants.

I like that proverb. It is not just the sense of warmth, of bringing light out of the darkness or providing for loved ones that speaks to me. It is the word *She*. She rises. She acts. She meets the day first and on her own terms, restored by a few precious minutes of quiet. She sets the fire and lays the table, yes. But she lays out more than that: she shapes the day for herself and all around her.

And so each morning I wake first and claim the day for my own.

Today it matters more than most.

The night is achingly cold. The cold that reaches long, bony fingers into your head like needles. But I come out to the garden nonetheless, to sit swathed in blankets on my patch of frozen, splintering grass, sugar-frosted in the tired moonlight. The thin air chills my fingers and chokes my breath, yet I need to be here on the lawn by the blue tits' hedge to speak to Henry: as if sitting on the same ground where he, Liza and I lay entangled with our picnic on our last day together can bring me closer to him. And I need him with me for this communion, to conjure the scene I must confront in my imagination, to see England's new ruler – my father – in my mind's eye.

I piece the scene together from the fragments of news that have reached me: Mother's account of it in her letter, the breathless telling by the official messenger from London, and the brash braying of the newspapers – both those of our side and the many others who attack us from myriad directions. Though I feel I am a world away from them, slowly, the figures of my family appear in the black haze before my eyes. Mother – quiet, nervous, sliding a finger underneath the double strands of pearls at her throat as she watches her life remade. My brothers – Dick drinking heavily in the corner, Harry eager and pacing in his best suit. Mall smiling shyly, seated close by Mother, Fanny shining in anticipation, her eyes roving the room.

But it is the vision of Betty which brings a lump to my throat and a blade to my heart, as she perches regal and resplendent in a new dress of evergreen silk edged with pink English roses. She is beautiful. A bountiful goddess, a new Puritan princess, little cherubic Cromwell on her lap and a baby growing in her womb. The favourite daughter and eldest grandson on his right hand tip their smiling faces in loving awe to the bulky sable-brown-dressed figure rooted in their midst like a great oak tree: Father, Lord Protector Oliver Cromwell. Now, suddenly, the ruler of three nations.

My mind paints a picture as vivid as those created for the late king and his family which I had seen at Hampton Court the day I came face to face with the tyrant himself. 'Van Dyck,' Father had told me with a nudge as we stood before the canvasses, his shining face as full of admiration as mine held contempt. And now it is to be my family, the Cromwells, who display themselves to all, living their new-modelled lives always ready to be captured in paint and verse. A new mythology has been born. A new dynasty to guide the Saxons so long under the Norman yoke and lead God's people out of Egypt. But will Father be the good Moses or the bad Pharaoh? I ask Henry's spirit. Can this truly be the path to the Promised Land?

Doubts crowd my mind even as I shake my head in amazement at the power now given to my father. How will he spend these riches? He could create the wide and tolerant Church he's always wanted. He could serve the Protestant cause in Europe and take on the great Catholic enemy of Spain. He could reform the legal system and Parliament's franchise as he has always urged. He could even license London's hackney carriages – how many times I have heard him grumble about them. He may do good things, yes, but does he have the right to do them? And what of the bad things? The choices I may not agree with? I trust Father more than any other but he is but a man with darkness and doubts within his nature as any other. My mind lurches back to Wexford; a place that bleeds only in the imagination of most Englishmen but which, only three or four days' ride from here, feels very real to me.

Should one man ever have so much power, even if it is my father? I return to Father in the picture, trying to read his mind. But this time, it is not he but the gaps in the family portrait that loom out to catch my attention. My dead brothers Robin and Olly appear as ghosts caught in specks of paint glinting in the candlelight, baby James a pencilled outline in Mother's arms. Our famous forbear Thomas Cromwell lurks in the shadows watching his kin. And of the living only I, the eldest daughter, am missing.

'Bridget!' my husband Charles calls to me from a window, his voice carried forward into the night silence on the trembling wind. Startled, I shake the scene from my head so the painted pieces fall shining through the moonlit sky like a shattered stained-glass window under the hammer of one of Father's crusading soldiers. The distracting images gone, the pure and tranquil Puritan world of the Word returns to me.

I had thought him Henry – just for a moment, a second when I heard only a man's voice on the air speaking my name. Perhaps it *was* Henry calling to me from Heaven, summoned to our sacred place to give his judgement on the scene I have watched in the air. What would you have thought of all that has happened this year? I ask him. Of Father – assured by the Rump Parliament that it would put itself back to the people for fresh elections, only to be betrayed when it hurried through a bill to perpetuate its sitting in his absence – provoked into the fury of Drogheda and Wexford and marching into the chamber like old King Charles to dissolve the Parliament by force? Of the assembly of nominated 'saints' that the Army Council summoned to govern in Parliament's place before Thomas Harrison's millenarians had squandered the opportunity and relinquished their responsibilities back to the army? Of the new written constitution – the first in England or anywhere in Christendom – drawn up by John Lambert, which made Father Lord Protector: king in all but name?

What would you have said to see so many of your own ideas, your own wording and clauses even, pulled together by Lambert into this extraordinary document which puts Father on the throne – the good parts borrowed from your *Heads of Proposals* offered all those years ago to the King? What would you have said to John Lilburne, returned once more to the Tower for threatening the Government and conspiring with Royalists, his *Agreement of the People* now good for nothing but privy paper, his baby Tower by now a tiny heap of bones shrouded in the earth?

And what, last but not least, would you say to see me here in Ireland once more, wife to the new governor, Charles, given the role when Parliament stripped it of its exaggerated vanities and title so that a furious Lambert and his wife felt they could not stoop to it for all the thousands they had laid out on their finery? What would you think of your children and me living in the same house in Dublin that we had shared for those precious months and listening to the next generation of the same blue tit family nesting in the garden? I see you lying on the lawn some days and come here to you, sometimes bringing little Henry to toddle and fall on the soft grass.

I hope you also feel us close by. I pray you are happy with the choices I have made.

Is this where we were always headed, I wonder as I pull the blankets tighter about my shoulders and look up at the stars in the ink-black and navy night sky – is this the end point Providence marked out for us through all three wars? All the protests and petitions, all the bloodshed and pain, all the lives lost and hearts broken leading us here to Father's Protectorate? Was it Father's star that mattered all along, like the star travelling across the Judean sky to shine above Bethlehem? And I too close to him to see it? And if you were still here, Henry, would it make a difference? How might events have altered if you had been in Parliament, if you had sat in the Nominated Assembly and been at Father's elbow, pen in hand? Would Father have still taken the supreme power rendered to him? He who once modelled himself on Gideon who won the war, killed the king, refused the crown and returned to his farm. I fly back through the years to our farm in St Ives and another early morning with my face tipped to the sky. 'Now I can serve God by my doing and not by my suffering alone,' my young father shouts for joy, Betty on his hip, 'and what things I shall do in the world!'

I will never know the answers to all my questions. No one will. All I can do is what Henry would have done – look to the future, turn my face to the east. I hear the soft mewl of new baby Anne waking deep within the house as if in answer and I rise to my feet. I had thought that Henry's death was the end of my story, but now I see the story of my family is just beginning. The age of the Tudors and Stuarts is set into dust, the age of the

Commonwealth and the Cromwells has dawned. And I must find my place within it.

Behind me, the house stirs, the first scraping sounds of chairs on flagstones and water rattling into pans drifting from the kitchen. I hear my husband's voice call to me once more as the first blush of dawn edges around the eastern rooftops.

'I'm coming!' I call in answer and turn back to begin the day.

ACKNOWLEDGEMENTS

The last two years have been very difficult and I must thank a number of people for helping my second book, *The Rebel Daughter*, to completion in spite of this. My agent Giles Milburn has continued to give me wonderful support and encouragement, brilliantly aided by the team at MMLA. I have also worked with several excellent editors at Orion Fiction and wish to thank Victoria Oundjian, Olivia Barber, Harriet Bourton and Charlotte Mursell as well as the wider team for all their efforts. My colleagues and friends at NRF and in the Cromwell Association continue to support me and my writing, for which I am very grateful, and I particularly wish to thank those experts who commented on early drafts of the book.

My first novel, *The Puritan Princess*, came out in the same week that my second son Orlando was born ten weeks prematurely, and at the height of the first Covid lockdown in April 2020. In those harrowing months, I could never have imagined that worse was to come but then it did: I lost my beloved mother Joanna Malins to a short and sudden illness in March 2021. I would never have coped nor finished this book without the love and support of my family and friends, particularly my sisters Annabel and Cressida, my brothers-in-law Jayesh and Andrew, my father Julian, Michèle, Stephanie, Jenny and Becca. Above all, I thank my wonderful husband Charlie and our two beautiful boys Theodore and Orlando (now thriving), who have carried me through every day with love, joy and solace.

But finally, and most of all, I acknowledge the many gifts made to me over my lifetime by my matchless mother Joanna who loved, championed and inspired me as no other. She always believed I would succeed as a writer and historian and did everything she could to help and encourage me. She took me on research jaunts and joined the Cromwell Association when I gave my first paper; she looked after Theodore on Fridays so I could write and looked after me when I needed to shut myself away for a concentrated weekend of work; and she pressed copies of *The Puritan Princess* into the hands of everyone she met, right to the end. I am who I am and where I am thanks to her. And so it is to her – the mother against whom I never needed to rebel – that I dedicate *The Rebel Daughter*.

Don't miss Miranda Malins' gripping and unmissable historical novel of family, politics and the price of love . . .

**Cromwell has survived the Civil War . . .
Now his daughter's fate hangs in the balance.**

1657. The youngest daughter of Oliver Cromwell, eighteen-year-old Frances is finding her place at England's new centre of power.

Following the turmoil of Civil War, a fragile sense of stability has returned to the country. Her father has risen to the unprecedented position of Lord Protector of the Commonwealth, and Frances has found herself transported from her humble childhood home to the sumptuous palaces of Hampton Court and Whitehall, where she dreams of romance.

But after an assassination attempt on the Cromwell family, Frances realises the precarious danger of her position – and when her father is officially offered the crown, Frances' fate becomes a matter of diplomatic and dynastic importance.

Trapped in the web of court intrigue, Frances must make a choice. Allow herself to be a political pawn, or use her new status to take control – of her own future, and of her country's . . .

CREDITS

Orion Fiction would like to thank everyone at Orion who worked on the publication of *The Rebel Daughter* in the UK.

Editorial
Harriet Bourton
Charlotte Mursell
Lucy Brem
Sanah Ahmed

Copyeditor
Marian Reid

Proofreader
Sally Partington

Audio
Paul Stark
Jake Alderson

Contracts
Anne Goddard
Humayra Ahmed
Ellie Bowker

Design
Debbie Holmes
Joanna Ridley
Nick May

Editorial Management
Charlie Panayiotou
Jane Hughes
Bartley Shaw
Tamara Morriss

Finance
Jasdip Nandra
Afeera Ahmed
Elizabeth Beaumont
Sue Baker

Marketing
Tanjiah Islam

Production
Ruth Sharvell

Publicity
Alex Layt

Operations
Jo Jacobs
Sharon Willis

Sales
Jen Wilson
Esther Waters
Victoria Laws
Rachael Hum
Anna Egelstaff
Frances Doyle
Georgina Cutler